SCORE ON YOU

USA TODAY BESTSELLING AUTHOR

HARLOE RAE

NOVELS BY HARLOE RAE

Reclusive Standalones
Redefining Us
Forget You Not

#BitterSweetHeat Standalones
Gent
Miss
Lass

Silo Springs Standalones
Breaker
Keeper
Loner

Quad Pod Babe Squad Standalones
Leave Him Loved
Something Like Hate
There's Always Someday
Doing It Right

I'd Tap That (Knox Creek Standalones)
Wrong for You
Yours to Catch
Score on You

Complete Standalones
Watch Me Follow
Ask Me Why
Left for Wild
Lost in Him
Mine For Yours

Screwed Up (part of the Bayside Heroes standalones)

To those who were raised to believe you're not
enough—it's a lie.
You're more than capable of chasing your wildest dreams.
Don't let anyone tell you differently. They don't matter.
Find a support system that makes you feel like you're
everything. Smash your goals. Don't surrender. Keep your
chin up. Choose your own destiny. Break free. And may
your version of Ridge Carter be waiting across the street.

This one is also for Jodie and Allison. Thanks for believing
in me and being part of my support system. Love you!

THANKS SO MUCH!

Guess what? I'm putting the acknowledgements in the front because I want you to know how grateful I am from the start. Score on You is book number twenty-one for me. That's a crazy amazing goal to accomplish. I can hardly believe I've been fortunate enough to have a career as an author. That's thanks to you. Please know how much I appreciate you for choosing Score on You to read. You're giving me the opportunity to continue doing what I love—writing swoony romance books. I'm eternally thankful. Then, now, and always.

Ridge and Callie have a very special story to tell. It's one I've been excited to write for years. Ridge is the type of hero that makes me passionate about writing. You'll see why soon. Callie's journey empowered me to push for more. I hope that enthusiasm comes across the pages. Fingers crossed you love them as much as I do.

I need to thank my patient and generous husband, along with my two adorable children, for giving me purpose along with unconditional grace. Especially as that deadline creeps closer. Major love to Heather, Shain, Renee, Jodie, Allison, Jackie, and Kate for being there to support me through the thick and thin. To Stacey, Candi, Alex, Keri, Leticia, Bobbie, Patricia, Lacie, and Kayla for being such a huge part of my publishing process. To Harloe's Hotties for being the best group ever. To the readers, reviewers, influencers, BookTokers, and Bookstagrammers for everything they do to support us. There are many more who deserve endless gratitude. You know who you are. I'm forever thankful.

And one more thing. If you enjoy Score on You—which I'm really hoping you do—I would greatly appreciate it if you could take a moment to leave a review. These are priceless and help new readers find my books, which allows me to continue following my passion. You're lovely!

Cheers to romance, books, and happily ever after.
xx
Harloe

PLAYLIST

"Belong Together" | Mark Amber
"Scared to Start" | Michael Marcagi
"Space in My Heart" | Enrique Iglesias & Miranda Lambert
"Stick Season" | Noah Kahan
"I Feel Like I'm Drowning" | Two Feet
"I Remember Everything" | Zach Bryan & Kacey Musgraves
"Lunch" | Billie Eilish
"Home" | Good Neighbors
"I Am Not Who I Was" | Chance Pena
"My Home" | Myles Smith
"Holy Smokes" | Bailey Zimmerman
"Who's Afraid of Little Old Me?" | Taylor Swift

Listen on Spotify!

A note from the author
Me again. Hi.

It's important that I mention Callie's background before you dive into the story. Callie was raised in a fictious society that's oppressive and views women as subservient. This plays a role in her behavior, as well as her progression throughout the book. The compound of Billmoore is from my imagination and not based on a real place. Any likeness to an actual location is purely coincidental.

There are some descriptions of mistreatment and violence against Callie, as well as her mother, that happened in the past and is mostly depicted off-page. These acts are in no way related to Ridge (the main male character/hero). He defends and protects her to the extreme, which might cross into morally gray territory for some. Be warned he's a bit over the top, but we love him that way.

Thanks for reading!
xx
Harloe

SCORE ON YOU

PROLOGUE

Calliope

"W HERE WILL YOU GO?" MY MOTHER HOVERS IN my doorway, her fingers knotted in worry.

I lift my gaze from the bag I'm packing to study her whitening knuckles. The lump in my throat doubles in size as I admit the truth. "I'm not sure."

"You mentioned a friend," she murmurs.

The term *friend* is generous. I met Harper Wilson last month when I was granted a rare leave from the compound. It's almost unheard of that a young lady such as myself is allowed to venture beyond the commune limits alone. Father declared that I'd proved myself to be trustworthy enough for a short trip. It was a test of my loyalty, a slice of freedom that I wouldn't take for granted.

That opportunity led me straight to a small town called Knox Creek. Harper spotted me and my wide-eyed wonder while I wandered aimlessly along Main Street. Her bold attitude immediately called to me. She was confident and outspoken and everything I'm not permitted to be. Unless I escape the narrow-minded community of Billmoore permanently.

Harper is little more than a stranger, but she's the only

option I have. I want to be like her. Desperately. Just for a day, or maybe a sleepless night. A few hours where I'm in control of my own destiny. The potential of making a single reckless choice is almost too appealing.

"Yes," I finally respond while breaking from my thoughts. I tuck the memory away for safekeeping and clutch tight to hope that she will accept me. "I'll visit the woman I told you about. That's where I'll go. Maybe she has somewhere I can stay until I find my own place. She might be able to help me get a job too."

Mother gasps and lurches toward me as if the idea is unheard of. She collects herself almost immediately, retreating to her spot at the threshold. "Calliope."

My shoulders bounce in a shrug. "That's normal. Women work. They're independent. Self-sufficient."

"But it's not…" She stops before finishing that rehearsed sentence.

"It's not our way," I recite for her.

But that's not true.

These restrictive rules are *his* way. The self-appointed dominant sex is in charge and dictates how we live. It's a core value in Billmoore. I've survived in this intolerant environment for twenty-one years. That's somewhat surprising since the urge to rebel and buck the system has been rooted within me for almost as long. I'm ready to break free from the oppressive cycle where I merely exist under Father's roof.

Especially now that I'm expected to marry and start a family. Several eligible suitors have already been selected and deemed worthy to be my husband. Not by me, of course.

The reminder squeezes my lungs until it's difficult to breathe. My chance to flee is slight to begin with, becoming less likely the longer I delay. The men are currently distracted by an annual event that kicks off the hunting season. This is the first year my brother was invited. It's considered a privilege to attend. Even so, that type of prey only holds their attention for a short stretch. They'll return in an hour or two, expecting gratitude for their efforts.

I begin to pack my meager belongings faster. "Will you come with me?"

It's not the first time I've asked her. This drastic move would be considerably easier with her beside me. She's my mother. My only source of support. Nothing competes with the comfort she provides. But the grip Father has on her is too strong. Those shackles have become more unbreakable over the decades.

Her continued silence proves as much. I still glance at her over my shoulder. She's shaking her head. Silent sorrow spills down her cheeks in rivers that she doesn't bother to stem.

"You better hurry," she urges.

I nod and zip the bag I've filled. "Okay."

"Send a message to let me know you're safe? Be mindful of his shifts at the mill." The reminder isn't necessary, but I pocket the advice all the same.

"Of course," I say and turn to where she's standing. "Maybe you'll be allowed to visit once I'm settled."

Her smile wobbles at the edges. "I'd love that. Very much."

And I'm sure she would. But we're both aware this could be the last time I see her. At least for a while. Which is why I hug her extra tight and let the embrace last longer than usual.

A hollow pang spreads through my chest. "Love you, Mama."

"I love you so much, baby girl. Don't ever forget that." Mother wraps her arms around me and slips something into my pocket.

My fingers curl around the wad of money, ready to return the generous gesture. "I can't accept—"

"You can." She stills my motion. "It's not much, but enough to get you started."

"Where did it come from?"

"That's not for you to worry about. Just take it."

I release my grip on the precious cash and slump into her hold. "Thank you. I'll spend it wisely."

"Use it to get where you need to go." She straightens from our embrace to cup my cheek. "Fly free and far. For me, okay? Do what I can't."

"But you can be free too. Come with me," I plead.

More tears spill down her splotchy cheeks. "No, I must stay. This is where I belong."

"He'll never forgive you." My stomach knots at the thought of his punishment.

The blame will fall on her alone in my absence. His wrath has the reputation of being brutal, which I can personally testify as truth. Mother is committing a grave offense against her husband by allowing me to leave. Worse yet, she hatched this plan. This is her selfless gift to me. More valuable than a million dollars. I could never muster up the courage to run. Not until she lit the spark that inspired my flight from the nest.

If Father discovers that she's behind this deception…

I feel my belly clench harder at the threat of his retaliation. My pulse accelerates as I grasp onto her hands. "He'll know—"

She squeezes my fingers that are locked between hers. "I'll be fine. Don't worry about me."

Heat flares in my eyes and I blink at the sting. "But—"

"Go. Before it's too late."

The clock on the wall ticks in mocking. I glare as more precious seconds vanish. "How will I get in touch with you? A simple note to confirm my safety isn't enough."

Her throat works with a thick swallow. "It's probably best if you don't contact me."

"Mother—"

"Please go, Calliope. I want better for you. Do this for

both of us. Find whatever calms that restless spirit and allow it to soothe your soul. You've always been too curious to stay penned in this fence."

I sniffle, attempting in vain to mask how much this farewell hurts. "What if I fail?"

She exhales, the sound heavy. "That's part of any adventure worth having. You'll try again and figure it out."

"But I'm scared. Where do I begin?" The possibilities seem endless after a life trapped in Father's confinement.

"Walk out of this house and don't look back."

I nod, but my heart feels heavy and ready to burst. The beating organ pounds harder as my departure quickly approaches. "Do you honestly believe I can do this?"

The question is for me as much as my mother. This is the first real decision I've ever made in my life. I can't survive on stifled breaths a minute longer. The eggshells I've been walking on are smashed into unrecognizable pieces. If I stay another day, I might be stuck for good. That's the risk I'm not willing to take.

Her grin is soft. "You'll get the answers you're searching for. I'm certain of that if nothing else. You're strong and brave. More than I'll ever be."

"Thank you," I manage to croak.

Mother gathers me in her arms for a hug that's too final. "Cherish every step of the journey, Calliope Rose. You'll know where you're meant to be when the moment arrives."

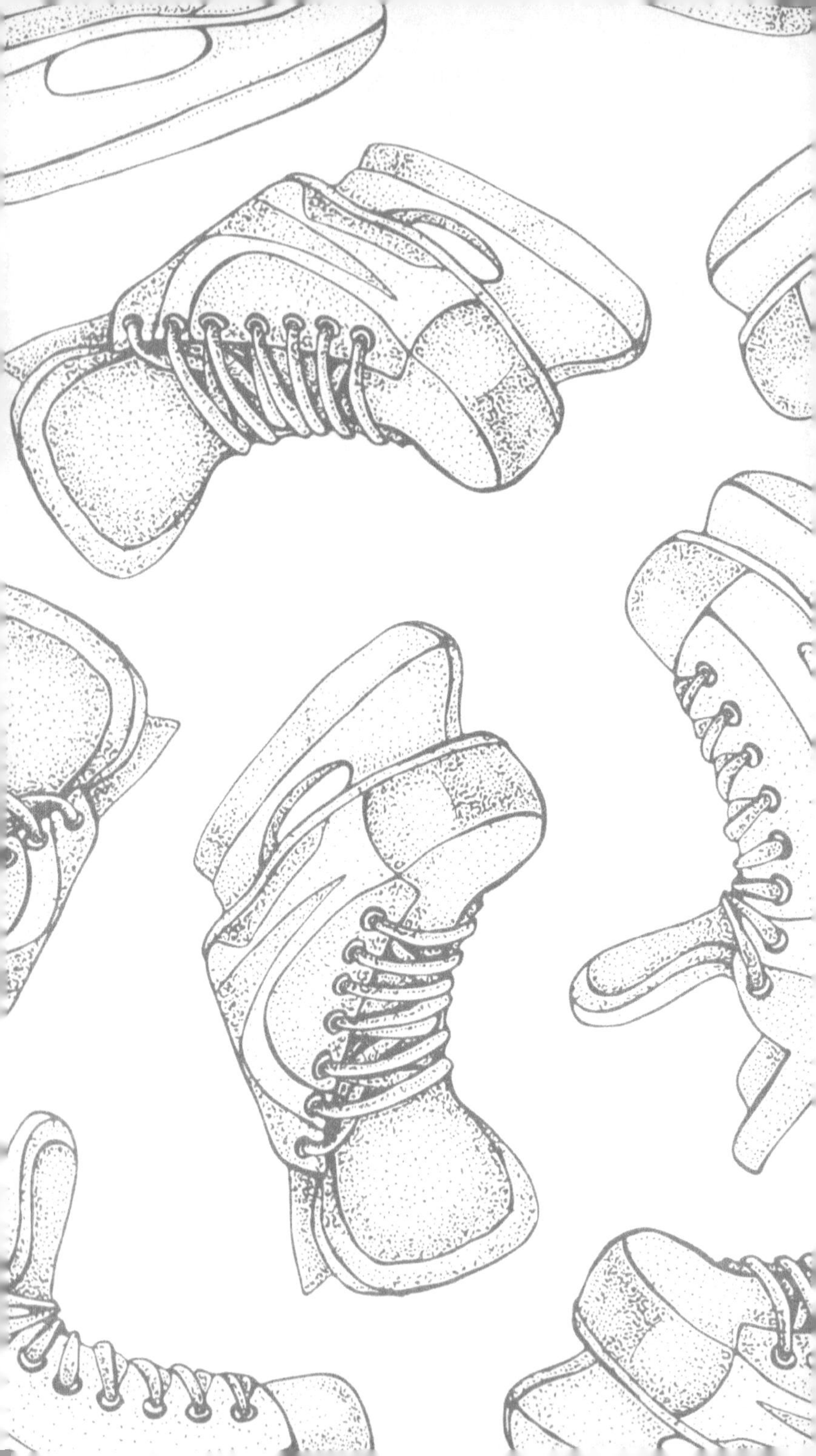

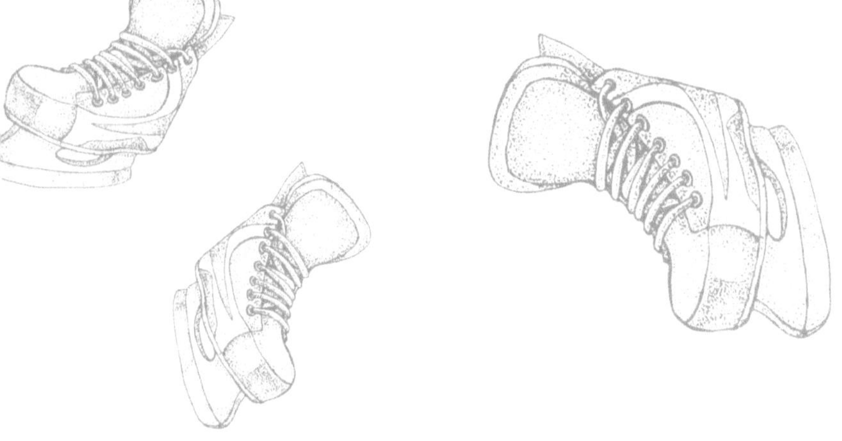

CHAPTER ONE

Ridge

I slide the freshly poured beer across the bar top. Amber liquid sloshes over the rim from the motion. The customer doesn't fuss about me spilling his booze.

Hell, he'd probably lap the excess off the counter if I turned my back. Although the thirsty gleam in his eyes suggests that he might lick the mess off the glossy wood with me watching. The patrons at Roosters are classy as fuck like that.

He tosses me a crumpled bill to cover his tab. "Thanks, boss."

I almost smirk at the title. "Be back with your change."

The customer waves me off, reaching for his tall glass like the contents are liquid gold. "Keep it."

Before I consider a response, the guy is suckling at his Surly and forgetting about me entirely. I turn away with a snort and scan the other regulars in my section at the rail. Full drinks and lopsided smiles greet me. With them satisfied, my gaze moves to Garrett and the performance he's serving the Friday night crowd.

His reputation as the favorite bartender is on full display as he flips bottles in the air before dumping a variety of liquor in a shaker. The women seated in front of him applaud his efforts. They lean forward in a fluid motion to give him a peek down their shirts. Unfortunately for them, he doesn't take the bait.

Garrett is completely devoted to his fiancée. Not that his lack of interest will discourage these chicks. If anything, they see the reformed playboy as a bigger challenge. This is proven when the brunette in the middle stretches to rest a palm on his forearm. He's quick to evade her touch, scolding her with a wag from his index finger.

"Didn't we talk about this earlier?"

The woman sticks out her bottom lip in an exaggerated pout. "Um, I forget. Maybe you should tell me again."

"Keep breaking my rules and you'll have to deal with Ridge." He hitches a thumb in my direction.

She doesn't spare me a glance. "But I like your tattoos."

"An even better reason to try your luck with him. He's got more ink than me."

Her eyes flick to where I'm standing behind the bar, several feet away from them. She frowns at my flat expression. "He doesn't look very friendly."

Garrett chuckles. "That's because he's not."

The blonde in their pack isn't shy about checking me out. Her stare penetrates deeper than an X-ray. "He's sexy as fuck, though."

My indifference cracks into a scowl. "Is that supposed to be a compliment?"

Garrett shifts sideways to block me from view and preserve their generous spending. Another wise choice. "Don't mind the grouch. I didn't hire him for his glowing personality."

One of the girls scoffs. "Why did you then?"

"He's just using me for money," I mutter.

Which isn't too far from the truth. It might've been Garrett's grand plan to open this place, but he couldn't do it alone. The best business decision he ever made was recruiting Drake and me as co-owners.

"You're more than a bank account to me, big brute." The guy I've known since freshman year of college tosses me a smirk.

"I suppose surrounding yourself with those you trust is a wise investment." There aren't many I can rely on more than Garrett and Drake.

"Quit playing. I couldn't run this cock den without you." He thrusts his arms wide and motions to what we've built over the last three years.

The ridiculous nickname our regulars gave Roosters threatens to make me smile. "It doesn't hurt to be associated with King Crusher from the Trojans."

The redhead chick sputters. "As in the condom brand?"

Garrett bends at the waist and cracks up. "Nah, as in the professional sports team."

She joins in his humor, but her laughter lacks true depth. "You're good friends, huh?"

It's no surprise this stranger catches the natural comfort between us. She probably would've noticed even sooner if Drake was out on the floor with us. Our brotherhood formed when we met in college during freshman orientation. The bond didn't break when I left campus after that first year to go pro.

These days, Knox Creek considers our trio a dream team. That's more than likely due to us putting Garrett's talents to good use.

"I only keep the best in my company." He flashes a broad grin at his adoring fans. "What can I say? Ridge is a big shot. Most of the jerseys on the walls belong to him."

The redhead's eyes stray to our collection of framed history along with other sports memorabilia blended in. "Football, hockey, or baseball?"

"Hockey," I grunt. The alternatives couldn't handle me.

A pitchy gasp responds to that tasty tidbit. The blonde peeks out from behind the barrier my buddy attempted to create. She has a hungry gleam in her wide gaze. "Oh, you're like really rich?"

"Fucking vultures," I spit.

"Okay, Thor. Quit swinging your hammer. She was just asking a question."

I feel my mouth twitch as Garrett attempts to soothe their ruffled feathers in that calm tone of his. It served him well on the football field and has a similar effect on this flock. If it were up to me, these ladies would already be halfway to Bent Pedal. Our competition just down the block will easily fulfill their needs if Casey and Adam are tending the bar. But chasing off customers isn't a great look, even for me.

"We can play nice, right?" Garrett knows my answer, which is why he sends me a warning glare over his shoulder.

"Is that my cue?" Even if it's not, I'm overdue for a reprieve.

Garrett shoos me away. "Yeah, yeah. Disappear into the shadows until you're capable of peopling without mouthing off."

"Don't hold your breath," I mutter while turning to the comfort a darkened corner will provide.

Conversations carry on as I make my retreat. One is louder—the speaker instantly identifiable—compared to the others. "Do you know of any available apartments in town?"

The inquiry is met with a giggle. "Already planning to flee your palace?"

A mulish snort responds. "As if. That man will never let me go."

"Damn straight," comes a grumbled reply.

Feminine coos fondle the unmistakable male's ego. "Then what's with the search?"

"Remember Callie?"

The mention of that very particular girl halts my progress while the exchange continues.

"Pssssh, duh. Love her," the unrecognizable voice gushes.

"Same, which is why I'm asking around. She just found out her landlord defaulted on his property taxes. He's been getting away with it for who knows how long and now his tenants have to pay the price. She has until the end of the month to find a new place to live."

I'm striding toward Harper before she's done speaking. "What about Callie?"

Our most recent hire startles at my abrupt interruption. She's great at slinging drinks, but her side hustle of socializing gets tiring. Except when the chatter revolves around a certain brunette beauty.

"Well, hello there." The bubbly bartender wiggles her fingers in my general direction.

"Tell me what's happening with Callie," I bark.

My reaction might be considered irrational, but that's what Calliope Porter does to me. I'm damn near obsessed even though we've never exchanged more than eye contact. There's something about her that's seduced me into submission. The shy glances and timid smiles—no matter how rare—have me hooked on her. I'm claimed. Taken. Hers. I plan to give Callie whatever she desires. That list better include me, or I'm fucked. And not in the pleasurable sense.

Her best friend is aware of my infatuation—mostly due to the fact that I respond like this—and she doesn't miss an opportunity to dangle the bait until I'm ready to pounce. It's been months of torture. This moment is no exception.

Harper quirks her brow, her arms loosely crossed, as she pivots to face me. "You're getting predictable, boss. I just have to say her name and you magically appear."

A muscle in my clenched jaw lunges impatiently. "Spit it out."

Instead, the sassy smartass flutters her lashes. "Didn't you catch the gist while eavesdropping? It's becoming a habit whenever my bestie is involved."

I pinch the bridge of my nose. "If you don't quit avoiding the subject, I'm gonna—"

"Better consider your next words to my wife," Jake Evans drawls from his usual stool. The asshole is a regular at Roosters and a general pain in my ass. His protective streak for those he cares about is his only redeemable quality.

Harper blows him a noisy kiss. "Love you, Jerky Jacob."

"For fuck's sake," I grind out.

Garrett tunes into my demise and begins cackling like this is a staged roast. Go fucking figure. "Ah, shit. Crusher is gonna do some damage if you don't spill the beans, Harps."

He isn't wrong, especially with the audience our spat has attracted. I rub my neck to ease the growing tension. It's a small miracle that Drake is nowhere to be seen. Two against one are odds I prefer to avoid.

"Okay, fine. I'll put you out of your misery and ruin my fun." She rolls her eyes, still stalling. "Callie is getting kicked out of her apartment thanks to that dumbass crook who calls himself a landlord."

The strain between my shoulders multiplies. "When does she have to be out by?"

"Missed that part, hmm?" Her tone is too smug. "She has until the thirty-first to relocate."

"That's less than a week," I mumble absently.

"Which doesn't seem legal. She's just expected to pack up and get gone," Harper gripes.

"Has she found somewhere to go?"

"Not yet. She just got the news yesterday. I would've offered to let her reclaim my spare room, but that's not an option since I surrendered my apartment to live in matrimonial bliss. Besides, she won't share a house with a man. Callie prefers to have her own space." Her shoulders lift in a defeated shrug.

Meanwhile, an idea is quickly forming. "How much is she paying now?"

"Five hundred, and the studio might as well be a shoebox. It barely fits her bed and dresser. Not sure how she's survived there for over a year."

My upper lip curls at Callie's current living conditions, shoving this plan full-speed ahead. "The house attached to mine is available."

Harper scoffs. "Like the other half of a duplex? She can't afford that."

"The rate is flexible. I'm willing to bet she can negotiate the price."

Her hip cocks out as she leans against the sink. "And why is that?"

My gaze narrows in on a smudge. "It's just sitting empty and collecting dust. Could she swing four hundred plus utilities?"

Her eyes bulge. "Is it a dump?"

"Do you think I'd live in a shithole?" I'm almost offended.

"No, but four hundred is crazy low." She clucks her tongue. "As in too good to be true."

"It's rent-controlled," I explain.

Her lips pucker tighter than a virginal asshole. "You just said the rate is flexible."

"It is, but there's a cap."

"Set by your grandpa in the forties?"

A dull throb begins to pound at my temples. "Does it matter? Just have Callie come by and check out the place."

Harper squints at me. "Do we need an appointment?"

"Nah, I'll make sure it's available whenever she's ready."

"Are you friends with the owner?"

"You could say that," I hedge. Even if I wasn't, this plan would sprout to fruition.

"Where was this magical property when I was renting?"

"Not an available option. You're not neighbor material." I grunt at the thought. "Behind the bar is as close quarters as I can manage, especially once Evans came back into the picture."

She glances at her husband, who's envisioning me as target practice, if the lethal intentions behind his glare are anything to go by. Harper's laughter confirms my suspicion. "Touché."

"So," I drawl. "You'll talk to her?"

"Yeah, yeah." She waves off the brimming urgency in my voice and flings a towel over her shoulder. "When are you gonna do the honors yourself? I told you to go easy with her, but that seems like forever ago. It's about time you break the ice, champ."

"Soon. It will be easier when she's next door," I mumble.

Her eyebrows damn near leap to the ceiling. "What was that?"

"Nothing." My scowl could beat Jake's if agitated further.

"Uh-huh, I get it. You have ulterior motives."

The clench in my gut is a warning I ignore. "Don't tell her that."

Harper smiles. The expression seems to reflect a scheme of her own. "Oh, trust me. Callie won't mind."

CHAPTER TWO

Callie

LET MY MOUTH DROP OPEN AS HARPER TURNS INTO THE driveway of our apparent destination. "This can't be right."

She points to the address displayed on her phone in Google Maps, which matches the numbers above the garage. "Welcome home, babes."

"That's a tad presumptuous." But my eyes don't stray from the stunning sight just beyond her windshield.

"As if you're going to turn down this fortress." Her thumb stabs at the two-story duplex.

I admire the structure that's beginning to resemble a castle. It looks like two separate buildings that are essentially glued together. An entire house could be mine. "It's too big for just me. I have nothing to fill it with."

"Are you complaining about excess personal space? I'm sure you could find a roommate—"

"No," I blurt. The pressure squeezing at my throat makes it difficult to swallow. "I'm not interested in living with anyone else."

Memories rise in a wave to crash against the barriers I've tried to build. Darkness swims at the edge of my vision as I attempt to silence the past. There's an echo of a voice I'll never escape. I force myself to inhale slowly, but my chest is rising and falling too fast.

Harper's hand covers mine that I didn't realize is clenched into a tight fist. "You're okay, Cals. No need to explain yourself."

I gulp and offer a slow nod. "Thanks."

She tips her head toward the rental. The afternoon sunshine glitters in her hair, spinning the strands into pure gold. "Should we inspect the inside? Or are the impeccable flowerbeds and wraparound porch enough to convince you?"

My focus roams over the dark brown window trim that pops against the beige siding. The contrast appeals to me, feeding my curiosity to explore. "We should probably take a quick peek at the very least."

Harper is quick to hop out and I follow her lead. Before I take a step, a figure appears on the cobbled path that leads to the house attached to mine. *Mine? Now who's being presumptuous?* But that thought becomes dust as my full concentration is commanded by the man watching me.

My heartrate spikes when Ridge widens his stance and crosses his muscular arms, taking on the appearance of an immovable force. A plain white shirt stretches across his broad chest. The colorful tattoos inked into his skin are more vibrant compared to when I've seen him at Roosters. He's larger than the males I've learned to fear, but I'm not afraid of him. I don't have the urge to cower or become invisible in his presence. Only that strange fluttery sensation swirls in my belly. It's becoming obvious this giddy feeling is connected to him.

A breathy sigh escapes me. His lips twitch in what some might assume is a grin, but I know better. Ridge Carter doesn't do smiles of any variety.

"Well, look who it is." Harper wiggles her fingers at him. "I believe she's who you were referring to as neighbor material. Do you approve?"

My gaze whips to her. "Huh?"

"Apparently"—she draws out the word while flipping her messy braid behind her shoulder—"there's a very short list of who this grump will share a wall with. I'm almost positive you're the one and only allowed to fill that role."

"Hush," I mumble.

Harper bumps me with her hip. "Don't be shy, babes. Just accept it."

Ridge doesn't respond, at least not verbally. There's an audible rumble rolling off him that could be considered an agreement.

I shiver despite the warm spring weather. As my cheeks heat into a rising flush, I steal another glance at the guy in question. The hat he's wearing shades his face, but the shadows can't snuff the molten fire in his eyes. Those green flames burn brighter the longer I'm caught in his unwavering focus.

Harper hooks her arm through mine. "Let's ditch this staring contest before I get turned on by secondhand smolder."

The suggestion in her words burns my face hotter, and I dip my chin to hide the evidence. "Quit it."

"Me? I'm an innocent bystander in this titillating foreplay. Tootles, boss." Harper waves at him in farewell. "We'll holler if there are any questions."

My foot catches on a pebble and I stumble. "We will?"

"Yeah, he volunteered to be our middleman."

I treat myself to a parting glance at him while Harper steers me toward the porch steps. "Why?"

Her fingers tap at a keypad above the knob to grant us entry. "The owner is some big shot real estate shmooze."

"Really?" I balk when there's a loud beep followed by a green light.

Without further delay, Harper shoves the door open. Keys aren't necessary to grant us entry. Noted.

She giggles at my sputtered reaction. "No idea what the

story is behind this place. Just making shit up. Ridge said we can contact him about the contract terms and such. He gave me the code to get in, but was skimpy on the details otherwise. It's a tad sketchy and secretive, which is totally on-brand for him."

"It is?"

She hums. "Except when you're concerned. He's made his intentions blatantly transparent."

"What do you—?" But my question trickles to a stop as I gawk at the paradise we've stepped into. "Um, wow. It's fully furnished."

"That's putting it mildly," she muses.

My jaw goes slack. "Is all this included?"

"I guess?"

Any concern about my lack of belongings whisks away. "Now I'm certain this isn't real. Are we in a dream sequence?"

Harper removes her sandals and strides toward the open area that's arranged as a living room. "Either that or we've walked into an interior design concept staged straight from Pinterest."

Once she mentions that, a realization surrounds me like a comforting embrace. I wouldn't know about the popular app—or have a cellular phone—if it wasn't for her. She taught me the basics, along with a crash course for social media. The overall style resembles an inspiration board I recently created. My feet are frozen to the foyer tiles as I digest the cozy aesthetic.

"Yeah," I breathe. "I wasn't expecting to find my vision brought to life."

"Don't be too shocked. Stranger things have happened," she chimes while skipping to the fireplace.

A smile automatically lifts my lips as I admire the simplistic layout. I slip off my shoes before wading deeper into the space that's beckoning to me. Plush fibers from the cream carpet tickle my toes. A bay window with a bench seat underneath allows natural light to spill in. There's an ethereal glow shining across every surface.

My approval continues to climb as I twirl in a lazy circle. It's neat and tidy. No dust or clutter in sight. The walls are bare. I realize there aren't many decorations either, as if the house is waiting to receive a personal touch. I'll gladly oblige. This room is bright and modern and exactly what I would've chosen for myself.

Neutral and cool hues partner into a cohesive blend. I study the combination that's pleasing to my taste. The crisp palate creates a relaxing atmosphere, which allows me to easily envision myself at home.

Pops of blue and green are splashed throughout. Navy throw pillows sit on the tan couch. Separate sections of glass stained in shades of emerald and jade are inlaid within the stone mantle. A patterned rug is spread out diagonally under a rustic coffee table. The wood is cut into an uneven rectangle that gives it a rare quality.

Every item fits together like pieces of a puzzle to create the big picture. If one thing is misplaced, the entire mood will be thrown off balance. I'm afraid to touch anything.

Harper doesn't share my hesitation. She flops onto the oversized chair near the empty bookshelf and then kicks her feet onto the matching ottoman. "Let's make a deal."

It's a challenge to keep my attention trained on her. "For what?"

"You move in with Jake, and I'll rent this masterpiece. Sydney can stay with me seeing as there's plenty of extra space." She motions around the generous floorplan.

My pulse stammers. "Um…"

Her stoic expression shatters when she begins cackling. "Your face is priceless. As if anyone but you could live here. Ridge practically said as much."

"I highly doubt that." But my belly swoops at the slight possibility of her comment being true.

The thrill of where I am and what this spot signifies diverted my focus off the man who consumes my thoughts. Momentarily, of course. Now my mind is straying back to him. I quickly find myself wondering what he's doing on his half of the duplex. He's probably lounging casually in his home, not taking me into consideration at all. Or maybe he's still outside waiting for my verdict.

That leads me to what the future could hold. Ridge is next door. This house shares a wall with his. It's intimidating to be in such close proximity to him. But more than that, I'm intrigued about the possibility. The change he will undoubtedly deliver to my dull existence. If I was daring, I could visit him whenever the mood strikes. That gives me pause. There's not a bold bone in my body. I can't even find the courage to talk to him. The curiosity might sprout into determination and push me into action. Maybe.

I float from those ponderings to discover that Harper is watching me. "Did you say something?"

Her already shrewd stare narrows into a squint. "You're just as smitten, huh?"

"That would suggest he's… interested in me." I'm still unsure how to comprehend a healthy relationship where both partners are equal. The idea of willingly engaging in one is another task entirely.

Harper clucks her tongue. "Um, duh. Have you seen the way he looks at you?"

"He's just being polite," I murmur.

She squawks in a pitchy tone. "That's the opposite of what he's doing. The man wants you. Badly."

"I don't believe that."

"Want me to go ask him? He'll give you the solid proof

you've been missing, if you know what I mean." She winks, which only serves to confuse me.

I shut her down with a rapid shake of my head. "No, don't go over there. Absolutely not. You shouldn't bother him with such trivial things." The consequences I visualize are enough to turn my stomach.

"Trust me, a bother is the very last thing you could be to him."

"I'd rather not test that theory."

Her forehead creases in a sign of disapproval. "Who else would create this queendom? The king wants you to sit beside him on the throne and rule these lands."

"You make it sound like a fairytale," I murmur.

"If the story fits." She forms her hands into the shape of a heart.

But I can't allow myself to get swept up in such an unlikely fantasy. "He's just being a nice guy."

Harper chokes on seemingly nothing. "There you go again. Excuses, excuses." She sighs dramatically. "Oh, my sweetly innocent friend. You're too kind. Ridge Carter is many things, but nice and polite aren't character traits I would use."

"I think he's wonderful." My breathy voice confirms as much.

"And I think the feeling is more than mutual. He couldn't suggest this spot fast enough after hearing you're on the house hunt."

"Really?

"Haven't you been listening? Pretty sure he decorated just for you." She hitches a thumb toward the kitchen. "Aren't those the jars you wanted from Target?"

"That's a coincidence."

"Uh-huh, one along with a dozen others. He said this place has been sitting empty and collecting dust. Neither of those appear to be true."

I inhale and absorb the calm energy. There's a noticeable crispness in the air that pairs with new beginnings. "It smells… fresh."

"And expensive. Only the best for his chosen one."

"Huh?"

"You're *the* neighbor material."

I heard her toss that title at Ridge earlier, but he didn't confirm her claim. He didn't deny it either. Still the doubt lingers. "Says who?"

"Nobody yet. But it's only a matter of time." She drums her fingers together in a smooth rhythm.

I'm transfixed on the motion for a moment. "Until what?"

"He finally tells you himself." She pauses before adding, "I suppose he needs to talk to you first. Maybe break the ice."

The room spins as I try to calculate the meaning behind her words. I'm overwhelmed in the best possible way. My knees quake and I fight the urge to collapse on what looks to be the most comfortable sofa in existence. Plans and ideas and anticipation are spilling in at a rapid pace. The apparent conversations I'll have with Ridge hold the most promise. And I haven't seen the rest of the house yet.

"I can live here?"

"Uh-huh."

"With it just like this?" I point at the appeasing layout.

Harper's eyebrows bounce. "According to Ridge."

"Shouldn't the owner be involved?"

"Beats me. He took charge of the situation."

A shiver pebbles my skin. I don't want to be controlled, but something about that man giving orders taunts an enthusiastic part of me. "Is he… bossy?"

"That's one way of putting it. Speaking of the grump, he asked me to pass this along for you to call or text." She pulls a rectangular card from her purse.

I smooth my thumb over the embossed lettering. "He wants me to contact him about the rental?"

"Yep, he's got you covered. Don't settle for any slim jimmy. Ridge will provide all the beef and jerky you need."

My nose wrinkles. "I'm not sure what that means."

"It's only a matter of time until you do." Harper leans forward, as if she's about to share a secret. "You're about to be very attached to him."

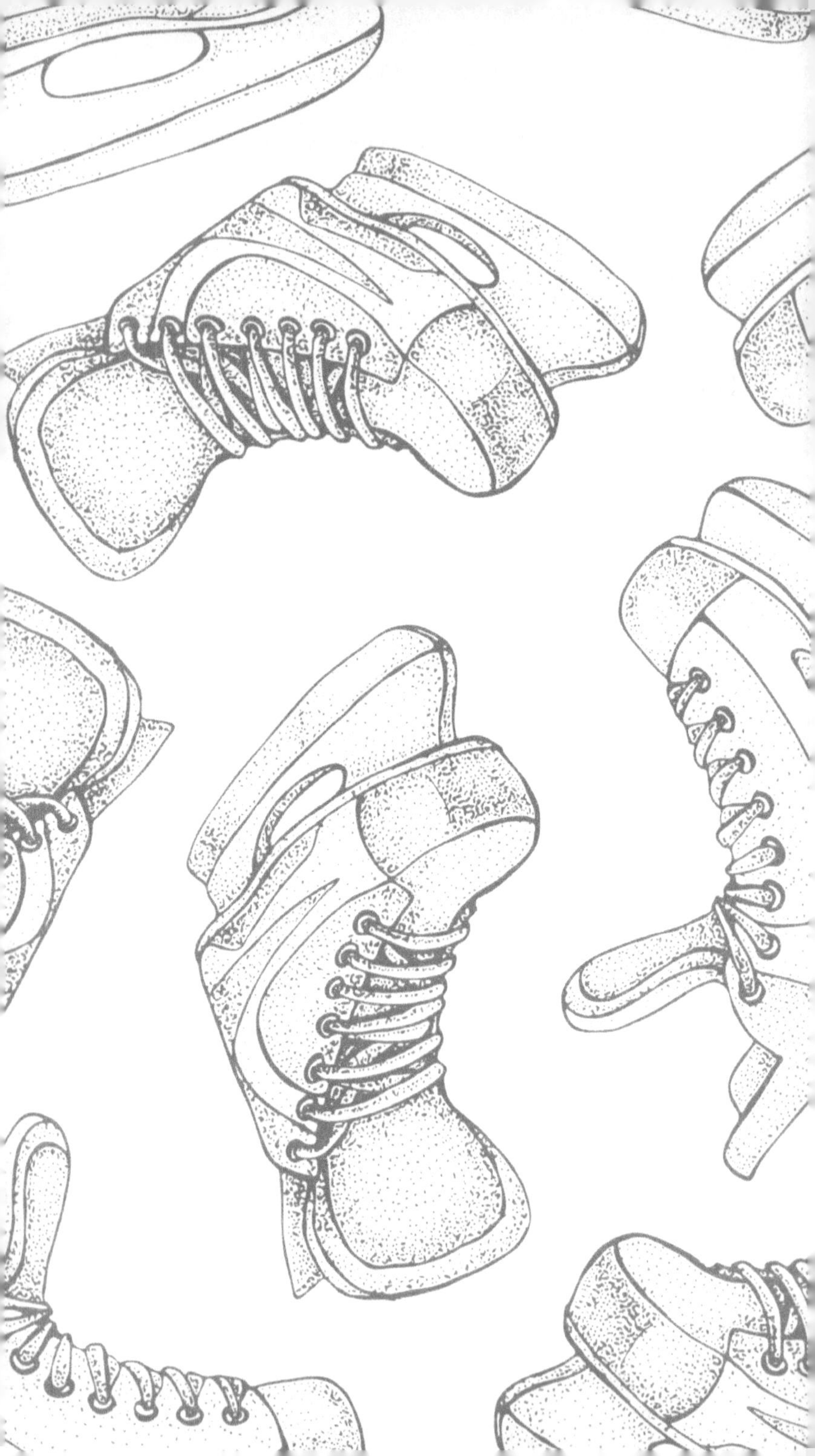

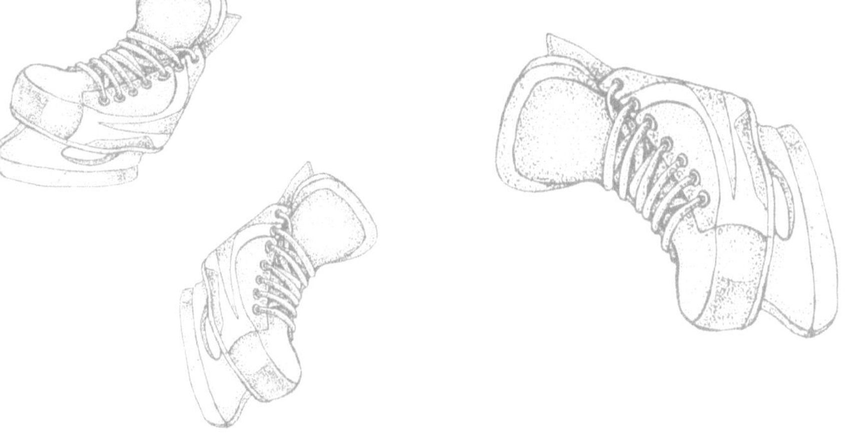

CHAPTER THREE

Ridge

D RAKE SHIFTS ON THE RECLINER FOR THE SIXTEENTH time in two minutes. I'm not counting on purpose, but the damn leather squeaks with each subtle movement from his ass. The grumbling under his breath is another annoyance entirely. It's as if he came over just to test my nonexistent patience.

At this point, I'm just waiting for him to make a monumental announcement. Either that or he has to take a shit. After another restless adjustment, he finally opens the floodgates.

"You're a hypocrite."

I don't bother taking my eyes off the game to glare at him. "Try again."

"Nope, it's true. You can dish it out, but you can't swallow your own advice. Look at how the key has slid into a different lock."

"That's not a saying."

Drake scoffs. "It is now."

My eyes roll at his determination to distract me from hockey. "Don't pretend you weren't part of that gang bang."

He takes a cheap shot at my knee. "Never said I wasn't. The difference is that if I had a sweet little thing—"

"You better not be referring to Callie as such." The warning vibrates from my harsh tone.

"What would you prefer?"

"That she doesn't cross your mind to begin with. Keep her name out of your mouth while you're at it."

"Well, shit. Someone ate his caveman cereal this morning." His chuckle is too amused, grating on my final frayed nerve. "As I was saying, I wouldn't be sitting here with your grumpy ass if the skate was on the other foot."

"Now you're fucking up sentiments on purpose."

"It's getting you to respond more than usual."

I scrub over my face to stave off an incoming migraine. "Want me to kick you out? Could've just asked."

"Add stubbornness to your list of admirable qualities."

"Don't question my methods."

"Straight madness? I wouldn't dare," Drake deadpans.

"This is coming from a guy who's notorious for choosing the wrong girl."

"Meanwhile, you haven't even talked to the one you're legit crazy about. How long has it been?" My so-called friend begins counting on his fingers. "Ten months?"

"Thirteen," I correct. That doesn't include the one or two she was in Knox Creek prior to my awareness of her.

Once again, there's no point in denying that I've kept track whenever Calliope Porter is concerned. After catching sight of her that random afternoon on Main Street, I made my interest freakishly obvious. Well, to everyone except her. My plan doesn't involve scaring her off before I have a chance to explain myself.

Drake's unintelligible grumbling drags me back to my living room. "Are you holding out for another year?"

"If that's what it takes." I'm nothing if not disciplined.

He curses under his breath. "Never took you for one to beat around the bush."

"That's your area of expertise. Nah, wait. You tend to miss altogether."

"Leave me be. I'm still licking my wounds." But his smirk suggests he's long since recovered.

"The fact you continue repeating the cycle is an insult to your pride."

"Good thing I have plenty of it."

Minnesota scores and I pump my fist before circling back to Drake's insanity. "You've got to be the only single dick who's desperate to have kids but can't find a chick to be your baby mama."

"When she's ready for me, I'll find her."

"Now you're sounding like Garrett."

He shrugs and slouches lower against the cushions. "Worked out in his favor. And don't think it hasn't escaped my notice that you're bordering on hypocrite territory again."

I grunt in response. Maybe I'm jealous. This pest won't hear me admit it. "The situation is under control. Quit bothering me and worry about yourself."

"Or you could share this ingenious slow play. Tell me what it is about her that gets to you."

"Why do you care?"

The silence that follows suggests he's scrounging for an explanation that will crack me. He should know better. His exhale sounds like a white flag, but my friend isn't a quitter. "I've never seen you give a shit about anything other than hockey and the bar. Maybe Garrett and me on a good day."

It's my turn to release a heavy sigh. If I divulge a tiny scrap, he might let me watch the game in peace. "She's different."

There's another pause. "Wow, that's deep. Did you come up with that on your own?"

"Consider yourself lucky that I'm entertaining your hopeless romantic questioning to begin with." Because even that crumb is more than I've given to Callie.

"C'mon, Crusher. You gotta give me more than that. Why does this specific woman twist you into knots?"

"Are you trying to get your ass kicked?" The urge to lunge at him regardless of his response flexes my muscles.

He pinches the bridge of his nose. "You're impossible."

"And you're nosy."

"For good reason. I might gain insight into my personal problems. We both know I could use the guidance." The sympathy card does little to penetrate my indifference.

But a ping from my phone earns an immediate reaction. That noise gives me an adrenaline rush similar to when I stole the puck or smashed an opponent into the boards. There's no doubt in my mind who the text is from. That doesn't mean my eyes don't automatically lower to feast on her message.

> Callie: Hello, Ridge. How are you? I was wondering if I could still ask you questions even though I've already signed the lease. You told me the other day it was all right, but I wanted to double check. Please don't hesitate to tell me if I'm bothering you. Harper insists I'm not. That doesn't necessarily mean she's telling me the truth. I know she's worried about hurting my feelings. You don't have to be concerned about that. Unless you want to be. I'm not trying to tell you what to do. I would never do that. Anyway, I just wanted to check. I hope I didn't interrupt anything important. Not that you would read my text if you were busy. There I go again. I better stop before I really do become a bother.—Callie

Damn, her formal texting is endearing as fuck. She's properly punctuated and grammatically correct. I get hard imagining her talking to me that eloquently. The strain in my jeans is a reliable companion, popping up whenever thoughts of the bashful brunette arise. It's safe to say the blood loss to my brain is almost constant at this point—and having adverse effects. Eventually, she might provide me with relief that's more physical than legible.

The fact she typed an entire paragraph when most don't bother with a full sentence reveals a notable distinction. Social norms haven't altered her free style. Callie radiates an innocence that's good and pure and infectious. That type of flawlessness belongs with an equally honest energy. But fuck that. I'm a corrupt bastard and she's all mine.

"Holy shit," Drake blurts. "Are you… smiling?"

The joy gets wiped off my face. Just thinking about Callie initiating contact has a way of smoothing my sharp edges. Regardless of the company I'm currently keeping. "You're still here?"

"Aww, grumpy bear. I didn't mean to ruin it. That must be from the one I'm not supposed to think about."

"Yet that's precisely what you're doing."

He chuckles. "What's she saying?"

"None of your business." I read her message again and then send a response.

> Me: hey, you. come to me for whatever you need. always. that's never gonna change

I'm aware that my behavior is intense. Some might believe I've already crossed several lines, and I plan to demolish many more. My infatuation isn't a secret. Callie has me hooked. At her mercy. Wrapped around her pinky tight enough to suffocate. That's what she does to me. I want to embed myself deep into her life, until she forgets what it's like to be apart from me.

And I'm willing to bet the feeling is mutual. Even if she doesn't fully comprehend what that means yet.

The bubble with three dots instantly appears to indicate she's writing a reply. She's eager and doesn't try to hide it. I like that. A lot.

"Damn, you're totally smiling. You're really gone for her, huh?"

"Fuck off," I grumble without looking away from my thread with Callie. But a fast motion on my left forces my attention to where Drake has his phone aimed at me. "What're you doing?"

"My due diligence and capturing this moment." His fingers begin flying across his screen. "Garrett is gonna lose his shit over this."

"You better delete—"

I cut myself off as a new message from her arrives.

> Callie: Hi again. Thank you for answering me so promptly. That's very kind of you. I appreciate having someone else to rely on. Harper has let me ask her everything, but I don't want to become a pest. I'm looking forward to being your neighbor. Is that okay to admit? I don't want to be too forward. But where I currently live, nobody is very friendly to me. I have a feeling you'll give me a warm welcome. Did you know I'm moving in tomorrow? Not that you pay attention to my schedule. I'm silly for even typing that. But maybe the owner told you. Either way, I might see you if you're home. Will you be? If you're not, I'll text you if I have any questions. I appreciate the help. You're already the best neighbor I've ever had.—Callie.

There's a noticeable warmth traveling through me as her words settle. I'm grinning like a fool and couldn't care less that Drake is beside me to witness it. Callie is getting attached to me. That's worth far more than whatever flack this asshole can dish out.

On cue, my friend lets loose a low whistle. "If you're nuts about her at this stage, what's going to happen when she's next door?"

"Destiny will come knocking," I mumble absently while giving her most recent text a third pass.

Drake hoots and kicks his feet like a toddler on too much sugar. "Oh, that's rich shit. You better jot that down in your memory book to reminisce at your wedding. Speaking of, when's the big day?"

I swivel my gaze to him as his meaning registers. "Huh?"

His snickering continues. "Fuck, this is too precious. It's adorable how distracted you get from a few simple messages. What's she saying?"

"Haven't we been over this already?" My sour tone doesn't diminish his amusement.

If anything, his smile stretches to creepy clown proportions. "Yeah, but I'm enjoying the variety of facial expressions you're putting on display. It's highly entertaining to watch your spirits brighten like the Stanley Cup finals arrived early."

"Well, I'd enjoy it if you got gone and let me be."

"Sure, sure. I'll kick rocks soon. First you gotta tell me when your neighbor is arriving."

"Tomorrow." And the wait tests every fiber of my restraint. I'm about ready to crawl from my skin as the hours tick down.

"Did you hire professionals or are you handling the heavy lifting yourself?"

"No to both." My jaw clenches at the reminder.

In return, Drake's mouth hangs slack. "You're not helping her?"

"Harper shut me down when I offered. She told me that Callie is particular about her space and who she allows inside of it."

Which is something I would've preferred to hear straight from the source, but she hasn't revealed those details yet. Not that I can blame the feisty blonde for protecting her friend. My natural instincts where Callie are concerned are territorial. Possessive at best. And we still haven't talked.

His eyes bulge. "Those two are gonna pack, move, and haul everything on their own?"

"It's not my preference, trust me." But I can only push so hard before I meet resistance. "Her studio is small. There shouldn't be too much stuff. Jake is letting them borrow his truck." Not sure what's wrong with using mine, but that's another grievance to address later.

Once she's living next to me, I'll handle her needs. Wants and desires too. Fuck, the potential of her relying on me for simple pleasures heats my blood.

My nosey friend grunts. "You got that asshole to do your dirty work? Quite impressive."

"The honor belongs to his wife. He's wrapped around her diamond-encrusted ring finger."

"Can't blame the guy. They're in newlywed bliss. Love like that is mighty fine."

"Speaking from experience?" My phone chimes to divert my attention away from whatever nonsense he's going to spew next.

> Callie: Hello, Ridge. It's me. Again. I noticed you read my text, but you didn't respond. Does that mean—?

Drake's hand clamps down on my shoulder before I can gorge myself on more of Callie's sweetness. "Nah, I haven't gotten lucky in the romance department. But you're about to be."

I shake him off me. "There'd be a better chance if you'd let me concentrate on what's important."

"Jeez," he gripes. "You act like I'm an infected ingrown hair on your ass, but she's blowing up your—"

"She's different," I reiterate.

Drake holds up his palms in surrender and rises to stand. "It's becoming clear that the gift of my presence isn't appreciated. I'll leave you two alone. You'll be very happy texting each other in companionable solitude."

At long last, something we can agree on.

"See ya later," I toss to him in parting.

"If you ever peel your eyes off the screen," his retreating voice calls.

Before the door slams behind him, I'm backtracking to start at the beginning of her latest message.

Callie: Hello, Ridge. It's me. Again. I noticed you read my text, but you didn't respond. Does that mean you're busy or you didn't like something I said? This is new to me. Could I be more obvious? I just don't want to upset you or push too far. That's not my intention. I'm mostly curious about everything. Uncertain too. There's much for me to learn. Harper says that I'm beginning to express myself openly from behind a screen, but not so much in person. From where I come from... well, that's a story for a different day. For now, I hope you're preoccupied instead of not responding on purpose. Am I too demanding? Or maybe impatient. Gosh, those don't sound good. Both is probably a safe bet. Are those two traits more appealing than needy? That's something Harper calls herself when... never mind. That's too personal. We can discuss that at a later date once we've known each other longer. If you still want to talk to me. Let me know if I'm bothering you yet. You

can be honest with me. I'd prefer that
over the alternative.—Callie

My thumbs are poised and ready when I've reached the end. I've never cared much for texting, but I'll sit in this spot for hours if it means this girl keeps giving me her words. She has plenty to share and I'm here for it.

Me: never too busy for you, sweetness. had a slight disruption to deal with. that's taken care of and I'm all yours

Me: the thought of you needy and demanding and impatient for me is what I've been waiting for. I like you just the way you are. trust me. don't hold back. give me the good and bad. whatever's running through your mind. I'll ease your troubles however I can

Me: let's start with you telling me about your day. no skimping on the details.

The three dots on her side bounce in their bubble almost immediately after my text is sent. I don't fight the grin that's forming or hesitate to sink deeper into the couch and prepare for the best night I've had in years.

CHAPTER FOUR

Callie

THE DRESSER MEETS THE CARPET WITH A QUIET THUMP. In contrast, Harper is making quite a racket. She groans while stretching her back. Several joints crack from the movement. A wince pinches her features that she has aimed at the ceiling.

"Don't tell my feminist side that I'm admitting this, but the moving process would've been significantly easier with some manpower." She releases another pained noise.

My hand automatically lifts to rub her shoulder. "I'm grateful for your help."

"It's my pleasure. Besides, now I have the perfect excuse to get a massage from my husband. Extra long and hard, if you know what I mean." Harper's eyebrows wiggle.

A blush heats my cheeks at the brazen visual of my new neighbor giving me a similar treatment. "That sounds… relaxing."

"What's got that dreamy look on your face? Other than the obvious." She motions around my bedroom that's in desperate need of organizing.

Predictable insecurity creeps in and replaces the fizzy

bubbles in my stomach. I knot my fingers until the knuckles turn white. "Do you think I text Ridge too much?"

"That's where your mind goes after we heaved massive hunks of furniture up too many stairs?"

"Yes?" More uncertainty. Shocking.

My friend must hear the doubt plaguing my voice. She grips my arms and gives me a reassuring squeeze. "Do you text him too much by most standards? Absolutely. But Ridge isn't an ordinary guy, especially where you're concerned."

I latch onto a specific piece of her explanation. A soft exhale deflates the tension from my posture. "You're right. He's certainly special. Unlike any man I've ever met."

"Good grief. I'm the one who just got married, but you're wafting love potion fumes all over me. I'll be begging Jake to knock me up if we're not careful." She laughs and fans her face. "To be honest, according to what I've witnessed, you're probably not messaging him enough."

My mood rebounds. "Really?"

"Um, yeah. I've got a seriously big hunch." Harper studies me for a moment, catching where my thoughts have wandered off to. "You want to text him right now, don't you?"

I chew on my thumbnail. "Uh-huh."

She giggles and shakes her head. "You're too cute. I bet he's just sitting over there waiting for you to message him."

That has me scrambling to get my phone. "Oh, gosh. He probably thinks I'm ignoring him."

Her hand stills mine before I can start typing. "Hold on. Does he ever initiate contact?"

"We haven't been writing to each other for very long. Just since you gave me his number last week," I murmur. "Usually I reach out first."

"Then let him do the honors." Her nonchalant tone doesn't pair well with this delicate situation.

My stomach sinks. "What if he doesn't?"

"Oh, he will."

I frown at my screen that remains blank in mocking. "How can you be so sure?"

Harper buzzes her lips. "Okay, Mopey Missy. There's no need to pout. You just moved into a beautiful house. Let's focus on that."

The reminder tugs my lips into a weak smile. "It's still hard to believe." Even with the proof surrounding me.

"Are you super happy?"

"Yes," I breathe and spin in a slow circle.

A bright future envelops me. That's the shove I need to ditch the gloom. There isn't a cause for upset. It's silly to consider it for even a moment. I've experienced true misery. If Ridge doesn't text me, I'll be just fine. The limp expression on my mouth lifts and spreads wide to announce this revelation.

She claps at what I feel as personal growth. "See? That's the spirit."

"The past year has been surreal. When I left the compound, I couldn't guess what was in store for me. I definitely didn't dream of living in a place like this. It just wasn't possible in my mind."

Harper's grin stretches to mirror mine. "Yet here you are. No dreaming necessary. Just goes to show that nice things can happen to those who deserve it, especially when you catch the eye of a broody bachelor with rental connections."

My face gets warm at the mention of Ridge, but I don't allow myself to focus on him. Instead, I create a mental list of things to get for my new home. There isn't much thanks to the owner providing everything except what I chose to put in this room. For whatever reason, this space was left completely untouched. Which makes it glaringly obvious that these are my belongings. The few items I own are in bad shape. I'm grateful to have the dresser and nightstand that I found for free, but the two pieces appear seconds away from disrepair.

It might be wise for me to begin there.

"Is bedroom furniture expensive? Like a matching set?"

"Depends on where you're shopping," Harper says. "You have money saved, right?"

"Not enough." Besides, that stash is for emergencies only.

She rocks on her bare feet. "Take on more shifts at the groomers. You're closer to Main Street now. The walk is only a few blocks."

I nod. "Yeah, that's a smart idea. It shouldn't take me nearly as long to get there."

"Or you could ask someone for a ride." Her thumb points at the shared wall.

"Ridge? Oh, no. I couldn't impose. He's too busy."

As if hearing his name, a telltale chirp draws my gaze downward. A message appears in our thread that I still have open on the screen. I'd already been smiling, but the expression hits comical proportions with his words.

> Ridge: how's it going over there? all settled in?

The relief I feel is equally ridiculous compared to my former distress. I begin typing a respond instead of overanalyzing the reaction.

> Me: Hello, Ridge. How's your evening? It's very considerate of you to check in on my progress. We're done moving my belongings inside. It wasn't too difficult, but I'm glad to be done. I still have some rearranging to do. That might be a job for tomorrow. Guess what? Harper and I were just discussing the texting pattern between you and me. Have you ever messaged me first? Like after we've stopped writing and haven't started again. I can't remember. She told me to wait until you did. I suppose that was good advice

since you did text me just now. I'll admit that I had my doubts. It makes me smile to think you must like our conversations. At least I hope you do. You must enjoy them somewhat to continue responding. Not to mention initiating contact. When I was worried about not hearing from you, I got very sad. I believe I'm growing quite attached to you already, just like Harper said I would. Is that okay? I don't ever want to become a bother, as I've mentioned previously. Probably too many times. It's an ongoing concern if that isn't obvious. Maybe that's enough from me for now. I look forward to your reply, Ridge.—Callie

"Is that him? It's like we summoned him or something." Harper approaches from over my shoulder and reads what I just sent. "Dude! You're not supposed to tell him all that."

My attention leaps off the screen to collide with her logic. "I'm not?"

She shakes her head. "Also, you don't have to greet him each time or sign your name at the end."

"Oh." I frown at my recent reply. "Do I look foolish?"

"Nah, he probably loves it. But you can save yourself time by cutting out the formality. Unless it's your first message that day or in a new exchange. It's like I told you when we first started chatting." Her grin is probably meant to be reassuring.

Confusion swirls into a thick fog. "But that's just your preference. Plus, you're my friend. He's a man. I want to make sure he knows I'm polite."

"Trust me, babes. He knows."

The oxygen in my lungs turns to stone and I wheeze. "Did you tell him—?"

Harper eyes widen. "No, no. Your secrets aren't mine to spill. But I told him just enough to explain that he needs to play a slow game."

I furrow my brow. "Such as?"

"That he should be careful with you"—she holds up a palm when I try to interrupt—"as in take things slow and be gentle. I wanted him to give you time to adjust. He's being patient on purpose. When you're ready for more, he'll be there. You control the situation."

That final statement stands out in bold. "I have control?"

"Yes. It's yours."

"Wow." That concept will take some getting used to. "I have so much to learn."

"Don't worry too much about it. Most of this is just general dating rules that don't apply in your case."

I blanch. "Dating?"

"Um, yeah. What else do you call this?" She motions to the ongoing thread in my phone.

"We're not dating."

"Ridge might think otherwise."

"But he hasn't expressed a romantic interest in me." Or maybe he has.

Once again, I'm out of my depth. Where I come from, there are no dates prior to an arrangement for marriage. I'm aware that's not how relationships are formed in Knox Creek, or most societies in this country for that matter. Even before fleeing Billmoore, I knew our customs weren't typical. To experience the divide is another rude awakening entirely.

The differences are staggering and have taken me the better part of a year to understand. To this day, it's difficult for me to comprehend Ridge's attentiveness as anything other than civil conversation. That means it's very likely he shows this common courtesy to others as well.

"What if he's dating someone else?" My voice holds a brittle edge.

Harper snorts, which becomes a choked cackle. "That's the funniest thing you've ever said."

"I didn't tell a joke."

"Maybe not on purpose," she giggles. "But you must be kidding. That man is already faithfully devoted to you. He even goes out of his way to avoid female customers at the bar."

"Really?" The idea clouds my judgment.

"Yes." Her tone leaves no space for argument.

"But we've never spoken about a mutual attraction to each other. Or having a date for that matter," I add after regaining clarity from my stupor.

"Ask him."

"About what?"

"Going on a date," Harper states casually. She's so at ease with this discussion. Just another variation in how we were raised.

Meanwhile, I feel sweat beading along my hairline. "Do you think he'll ask me out for a date?"

"Or you could ask him on one."

A gasp wrenches from me. "I can't do that."

"You certainly can. We're fortunate to be in the modern age. Women are very capable of ruling the roost. Be empowered." She shakes her fist.

My head is spinning as usual whenever we get on the subject of men. I stumble toward the bed, barely catching myself on the edge. "Oh, my."

"Welp, my work here is done." She brushes her hands together. "Gonna get a rub down from Jerky Jacob."

"Huh?" I barely hear her over the brewing chaos in my mind.

"That massage I mentioned," she clarifies while shaking her hips. "And then some."

Even my sheltered awareness can gather her meaning. "You're bad."

"Eh, a little debauchery is good for the soul." My friend

saunters to the door, but peeks back at me before leaving. "Better answer him before he comes over here."

"What?" I glance down and notice several messages I've missed from Ridge flashing on the screen.

With the pressure from the dating topic, I'd forgotten to reply. That's a first.

Ridge: glad you're over there. things will be easier now. and thx for telling me you want to hear from me more often. I'll be texting you first thing each morning. might as well since you're my every waking thought

Ridge: that might've been the longest text I ever sent someone

Ridge: did I shock you into silence with that? hope it wasn't too much

Ridge: sweetness?

Ridge: callie. gonna need a reply soon

My jaw hangs slack. "He sent me five consecutive messages. That's a big deal, right?"

But Harper is gone, and I'm talking to an empty room. That gives me the freedom to return his messages without being rude. Not that her presence would stop me.

Me: Apologies for the delay. Harper just left. I'm glad you'll text me every morning. That sounds like a lovely start to each day.

I assume his response will take a few minutes. When my phone pings within seconds, my breath catches.

Ridge: what's wrong?

Me: With what? I'm very happy in this house. Didn't I tell you that?

Ridge: you're not giving me all of your words like usual

Me: That doesn't mean there's anything wrong. I'm trying to keep my messages short.

Ridge: why?

Me: Harper told me I should be more concise.

Ridge: didn't I tell you the opposite?

I scroll through our previous messages to recall what he actually said.

Me: You told me not to hold back. That you want to hear the good and the bad. Whatever is running through my mind.

Ridge: sounds like the opposite of concise to me. lay it all on me, sweetness. our conversations are the best part of my day

Nerves bubble to the surface as I consider where to begin. The possibilities are endless. I can't ask him on a date. That feels too personal and inappropriate. It would be nice to become better acquainted. I suppose asking questions is the easiest option to accomplish that. My phone dings while the freedom to choose continues tripping through me.

Ridge: did I lose you again?

Me: No, I'm here. I'm just thinking about what to say.

Ridge: that didn't seem like a problem before

Me: Okay, I'll just write everything that decides to flood forward. It just felt like too much pressure suddenly. Like I was put on the spot. Does that make sense? Then I froze and didn't say anything, which led to you believing I was ignoring you. Again. Although, to be fair, I wasn't really ignoring you before. Not on purpose. Harper and I were talking about something kind of serious, at least for me. The topic distracted me to the point that I didn't see you had sent so many messages. It wasn't my intention to make you worry or wonder why I'm not responding. Not that I'm assuming you were worried. That's something I would do if you stopped replying to me. Worry, I mean. You've probably figured that out about me. I'd like to know more about you, if that's all right. Can I ask you questions?

I sigh as my message is sent. It feels as if a weight as been lifted off my chest. Maybe I should follow Ridge's advice and allow my words to flow freely. At least when I message him. He seems to prefer my lengthy responses. A text arrives to mark that assumption as fact.

Ridge: there we go. that's much better. I like it when you let go and speak your mind. that includes asking me anything

Me: Thanks for embracing my rambling. Your support means a lot to me. I'm still adjusting to this way of life. You're already helping me. In more ways than one. There's usually a desperate urgency inside of me that's clawing to escape. Maybe that's why I write so much. It just pours out. All right, now for a question. Do you like animals?

Ridge: first, knowing that I'm helping you does crazy things to me. I enjoy seeing that spelled out in your words. a lot. I appreciate you telling me. maybe one day you'll share where this urgency comes from. second, I love animals. who doesn't?

Me: I'm glad you enjoy my words. There are plenty of people I used to know who didn't like animals. Where I grew up is very different from here. My voice wasn't heard, if that makes sense. I think that's why I have this sudden urgency to speak when there's a chance.

Ridge: your voice will always be heard by me. that's a promise

Me: This might be too trusting of me, but I believe you. I can tell you're different from the rest. Maybe one day you'll explain what these crazy things are that you're referring to.

Ridge: I'd rather show you, sweetness. when you're ready

A flush rushes under my skin and I'm burning from curiosity. The unknown makes me squirm. There's a strange sensation warming in my belly. I wonder what will happen if he says more things like that. Perhaps I'll catch a fever.

Ridge: that was too much, huh? I can practically hear you tossing and turning

I stop fidgeting, only to realize that I've reclined onto the bed at some point. His words remind me of an earlier thought that occurred to me.

Me: Are the walls thin? I'm certain your statement is purely fiction, but now I want to know if you can hear me from your home.

Ridge: do you hear that?

I strain my ears, but there's no sound other than my rapid pulse.

Me: No. Should I hear something?

Ridge: I'm pounding on the wall

Me: Well, it seems we've settled that the walls aren't thin.

Ridge: how unfortunate

Me: Why is that?

Ridge: I wouldn't mind listening to your voice

Ridge: is that creepy? didn't think before I sent it

My belly swoops and dives in an impressive acrobatic routine. As the tumble sequence settles, I gather the courage to respond.

Me: I wouldn't mind listening to your voice either.

Ridge: damn, sweetness. probably shouldn't have told me that. now I won't be able to stop picturing my name falling from your lips. it's taking an unholy amount of restraint to stay put and not come knocking on your door.

Me: Oh! I'm about to abruptly change the subject. Does that make me rude? I really hope you don't think I'm being rude. You just reminded me that I want to paint my door. Do you think the owner would mind?

Ridge: if anyone's rude, it's me. it's for the best that we talk about something else. what color do you wanna paint it?

Me: I think green would look nice. A bright spot against the neutral siding. What do you think?

Ridge: that suits you

Me: Really? Do you think the owner will allow me to do it?

Ridge: consider it approved

Me: Just like that?

Ridge: yeah, sweetness. just like that

Me: How can you be so sure?

Ridge: you'll see. until then, I'm ready for another question

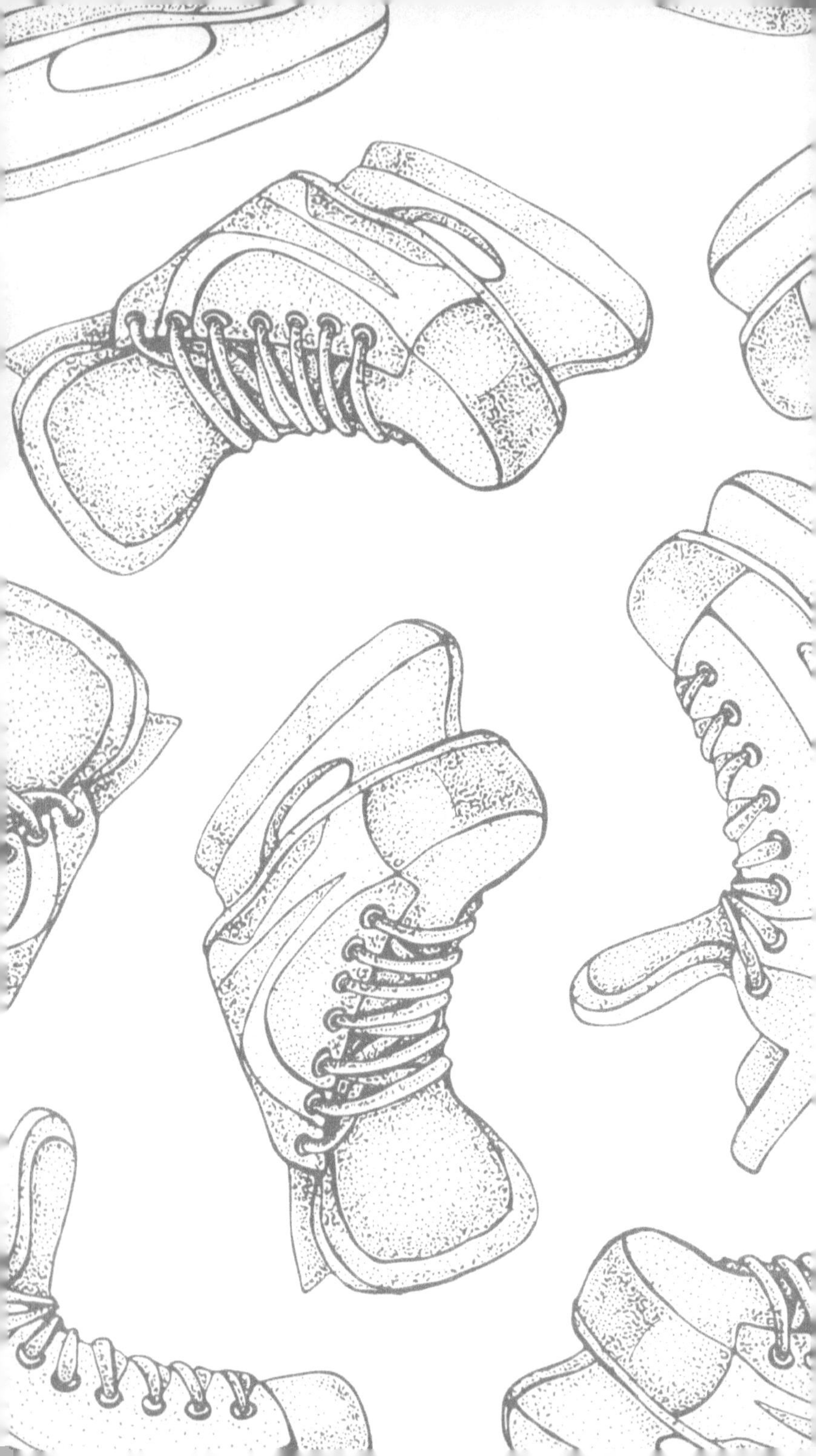

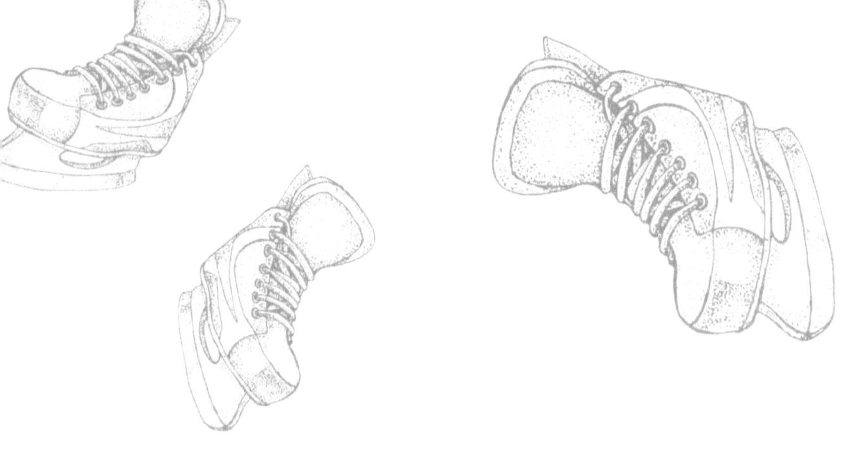

CHAPTER FIVE

Ridge

SWEAT BEADS ON MY FOREHEAD FROM THE PRESSURE to finish in such a short amount of time. I didn't think it would be this hard. The final touch is applied with an upward stroke. Relief fondles me while my knees hit the porch floor. Pride soon follows. A slow exhale grants me a moment's reprieve.

My task is complete, and I wasn't caught in the process. The surface is smooth, wet, and covered in its entirety. Just as I'm about to straighten and inspect my handiwork, a gasp confronts me.

Spoke too soon.

I'm on my feet and turn to face her judgment. Callie stares at the fast motion through unblinking eyes. The sight of her in front of me is staggering and I almost fall flat on my ass. At the last second, I grab onto the railing for support. This leaned position gives me a calm and confident appearance. Or I look ready to pounce. Nobody could blame me for acting like an alpha male in the presence of his mate.

Fuck, she's beautiful. The early afternoon sun sparkles in her dark hair. My hands curl into fists, desperate to comb through those glossy strands. I bet she feels like silk. *Everywhere.*

There's a twinkle in her gaze that remains fastened on me. The blue is soothing and offers me peace even though my heart is racing. It also spurs me into action.

I take a chance and step off the porch, closing our distance until a few long strides separate us. She watches me approach but doesn't move otherwise. Fresh paint dances in the wind along with a vanilla sweetness that I can only assume comes from Callie. I want to drag her scent deep into my lungs until she's all I breathe. The temptation dangles on the next breeze, stirring my arousal.

Through the haze, a thought occurs to me. We've never been alone until now. It appears that the same realization strikes her as she glances at the quiet street. I should probably excuse myself and stop making her uncomfortable, but my soles are rooted to the ground. Callie's wide astonishment returns to me, and I'm lost.

As a former professional athlete, I know how it feels to be put on a pedestal. Fans still flock to me when I'm out in public. Those years in the league also taught me what it feels like to be put on the spot and handle the stress that accompanies such a bright spotlight.

I was always able to manage the chaos in a packed arena. Block out the noise to get the win. Nothing could shake me. Past tense.

As it turns out, silence from Calliope Porter is what tests my limits. This timid woman snatches every ounce of composure I possess just by giving me her attention.

The quiet yawns and stretches, then demands a snack after such a lengthy nap. My jaw itches and I scrub at the stubble there. I need to say something. She just stumbled upon me painting her front door. This was her idea. Kind of. But that's not the point. As the trespasser, it's my responsibility to explain myself.

My tongue swells to the point where speech is impossible. Only a muffled grunt is audible from me. *Real fucking eloquent.* I clear my throat and try again.

"Hey, Callie." My palm lifts to wave at her as if that small gesture will ease the tension. "As you can see, I went ahead and took care of the update you suggested. Now you don't have to get your hands dirty. Not that it would be a bad thing if you did. It wasn't my intention to cross a line. I just wanted to handle the project for you. Consider it a housewarming gift. A personal touch from me to you."

That's not grounds for calling the cops or anything. I tuck my chin and fire off a round of foul expletives aimed directly at my mouth. The fact I'm stumbling over my words like a toddler in ice stakes isn't doing me any favors. As if agreeing, Callie's lips twitch in what I trick myself into believing is amusement. At least I'm useful for something.

The affirmation—self-proclaimed or not—loosens the strain in my lungs, allowing me to breathe freely. "I meant to have this done before you got home."

A crease appears between her brows. She still doesn't speak, which is a stark contrast to the girl who has been rambling to me over text messages longer than my dick. This timid version can barely look me in the eye. It seems her fondness for conversation is reserved for our text thread. That's just fine. I'm the one who sprung this unannounced visit on her.

"This isn't how I planned for us to officially meet," I rush to explain. "But here we are. I saw you leave and figured the time was right. It was meant to be a surprise. Guess I took longer than necessary to finish."

Callie peers around me to inspect my artistic ability. The hint of a smile from earlier expands into a full grin.

I follow her line of sight to stop myself from gawking.

The effort is commendable, but worthless. My focus returns to her within seconds. "Do you like it?"

A soft hum is paired with a nod.

"If the shade isn't right—"

"No!" She startles at her own voice. "It's perfect."

And just like that, I feel ten feet tall and capable of anything. "Good. That's, uh… really good." I scrub at the prickles spreading across the back of my neck. "I'm glad."

"Thank you," Callie murmurs. She dips her face, but there's no hiding the smile that's likely to spark a heatwave. Or the way she bites her bottom lip.

It's no wonder that I find myself staring at her. Shamelessly. But I quickly recall how our exchange began. Those handful of utterances she gave me are a big step. I won't test my luck.

"Um. Is there anything else I can do for you? While I'm here, I mean?" The initial deed is done, but I'll gladly stick around for more.

Red splotches appear on her cheeks. Before my mind can take a dirty turn trying to picture what's causing that blush, she shakes her head.

I shove my hands in my pockets and prepare to leave. "Well, I did what I came to do. I'll be next door if you need me."

Callie peeks at me from beneath her lowered lashes. "Bye, Ridge."

My foot catches in the grass and I barely keep myself upright. Damn, I've been waiting a long time to hear that. What I've been imagining doesn't come close to the real deal. My name from her lips is a burst of sweetness wrapped in sinful delight. I'm already addicted and thinking of ways to have her call out to me on repeat.

But first, I need to regain control of myself. Weak knees and an elevated heart rate aren't the physical responses I'm concerned about. A groan threatens to expose my desire. There's no concealing the hard bulge in my jeans, which means I need to put distance between us. Now.

I glance back at her over my shoulder, keeping my cock pointing in the opposite direction. "See you soon, sweetness."

And that's the extent of my restraint.

Once I've crossed from her property to mine and shut myself inside, I wait for the frenzied lust to fade. But clarity doesn't return. The solid surface at my back doesn't add stability. All I hear is my name spilling from Callie's lips like a chant.

My boots hammer on wood as I rush upstairs. Arousal chases me faster with each step. This intensity is foreign and reserved strictly for her. There's a singular goal leading me to the spot that connects her home to mine. That section of wall above our attached garages has become a sanctuary of sorts. As I enter my room and reach that place, the desperation has grown into a caged beast.

I rip open my pants to free the insistent throb. Relief wheezes from me while I get a solid grip. I begin to fuck my fist and plant the other palm firmly on the wall. That contact grounds me. My mind makes quick work of picturing Callie on the opposite side. The visual is enough to fuel my desire to intoxicating levels.

My hips thrust at a feverish pace. I'm already teetering near the edge from visions of her hand replacing mine. I pump my dick harder at the fantasy. It takes true shape in the form of her lush mouth while she beckons for more. There's a sweet scent floating in the air that has my mouth watering. I'm compelled to increase the speed, rolling my wrist until the motions are a blur. Shivers ripple over me and I expel the groan trapped from earlier.

"Fuck," I grunt. "Almost there."

Need thrashes under my skin, tightening until it's difficult to breath. Just a few more strokes. The peak appears when I squeeze my base and give a final upward tug. Heat bursts forward, shooting out with the force of my climax. That warmth crashes in waves from one to the next until I'm dizzy. Pressure flows from me in a steady stream until I'm sagging under the weight. My fingers curl along the wall as if I can anchor myself. But the release is too powerful.

White spots speckle my vision as the last of my pleasure is wrung dry. I rest my forehead on the wall while my chest heaves. There's an empty ache in my balls as if this process hasn't been a daily occurrence since Callie showed up in Knox Creek.

My ears are ringing when reality comes into focus. I soon realize the sound is from a notification alert and the mess on the floor becomes an afterthought. There's a tremble in my hand when I tug my pants up and grab my phone. Through a bleary squint, I manage to read the text.

> Callie: Hello, Ridge. I wanted to thank you again for painting the door. It's perfect, just like I told you. Did you get permission from the owner? Or maybe you didn't need to ask because you're him. Is that jumping to conclusions? Hopefully not. Either way, you've made my day. You've also made me curious. I'm almost certain you're not only my neighbor, but also my landlord.

> Callie: Oh, I almost forgot. It was lovely talking to you. Even if I didn't say much. You kind of caught me off guard, but I wouldn't change a thing. Other than maybe speaking a bit more. I was struck silent by your presence, if you couldn't tell. In a really good way. Being that close to you alone had me tongue tied. I'll do better next time.

I smile into the afterglow. My eyes still struggle to focus as I reply.

Me: hey, you. glad you like the door. it was the least I could do after everything you've done for me. just let me know about any other changes you want to make. as your neighbor and landlord, but hopefully as a more significant role soon. it seems promising and likely considering you're already thinking about next time

Me: also, I'm always struck by you

Callie: Um, wow.

Callie: You made me speechless again.

Callie: Okay, I've recovered. Mostly. That's just really nice to hear. It's like my feelings are validated, or I'm jumping to more conclusions. But I'm not sure I understand. What have I done for you?

Me: gave me a purpose. revived my passion. made me smile. just to name a few

Callie: I did those things for you?

Me: only you, sweetness

Callie: There's something I want to ask, but I'm not sure I should.

Me: you can ask me anything

Callie: Okay, remember you said that. Do you have plans tomorrow? Can you come over for dinner? I'd like to cook for you. As a show of gratitude, but also as more. Like maybe a date? If you're interested. Gosh, I can't believe I typed that. I'm going to send this before I second guess myself and delete it.

My stare locks on the screen. She's not the only one who needs to recover after such a huge blow. It takes several seconds for her message to register.

Me: you wanna go on a date with me?

Callie: Yes. Very much so. The maybe I included might've led you to believe I was unsure. That's not the case. I'm extremely interested in you. That's why I'd like you to come over for dinner.

Me: are you ready for that? to have a man in your home

Callie: You're not any man, silly. The invitation is extended to you. Only you.

I'm depleted, or so I thought. The significance in her text grasps me in a gentle hold. Her trust is precious, and I clutch those delicate threads to my chest. A wide smile forms on my lips as I bask in the moment. She only wants me. Damn, that sounds better than a fantasy. My dick is suddenly rising to the occasion, eager for round two as if coaxed from slumber.

Me: I'll be there

CHAPTER SIX

Callie

WRING MY HANDS UNTIL A STING CRIES OUT TO STOP ME. My sore knuckles are the least of my troubles. I turn on my heel and pace back to the fireplace. At this rate, I'm going to wear a path into the carpet.

The clock mocks me, ticking away time without a concern for my nerves. Ridge should arrive any moment. That only serves to send my pulse into a tailspin. I pivot to make another pass across the room.

My gaze whips from left to right while seeking a distraction. I need to occupy what's left of this wait or I'm likely to faint. Our meal is already cooking in the oven. A page in my scrapbook is prepared for the event. It's sure to be one of my best creations yet. Maybe we'll take a picture together to capture the memory. That giddy thrill skips in my belly at the thought.

Hopefully Ridge will think I look nice. The dress I'm wearing accentuates my curves in a subtle sense—according to Harper, at least. It makes me feel exposed, but tonight is about pushing boundaries. I'm exiting my comfort zone.

I peek in the mirror to check if the makeup I applied is

still on. My mascara hasn't smudged and the red tint on my lips pops. Minimal and classy, just like the loose curls styling my hair. Harper's reassurance is playing through my mind once again.

Nothing needs to be done other than the actual date itself. That term sets off a fresh buzz in my pulse. Doubt soon follows.

Maybe this was a bad idea. It's too soon. I'm rushing into things. He's going to be disappointed. The night will end badly.

My stride comes to an abrupt halt along with the trail of negativity. Those concerns feel wrong. The cramp in my stomach confirms it.

That's when the doorbell rings. I just about leap to the ceiling from the sound. With a palm pressed to my chest, I rush to greet him.

The breath whooshes out of me as he comes into view. It takes me far too long to process that he's actually standing on my stoop. A formal welcome is required. I shake free of the stupor, forcing a smile that wobbles.

"Hi." That's the limit on my communication skills in this instance.

Ridge's mouth slants into somewhat of a grin. "Hey, Callie. You look"—he pauses to take his gaze over me in a slow caress that curls my toes—"like my dream come true."

Warmth rushes through me and I'm suddenly light-headed. The compliment breaks the barrier that held my voice hostage yesterday. "Oh, that's… very nice of you to say. I like the way you look too."

A raspy chuckle rumbles from him before he reveals something from behind his back. "These are for you."

I gasp at the large bundle that's clearly a bouquet. "You brought me flowers?"

Never in all my years at Billmoore did I witness such a romantic gesture.

"A pale comparison to your beauty, but I believe these will be adequate."

With trembling fingers, I peel back the thick paper to peek at the arrangement. My knees threaten to buckle and I sway into the doorframe. "Chrysanthemums are my favorite. These ones in particular are stunning."

"I chose well then." His tone is velvet against gravel— an unlikely combination, which makes the gentle rasp more alluring.

The lump in my throat expands. "You picked these at random? I find that hard to believe."

"Call it a hunch."

"Mhmm. How did you know I'd like these?"

His stare bores into mine until I feel trapped, very willingly. "I pay attention. Besides, they represent optimism and happiness. Seemed more than fitting."

"You're very charming." I bury my blush behind the bouquet.

A gruff noise shoots from him. "Not many would make that claim, but your opinion is all that matters."

"There you go again." My face flames hotter.

"I better cool it, huh?" Ridge inhales deeply. "Something smells tasty."

"Oh! Where are my manners? Please don't hold it against me."

"Never."

I step aside and sweep an arm forward. "Come in. Dinner will be ready soon."

"My nose tells me I'll enjoy whatever you're making."

"Well, good. I hope you're hungry." My heart flutters as I walk toward the kitchen.

"Famished," he murmurs.

When I peek back at him, he's following me closely. "I'll just put these in water quick."

After fetching a vase, I add the fertilizer and trim the stems. The green chrysanthemums add a fresh burst of color on the counter. A satisfied hum sweeps from me. In return, Ridge releases a pleased rumble of his own.

I glance over my shoulder to find his focus locked on me. "Shouldn't be much longer."

He remains standing near the table. "Can I help with anything?"

I blink at him and this unfamiliar territory. "Um, no. That's not necessary."

"You sure? I can be useful."

The idea is outrageous, even after many months apart from those instilled values. A decade separated from Billmoore probably wouldn't be enough. "You're my guest. Not to mention a man."

He quirks a brow. "What's that have to do with it?"

I swallow the explanation that sits too heavy in my throat. "Just stay put."

Ridge guffaws. "Telling me what to do?"

"N-no. I wouldn't dare." My chin dips on instinct.

He moves closer. "Hey, don't get shy on me again. I was just teasing."

That has me peeking at him. "Okay. Can I get you a drink? I'll serve you."

A low rumble rolls off his chest. "I'd prefer if we served each other."

My thoughts race as I search his expression. Honesty and warmth reflect back at me. I slump against the solid surface behind me while soaking in the comfort he provides.

Sparks ignite when our eyes meet and lock. I shiver, but there's no trace of chill. In fact, the temperature seems to spike. Most likely from his unwavering stare. Heat practically wafts from his smolder. That warmth sweeps through me, settling in my lower belly. I press a palm there to cradle the foreign sensation.

My gaze refuses to stray. Not that I'm trying to look elsewhere. I fall into a trance while getting swept away into the green depths that appear bottomless. He pulls me deeper under the spell as his lips part. At least until the unmistakable stench of burnt food filters into the air.

"Oh, shoot." I whirl toward the oven and wrench open the door, my hands already wafting at the smoke in a futile effort. "No, no, no."

His presence looms beside me as if offering unconditional support. "What's wrong?"

I bite my inner cheek to stave off a cry of outrage. "Dinner is ruined. This was meant to be foolproof. I've made this dish dozens of times."

"We can still eat it." But the uncertainty in his voice is paired with a slight grimace while he peers at the charred lasagna.

"No, it's beyond saving. In my flustered state earlier, I must've forgotten to set a timer." I lift my hands to shield the threat of tears. The last shred of my dignity can be salvaged, even if a sharp cramp replaces the calm in my chest.

Suddenly, he's lunging forward. His hurried motion stops just short of colliding with me. Ridge is towering over me, near enough to smell. I take advantage. My next breath is spiced pine mixed with reckless abandon. The scent is unique, fitting for him and this moment.

It's only then I recognize our position. I've never been this close to a man who wasn't family. Warmth explodes in my cheeks and quickly spreads like a wildfire. I fight the ingrained instinct to look away.

He lifts a palm to hover over my forearm to drag me back to the moment. "What happened?"

I lower my wrist to inspect the faded memory. "I burned dinner."

"No, I mean this." Ridge gestures to the inflicted area with his open palm, almost touching me.

"I burned dinner," I repeat. "That was my punishment."

Too many emotions flicker across his features. The kaleidoscope is almost fascinating to witness until he speaks. His tone lacks its usual vibrancy when he utters, "Someone did this to you? On purpose?"

I gulp at the prospect of pain, but manage a jerky nod in confirmation. It's my fault and I'll accept what he deems acceptable. "Are you going to teach me a lesson?"

"The fuck?" His voice borders on a roar. "Absolutely not. I could never hurt you. Please tell me you believe that."

In any other circumstance, I'd shrink away from the curse launched in anger. Instead, my posture remains straight with renewed confidence. Ridge is responsible for providing that.

"I trust you to never hurt me." My gaze admires the gleam that crosses through his.

"Who did this, Callie?" Now he sounds too calm. The steel of a blade preparing for battle.

"My father," I whisper.

"Your—?" He sputters while struggling for a full breath. "Your father did this to you?"

"Yes, as he should have."

His mouth opens and shuts twice without him uttering a sound. "How can you be so nonchalant about this?"

"I deserved the mark. It was a fair exchange after I burned our family meal." At least according to them.

Ridge rolls his shoulders, standing to his full height. "Where can I find him?"

"Why?"

"I plan to teach him a lesson of my own." His knuckles

crack as he forms a fist. "He dared to lay a hand on you. That was a big mistake."

"What're you going to do?"

He takes several steps backward. "For starters? Burn his arm."

"You can't!" I reach out as if I have the ability to halt his retreat.

"How can I not? Your own father hurt you." He turns away and my stomach drops.

"Are you ashamed of me? I've been bad." A sob catches in my throat. "I'm scarred and damaged. Unfit to be a wife. I won't blame you if you never want to see me again."

Ridge whips around to face me before I can blink. There's a storm in his gaze, but I'm not afraid. Never of him. Especially when his arms lift, inches short of embracing me. I almost beg him to close the remaining distance. But that's too bold. Even for me on this night when I've been more brazen than ever before.

His thumb brushes over my ruined flesh. The touch is soft, barely noticeable. Yet I feel his finger along my skin as if he's reaching into my soul. "You're perfect, sweetness."

"I'm far from it."

"Not to me." Ridge pauses and his wild heartbeat thumps loudly in the silence. "To me, you're all that matters. Meeting you is the best thing to ever happen to me."

Fuzziness clouds my brain and I'm unsure how to respond. "We only just met."

"Doesn't make it any less true. I've felt very… attached to you, from the first moment I saw you."

My eyes lift to collide with his. "Then why would you harm my father?"

He drops his thumb from the permanent reminder of my error. I feel the loss of his touch like a physical pain.

"I'm very upset, Callie."

"With me?"

"No!" Thunder booms in his expression, shaking his entire frame that's already rigid. "Never with you. I'm furious at your dad."

"But why? He was just doing what's expected." Which is just one of the many reasons I was desperate to escape. The emotional damage still impacts me to this day, but I'm getting better. "That's just the way things are where I'm from."

"It doesn't matter what fake rules he's using as an excuse. What he did is wrong. My fury is the least he deserves. It bothers me beyond reason to imagine you hurt, especially by someone who should be protecting you. Not that his position matters anymore. I'll do the honors from now on."

My breath hitches. "You want to… protect me?"

"Always."

"Then stay. Don't hunt the past. Let's focus on the future." I bite my bottom lip. "Together."

"Ah, damn. Who am I to argue with that?" His focus slides to my mouth. "Are you giving me permission, as we move forward, to deal with anyone who's careless enough to mistreat you?"

"If you insist."

"I do. I'd also kick their ass regardless."

"You're charming and a brute," I sigh wistfully.

His fingers flex, almost making contact with mine. "The second trait I'm very familiar with. I used to check guys into the boards for a living. Penalties didn't stop me. My busted rotator cuff did." A dangerous glint enters his gaze. "But I can still deliver a swift beating. They don't call me Crusher for nothing."

I wince. "Please don't fight him over this. It's old and healed. I'd rather you stay with me and forget about punishing my father. Let's make new memories. This is our first date."

"Fuuuuuck," he groans. "I'm an asshole. An insensitive one at that."

"You're not. Trust me. It's admirable that you want to defend my honor. That's just not necessary."

Ridge tips his face to the ceiling, exposing his thick throat that works with a swallow. "You make me weak, woman."

"Is that bad?"

His eyes return to mine. "Nah, nothing you do to me could ever be bad."

The slew of compliments has my head spinning. I glance to the side where our ruined dinner rests. "It'll take me a while to remake the lasagna."

He makes a disgruntled noise. "You've done enough already. I'll order something instead. It appears you were in the mood for Italian."

"I'll never say no to pasta."

"Pesto tortellini with broccoli?"

My jaw drops as my belly gives a very unladylike grumble. "That's my favorite."

"Is it? Interesting." The sneaky tilt to his lips suggests there's an interesting backstory to his knowledge.

My squint narrows on him, determined to get answers eventually. "I bet you know just the place to get it too."

"Sure do." Ridge digs his phone from his pocket and begins tapping at the screen. "Coming right up, sweetness."

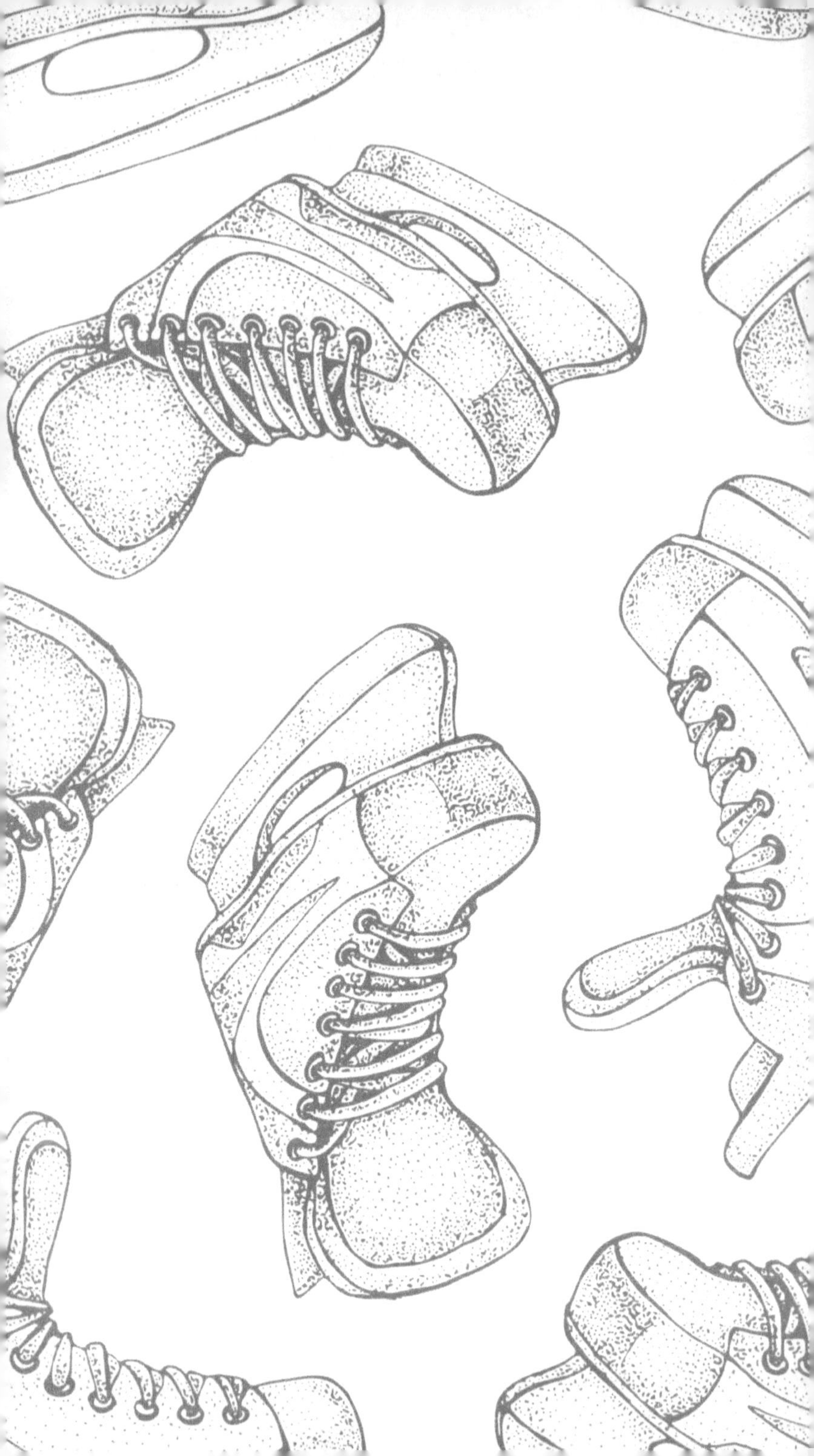

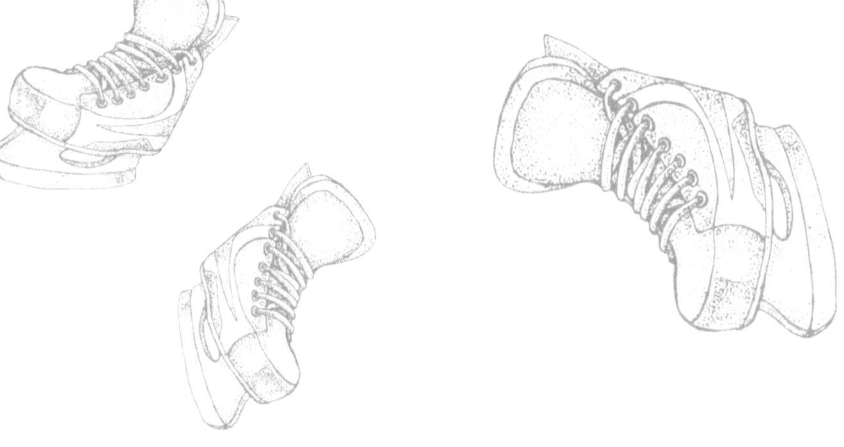

CHAPTER SEVEN

Ridge

MY FURY HAS SIMMERED TO A MUTED RAGE. The definition of peace sitting across from me is the only reason I'm stuck to this chair rather than seeking revenge on her behalf. Callie appears oblivious to my stewing resentment toward her father. As if I could so easily forgive and forget and fuck off. My fists demand justice, crushing the napkin in my grip into unrecognizable shreds. But I'm trying to remain calm. At least outwardly.

The reminder that this is our first date plays on repeat. I wasn't lying earlier. She's all that matters. Nothing can ruin the night for us. Especially not my foul mood provoked by a man I'll never meet. He's not worthy of intruding on us.

If Callie overheard the madness wreaking havoc in my mind, she might ask me to leave. I wouldn't blame her. It doesn't mean I won't drag my heels on the way out. But that's my obsession talking. For her. Only her.

I might be overbearing, but she hasn't told me to back off. If anything, her reactions entice me. My gaze feasts on Callie as she devours her favorite meal. I'm captivated instantly. She's too gracious, offering me endless praise as if I cooked the food from scratch. The internal conflict and what's left of my anger melts away.

Every smile and pleased sound is like a badge I've earned. Her happiness is infectious. I unclench my hands and rest them flat on the table. My chest expands until pressure warns me that I'm about to burst. That doesn't stop me from continuing to stare at her, getting more than my fill. I can't remember the last time I've felt this lucky.

But then I glance at her arm. That scar taunts me as if I've already failed her. I vow to never allow harm to strike her again.

"Ridge?"

A hot surge floods my veins, and an involuntary groan is forced from me. The potency is more intoxicating than scoring a goal to win the game with two seconds left on the clock. It's safe to say I'm not immune to her uttering my name. I probably never will be.

The control she wields over me might be cause for concern, but I willingly hand over the reins. She gets all of me.

Other than my undivided concentration to conversation, seeing as she has to clear her throat for me to notice the silence is mine to end.

Once again, I'm rendered useless just from a simple mention. Fuck, I need to get a grip.

"Yes, sweetness?"

"Are you okay?" She scoots her fingers toward where mine are planted.

I wonder if she realizes the subtle movement puts her within touching distance. Or how easy it would be for me to engulf her palm with mine. Shit, there I go again.

"Couldn't be better. Why do you ask?"

Callie tortures her bottom lip with a gnawing bite. "You look… bothered."

I smooth my features. "Really?"

Her squint digs beneath the exterior. "Please don't concern yourself with what happened before we met."

"Might as well ask me to quit breathing."

"You couldn't have changed the outcome regardless," she urges.

"Doesn't mean I can't wish things were different."

Her smile lacks its usual sparkle. "In my father's eyes, his actions were justified."

"And I'll gladly rearrange his face to extend my gratitude. Maybe then he'll see clearly."

The thoughtful tilt of her head suggests she isn't completely opposed to the idea. Progress. "Did Harper tell you about where I came from?"

"No, I never asked."

"Oh." Her wounded expression is a blade sinking into my gut.

"Hey." My thumb nudges hers. The slight contact has the desired effect, earning me a gasp. "Don't think that means I'm not interested. I just wanted to hear the story from you."

Relief washes her expression of the defeat pinching between her brows. "Oh, okay. That makes me feel better."

I'm riveted to the glow returning to her complexion. "Is your background difficult to talk about?"

"Not really. It's probably harder for you to hear than it is for me to share."

"Shit," I grind out. The history burned into her skin nearly tossed me over the edge. Whatever she's about to reveal is likely to put me in a tailspin.

"We don't need to discuss it." Her meek tone prods at the protective instincts she's established in me.

"It's part of you, sweetness. That means I want to know."

"Have you heard of Billmoore?"

The name rattles around, but doesn't connect. "Is it nearby?"

"About two hours south. Some say Knox Creek is in the middle of nowhere, but they clearly don't know how isolated a place can be." Callie laughs, but the sound lacks humor. "Billmoore is a secluded community that's built on particular… beliefs. The compound is spread across hundreds of acres and includes numerous families."

"Like a cult?"

She flinches. "Um, no. That's not a term the elders would allow. It's a private civilization set apart from typical society by these… outdated standards."

"Such as mistreating someone for burning dinner?"

"Women are raised to be subservient," she whispers. "We're taught that men are in charge. No argument. Like what I texted you, my voice wasn't heard."

"And I won't break my promise. Your voice will always be heard by me."

"I believe you. Now more than ever." She bumps her index finger against mine, making a move of her own.

"Good," I mumble. "That's real good. I'll prove myself worthy of your faith in me."

"You already have."

"Compared to the men you're used to, that's not a major feat. No offense," I add.

Her hand swats at the air to wave me off. "None taken. My expectations are skewed, but you'd exceed them regardless."

I release a heavy breath. "Too easy to please, sweetness."

"Perhaps. Or it's your special influence on me, which is most likely. Harper has spent the better part of this past year explaining how different traditions vary beyond the walls of Billmoore. It's still an adjustment. Where I was raised, if girls didn't follow the rules or were caught misbehaving, a proper punishment was provided."

"Proper punishment? Damn, they did a number on you to believe you deserved that pain." The fact she used past tense is a small miracle. "How did you cope in such an oppressive environment?"

Her throat works with a gulp. "I kept pushing forward to survive."

"Or merely existed like a trophy to be won."

"That makes me sound like a coveted prize. Nobody would treat me as such."

"I will, but as an equal. You won't be stripped of control ever again. That's another promise, so long as my heart is beating. It's yours." I'm referring to more than her right to choose, but that's her realization to arrive at. My concentration is riveted on her and the cascade of emotions she's reflecting.

"You're even more noble than I anticipated," she whispers.

"Noble?" I take a hand through my hair. "An hour ago, I was prepared to seriously injure your father."

"In my defense like a white knight. But you stayed instead."

"Still considering it," I admit.

"Yes, you'd like to rearrange his face." Her lips twitch as she recites my earlier comment.

"Grant me permission and consider it done."

She shakes her head. "He's highly respected at Billmoore. A leader among the people. Provides for his family. Sets an example for those that need guidance. Just view it as a very different perspective on reality, if that makes sense."

"The fact you can justify his actions is… something else."

"I don't expect you to understand. Trust me, now that I'm removed from that life, I see how damaging it is. But he's still my father." Callie shrugs and sits straighter. "Rather than wallow over what's done and can't be fixed, I'm choosing to look ahead. I get to choose my own path despite how I was raised. That's a major accomplishment."

"You're a better person than me," I commend.

"Agree to disagree."

A lull settles between us, but the pause isn't awkward.

It's a break to gather our scattered thoughts. I take a moment to glance around the room, noting most pieces are what I purchased prior to her moving in. Maybe Harper was right about Callie's lack of personal belongings. Either that or she prefers what I bought. The latter strokes my pride in a tight fist.

Lust climbs my throat in a lazy caress, teasing at how this evening might end in pleasure rather than haunting memories of pain. I force myself to focus on the less desirable option. Otherwise, she might pull the plug prematurely, assuming there's nothing left to say.

"Have you been back to visit?"

Callie pulls herself from wherever her mind had wandered. "No, it's not allowed. I'm considered an outcast. Banished. It doesn't bother me except that I can't talk to my mom."

"Does she know where you are?"

"I think so." She worries her inner cheek to suggest the opposite. "I've called but she only answered once. She told me not to contact her again. It's too risky. If my father were to find out…" Her voice trails off, but the words left unsaid might as well be shouted.

"Does she stay there by choice?"

"Maybe by circumstance and out of habit. Some warped loyalty to my father. I tried getting her to leave with me. She refused." A glassy sheen glosses over her eyes. There's a noticeable weight slouching her shoulders as well.

I read the mood for what it's become. "Thanks for sharing all that with me, sweetness. The trust you've placed in me won't be taken for granted."

She blinks in rapid succession to chase away unshed tears and haunting memories. "I appreciate you listening. It's not the most glamorous tale."

"Anything you have to say is what I want to hear." I smile, but the expression probably resembles a rusty gear. "Should we change the subject?"

Relief expels from her. "Yes, please."

I push away from the table. "How about I take care of these dishes first? It's your turn to stay put."

Callie emits a strangled shout that would startle most wildfire. "No."

The refusal halts my motion and I remain seated. "No?"

Her wide stare is locked on me. "It's not allowed."

"I beg to differ."

"There's only so much change I can manage in such a short period of time. This"—she motions between us while red splotches spread across her cheeks—"is an inappropriate practice where I came from. Unwed couples don't socialize unless there are chaperones present."

"Is this uncomfortable for you?" And then I recall how close we were in the kitchen earlier. I crashed into her personal space without consideration. "Have I pushed your boundaries? If you'd prefer to invite others to join us—"

The flash in her eyes cuts me off. "I'm comfortable with you, Ridge. Very much so. But your concern is very considerate. Admirable even."

"Real glad to hear it, sweetness. Puts me at ease." I wipe fake sweat off my forehead.

A brief rest follows where her thoughts fill the room. I watch as indecision plays out across her features. A fresh blush colors her face and it takes heroic effort I didn't know I possessed to remain on this side of the table. After what feels like a painfully long delay where gratification dangles just out of reach, she rises from her chair.

"Would you do me a favor?"

"Yes," I answer without hesitation. "Whatever you need or want."

Her responding grin is small but bright. She could request anything, and I'll agree for the sole purpose of keeping that happiness aimed at me. "Can we take a picture together for my scrapbook?"

My brain misfires and screeches to a standstill. That is… not what I expected. I might blackout momentarily from the sweetness overload. This fucking girl. Always keeps me guessing. She's innocent and adorable, but there's a bold spark suppressed under the surface. That flicker is desperate to expand. I plan to coax that flare from hiding and nurture the flames as they grow wild. There isn't a better way to spend the rest of my days.

Others in her position would crumble and sacrifice their identity. She fought for herself, leaving everyone and everything behind. Talk about admirable. She's my sweetest reward. One that I didn't earn. At least not yet.

"I'd love nothing more than to capture this moment with you," I eventually croak. "It's an honor to be featured as a worthy memory."

That plump bottom lip is trapped between her teeth again. "You don't think it's silly?

"Absolutely not. I'm all for documenting our progress. Maybe you'll show me what you're making."

"Maybe. It's very personal for me."

After dropping that declaration, Callie disappears down the hallway and returns a minute later. A Polaroid camera that looks like the original model is clutched protectively in her grip.

I gawk at the relic. "Where did you find that? Memory Lane?"

Her brow furrows at my mention of the antique store in town. "It was a gift from my mom. To be honest, it's difficult to find film that fits. A package of ten exposures is expensive. I only use it for special occasions."

"Damn, you know how to compliment me."

I'm transfixed as she creeps forward. Each step closer whips my pulse to a full gallop. My arm lifts in invitation and she only hesitates for a measured inhale before pressing herself into my side. I fight the urge to tighten my grasp while she melts against me.

"Smile," Callie prompts.

I don't bother glancing at the lens, not when she fills my entire field of vision. She's all I see, and I hope that comes across as her finger pushes the shutter button. The whir from the camera churning out the image cracks our pose. She snatches the picture that's spit out.

"It takes a few minutes to develop." There's a tremble in her fingers when she sets the shot face-down on the table.

I chuckle and am almost startled by the raspy notes. "You're hilarious."

"Am I?"

"Haven't laughed in what feels like ages."

Callie beams at me, bright enough to bathe my face in warmth. "Thanks for making my first date memorable."

"Your first? Never been on a date before?"

She looks scandalized by the idea. "Of course not."

The story she shared earlier loops back to remind me how impossible that would've been in her previous situation. My chest swells from the claimed honor belonging to me. "Well, this is just the beginning. I have a good feeling this is the first of many things for us."

"Really?" She twists her lips. "You've probably experienced everything already."

"Not what truly matters. Those I've saved for you."

Callie gasps, searching the honesty in my gaze for any cracks of deceit. "Promise?"

"Yeah, sweetness. I promise."

CHAPTER EIGHT

Callie: As if you could ever do that. But I appreciate you being considerate. To be honest, I'm a bit sleepy.

Ridge: go to bed, sweetness. I'll text you in the morning

Callie: Oh, wait! I almost forgot. Our picture turned out really well. Too bad we don't have another copy for you.

Ridge: sounds like that gives us an excuse to take more

Callie: Oh, yay! Photos are great material for my scrapbook. I'm glad you're willing. I wasn't sure since you're not looking at the camera in this shot.

Ridge: that wasn't an accident. I couldn't look away from you

Callie: There you go again. Is this flirting? I wouldn't know. But I feel like you're flirting with me when you say such nice things to me. It's similar to the swoop in my belly when I saw how you stared at me in the photo. Is that okay for me to admit?

Ridge: lol. I'm very much flirting with you. don't ever doubt that. since you're still in a chatty mood, tell me more about these private thoughts and belly swoops

Callie: I'm not sure that I should...

Ridge: I disagree, but only if you're willing

Callie: Both of those things happen when I think about you.

Callie: Ridge? Did you fall asleep?

Ridge: still here. just trying to stop myself from coming over there. I bet your blush pairs well with these private thoughts and belly swoops.

Callie: Yes, and I'm blushing right now. LOL

Ridge: probably shouldn't have told me that

Callie: Why not? Is it bad?

Ridge: nothing you do could ever be bad. you're a good girl and your sweet words do certain things to me like I've told you before.

Callie: I remember. You'd rather show me those things than tell me.

Ridge: that's right, but you're not ready

Callie: How do you know?

Ridge: we've only had one date

Callie: And these things require more than that?

Ridge: in our case. there's no rush. time for bed?

Callie: Can I ask another question first?

Ridge: ...

Callie: We talked about my family tonight, but I don't know anything about yours. Where are you from? Do your parents still live there? How's your relationship with them? Are they still married? Do you have any siblings?

Ridge: That's more than one

Callie: I got carried away. Do you mind?

Ridge: not at all. you should know by now I want to hear whatever you're thinking

Ridge: I'm from a town two hours north of here called Nowthen. ever heard of it? probably not. it's very small

Ridge: yes, and you'll just know

Callie: How can you be so sure?

Ridge: I'm already at the point of no return. you're stuck with me, sweetness. whether you're ready or not, I'm yours

CHAPTER NINE

Callie

L IKE A PREDICTABLE ROUTINE, THE CHIME FROM THE front door sensor sets off a chain reaction. A chorus of yips and howls erupts in the large breed room. In response, the small dogs begin barking. That gets the few held in the grooming area to join the hype squad. The collaborative effort creates a deafening symphony to greet whoever just entered Pampered Pooch.

The excitement surrounding me automatically stretches my lips into a wide smile. Just another day in paradise.

"Callie," my boss yells across the room. "You've got visitors."

I offer a quick nod in response. There's no chance of her hearing me over this noise.

Stacey disappears from view, returning to her position at the counter. I don't manage the desk for obvious reasons. On the rare occasion someone asks for me, I'll venture from the safe haven of the dog rooms. It's safer back here.

A fluffy mutt spins circles around me as I pad across the rubber mats. I step into the lobby and shut the soundproof divider to leave the chaos behind. My eardrums are thankful for the reprieve.

A loud squeak shatters the brief quiet. "Hi, Callie!"

I brace myself as Sydney crashes into my legs. "Hey, you. What's up?"

"Chicken butt," Harper's daughter giggles.

"Very funny." I look over at my friend. "This is a nice surprise."

"We were in the neighborhood." She laughs. "Get it? Small town. We're always close by."

"And I'm glad for that."

Sydney tugs on my shirt and beams up at me. "Can we eat lunch? My tummy is super fussy. I gotta feed the grumbles."

"Ah, yes," Harper chimes in. "There was a slight ulterior motive of sneaking you off for a quick break."

"Um…" I glance at Stacey to gauge her reaction. She's already nodding, and then makes a shooing motion toward the street. "Looks like I'm free."

"Yayyyy!" Sydney twirls to show off her ballerina talents.

"We just need to get this little cutie logged in for an hour or two." Harper points to where their Pomeranian is patiently sitting by the gate. "She's ready to play."

"I'll take care of checking her in," Stacey smoothly interjects. "Enjoy your lunch."

"Thank you," I reply.

Sydney swoops down to pepper her beloved pooch with several kisses. "Be back soon, Glitzy. Don't miss me too much."

"She'll have a blast," Stacey insists.

In response, Glitzy yips and begins scratching at the gate.

My boss grants her entry into the small breed room, temporarily flooding the lobby with happy barks. "As for you three, go feed those bellies."

We wave to her and walk out into the warm spring weather. I tip my face to the sunny sky. "Where to?"

"Bent Pedal is next door." Harper motions at the building.

My brows shoot to the clouds at her treason. "Isn't that a direct competitor of Roosters?"

"Yeah, yeah. I thought that once upon a time, but it's more about supporting our local businesses."

"I dunno. Feels unfaithful." My mind immediately goes to an image of Ridge seeing me at another restaurant when I rarely go to his.

"Would you feel better about Bean Me Up? Their patio is open."

"Oh, yessss!" Sydney bounces on her toes as we start strolling in the direction of the bistro. "They have the bestest ice cream. Maybe Bradley will be there."

I squint at the unfamiliar name. "Bradley?"

"You've met Garrett's fiancée, right? Grace is Bradley's nanny and we bumped into them At Bean Me Up once. Now he's in kindergarten at the same school as this smitten kitten." Harper rolls her eyes toward the little girl skipping along beside us.

"He's super cute." Sydney flutters her lashes to confirm her mother's claim.

"Don't even get her started," my friend murmurs to me from the corner of her mouth. "And if your daddy hears more about this crush, he's never gonna let you leave the house again."

Sydney wrinkles her nose. "He's a fun sponge."

"What?" I laugh as we arrive at the patio entrance and find a table.

"He soaks up all the fun." She makes a slurping noise that resembles moisture getting sucked into a hose.

"Oh, I see what you mean. Well, to be fair, you're very young. Maybe it's better to wait several more years before you think about boys that way." I choose the chair that has a view of the lake in the distance.

She parks her little fists on her hips before sitting down. "I'm seven."

"No way. When did that happen?"

Sydney frowns. "Did you forget my birthday? You were at the party."

"I would never," I rush to say. "November twenty-first is a very important date. It should be a holiday."

Her eyes sparkle. "That's a fantabulous plan. How do we make a holiday?"

"We just declare it as such."

Harper claps while Sydney leaps from her seat to perform several impressive dance moves. "Okay, superstar. Let's fix those hungry pains before this celebrity status goes to your head."

On cue, a server stops over to give us menus and take our drink order. Sydney doesn't hesitate to set her focus on completing the provided activity sheet. That allows Harper's burning curiosity to unleash on me.

"So," she chirps. "Yesterday went well?"

"Oh, yes. It was perfect." My heart flutters at the reminder. "Ridge is such a gentleman."

She snorts. "Didn't know we were telling jokes, but that's a good one."

"He is," I defend. "Just like a fairytale hero, he wants to storm in and to protect me from my father."

"That totally tracks."

"Some of the stuff he said was so romantic." I chew on my bottom lip while deciding what to share. "Such as he'll treat me as a coveted prize, but as his equal. I'll never be stripped of control again so long as his heart is beating."

Harper whistles. "Wow, the brute sure puts on the moves fast when he wants to. Guess he saw a green light."

"What do you mean?"

"That man has been crazy about you since last year, but he didn't do a thing about it. Until now." This isn't the first time she's mentioned something along those lines.

"I guess the moment was right."

She nods. "You're the neighbor material he's been waiting for."

Which reminds me. "Did you know Ridge owns the duplex?"

"No, but I'm not surprised. He has plenty of money stashed away from his professional hockey career."

"I would've loved to watch him play." There's a wistful edge to my voice.

"Yeah, girl. It's hot on the ice. I bet he was a beast out there. Google his best games."

"Oh, that's smart. I bet there's a lot of footage."

"Keep a towel close by to mop up the drool. Better yet, sit on one so you don't make a mess on the couch." Harper winks.

It takes me several seconds to gather her meaning. Heat floods my cheeks. "You're bad."

"What else is new?" She leans forward. "Have you kissed him yet?"

My blush burns hotter. I think back to how our date ended last night. He politely excused himself shortly after we took the picture together. Something about not wanting to overstay his welcome, which is similar to what he said in our texts. As if it's possible for him to do either.

I shake my head. "That's probably not going to happen for a long while. We just had dinner."

"No dessert?"

A gasp wrenches from me. "Was I supposed to bake cookies or cupcakes? Maybe a pie would've been more to his liking. I totally forgot."

She bursts into a fit of giggles. "Gosh, you're adorable. I wasn't referring to that type of sugary treat." She seems to consider something. "But now that we're on the subject of baking stuff in the oven, have you thought about protection?"

I furrow my brow. "Like pot holders?"

"Good grief, I can't even with you. For when your relationship with Ridge progresses to"—she peeks over at Sydney who's now concentrating on coloring a picture—"the intimate phase."

"Why would I need protection from him?"

"It's mostly his swimmers you should be worried about." She wiggles her index finger to imitate a worm.

"I'm not sure what you're referring to. This isn't a topic they taught us," I groan and rub my temples. "Even more so, that's private. What happens in the bedroom is sacred between husband and wife."

Harper's blink is slow. "Oh, you're going to wait for marriage."

That gives me pause. "I suppose those traditions belong strictly to Billmoore."

She shrugs. "Not necessarily. It just depends on your personal beliefs. Plenty of couples wait until their wedding night."

My mind whirls fast enough to make me dizzy. "I haven't given it much thought."

There hasn't been a reason to, until recently it seems. Sex is so far off my radar that it doesn't even appear as a speck. But I do find Ridge extremely attractive. The thought of being intimate with him is definitely appealing. Warmth collects in my lower belly, and I shift on the seat.

"This is happening very quickly," I add.

Harper must catch the stress tightening my features. "Hey, don't worry. You're not rushing into anything. But there are many options for when the time comes for the next step, and you want to prevent… you know. That way you don't expand your waistline until you're ready." She widens her eyes and makes an arc over her flat stomach.

Sydney chooses that second to be done with her drawing. "Are you pregnant, Mommy?"

The idle chatter surrounding us abruptly ends. It feels like every pair of eyes shifts to stare at our table. Even our server pauses on her return to us with the drinks held in midair. Secondhand embarrassment flares in my cheeks and I duck my chin. Meanwhile, Harper winces and faces her daughter.

"No, I'm not expecting a baby," she says loud enough to

appease the crowd. Then she leans closer to Sydney. "And please don't shout that. People are listening."

The little girl glances around. "Why are they spying on us? That's rude."

"It's just what folks do. Daddy will hear about this before I even get the chance to call him. Rumors in this town spread faster than"—she cuts herself off with a quick glance at her daughter's rapt focus—"jelly on toast. We should probably put a lid on discussing your… reproductive safety choices until later. Otherwise, everyone will assume you're preparing to do the deed with your grumpy neighbor."

"Oh, no." Flames erupt across my face. I peek at those seated nearby. Most appear to have lost interest in us. "The gossips aren't that bad."

"You're not giving them enough credit. I heard about Ridge painting your door before he even finished the job."

"That's unbelievable," I whisper as my stomach somersaults. "I still can't believe he did that."

Harper swats at the space between us. "Puh-lease. That man would do anything for you."

"That's not true," I mumble.

"Wanna bet?"

"I don't like to gamble."

She laughs. "Then how about giving him a surprise? I think it's your turn."

"Like a plate of cookies?"

"Sure, he's gonna love that." When Harper wiggles her brows, concern spikes my heart rate. "But I have another sug-gestion that will satisfy more than his sweet tooth."

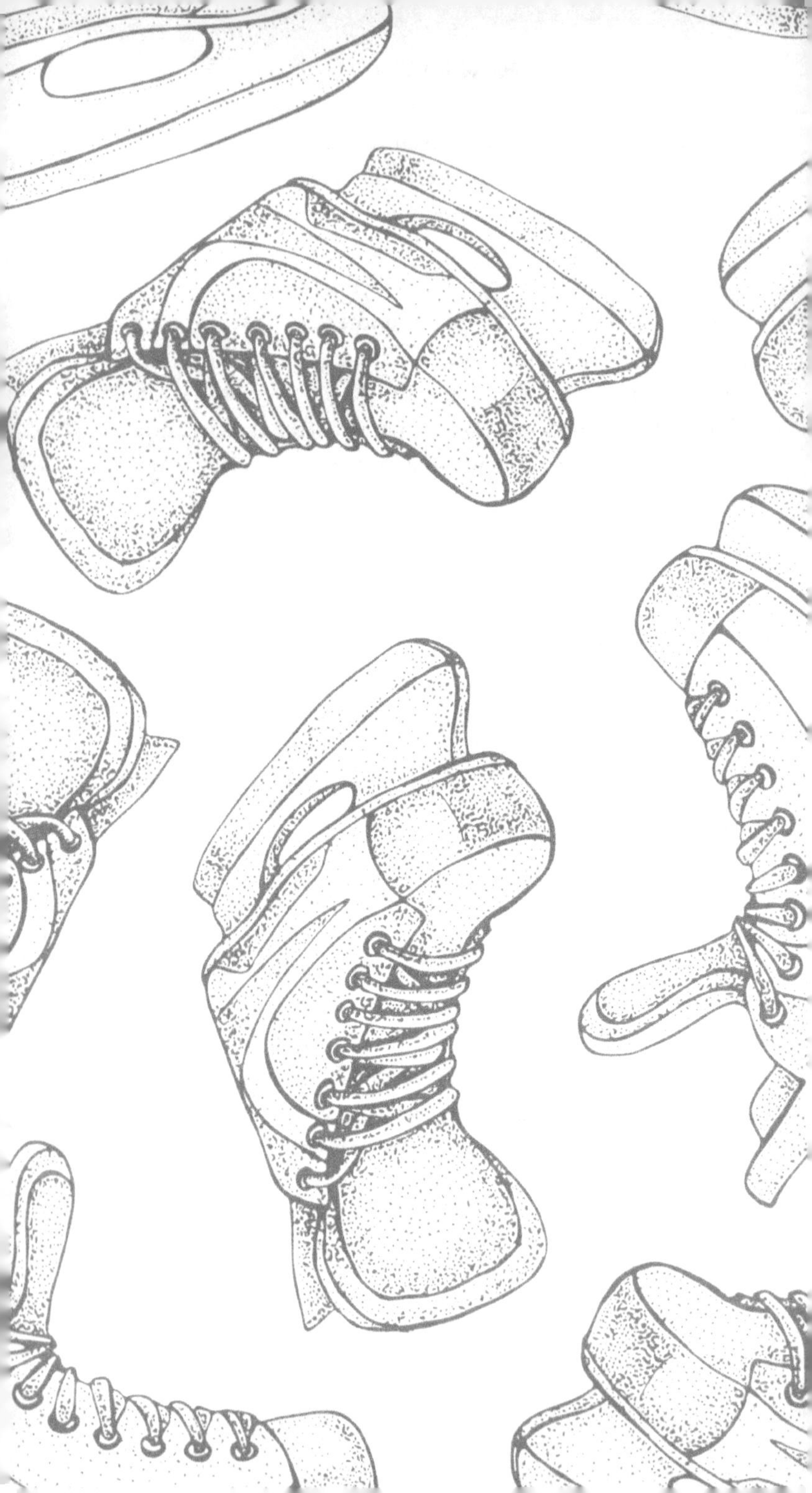

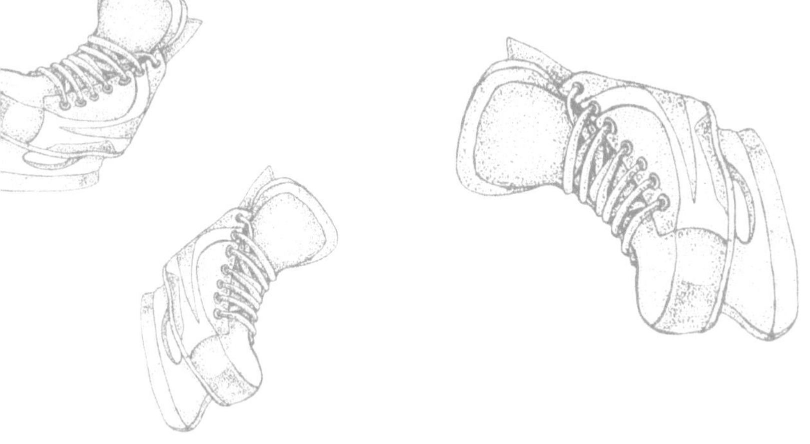

CHAPTER TEN

Ridge

A GIGGLE THAT'S RIPE WITH SNEAKY UNDERTONES demands my attention. I glance over to where Harper is typing on her phone. The grunt I aim at her does little to pause whatever she's writing.

"Could've sworn you were on the clock," I gripe.

"Oh, hush," she retorts without bothering to look up. "You're the last person who can give me shit for texting on the job."

Yet I haven't since this shift started. The only person I'm interested in hearing from is busy. With what, I'm not sure. As if I'm not already suspicious, another giddy noise comes from the blonde who's supposed to be bartending.

My gaze shifts from Harper to her husband. Jake is firmly planted on his usual seat, a beer clutched in one palm. The fingers of his other hand drum on the wood counter as he watches his wife slack off on the job. No phone in sight.

I pin a glare on the so-called exemplary employee. "Are you talking to Callie?"

"Maybe." She averts her screen but not before I see the

length of the blue bubble that's a signature style for a certain text-chatty brunette.

I frown at my screen that remains blank. "What's she saying?"

"None of your business, boss." A distinct chime announces a new message. Harper's grin spreads to concerning levels. "Right on time."

I'm confused by her vague statement until another recognizable sound carries across the room. The front door opens with a whoosh that wafts a gust of sweetness directly to me. My undivided attention is immediately locked on the blue-eyed beauty who's responsible for turning me into a lovesick sap. I'm hers—irrevocably—and she doesn't even know it yet.

Callie commands me from where she hovers out of reach. As if to prove my devotion, the racket from rowdy patrons and slackened inhibitions ceases to exist. Vanilla and unbridled temptation perfume the air until I can taste the addictive flavor on my tongue. My muscles flex while preparing to launch at her, but my feet remain firmly planted behind the bar. There's nothing I can do except wait for her to end this agonizing separation.

Her eyes dart from left to right as she surveys the thick crowd. She hasn't moved from the doorway. The frozen state of her stance reveals that she's seconds from fleeing the scene. I can't have that.

"C'mere, sweetness. I saved you a spot." My spread arms beckon her toward me. As she begins skirting forward, I glare at the random Joe hogging prime real estate at my section of the rail. "Move."

The guy drops his jaw. "Excuse me?"

"You're in my future wife's seat."

"Holy shit," Harper sputters.

I'm barely listening as I motion to a preferred place for

this dude to relocate his ass. "Go sit over there and I'll buy you a drink."

He ambles off, but mutters under his breath about me being whipped on pussy. I'd give him something to really complain about if the woman of my obsessions wasn't approaching.

Harper is still choking on perfectly good oxygen. "What was that?"

"You heard me," I growl without taking my focus off Callie.

"Talk about staking a claim. Damn," she whistles.

I ignore her while Callie eliminates the remaining distance between us and slides onto the stool. "Hey, sweetness. This is a surprise."

She glances at her friend beside me. The instigator looks far too pleased with herself. Callie doesn't seem to notice before she returns her gaze to me.

"Hopefully a good one," she murmurs.

"The best. Do I have this one to thank for it?" I blindly motion toward Harper.

She scoffs at me in return. "Nope, Callie gets all the credit."

"Even better," I rasp and lean forward on a bent elbow.

Callie's cheeks blaze a bright red in the dim lighting. "I brought you something." She whips out a covered dish of cookies from seemingly nowhere and sets them on the bar top between us. "Are you allergic to anything? I should've asked first. To be on the safe side, these are free of nuts and gluten."

My tongue is tied tighter than a jockstrap. I manage a croaked, "Thank you."

"Awww, that's very thoughtful. Can I have one?" Harper pinches at the air as if she's about to steal a cookie whether I grant permission or not.

"No." I swipe the container out of her reach. "These are mine."

"Jeez, boss. Thanks for sharing." She rolls her eyes, but winks at her friend in the next second.

Callie giggles. "I hope you'll like them."

"Are you kidding me? These are about to be my new favorite dessert." I crack open the lid to take one out, quickly shoving the entire thing in my mouth. Can never be too cautious with the company I keep back here.

Melted chocolate bursts across my taste buds. There's a hint of vanilla, which is fucking perfect. It's baked just right. Not too gooey, but soft enough to crumble. A rumble creeps past my sealed lips.

"You know what they say," Harper croons. "The way to a man's heart is through his stomach."

Callie's wide eyes are fastened on me while I finish chewing. "What do you think?"

I swallow the last bit and rub my abdomen. "Might be the best thing I've ever put in my mouth."

Her blush makes a rosy reappearance. "You need to try my tater tot hot dish."

"I'll eat whatever you're willing to feed me," I freely admit.

"He's gonna lose his mind once your cherry casserole is on the menu," Harper intrudes.

Callie crinkles her forehead. "Cherry casserole?"

"Ridge will gobble that cobbler. Even better than casserole. Finger-licking good." She does the motion for a chef's kiss.

"I'll need to find a recipe for that," Callie mumbles absently.

While my innocent girl jots down a reminder for herself, I shoot a glare at Harper that promises retribution. It would have most grown men shit their pants.

"That sounds like my cue. What's that, Jerky Jacob?" She

cups her ear and begins trotting off in his direction. "I'll be right there."

With that nuisance occupied, I'm able to concentrate on the only one who matters. Callie is already looking at me when I catch her stare. She lowers her lashes, but peeks back at me a moment later. I like to think she can't keep her eyes off me. The compulsion is very fucking mutual.

"Thanks again for the cookies. I'll treasure these." Which starts with tucking them under the counter in a secure location.

She peers over the edge. "I can make more."

"That's an offer I'll never refuse. Just like having you in my bar. It means a lot that you stopped by."

"Really?" Callie's gaze sweeps over the others who chose Roosters to take a load off, but I don't acknowledge their existence.

"Yes, really," I confirm for her instead. "And now I finally get the pleasure of serving you."

She gasps as if our roles in this scenario just occurred to her. "Oh, my."

"What's it gonna be, sweetness? Just name it and I'll deliver. On the house."

Callie surveys the variety of options on display. "Um, I've never had an alcoholic beverage before."

Can't say I'm all that shocked by her response. "Would you like one?"

"Only if you make it for me." Her lips pinch into a firm line as if she can't believe those words spilled out.

"Damn," I grunt and clutch at the area above my heart. "You're giving me the privilege of creating your first cocktail?"

"We have many firsts to share, right?" The blue in her eyes reflects a sacred vow.

I eagerly dive into those depths, allowing the calm waters

to submerge me. "Absolutely. I'll take as many as you're willing to give me."

Callie's timid smile is a gesture of trust and I clutch those fragile strands close to my chest. "What do you recommend?"

My mind whirls with the base ingredients of a few staple combinations. "I'm gonna let my creativity take the lead, which is a first for me."

Her expression brightens as I get to work.

I grab the coconut rum that has a reputation for its smooth flavor. Just a small amount gets added to the blend.

She studies my movements like the process is fascinating. That riveted focus doesn't stray as I flip a shaker in my hand as if this is common practice. The rusty motions gain the attention of an actual flair expert.

"Those are some smooth moves, Crusher Carter." Garrett saunters over and claps me on the back. "A real crowd pleaser tonight, huh?"

"For a solo audience," I mutter while dumping a generous amount of pineapple juice in the container. A few other fruity components go in next.

"That's cute. Not sure why I'm busting my ass running interference for you. What's the deal with this disgruntled customer saying you booted—?" His question cuts off when he spots Callie sitting in her designated seat. "Oh, hey. Didn't see you there."

She dips her chin and offers him a quick wave.

"Always a mood booster when you're at the cock den," he squawks.

Callie nods in gratitude but doesn't speak.

Meanwhile, I snort at his antics. "Is there a problem?"

"Nah, got it sorted."

Just then, a pained yelp comes from his section of the rail. "Ow, ow. Shit. That stings."

Garrett whips around to face his fiancée. "What's wrong?"

"Got squirted in the eye," Grace whimpers. There's a freshly squeezed lime in her grip that appears to be the guilty offender.

He chuckles. "Aww, shucks. We've talked about you getting too close to the splash zone, soulmate. Didn't you learn your lesson on my birthday?"

She tries to glare at him, but the watery side effect just looks pitiful. "Not funny."

"Let me assess the damage." Garrett wanders off to tend to her, which allows me to complete my task.

I turn my attention back to my concoction. Vanilla syrup is a must. Three mint leaves join the party, chased with two pumps of grenadine. An orange slice slides onto the sugared rim. The end result should taste like a trip to the Caribbean.

Callie's giddy satisfaction bounces between me and the finished product. "That's too pretty to drink."

"I beg to differ." Otherwise, I won't be able to gobble her cobbler or whatever gibberish Harper spewed earlier. "Beauty like this shouldn't be wasted on simple admiration. It's meant to be consumed. Ravished. Devoured. Feasted on until the insatiable cravings are content." I pause to cool the fire that's incinerating my filter. "It's all about moderation, of course."

"Um… okay." She tilts her head while pondering my ranted nonsense. "What do you call this masterful creation?"

I chuckle at her praise, but a suitable name fails me. Garrett's romantic ass already claimed several titles for the signature cocktails he regularly whips up for Grace. Not only that, but the concoction I'd originally considered might be a bit too strong for her to swallow. For several reasons. I'll play it safe for now.

"How does Neighbor Material sound?"

Callie's gaze leaps to mine. "Rather familiar."

"As it should."

"Have you made this before?"

"Never. That label belongs to you. Exclusively," I rasp. "Please try this liquid version and put me out of my misery."

Our fingers brush as she reaches for the smooth stem. A zap travels through me from that brief touch. She gasps and her gaze leaps to mine. It seems I'm not alone in this madness.

After another stuttered exhale, she picks up the glass in her delicate grip. The smallest sip passes her lips. A delectable moan follows. Her eyelashes flutter shut as if she's in ecstasy from suckling at this extension of me. My mouth waters as I imagine her tongue sliding along mine while she swallows.

Warmth pumps into me at a feverish rate and I grapple at the counter for support. "You like it?"

"Mhmm. It's fresh and fruity and different from anything I've ever had before." Callie takes a generous pull, her throat bobbing with the effort. "Delicious."

"Does this mean I'm corrupting you?" My question gets the desired reaction.

Her cheeks turn redder than the rarest ruby. "If you are, then I approve."

Before my thoughts lead us to the gutter, a suggestion that's appropriate for public strikes me. "Did you bring your camera?"

"I never leave home without it."

"Should we capture this special occasion? Maybe it'll be memorable enough for your scrapbook."

Callie is already swiveling on her stool with the Polaroid poised in midair. I position myself over her left shoulder. My eyes automatically shift to where she's smiling at the lens. A flash signals the moment caught on film.

"That's going to be a keeper," she croons while turning back to face me.

"Of course," I rasp. "You're in it."

A flush burns a splotchy path along her slender throat. "I think most would say that you're the one they want to see."

"Good thing nobody else matters."

The grin she gave for the photo doesn't compare to the one aimed at me. "Did you look at the camera this time?"

"Absolutely not."

Her lips twist. "You're a stinker."

This woman can call me whatever she wants so long as her attention remains on me. I'm hanging on her every word. A puddle of drool is probably collecting on the bar top, but that's the furthest thing from my mind as she sips at her drink again. The glass will be drained very soon at this rate.

"More?"

She giggles. "Are you trying to keep me here all night?"

My gaze burns into hers. "Only if I'm lucky, sweetness."

Callie returns my stare with unwavering intensity. "I think luck is heavily in our favor, Ridge."

A cheesy imitation of cracking a whip bursts our bubble. The mocking sound deserves immediate action for breaking my concentration. I'm forced to rip my gaze off Callie and losing that connection to her is critical. For the offense, I stab the guilty party with a glare.

This asshole's interruption is a spear of ice that attempts to freeze my bloodstream. It's as if I just got dunked into a frigid lake. Based on how the douche canoe is cowering, my expression must reflect the intention to kick his ass. But just in case, I decide to spell it out.

"Fuck off." My voice vibrates with the need for retribution.

"Shit," he mutters. "Didn't mean to make you mad, Crusher. I was just screwing around."

"Do you think I'm the type of person who appreciates such juvenile fuckery?"

His scrawny frame trembles on the stool he's fortunate enough to still occupy. He's probably seconds away from pissing himself. "Nope. That's my mistake. Sorry, man."

"Don't apologize to me." My head tips in Callie's direction.

His wide stare shifts over to her. "I'm sorry."

She scrunches her forehead, but doesn't respond to his bullshit apology. Instead, her baby blues search my gaze that's faithfully returned to hers. "I think he's scared of you."

"As he should be." But then an ugly thought occurs to me. "Are you afraid of me?"

She shakes her head, sending brown hair tumbling around her shoulders. "I don't think that's possible. You're not scary to me."

"Thank fuck for that, sweetness. Now," I drawl and lower myself to her level. "Where were we?"

CHAPTER ELEVEN

Callie: Hello, Ridge. Are you next door or did you go back to work? Thanks for driving me home. You didn't need to do that.

Ridge: I wasn't about to let you walk in your first ever drunken state

Callie: Walking is my only form of transportation. I don't know how to drive.

Ridge: well, shit smh had I known that's how you got to the bar, I would've picked you up to begin with

Callie: No way. That would've ruined the surprise.

Ridge: nah, sweetness. every moment with you is a surprise

Callie: How do you figure?

Ridge: I never thought I'd find happiness like this. just opening up about my feelings is a foreign concept. you're a shock to my system

Callie: That sounds like unexpected bliss.

Ridge: yeah, you get it

Callie: I do, and I feel the same.

Ridge: that validation makes me want to reveal stuff you might not be ready to hear

Callie: Will you? Please? I really enjoy your romantic side.

Ridge: only for you, sweetness. you're the reason I feel like this. each smile you gift me is precious. I cling onto every word like the softly spoken syllables are my sustenance

Ridge: oh, and now I have your cookies to consume as a midnight snack. it's as if you've rebooted me to operate on whatever you're willing to give me

Ridge: you've also turned me into a sap, but I'm not complaining

Ridge: and don't even get me started about what seeing you perched on that stool in my section of the bar does to me

Callie: The flutters and belly swoops have returned.

Ridge: tell me more

Callie: It's such a giddy sensation that I'm unfamiliar with. I'm glad you liked the surprises tonight. There's something I need to tell you, though. I can't take credit for both. The cookies were my idea. Harper suggested I visit Roosters. To share a bit more honesty, stopping by unannounced is way out of my comfort zone. I had to talk myself into following through with the plan. It almost didn't happen. But you know what? The unexpected bliss we just talked about was on your face when I walked into the bar. Seeing that was worth the nerves. It radiated from your expression. I can't properly describe it, but that look stunned me for several moments. You make me feel things I didn't know existed. Just like whenever I open my scrapbook to see our pictures. It's the same joy on your face. I think you might like me, Ridge Carter.

Ridge: I more than like you, Calliope Porter.

Callie: Does this mean you're my... boyfriend?

Ridge: I thought that was obvious

Callie: Not to me. I'm clueless when it comes to dating, remember? The little I've learned is from you, Harper, and romance books. That still isn't much. We haven't even... held hands yet.

Ridge: would you like that?

Callie: Very much so.

Ridge: consider it done. just like how I'm very much your boyfriend. or if not, I'm still waiting

Callie: For what?

Ridge: for you to claim me as yours

Callie: You're mine?

Ridge: undeniably

Callie: Does that make me yours?

Ridge: absolutely. if you agree

Callie: Yes, I like the sound of that.

Ridge: then it's official. no refunds

Callie: That's another first for me.

Ridge: ditto

Callie: No way. You've dated before

Ridge: sure, but nothing serious. this is the first real relationship that counts

Callie: Oh, Ridge. That's such a great answer.

Callie: And now I've decided something else.

Ridge: that sounds like trouble

Callie: Don't worry. It's nothing bad. You need a nickname.

Ridge: other than Crusher or Carter?

Callie: Other people call you those. I want this one to be special between us like how you use sweetness for me.

Ridge: what're you thinking?

Callie: It can't be too cute since you're so... masculine. Pookie Bear wouldn't do you justice.

Ridge: you don't think so?

Callie: Nope, especially when it could be shortened to Pooh.

Ridge: I dunno. seems fitting

Callie: We can do better. I'll think on it. Until then, I should probably go to bed. I have the early shift tomorrow.

Ridge: one last question before you doze off

Callie: I'm here for it.

Ridge: how do you take your coffee?

CHAPTER TWELVE

Callie

T HERE'S A NOTICEABLE BOUNCE IN MY STRIDE THIS morning. That extra pep seems to get more springy with each passing day. It's no secret as to why.

The ongoing chat I have with Ridge is open on my screen. My boyfriend—cue an internal squeal—makes it a point to text me the moment he wakes up. Usually the context is romantic and flirty. As of late, a boldness is coming across from him. His most recent message had me blushing hard enough to spike a fever. I'm still recovering from what he typed. That unbalance hasn't allowed me to form a worthy response.

Besides, the clock reminds me there isn't time to waste for fantasizing. My shift starts in thirty minutes and to walk there takes me at least twenty.

I step out onto the porch, allowing the door to shut behind me. The keypad whirs to announce the deadbolt is locked. That secure confirmation sets me off down the stairs into the pleasant mid-March weather.

My forward motion screeches to a standstill when I see who's parked in the driveway.

Ridge sits behind the wheel of his idling truck. The black

paint glimmers from the sun. I shield my eyes from a particularly bright streak that threatens to blind me.

Meanwhile, he isn't shy about letting his gaze devour me. His upper half leans out the window to get an unrestricted view. Green flames engulf his stare to burn the distance separating us. That hungry perusal licks along my skin, leaving heat behind. I tremble but my knees remain locked to keep me rooted on the spot.

Ridge tosses me a crooked smirk. "Hey, sweetness."

"Hi... boyfriend." My face bursts into a blaze and I duck my chin too late to hide the evidence.

Ridge releases a low groan that sounds like approval. "I was right."

The embarrassment is chased off by that gravely tone. Our eyes meet and hold once I'm brave enough to peek. "About what?"

"You look sexier than a fantasy come true."

He's referring to that last text that had me burning up. A squirm shifts my hips, a sudden warmth gathered there. It's a sensation I was unfamiliar with until meeting Ridge. I now understand the thrum located in my lower belly is desire.

The awareness reignites my blush. "Oh. That."

He chuckles at my obvious shyness but doesn't tease me. "Need a ride?"

"I have to work."

"Yeah, I'll drop you off."

My lips part. "You want to drive me?"

"Just one of my many boyfriend duties." Ridge studies my unmoving stance. "Unless that would make you uncomfortable."

My legs quake and then I'm moving to accept his invitation. Maybe I should consider how quickly he's integrating himself into my routine. But that's my choice. I'm glad he's often nearby. My newfound independence isn't at risk. If I asked him to back off, I know he would. Immediately. There's not a chance he'd refuse me.

He suddenly leaps into action. Before I can process his intentions, he's jumped out and rushed to the passenger side. The door is swung open for me as I arrive.

"What service," I gush.

"Only the best." His arm hovers in midair as if he wants to provide additional assistance.

My skin tingles at the anticipation of contact. It's easy to imagine the comfort a simple touch would deliver. If I falter long enough, he might hoist me inside. Would he? The air crackles as I delay stepping onto the running board.

As it turns out, Ridge is too much of a gentleman. He's probably worried about my reaction. I try not to let my disappointment show when he respects my personal space.

"Thank you," I murmur as I get buckled into the seat.

He hovers for a moment, like he's fighting an internal battle. In the end, he tucks his chin and moves away. "You're welcome."

After shutting me in, he retraces his steps to the driver's side. I occupy myself by inspecting the truck's interior. The beige leather is supple and soft. There's no litter on the rubber mats. It's almost as if the vehicle is fresh off the lot. Other than the distinctive scent. A woodsy spice hangs in the small space and I pull in a deep breath. That's unique to Ridge.

There's also a faint smell of freshly brewed coffee. That's when I notice two covered cups in the center console.

In a fluid motion, Ridge returns to his spot behind the wheel. "Ready to go?"

"Yep, but what's this?" I point to the beverages.

He passes me the one with a pink lid. "A caffeine boost for you. Hazelnut with skim milk and whipped cream."

"Thanks so much." My fingers curl around the protective sleeve as I sniff the rich aroma. "Just the way I like it."

"That's what I was going for." His gaze is riveted on me while I take a cautious sip. "And there's something else."

Before I can ask, he reaches into the backseat. I gape at the present he deposits on my lap. It's a stunning display of shiny green and sparkly blue embellishments. Shock spreads through me at the unexpected sight.

He took the time to actually put the gift in decorative packaging rather than tossing an unwrapped object at me like an afterthought. Not that I'd make a fuss about presentation. The second option is common practice where I come from. As if I should be grateful that I crossed his mind at all regardless of the item. That's how my mother would react to any offering from my father. It's pathetic when I look back on those memories. She deserves so much better.

My watery gaze focuses on a curled ribbon. A loud crinkle warns me that I'm squeezing too hard. This pretty box just proves that Ridge spent additional effort on me. Like usual.

"Are you okay?" He asks after several minutes have passed and I'm still caught in a stupor.

My nod is disjointed. "This is just… really special."

"Open it," he urges.

I peel away the taped seal, trying not to rip anything. This will make a stunning background for a scrapbook page. My astonishment gets the best of me once the label is visible. The remaining paper is torn off without concern.

"Oh. My. Gosh." I suck in a sharp breath. "This is the latest model. Are you for real?"

"Appears that way." He flexes his biceps.

My gaze is instantly drawn to him. Another plain shirt stretches across his broad frame. The white fabric does little to conceal his bulk and brawn. His forearms are exposed thanks to the sleeves pushed to his elbows. Ropey veins and colorful tattoos are a distracting combination.

He's close enough to touch but I don't dare. Not after he

didn't make a move earlier. I take the safe route and inhale him again. The crisp pine and masculine energy are addictive. My mouth waters as if I can taste him. Warm fuzzies skip in my stomach as I get lost in a daze.

"Callie?"

"Huh?"

A raspy chuckle enters the scene, beckoning my imagination to wade deeper. "Do you want to take a picture?"

"Yes," I mumble absently. His beauty should be captured and plastered on the wall. But only for me to see. He's mine now.

Ridge's amusement rumbles from his chest. "Might want to take the camera out of the box then."

I blink back to reality. "Oh! Right."

He points at the Instax Mini. "Now you have one for regular use and can save the other for extra special occasions."

"You don't have to buy me things." Yet I'm undoing the cardboard flap.

"That's hilarious. I plan to buy you anything your heart desires."

"What if my heart just wants you to like me?" My breath catches. How did I get so bold?

The lingering hunger is his stare suggests he wants to eat me for breakfast. "You're selling yourself short, sweetness. I already more than like you, remember?"

"It's impossible to forget." The texts from last night play on repeat. "That's why you're my boyfriend."

"Until I get upgraded." He winks and something clenches inside of me.

Heat blooms in my cheeks. "We just started dating."

"I'm a patient man," he reminds.

"But once I'm ready?" For what, I'm still unsure.

"You'll discover just how obsessive you've made me. I'll

be insatiable." The certainty in his voice is a caress along my most sensitive flesh.

I gasp when my nipples pebble into hardened points. The friction against my bra sparks that unfamiliar heat between my legs. When I press my thighs together, the needy sensation expands. It's all I can do to trap a moan.

A knowing glint flickers in Ridge's unwavering stare. He must notice a change in me. Questions flood my mind and I'm desperate to ask for details. But he's determined to make me wait. I'll figure out this secret sooner or later. Based on my body's signals, there's a new phase approaching.

Rather than extend this awkward tension, I fixate on the camera in my grip. "I can't believe you did this. Thank you. Again. So many presents and the sun is barely over the horizon. It's very thoughtful."

He hangs an arm over the steering wheel, which brings us closer. "That's a fitting sentiment, since I'm always thinking of you."

"Holy moly." I fan my face. "You say the nicest things."

"Trust me, sweetness. This isn't my standard setting. There's plenty of dirt and filth up here too." He taps his temple. "But that's reserved for another day. Should we capture the moment before you're late to work?"

"Yes!" I fumble while putting in the batteries and film. This model is significantly lighter than the antique my mother gave me. The compact build allows me to effortlessly point the lens at the optimal angle. I pause before I press the shutter, peeking over at Ridge. "Are you going to look at the camera?"

"Nope." His breath fans the flames on my cheek.

I allow my eyelids to slide shut as a smile stretches my lips. "What am I going to do with you?"

"Love me."

"What?" I twist toward him just as my finger slips and snaps the shot.

"That's gonna be the best yet." He snatches the exposure as it gets spit out.

"What?" I repeat as his earlier words whirl in a spiral until I'm lightheaded.

"Candids can't be replicated," he explains.

A crease forms between my brows. "You said that for shock value?"

"Nah, but your expression will be priceless."

"You should have this one," I insist when he tries to hand over the image.

"Are you sure? It'll fit with your collection."

"That just gives us an excuse to take more, right?" I jostle the Instax in my hold.

"I won't argue with that." He slides the developing photo into a crack on the dash.

"That doesn't fit with your minimalist vibe." A cringe tightens my features while I motion to the spotless interior.

"Sweetness," he chides. "There's nothing minimalist about me. I've just been waiting for you to fill in the gaps."

And there go the belly swoops. "Um, wow. You might be perfect, boyfriend."

"Far from it," he chuckles. "But for you? I'm giving it all I've got."

I rest a palm flat on the somersaults wreaking havoc in my stomach. "It's working."

"Good. Which reminds me, the pups are waiting for you. I don't want you to be late." Ridge reverses out of my driveway and begins the short trip to Main Street.

My shift at Pampered Pooch hasn't crossed my mind. "Smooth transition."

"What can I say? I'm not just hard edges and cheesy lines." He knocks on the divider that separates our seats.

"No," I breathe. "You're much more."

A comfortable silence settles between us as the tires bump

along the pavement. It doesn't escape my immediate notice that our hands are inches apart. As if listening to my inner dialogue, Ridge glances at where we're almost touching. My heart begins to race while I consider eliminating the space. I can be brave.

But before I can make the move, his palm shifts to cover mine. The touch is tentative. A test to my untried limits he's often referencing. The slight contact still shoots a rocket off in my chest and it takes saintly effort to sit still.

Ridge probably catches the struggle twitching across my expression. "Is this okay?"

My pulse is galloping to the point that I hear hoof beats. "Very much so."

With permission granted, he clasps our hands together. A riot of giddy bumblebees take flight in my belly when he threads my fingers between his. Uncertainty begins to assault me. My skin is clammy. Oh, gosh. He's going to think I'm a sweaty mess. And I'm probably too stiff.

After a long exhale, I sag into the leather. Ridge gives me a gentle squeeze that I feel straight to my toes. I rub my thumb along his in response. All too soon, he's pulling over at the curb in front of my job. I sit for several moments while debating with myself. Releasing his grip isn't on my preferred tasks to complete this century. It's not as if I can stay glued to his side all day, though. The appropriate solution is to get my butt into the doggie daycare.

Ridge's deep timbre puts a halt to the hasty retreat I was about to make. "Hey, sweetness?"

"Yeah, boyfriend?" I toss at him in return.

His mouth quirks and I could just about melt. "Do you have plans this weekend?"

I pretend to think it over, but my calendar is empty. "Not that I'm aware of."

His gaze travels from mine to where our fingers are still

interlaced. "Want to go somewhere with me? I have a specific place in mind."

"Is it a surprise?"

He nods. "And a date if you agree."

"As if I'd deny you."

A glint sparks in his eyes. "Probably shouldn't admit that."

I trace over his knuckle with my nail. "Why not?"

"Your modesty might be in jeopardy."

A laugh bubbles from me. The sound is freeing. "I'm willing to risk it."

"Don't say I didn't warn you." There's a teasing note in his tone.

Our bodies tilt inward as if drawn together by a magnetic force. It gives me the courage to taunt him in return. "Do your worst, boyfriend."

An audible gulp bobs his Adam's apple. The air separating us turns static. His palm seems to heat against mine like a brand is forming. I welcome the burn and refuse to shy away. He searches my gaze as if seeking further permission. Whatever he wants, I'll likely agree. But then he straightens to douse the flames.

"Well, would you look at that? I was right again." He nods at our most recent picture that's completely developed.

Our eyes are locked on each other rather than focusing straight ahead. It's like we're looking at what truly matters.

"Unexpected bliss," I sigh.

"Yeah, sweetness." Ridge's attention on me feels bottomless in this instant and all those that will follow. "That's us."

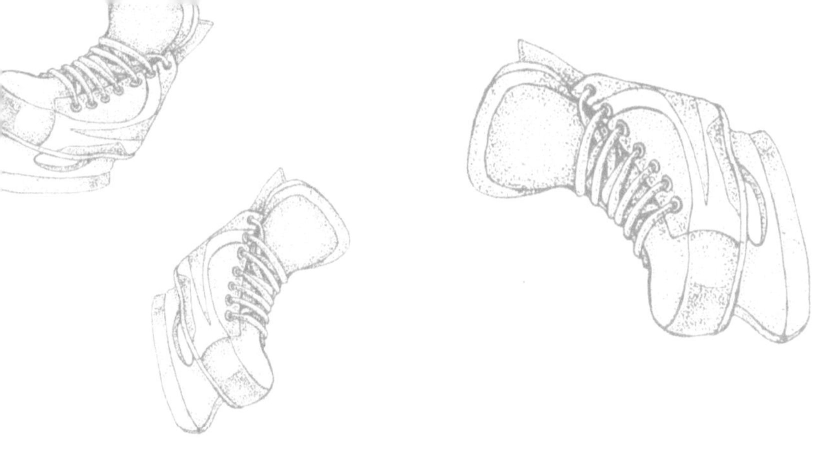

CHAPTER THIRTEEN

Ridge

MY THUMB TAPS ON THE STEERING WHEEL AS THE freeway curves toward our secret location. That rapid beat mirrors the thunder in my chest. For whatever reason, this date feels like a turning point. There's only one direction I'll allow.

Callie is beside me in the passenger seat. It's easy to consider that as her rightful spot as we move forward. I could sense a shift in our dynamic when we were in a similar position the other day. Just like then, her hand is clutched protectively in mine. The comfort from such casual contact is a natural high.

A constant buzz thrums through me whenever we're connected. Callie releases a long exhale as if the static charge surges in her veins too. That content sound confirms that she welcomes my touch. If pressed, I'd be willing to assume she wanted to initiate contact the moment I picked her up. I sure as shit did, and here we sit. Interwoven.

My relationship with Callie is progressing faster—and better—than I dared to anticipate. We're transitioning into a more physical stage and it excites me. Warmth rushes under my skin and I shift against the cool leather. Arousal is always on tap whenever Callie is nearby or I'm thinking about her, which means my body is constantly on alert. The steady thump from tires on pavement anchors me before I get carried away.

Callie has been noticeably quiet since blocks of buildings replaced rolling fields. I take the opportunity to glance over at her. A grin automatically crooks my lips as if I'm the smiling sort. Only this girl can get the expression to rise from me. Not that many would be immune to her in this situation.

Her round eyes and unblinking stare are adorable. She presses her right hand flat against the window. A foggy imprint appears from the pressure.

Then just as suddenly, her body sways toward mine as if reeled in by our linked fingers. The liberty of touching her freely is heady. I've been granted permission and I'm taking advantage. She accepts me. Once again, I'm fortunate enough to cradle her delicate trust in my grip. Quite fucking literally. I trace along her inner wrist with my thumb as the smog grows thicker in the sky.

"Do you know where we are?"

"Far from home," she breathes.

"This is the capital of Minnesota." I point straight ahead to where we're going.

"St. Paul." She peeks over at me. "Our basic education didn't skip geography."

"Have you ever seen a big city?"

"No." There's wonder in her voice as her attention returns to the urban landscape.

"There are far larger than this. Minneapolis is just down the road."

"Incredible." Her fingers curl against the glass as if she can touch the skyscrapers. "I'm sure this is nothing new for you."

"Nah, I've been around." As in all fifty states before I

graduated high school. Traveling sports and the potential of going pro will do that to a kid.

"What's your favorite place to visit, boyfriend?" Callie pauses to think her question over. "For a… vacation." The hesitation in her tone makes that last term sound like a mythical concept.

I flick the blinker and switch lanes. "Well, that depends on the type of trip you're interested in. A beach resort is ideal for relaxing, but the main strip of a popular downtown area will provide a weekend full of debauchery and reckless decisions."

Her lips twitch. "That's not what I asked. I want to know your dream destination."

"Anywhere with you, sweetness. Your choice."

"As if," she giggles.

"Test out your power and find out."

"Power?" Callie shakes her head. "I don't need that."

"Regardless, you have it."

"I wouldn't know where to start," she muses.

"It's something to think about. There's no hurry."

Without releasing my hand, she digs out her phone and opens a fresh Google search. "The possibilities are endless."

A quick glance at her screen reveals millions of results. "We can narrow it down. Would you prefer beautiful scenery from nature or attractions that are mostly indoors?"

Callie hums. "The first option."

"See? That already eliminates a ton of locations."

She continues scrolling for another moment. "Would you take a vacation with me?"

"Didn't we already establish that? Where you go, I'll follow." Which would make not inviting me awkward as fuck.

She bites her bottom lip. "Just checking."

"I love your ambitious spirit. How do you feel about flying?"

Her wide eyes find mine and she goes very still. There's a

frantic urgency in those green depths that suggests she might find the nearest spot to hide. "Like in an airplane?"

My fingers squeeze hers in what's meant to be reassurance. "I take that as not great. We can make it a road trip."

She expels a loud breath and relaxes against the seat. "I like the sound of that. Staying on the ground feels safer."

I exit at the next off ramp and turn right on Kellogg Street. "Whatever makes you comfortable. It'll be an adventure regardless of how we get there."

Her lips part as if she's about to admit her unwavering devotion. Then she does a quick scan of our surroundings as the city envelops us. The thrum of activity spreads far and wide in this area. Traffic is thick on the road. People crowd the sidewalks. Vibrant displays are splashed across store fronts to draw attention. Music blasts from an unknown source.

There's much to see—other than greenery—and the woman beside me has taken notice.

"Do you care if I take a picture?" She stares meaningfully at the one that's permanently attached to my dashboard.

Confusion swirls as I pause as a traffic light. "Why would I?"

Callie makes a point to look down at our clasped palms before lifting her brows. "I need both hands, boyfriend."

"Do you? I thought the latest model was a point and shoot? One finger should do the trick." And that's definitely what she said.

"Unlikely. I'm not that talented," she laughs.

"I disagree." But I release her from my hold.

A grateful smile gets sent my way. "You can reclaim your grip in just a moment."

The window lowers and a breezy gust whips at her hair. "Whoa."

"It would've been worse on the interstate," I chuckle.

Callie attempts to tuck wayward strands behind her ears. "I'll be quick."

"You can't rush beauty."

Her eyes roll in my direction before she returns her focus to the passing street view. "You humor me."

A rumble rolls off my chest. "I hope I do more than that."

She visibly shivers. "Much more."

Heat travels through me faster than the speed limit. If I wasn't driving, I'd be fighting my restraint against kissing her. "How 'bout that picture?"

That snaps her from the stupor. "If you'd quit distracting me."

"You make it too easy."

"What can I say? I like it when you flirt with me." Her blush teases me while she captures an image of the sleek architecture.

The hum from the film being exported is drowned out by the wind. Not that I'd notice. My chest is too preoccupied swelling with pride as Callie takes another picture. She's no longer concerned about limiting herself and that plucks a triumphant string within me.

A thought occurs to me while she aims the lens at a mirrored structure. "Why don't you use your phone to take pictures? The camera is much better than an Instax."

She twists her lips, but nods. "Technology is strange. I'm still getting used to having a handheld device that grants me access to just about everything. Call me old-fashioned, but there's something about holding an actual camera in my grip. I don't have to be a photographer to understand the significance. Plus, it spits out pictures instantly! Way cooler than just staring at them on a screen."

There's no stopping a smile from forming at her enthusiastic explanation. "I get that."

Shock steals her voice for several seconds. "Really?"

"Yep. Plenty of stuff is just fine the way it is. Not everything should be updated or replaced just because a new version is simpler or supposedly 'better.' I won't abandon a good thing that's proven itself. Such as the local company who made my pads and equipment even when I was pressured to use a big manufacturer. I did several ads for their business to put them on the map." My chest puffs up a bit at the reminder.

"Exactly." Her eyes sparkle as she gazes at me. "You totally get it."

"Does that mean I get you?"

"Yes?"

"The uncertainty doesn't bode well for me."

Callie giggles and focuses on a skyscraper stretching for the clouds. "Would it be better if I said that I'm not uncertain about you?"

"Abso-fucking-lutely," I blurt. "Very much so."

"I've never been more certain of anything in my life." Her tone is barely a whisper, but she might as well have screamed the declaration.

Now I'm the one struggling to respond. The need surging through my system is too demanding. "Damn, sweetness. That's how you bring a man to his knees."

Her posture stiffens in visible alarm. "But you're driving."

"Figuratively speaking," I amend. At least until she's ready for me to properly worship her.

The redness that blooms in her cheeks suggests she can hear my plans for our future. "Silly me. I was concerned for your health."

"Nah, don't worry. I'm not going anywhere."

"Thank goodness." Her relief swirls along with the early evening breeze before she closes the window.

A bright flash in my periphery makes me blink. "Whatcha doin' over there, sweetness?"

"Saved the best for last."

"A picture of me?"

"You look very mysterious while driving us on this seemingly endless journey." Her arm flails toward the windshield.

"Is someone getting impatient?" Not that I can blame her. We've been on the road for over an hour.

"More like morbidly curious." She tucks her new prized possession away. "That's enough photos for now. I'll take more once we get to where we're going. And on that note, are you planning to reveal this secret location?"

"You're about to find out," I say as the Xcel Energy Center comes into view. My empty hand seeks to reclaim hers. "We're here."

"Where?"

I point at the domed fortress on our left. "This is where the Minnesota Trojans play."

Callie gasps. "That's the hockey team you were on."

"Yep, and I still have access to the rear lot. Free parking this close to the arena is a golden goose."

"Sounds like a fairytale," she muses.

"That's what I'm going for." I pull into a spot in the center row.

"Your choice in attire makes more sense now." She glances at my matching hat and shirt before frowning at her outfit that doesn't have a stitch of gold or green. "Is there a souvenir store where I can buy a jersey or other clothes? Then I'll look like I belong."

A jealous wave crashes over me to give our surroundings a green hue. My hand slips from hers and I shift into park. Then I grip the steering wheel hard enough to make the leather creak. "You want to wear another man's name across your back?"

Callie frowns. "Why would I do that?"

"The jerseys in the pro shop are from the team's current

roster." I kill the ignition with more force than necessary. "You'll be supporting whoever you choose."

A disgruntled squeak escapes her. "I'll just get a generic option."

"Or you could wear this."

She watches me pull a wrapped bundle from the backseat. "Another gift?"

"Consider it mutually beneficial."

Her fingers lift the tissue covering to reveal a familiar color pattern along with the Trojans' logo. "You got me a jersey?"

"It's somewhat of a retro throwback," I joke.

Callie holds up the oversized garment. After flipping it over, she traces the letters of my last name boldly displayed for all to see. Imagining that caress against my bare flesh is an erotic visual. Her gentle touch lowers to fondle the twenty-three that monopolizes the center, which only adds to the temptation.

"This is yours," she says softly.

Just like you are, I nearly groan. Rather than allow my obsessive side loose, I settle for a gruff, "Sure is."

"I love it. Did you know twenty-three is my favorite number?"

"That's very convenient." And just one more reason we belong together.

"Mhmm, it's my—"

"Birthday," I finish for her.

"My golden one is this year." She taps the trimmed stitching that matches the milestone. Another coincidence.

"We'll have a big celebration in September."

"That's many months away. For right now and always, I get to support you whether you're on the ice or not. Which is how it should be since you're my boyfriend." She slips the mesh fabric over her head and my cock is ready to punch a hole in my jeans.

"Damn," I croak.

"What do you think?" She tugs at the hem, which rests at mid-thigh in her current position. The baggy material will probably fall to just above her knees once she's standing.

"Perfection," I rasp. My gaze feasts on her tagged with my name and number while I wrestle the arousal thrashing through me. "You're the most stunning sight I've ever seen."

"Thank you," she murmurs. "For everything."

"Trust me, sweetness. It's my pleasure." I discreetly push at the bulge behind my zipper.

Her stare slides to the steady flow of people entering the Xcel. And that's just one of many access points. "There are a lot of people at these games, huh?"

I chuckle. "You could say that. Does it bother you?"

Her bottom lip gets tortured between her teeth. "I'm not used to crowds of this size. Knox Creek is big compared to where I grew up. It's still an adjustment."

My hand scoops hers into a reassuring hold. "I reserved a private suite to keep us separated from the masses. We'll have a large room and box seats entirely to ourselves. But if you're not comfortable, we can do something on a smaller scale."

"No, I want to try."

"Are you sure?" I give her fingers a squeeze.

Callie's blush reignites to replicate a rose garden in full bloom. "With you at my side, I'm sure I can do just about anything."

CHAPTER FOURTEEN

Callie

Nerves form an unforgiving knot in my stomach. I gulp against the dry desert my throat has become while Ridge leads us closer to the imposing building. People swarm from every direction and create a funnel at the entrance. Sweat prickles at my neck as we approach the fluid stream that flows into the unknown.

What I focus on is the section of glass doors straight ahead. In the center is a circular opening that appears to have a spinning mechanism. That's precisely where Ridge is steering us.

I slam on the brakes just as a gust from the whirlwind contraption hits my face. "What is that thing?"

He scans the general area as if searching for an invisible problem. "What thing?"

"That." I point at the strange spiral device.

His gaze shifts from me to the object in front of us. "The revolving door?"

My mouth works silently for several moments. "That's a door?"

"Yeah…" He drags the singular word through mud. "Haven't you seen one before?"

"Is this a response from a person who sees them regularly?" I motion to my wide eyes and locked knees. "In case that isn't obvious, I've never seen one before."

He scrubs at his mouth, trying and failing to hide a growing smile. "You step inside, and it moves automatically. Think of it as a hands-free option."

"Fancy technology," I mumble.

"Nah, these have been around for ages." Ridge no longer bothers to smother his grin. "Just wait for the elevators and escalators."

The first is a recognizable term, but the second draws a blank. Not that I have personal experience with either of them. "Are they weird like this?"

"That depends on what you mean by weird. They're fairly common in buildings with at least two stories, especially elevators."

A memory clicks on in my mind. "Do they go up and down?"

"Fuck," he chuckles. "You're too adorable. Yes, they're both motorized alternatives for stairs."

"There's still much to learn," I mumble.

"Let's just go this way." He hitches a thumb at a regular door.

"Nope, I'm going through the spin cycle. The entire purpose of fleeing the compound was to experience everything I'd been missing, and that's stating it mildly. But a revolving door is on the list regardless."

Ridge's stubbled cheek twitches with a renewed smirk. "I can't argue with that."

I pull in a deep breath until my lungs complain. "You won't let go of my hand, right?"

"Wouldn't if you begged."

"Really?"

His expression turns smug. "I'd consider it, but probably not."

"That's what I thought. Okay, I'm ready." I creep forward to what might be a torture chamber, or a time machine if I'm being fanciful.

Ridge takes charge of the situation. My feet are practically lifted off the ground as he casually strolls into a triangular enclosure that's fit for two. He's so tall surrounding me, like a protective shield. I hold my breath while the glass cylinder envelops us. We shuffle to keep pace with the lazy speed. The frantic thrash in my pulse slows. This isn't scary. Well, not unless we get stuck. But we arrive on the other side without incident.

"That wasn't so bad, right?" He guides me forward to allow those behind us to exit the rotation as well.

"Nope," I chirp. But then I catch sight of the massive space we've stepped into. My shoes stick to the concrete while I gawk at the ceiling that appears sky-high. "Holy shit."

Ridge chokes. "Did you just curse?"

"Can you blame me?" I fling an arm toward the curved wall made entirely of windows that stretches farther than I can see. Across from that impressive sight are display cases filled with awards and memorabilia that probably costs a fortune. The awe goes on from there. "This deserves an expletive. I wasn't prepared for… all this."

An amused rumble rolls off the man I'm glued against. "If the concourse gets this type of reaction, you're gonna lose your mind once we get to the ice."

Without releasing my grip on him, I turn in a slow circle. "That's highly possible. It's already surreal out here. My mother wouldn't believe me if I told her," I breathe.

He peers down at me. "I haven't heard you mention her

very often. Are you worried about how she's doing since you left?"

"Yes, constantly. It's hard to think about her. I feel extremely guilty for leaving her behind." My chest aches as I wonder what she's doing at this very moment. "But I'm trying to live a better life for both of us. That's what she wanted. For the past year, I trained myself to shut off the pain from the past. I struggled at the beginning, but I won't take her sacrifice for granted. Maybe one day she'll get to explore beyond the limits of Billmoore. In the meantime, I'm trying to capture every moment in her honor."

The reminder has me blindly grabbing for a one-handed grip on my camera. I aim the lens down the long corridor that's bright with natural light. As the gears grind to spit out the film, Ridge stoops to my level.

"Should we take one together?"

"Of course." I'm giddy with the possibility of another shot with him. If he knew how badly I want to fill an entire album with pictures of us, he'd probably never speak to me again. But a sideways glance finds his focus locked on me. On second thought, he might enjoy that.

"May I?" He holds open his palm for me to pass over the Instax.

There's no hesitation from me to fulfill his request. His fingers release mine in order for him to loop an arm around my waist to pull me close. The motion is seamless, never severing our contact.

The height difference between us is laughable, but he doesn't complain while bending lower. Our cheeks almost touch as we pose for the photo. I don't have to ask if he's going to look at the lens. It seems to be his signature style. Plus, I like the idea that he can't look away from me. He presses the button while I smile from the inside out. The flash has spots dancing in my eyes that might as well be stars and hearts and—

"Can I be next, Crusher?"

My eyes scan for the owner of the feminine voice, finally landing on a beautiful blonde. Confidence practically shines from her flawless complexion. My own shrinks and cowers beneath a familiar layer of insecurity.

A loud buzz fills my ears as I begin scooting from the frame to let her replace me. It's physically painful to separate from him, but the sting doesn't get a chance to spread. Ridge's grip on me doesn't loosen. If anything, he holds me tighter.

"Where do you think you're going, sweetness?"

"She wants to take a picture with you." My whisper is weak and pathetic.

"Do you think I'll allow that?" The steely edge in his tone gives me the answer.

But my pride is still wounded. "You should. She's very pretty."

"Is she? I didn't notice."

"How's that possible?" A sideways glance confirms she's hovering just beyond our previously intimate bubble.

"I only see you." The devotion in his statement reclaims my full concentration. "Now that you're really listening, I'll ask you again. Do you think I'll allow another woman to stand beside me?"

My swallow is thick. "No?"

"No," he states firmly. "Especially after I promised not to let you go. Even if I hadn't, it's a known character flaw that I don't do photos in public. Until now. You're the only one who gets that from me."

The breath whooshes from my lungs and I nearly sway into him. "Oh."

His gaze drops to my parted lips for a moment before

he returns his stare to mine. "Yeah, sweetness. You're getting there."

Before I can ask for clarification, someone bumps into my shoulder with enough force to knock me off balance. Ridge is there to catch my fall and set me upright. As I'm regaining my bearings, a menacing growl threatens to topple me in the opposite direction. I realize the noise is coming from the defender of vengeance who refuses to relinquish his hold on me.

"Apologize to my"—he pauses as if chewing on a suitable term to regard me—"girlfriend."

The man stumbles backward and visibly pales at Ridge's seethed command. "Shit, it's Crusher. Sorry. I'm so fucking sorry."

He runs off before I can process what happened. Not that my concentration would've stayed on him long. The events spread over the past three minutes gathered a large following.

Everyone blends together as a cohesive unit. A sea of green and gold to support their beloved Trojans. Several pairs of eyes are aimed directly at us. Others are more polite, only peering over at curious intervals. A handful of bold individuals point and whisper within their social circles.

I look down at my jersey to see if it's crooked. The garment drapes my figure evenly like a loose gown. A peek at Ridge reflects his stony mask that's reserved for everyone but me. He doesn't appear the least bit concerned about this extra attention.

"People are staring," I murmur.

"They can't help themselves. You're a captivating beauty like the sun. They'll go blind before averting their gaze."

Even if I was vain enough to believe him, it's obvious I'm not the target of their attention. "You're a big deal, huh?"

"I'm somewhat recognizable."

"Somewhat? Everyone is looking."

He tugs the brim of his hat down lower to conceal the upper half of his face. "Not really."

"Why are you hiding then?" I cup the side of my mouth and stage-whisper, "It's because you're super famous."

"Only to hockey fans," he relents.

"And you're dating me?" My voice is a shrill squeak.

"It's a shock to the system, huh? I'm aware that I don't deserve you. It's very generous of you to lower your standards for me."

I scoff, which turns into a dry laugh. "You must be joking. If anyone is lucky in this scenario, it's me."

He shrugs. "Not the way I see it."

It goes against my nature to argue with him, even if he's acting delusional on purpose. "Agree to disagree."

A piercing whistle interrupts us. "Woot, woot. Crusher is in the house!"

His nostrils flare as he assesses those fascinated by his presence. "Fuck, maybe this was a bad idea."

A gasp rattles me. "How can you say that?"

"People aren't respecting you." He signals to a girl who's probably recording our exchange.

I squeeze his hand, which is securely fastened against mine again. "Would it put you at ease to know I feel very well protected while I'm with you?"

Ridge's eyes heat and there's a noticeable upward curve to his mouth that betrays his neutral expression. He tugs me forward before anyone else can witness the crack in his armor. "C'mon, sweetness. Let's get to the suite before another dumbass decides to test your personal space."

Staying true to his promise, I'm tucked safely into his side as we wade into the sea of bodies. An impenetrable barrier encircles us. He might as well be a shield against the crowd. I rely on his towering height to protect him. No harm will touch me while he's here. That sense of safety allows me to ignore the lingering stares burning into my hunched form.

Ridge maintains a measured pace while steering me through the maze of this building. Our slow speed is most likely for my benefit. I'm grateful; it seems he knows what I need without me having to utter a word. The same goes for how he absently strokes the ruined flesh on my forearm with his thumb. It seems like he can't stop touching me, which frees a dozen butterflies in my belly.

We climb two flights of stairs rather than take a risk on the escalator. That motorized alternative might eat my shoes. As we approach the third-floor landing, Ridge tilts his phone screen at a uniformed attendant. The man grants us access to wherever we're headed. This corridor isn't nearly as congested. A brisk stroll delivers us to a door where another security personnel waits. He barely glances at what I assume are electronic tickets on Ridge's screen before allowing us inside.

Once again, my stride stumbles to an abrupt halt just as I cross the threshold. The room we've entered is immaculate. Leather chairs and polished tables are arranged on the left side. A long table occupies most of the right. Its surface is covered with an assortment of bowls and platters. Framed achievements from previous hockey games and other events hosted by this venue are hanging on the walls. But the massive viewing window straight ahead steals the scene. From what I can see just beyond the glass, there's a private section of seats on a balcony of sorts. Those must be reserved for us.

"Welcome to our suite." Ridge gestures at the upscale vibe.

I shuffle forward. "Consider my mind officially blown."

"Totally called it."

"We get this entire place to ourselves?" My slack jaw will collect flies soon.

"Yep, just you and me for the next several hours."

"This requires proof for posterity." In the next moment, I have my camera pointed at the elegant furnishings. I immediately aim in the opposite direction for another shot.

"Are you hungry? We have about thirty minutes until the game starts." He redirects my attention to the variety of choices arranged in a buffet.

After a cursory appraisal, it appears the options include my favorite foods. The rich scents in the air confirm as much. There's pesto pasta with toasted garlic bread. Ripe pineapple, strawberries, and peaches. A Greek salad with extra feta and olives. Bottles of unsweetened iced tea. Snacks and sugary treats for later. There's an obvious theme to this spread, which sparks my suspicion.

"Did you choose the menu?"

"Is it that obvious?" He ducks his chin, almost appearing shy.

I squint at him. "Which of these options did you pick for yourself?"

Ridge peruses the choices. "I'll eat whatever. I'm not fussy."

"But what do you like to eat?"

His gaze feasts on me until he's had his fill, and then he binges on a second serving. "Anything you're willing to give me."

I blink at the evasive response. "Um, okay. I'll get you some of everything."

"That won't be necessary but allow me to serve you." He begins filling a plate for me before I can protest.

A chiding look settles on me when I try swapping roles. I'm not allowed to lift a finger, other than to stay connected to him. He won't hear me complain. That comfort from contact goes both ways.

We sit at one of the tables and dig into our dinner. An explosion of flavors pampers my tastebuds. I barely manage to stifle a moan around the next mouthful. Savory spices and rich sauces stir a pleasurable warmth within me. Every bite is better than the last.

To stop from licking my fork, I watch Ridge devour what remains of his meal. It seems only fitting since he hasn't looked away from me as I thoroughly inhaled the cuisine. That trails my gaze to the secure grip he has on his own utensil. Then the muscles and thick veins in his forearms demand recognition.

I dab at my lips with a napkin. "You have a lot of tattoos."

A teasing glint flickers in his eyes. "Are you just noticing?"

Fire blazes in my cheeks. "As if I could miss the colorful ink on your skin. I didn't have the courage to mention them."

"Until now," he rasps.

"You make me brave." I gulp as nerves threaten to bubble up. "It's a new development."

"That inner spark is shining through, sweetness." He toys with my fingers that are once again weaved through his. "I'm honored to be the one fanning your flames."

The smoky tendrils curling off his tone suggest that he's referring to more than my newfound confidence. But I'm not sure how to broach the provocative context. Instead, I swerve back to where my interest often lands. Along with his willingness to talk about himself. There's no resisting an open invitation like that.

"How many tattoos do you have?"

"I stopped counting years ago. There are at least fifteen combined to create this"—he points to the heavily-inked flesh on his right arm—"full sleeve design. The left one only has a half, but there are still plenty blended together. I have many others on parts not as visible."

The potential of locating those alerts my belly to swoop and flip faster than normal. "Which one did you get first?"

"This." He circles a hockey stick with a puck balanced on the wider end. "I added the jersey after the Trojans signed me from the draft when I was nineteen. Seems like ages ago."

There's longing in his revelation and those sad notes give me pause. I don't want to pry. "Which is your most recent?"

Ridge smirks. "Roosters is written along my ribs. I included the cock den too."

The urge to ask if I can sneak a peek dances on my tongue, but that would return us to inappropriate territory. "How long ago did you get it done?"

"After the bar opened, which was over three years ago."

My brows lift. "Are you done getting tattoos then?"

"Nah, I have plans for another design. Already set an appointment."

That intriguing strand tethers my concentration. "What're you going to get?"

His chuckle is warm and gooey and very unlike him. "You'll see once it's done."

"You won't tell me?"

He shakes his head. "I'd rather show you."

My smile wilts slightly. "I've heard that before."

His focus slides to the arena center. "Should we go to our seats?"

I follow his gaze to see a countdown displayed on a large screen. A furrow creases my brow. We had half an hour not too long ago. Now only four minutes remain. "Time runs quick when I'm with you."

"That means we make each second count."

"Oh," I exhale. "You're being very romantic tonight."

"Just tonight?"

I bite my bottom lip while forcing myself to hold his gaze. "No, it seems to be a regular occurrence."

"Ever since I met you." He winks and rises to his feet.

I'm struck still as he gathers our dirty dishes. After dumping them in the labeled tub, he refills my tea along with his water. My focus is fastened on his fluid movements. That leads me to appreciate how well his jeans fit him. The denim molds to his athletic build like the fabric was stitched just for his measurements.

He glances over his shoulder to catch me. "Like what you see?"

"Very much," I blurt. My eyes widen at that bold statement. A fiery heat floods my cheeks as I wait for his reaction.

A pleased rumble rolls off his chest and he prowls to where I remain frozen in place. "Damn, sweetness. Do you have any idea what this does to me?"

I don't breathe while his bent knuckle traces a warm patch that's bloomed on my face. "Constantly blushing exposes me as innocent and shy. I'm embarrassed by how easily it happens."

"It's sexy," he murmurs. "Especially when I'm the cause of it. You drive me to the brink of madness no matter what you're doing." His finger strokes a pattern into my flesh. "But when you're flushed? I'm shoved over the edge into blind obsession. Consider me lost in you."

My inhale hitches from his admission. Ridge is barely touching me, but it feels as if he's delving beneath the surface to cradle my very essence. There's a blatant need in his gaze that even I can recognize. That desire awakens something in me. I whimper as a spasm clenches in my lower belly. He must sense the change in me because his hand drops with a suddenness that's startling.

"We need to get out there"—he motions to our empty chairs on the other side of the window—"before I take a liberty you're not ready to give."

I want to argue that he can have me, but the retort stalls on my parted lips. In truth, I'm not sure what that means. "Okay."

With a palm notched at my lower back, Ridge escorts me to the front row of our sectioned-off box. I watch from above as people fill the stadium seating below. Green and gold covers the space. Soon the entire arena is full and neon lights pass over the crowd in an erratic sweep. Music blasts from hidden speakers. My breath catches as smoke spews from canisters attached to the plexiglass. It's quite a spectacle. The pile of pictures beside me is growing rapidly.

"Welcome, hockey fans! I hope you're in the mood for a great game. Tonight, your Minnesota Trojans take on the Chicago Grizzlies. We'll see who comes out on top."

The announcement comes from an unknown source. Not that it matters. We're all focused on the ice as players enter and begin skating around. A few names are called out, which are recognized as the starters. I'm transfixed while many drop to their knees. The motions that come next are unexpected. Their performance threatens to scandalize me.

I scoot to the edge of my chair. "What're they—?"

"This part isn't important," Ridge grumbles.

"Really? Everyone seems very interested." In fact, the women in attendance appear glued to the act of several players stretching.

"It's mostly for views. The routine is staged these days." His tone is sour.

"Does that bother you?" Maybe it takes away from the authenticity of the sport.

"Other men trying to steal your attention by lewdly thrusting their hips? Abso-fucking-lutely."

I chance a peek at one in the center. His movements are especially vigorous. It almost seems like he's imitating an intimate act. And once that occurs to me, I can't unsee it. "Oh, my."

"Do you like what he's doing?" Ridge's harsh exhale wafts across my neck.

I squirm in my padded chair as flames travel through me at an alarming rate. My brain misfires while I replace the player on the ice with the man beside me, and I'm splayed underneath him. The visual is vivid and graphic and I want more. I can almost smell carnal lust circulating in the air.

"Sweetness?"

"Um…" I stutter. It's difficult to look him in the eye after imagining that.

"Tell me what you're thinking."

"I can't." The reply is a breathy rasp.

He straightens slightly. "Am I making you uncomfortable?"

"No," I blurt and blindly grab for him. "Our nearness is what calms me."

His eyes flash in a passing streak of light. "Are you picturing something that involves him?"

My hair becomes a whip as I give a sharp denial. "It's you I see."

His fingers slide between mine and I trap a moan. "That's all I needed to hear."

I sag in relief that he doesn't press for more detail. "Okay."

"You're getting ready for me."

"Ready," I mumble.

"Yes, you're almost there. Soon, sweetness."

A deafening buzzer shatters our moment. The puck drops on the ice and a flurry of movement immediately follows. I'm riveted by the intensity. The players move fast enough to become a blur before my eyes. My gaze sweeps from left to right in a pitiful attempt not to miss a moment.

Ridge must notice my struggle. "I usually try to focus on who has the puck. That's where it counts."

"Good tip." And it works. My brain doesn't hurt as I soak in each frenzied play.

The crowd goes wild when the Trojans score. We leap to our feet and join in the celebration. My usual meek demeanor melts away while I cheer until my throat burns. Ridge glances over at me. A wide smile brightens his expression. I return the gesture, squeezing our clasped palms. We collapse into our seats without losing eye contact.

Once the noise level lowers to normal, he bends toward me. "Are you having fun?"

"Um, duh. I'm on a date with my boyfriend." I giggle at the sassy response. Just then, the action on the ice turns brutal. Two players collide hard enough to crack their helmets together. The resulting echo makes me wince. If that isn't painful enough, the two begin punching each other. "It's more violent than I thought, though."

"You can hear the Grizzlies squeal for mercy from up here." He leans forward as if he's about to launch over the railing to enter the fight.

I think back to his shift in mood when talking about playing for the team earlier. "Do you miss it?"

He's already nodding. "Every damn day. The adrenaline rush is addictive."

My confidence wavers, but I scrounge up the courage to whisper, "What happened?"

Ridge blows out a heavy exhale. "It was like any other game. I just took a wicked hit and immediately felt the damage. There was a blast of fire in my shoulder. Completely blew the whole joint. I couldn't move it. That type of injury ends a career. The scar left behind is gnarly."

I cringe. "That sounds awful."

"Don't pity me too much, sweetness. I had almost seven complete seasons with the Trojans. That's more than most get. I'm set to live in luxury thanks to my generous contracts."

Money is a sticky subject to broach. It's also none of my business. Instead, I decide to get an answer for a question I've been meaning to ask. "How old are you?"

"Wise beyond my years," he jokes.

"Seems that way," I quip.

"Just turned thirty-one last month."

My heart lurches. "What? No way. I didn't get you a gift."

"You did."

"I think I'd remember."

"You're the only thing I wanted." His stare is heavy with meaning. "And here you sit."

Before I can respond, there's a break in the game. A cheesy tune blasts from the speakers and an eruption of excitement screeches from the audience. There's a live feed of the packed arena, panning quickly across the seats. Then a cutout heart flashes on the oversized screen. Inside the shape is a title of what I assume is a scheduled segment for entertainment purposes.

"The Kiss Catcher?"

"It's exactly as it sounds," he explains.

On cue, the camera lands on a couple in the audience. They immediately embrace in a passionate smooch. The second pair engage in similar affection. Then, to my utter shock, Ridge and I are on display. I don't move other than my eyes, which bulge to comical proportions.

Once again, my dependable boyfriend takes charge of the situation. He lifts our joined fingers and proceeds to pepper my knuckles with chaste pecks. Fireworks boom in my stomach as he repeats the action on my other hand. But the crowd isn't satisfied.

"Kiss her, kiss her, kiss her," is shouted as a unified chant.

The volume is thunderous, but I drown them out when Ridge dips toward me. He flips his hat backward in a fluid motion. His spicy pine aroma invades my senses and I suck in a deep breath. My pulse gallops into a sprint. I get dizzy as his warm exhale ghosts across the shell of my ear.

"Do you trust me?"

My nod is automatic. "More than anyone else."

"I refuse to have our first real kiss be broadcasted for public approval, sweetness. But we've gotta give 'em something." Then he shifts until his lips press to my overheated cheek.

Our captivated audience roars. A quake vibrates the floor

beneath my shoes. The announcer attempts to speak over the chaos. I ignore everything except the soft pressure from Ridge's kiss.

He smiles against my skin. "I was wrong earlier. This was the best idea."

My face turns into his. I'm certain he can feel the corners of my mouth curve upward into his stubbled jaw. This is a moment I'll cherish forever. "I couldn't agree more, boyfriend."

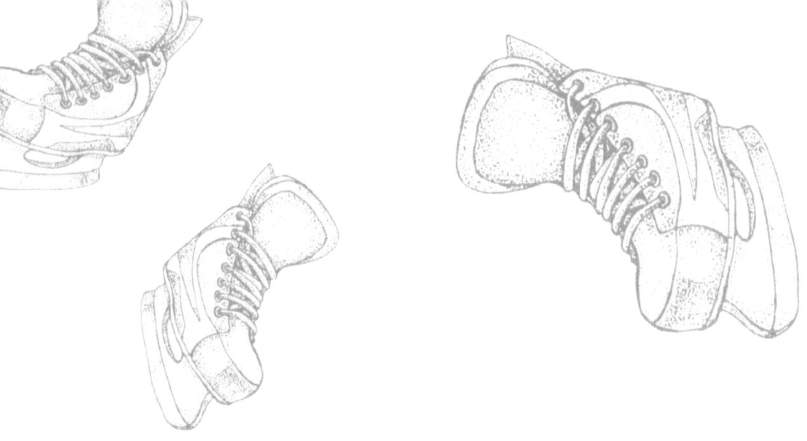

CHAPTER FIFTEEN

Ridge

> Callie: Hi, Ridge. Did I tell you that I had a really great time tonight? If I forgot, now you know. It was extraordinary. There's just one thing that could've gone better.

My fingers fly across the screen in my rush to solve this grievance.

> Me: tell me what went wrong

> Callie: Oh, gosh. Don't worry. It's not that serious. I just thought you might do this one thing at the end of our date, but you didn't. You're always saying I'm not ready. Maybe that's why you're waiting. I think I could be ready for this. In fact, the idea of it gets me rather… excited.

The phone almost cracks in my grip.

> Me: are you gonna tell me what're you ready for, sweetness?

Callie: I'm not sure if I can be so bold.

Me: would it help if I said please

Callie: Maybe.

Me: please tell me, love. I'll put extra sugar on top

Callie: Love? Now I'm really trying not to panic.

Me: you said it wasn't that serious

Callie: It isn't. Or wasn't. Especially not for you. But you called me love and that makes me even more eager.

Me: I'm going to need you to tell me before I assume the worst

Callie: Okay, here it goes.

My heart thunders as I wait for her next message. I've never needed her words more than this moment. But the silence mocks me.

Me: did I lose you?

Callie: No. Never. I'd been working up the nerve to admit that I was hoping you would've kissed me at the end of our date.

I blink at the screen. It takes far too long for her request to process. Once the shock computes into sense, I'm swiping at my screen for her number.

Her breathy exhale is the first to greet me. "Ridge?"

"Sweetness," I rumble in return.

"Um, hi. I wasn't expecting you to call me."

"And I wasn't expecting you to tell me that I should've kissed you."

Her gulp is audible. "Is that bad?"

"No, it's the total opposite. But there's a problem."

"What?"

"Now all I'll be able to think about is kissing you. I won't be able to rest until it happens."

"That sounds challenging." She pauses. "Maybe you should… come over."

I'm off the couch in an instant. "On my way."

"Really? That was fast," she giggles.

"I'm a very motivated man." The soles of my bare feet scrape against concrete and stone until I stop at the bottom of her porch stairs. "Were you serious?"

"Yes."

"Then come outside."

She appears in the doorway a moment later. The glow from the overhead lamp gives her an ethereal appearance. It's only fitting seeing as she's the one who restored my faith in genuine goodness. My own personal angel sent from above.

Then my gaze lowers to notice she's still wearing my jersey. She's removed her jeans, and the hem hangs long enough to hide whatever she has on underneath. Maybe nothing. That thought, along with the sight of her bare legs, could bring me to my knees. I'd go down willingly.

For now, I go dizzy with need and reach for the railing. The wood creaks from my weight. "Were you already in bed?"

"Yes."

"You're going to sleep in that?"

Callie fiddles with a patch near the bottom edge. "Uh-huh. It's very comfy."

The once-sturdy banister is ripped from the boards. "Shit."

Her eyes widen as the piece dangles free. "Are you okay?"

"Too soon to tell," I rasp.

She descends the first two steps and then remains standing on the last one. This puts us at a similar height and within touching distance. Only a few inches separate us either way. I lift my arm slowly toward her waist, giving her plenty of opportunity to dodge my advance. A thrum pulses through me when she doesn't stop me. On the contrary, Callie sways forward to accept my embrace at her middle.

My fingers clutch at the mesh fabric near her ass while I cradle her face with the other palm. "You've never been kissed, huh?"

She gasps and her cheek burns hotter beneath my touch. "No, of course not."

"But you want to be?"

The stars above reflect in her open gaze. "Yes."

"And you want to grant me the honor of being your first?"

"Yes," she repeats.

My thumb tugs at her bottom lip to free the flesh from between her teeth. "Have you pictured this?"

"More often than I should admit." She tips her chin up as if seeking my mouth.

It takes every shred of my willpower to not surrender. "How do you think it will feel?"

"I'm not sure. Show me," she urges.

"Tell me first."

Callie's tongue pokes out, weakening my resolve. "I have very little to go on, boyfriend."

"Just humor me."

"Fine," she relents. "For you, I'll be foolish and take a guess."

"You could never look foolish to me. Would it make you more comfortable if I told you first?"

"Very much so."

I swallow the itch that demands instant gratification. "The

moment our lips touch, I'll discover paradise. This restlessness inside of me will finally be calmed. Your energy will consume me. More so than now. That untapped source will fuel my entire being. Breathe life into me. Grant me worthy. Give me renewed purpose. I'll feel everything I've been missing. More than that, I'll be gifted everything I didn't realize I've been surviving without."

Callie is silent for several moments. Her gaze dips to my mouth. "Are you real?"

"Wanna pinch me and find out?"

Her giggle is pure elation. "No, but can I copy your answer? I can't do better than that."

"Just try. For me," I plead.

She hums before shutting her eyes. After a brief pause, she flutters her lashes and stares at me again. "Our kiss will be a thrill I've never experienced. I imagine it like standing on a cliff with my arms spread wide, letting the wind tunnel through my hair. A gentle breeze that gains momentum through our connection. I'm free to fly and soar and reach new heights."

"Damn," I exhale. "That sounds incredible."

She nods. "Will you kiss me now?"

"I think so." Yet I force myself to remain disciplined and strive for a measured pace.

An impatient huff escapes her. "You're teasing me."

Before I can soothe her upset, Callie rises onto the balls of her feet and presses her lips to mine. Shock barrels through me, keeping me stiff and unresponsive. The kiss is chaste and soft and over before I can react.

Her eyes avoid mine as she retreats, lowering until her heels return to the floor. "I couldn't wait any longer."

The uncertainty in her voice punches me straight in the gut. A pit forms there and guilt swoops in. Dammit, I've failed her. And that's unacceptable.

With the arm that's still cinched around her waist, I haul her against me. Our mouths meet in a clash of fire and passion. Her posture is rigid for a split second before she melts into my embrace.

I fight against the frantic urgency to push for more. It's vital that Callie is comfortable, and we progress at her pace. She's timid at first. Her lips barely move over mine. That gentle exploration is more than enough to provoke me.

An electric zap surges through my veins and I groan into her. The erratic pulse in my ears derails my composure. I feel clumsy and sloppy, as if I'm a novice and this is my first kiss too. It might as well be. Everything prior to Callie fades into a forgotten heap. All that's left is us. The significance isn't lost on me. This woman is the only one who can satisfy me, as if I wasn't already certain.

That realization sets me in motion. I'm on a mission to make this experience unforgettable for her as well. The palm I have on her jaw begins to roam. My fingers drift to her neck, then travel to her nape before settling on the back of her head in an attempt to stay grounded. Callie mewls at the change in angle this position presents.

I inhale her gasp, using the opportunity to slide my tongue along hers. She falters at the sensation while I indulge in her taste. Vanilla explodes across my senses, and I'm consumed by her, just as predicted. She experimentally licks at me. A delicate push and pull begins. Soon enough, our rhythm syncs into a smooth glide.

Heat spreads between us. Each stroke of her tongue is hotter than liquid flames. It's no surprise I'm instantly obsessed and want more of her warmth. My palm at her waist tugs until she's pressed flush against me. I clench the other hand into a fist to stop myself from overpowering her completely. She whimpers when that action yanks her hair at the roots. Fear sluices down my spine in an icy chill. My desire is too raw and exposed. I'm liable to scare her at this rate. But she shocks me by grabbing the front of my shirt and using that as an anchor to hold me tighter.

She bumps her hips forward as we sip at each other. I don't require further encouragement, but her tiny movements only entice me. My palm grasps her ass to bring us impossibly closer. A blissful sigh welcomes my affection. Her enthusiasm ignites my lust to burn.

Our motions become frantic, tapping into what I've kept pent up. She digs her nails into me until it stings. I relish the bite of pain. An inferno blazes in my blood. Hunger becomes ravenous. The last strand of control snaps and heads south.

Callie might be inexperienced, but there's no mistaking my cock for anything other than blatant arousal. I muffle a grunt when she nudges me there. If she repeats the process, I'll be tempted to wrap her legs around me and dry fuck us into oblivion. Either that or I'll explode in my pants.

Rather than grind myself against her like a horny teenager with zero stamina, I pry my mouth from hers in an act of sheer restraint. I rest my forehead against hers while trying to gather my frayed bearings. Labored breaths slice in and out of me at a pace better served from running a sprint. Callie doesn't shy away, but her blush would be visible even in the pitch dark.

"Oh, my." There's no describing her expression as anything other than dazed. "That's how a first kiss is meant to be shared."

"Was it everything you were expecting?"

She shakes her head. "So much more. Everything I imagined can't compare. You've blown my expectations again."

A contented rumble is my initial response. "Likewise, sweetness. Not that I had any doubts."

There's a brief pause where we just admire each other after crossing this line. Her accelerated exhales bathe my lips that are wet from our kiss. I cup her cheek and she turns her lips into my palm. Her mouth drags along my skin.

"Thank you," she murmurs against my wrist.

"If anyone should be voicing appreciation, it's me. Somehow, you soothe this unfulfilled want caged inside of me." I rest her palm flat at the center of my chest. "You give me peace."

She stares at her hand that's planted on me. "Just from a kiss?"

"In addition to everything else." I tug on the jersey that's caressing her curves. "It's your effect on me."

She presses two fingers to her swollen lips. "Is it always like this?"

"I wouldn't know."

"Don't pretend you haven't kissed others."

"Whatever happened before you doesn't clog wasted space in my memory."

Her scoff coasts along the evening wind. "I'm not that naive."

"Believe me, sweetness." I press my mouth to her warm cheek. "After seeing you, nobody else matters. Simple as that."

Callie leans into my touch. "I think you might be my dream come true."

"Yeah?"

"Yeah," she confirms.

"That's good, sweetness." I kiss her again and murmur against her lips, "I'm certain you're mine."

CHAPTER SIXTEEN

Callie: Hey, troublemaker.

Ridge: uh oh. what'd I do to deserve a change in nickname

Callie: Stacey asked if I was sick. Want to know why? I'm blushing at work and it's totally your fault. That last kiss before you dropped me off is playing on repeat in my mind. It's all I can think about. The belly swoops won't quit. Clearly my cheeks are flushed to the point of notice. I can't go thirty seconds without my thoughts wandering back to you.

Ridge: that doesn't sound like a problem

Callie: Yeah, yeah. You love it when I'm thinking about you.

Ridge: it seems only fair. plz don't stop

Callie: As if I could. I can't manage to get anything done, but you go about your day without an issue. What're you doing btw? Are you at Roosters?

Ridge: at the gym. Drake is glaring at me

Callie: Why? Are you distracting him too?

Ridge: nah, I'm distracted by you. supposed to be spotting him

Callie: What? Jeez. Don't let him get hurt.

Ridge: his head is too hard for that

Callie: Are you sweaty from lifting weights?

Ridge: not yet, but thinking of you hot and bothered is elevating more than my heartrate

Callie: Oh! That reminds me. Did you get my rent money?

Ridge: not sure how that relates but no

Callie: Well, it's been bothering me. I have direct deposit set but the payment didn't seem to go through.

Ridge: weird

Callie: You don't seem too upset about not getting paid.

Ridge: if you want the truth, I cancelled your payment

Callie: What? Why would you do that?

SCORE ON YOU

Ridge: I don't need your money. I want it even less than that

Callie: But I have to pay you rent.

Ridge: trust me, sweetness. you don't

Callie: This doesn't seem legal. I want to be a legitimate tenant. What's stopping you from evicting me?

Ridge: my honor

Ridge: but more than that, you're my girlfriend. you're not going anywhere

Callie: I don't feel right living at the house for free.

Ridge: you're doing me a favor. it would sit empty otherwise

Callie: That reminds me of something else I wanted to ask. Why haven't you rented it out before?

Ridge: I hadn't met you yet. you're neighbor material, remember?

Callie: Good grief. How am I supposed to stay frustrated about this situation when you're flirting with me?

Ridge: easy. you just forgive me and accept free rent

Callie: It's not that simple. You're still a troublemaker.

Ridge: so long as I'm yours

Callie: Always XOXO

Ridge: hugs and kisses? damn. you just made my day

Callie: Didn't I already?

Ridge: love when you get sassy

Ridge: you've made my whole life a helluva lot brighter

Callie: Consider yourself forgiven. But why did you buy a duplex if you didn't plan on renting the other side until meeting me?

Ridge: mostly to give my family a place to stay when they come visit

Ridge: like I told you before, they're overwhelming

Ridge: it's in my best interest to provide them with their own space

Callie: Which you've now rented to me. For free. Where are you going to put your family when they visit next?

Ridge: they can take my house. I'll crash on your couch

Callie: There's no way I'd make you stay on the sofa.

Ridge: You're gonna let me sleep in your bed?

Callie: Maybe...

Ridge: what can I do to seal the deal?

Callie: Let me pay rent.

Ridge: something else

Callie: Am I allowed to get a dog?

Ridge: why wouldn't you?

Callie: Not sure if you had a rule against them.

Ridge: we're a pet friendly establishment

Callie: LOL That's reassuring. There's a golden doodle who frequents Pampered Pup and he might need a new home. Walter is such a good boy. He doesn't shed either, which is a bonus.

Ridge: can't wait to meet him

Callie: That can be arranged. Like when you pick me up after my shift. Until then, you better get back to lifting weights or Drake will yell at you.

Ridge: I'd like to see him try

Callie: And I'd rather you didn't risk it.

Ridge: lol later, love

CHAPTER SEVENTEEN

Callie

THE SHADE FROM THE OVERHANG OFFERS A GENEROUS reprieve from the mid-morning sun. This spring has been unseasonably warm, and the late April heat is no exception. That's just one reason this outdoor feature has become a haven for me.

A gentle breeze shakes through the nearby trees. That gust frees stray hairs from my ponytail. Before I can blink, those strands glue themselves to the balm slathered on my mouth. I barely notice the sticky tendrils. The reminder of why I applied the goop so thick steals the spotlight.

Tingles spread across my flushed cheeks while the memories flood in. It's been almost two weeks since my first kiss. I'm ashamed to admit that I've lost count of how many we've exchanged since. What's for certain is that my lips are chapped from our frequent—and spirited—affections.

My throat is suddenly dry, and I reach for my glass. Chilled lemonade soothes the ache that seems constant as of late. That relief lasts for three seconds at most. The distant hum reminds me of who's right around the corner.

I'm caught in a daze when a recognizable car pulls into

my driveway. A blinding reflection streaks off the blue paint to knock me from the stupor. Harper appears from behind the wheel. Her arrival suggests that's it's already ten o'clock. The chair creaks as I shift slightly, but make no move to stand.

My friend quirks a brow as she approaches. "Well, hello to you too."

"Hey, what can I say? It's a lazy Tuesday," I explain.

"Mhmm, it looks that way. We should rhyme in the bay." She climbs the stairs and sits down beside me. "Enjoying the scenery? You look preoccupied."

"No more than usual." I can sense her rapt focus boring a hole into my avoidance. It's necessary for my attention to remain firmly planted straight ahead. One glance at my flushed expression is all it'll take for her to read my salacious musings.

"The artist in her element. What's captured your attention?" Her chin points to the camera in my lap.

That's when the distinct buzz grows louder to interrupt our conversation. Harper whips her head toward the sound. Ridge comes into view from the side of my house, pushing the lawnmower. I shamelessly admire his naked upper half. Inked skin gleams with a layer of perspiration. Defined muscles ripple and flex from the effort of steering the motorized tool. Green flames smolder into mutual attraction as he meets my stare. Meanwhile, a screech spills from my bestie. She flails like a rag doll and tosses an arm over her face.

"My eyes! They're bleeding. I'll never recover," she wails.

I snort at her theatrics, but this reaction is preferable compared to her drooling over him. "Bummer, babes."

"You don't even care about my wellbeing. The image of my shirtless boss will haunt me." Harper points in Ridge's general direction.

"Maybe you shouldn't be looking."

"I wouldn't if I had a choice, sassy pants. Way to warn a woman." She shudders.

"Not sure what you're complaining about. He's yummy." I wiggle my fingers at him.

My boyfriend reciprocates by blowing me a kiss, which I pretend to catch. In. My. Mouth. Not sure what's gotten into me, but I'm positive it has everything to do with this man.

"Um, wow. Why don't you lick him while you're at it." Harper sticks out her tongue for emphasis.

"I just might."

"Those twat flutters are ready for flight, huh? Horny duck."

"Isn't it toad?"

"You would know," she quips. "Not that I can blame you when your favorite flavor of man candy is flaunting his physique."

I disguise my squirm as an adjustment in position, skipping my toes along the wood floor. "But unfortunately, I'm not sure what to do about it."

Harper waves off my concern. "The unknown won't last much longer. It appears your relationship is progressing rather quickly. Has he asked to trim the hedges?"

My gaze scans the freshly cut grass. The natural fragrance is ripe in the air. "Huh?"

"How about plowing the field?"

"Do you mean the flowerbeds? He planted chrysanthemums for me." Which earned him several boxes of freshly baked cookies.

She giggles. "Did the smitten kitten pull your weeds while he was down on his knees?"

I twist my lips. "Oh, you're using euphemisms to be sexually suggestive."

"Obviously. A little debauchery is good for the soul," she reminds. "You catch on quick."

The sarcasm doesn't escape me. I raise the Instax from

its cradle on my thighs and snap a picture of my main muse. "Like you said, I'm preoccupied."

"And now I see why." She peeks over at Ridge long enough to notice the gauze on his left pec. "Did he hurt himself while whacking your bushes?"

"No," I laugh. "That's his new tattoo."

"Have you seen it?"

A thrill skitters through me. "He sent a picture."

"Care to share with your bestie?" Harper huffs and opens her palm.

Mine reaches for my phone. "I don't see why not."

She gasps at the image. Her shock lacks the mock-horror from moments before. "Oh, that totally tracks with his claim at Roosters."

I straighten in my chair. "What claim?"

"That's for him to tell you. Have you touched it?"

"No," I blurt.

"But you want to?"

"Yes. Very much so."

"Holy moly, this is major." She claps with enthusiasm.

"It seems like a big deal," I agree.

"Duh, babes. He branded himself for you."

The belly swoops choose that instant to perform an impressive routine. My gaze automatically lands on Ridge across the yard. As if sensing my stare, he glances over to where I'm perched in the shade. A smirk slants his mouth and I'm possessed by a sudden urge to kiss him. Not just because he's mowing my lawn or gifting me with a rare expression of happiness. It's just him. Everything he does.

In this moment, the future we could have spreads out before me. The visual is breathtaking and magical and more than I dare to dream of. That doesn't stop me from latching on tight.

Without looking away from him, I tilt toward Harper. "I think I'm ready for the talk."

"More context would help," she replies.

"About… you know." I point at the most intimate part of me.

Her eyes widen. "Oh! You're like… really ready."

I nod. It seems like I've been waiting forever to hit this elusive point. "Tell me what I need to do."

"Have you mentioned this to him?" She motions to where Ridge is turning to cut the final strip.

The guts to broach this topic wither slightly. "No."

"That's completely fine," she rushes to say. "It's important to be prepared for when the time comes." Harper snorts, which morphs into a cackle. "That won't be the only thing coming."

"An orgasm would be nice, but not expected." My mother was kind enough to pass along a few pieces of wisdom.

She balks at my statement. "Holy shit. Did you just say orgasm? What's in that lemonade?"

I glance at the sweaty pitcher. "Sugar and ice?"

"Did Molly slip in there?" She leans over to inspect the contents.

"Who?"

She laughs. "Just messing with you. But for real, I'm proud of you for taking the initiative. I have quite an extensive collection of romance books if you want to borrow one or an entire shelf for inspiration. Grace has plenty too."

"That's a good idea. I want to… please him." My face goes up in flames at the thought alone.

Harper fans herself. "Damn, that man is rubbing off on you."

My bottom lip gets clamped between my teeth when Ridge scratches at his chiseled abdomen. "I wouldn't mind if he did."

"Yep, you're certainly ready." She whistles and then drops her gaze as if I could possibly scandalize her. "What's that?"

I squint at what's caught her attention. "A welcome mat."

She shoots me a flat look. "Jeez, thanks for that brilliant hint. But why did you choose one that says, 'No Pricks Allowed'? Seems a bit counterproductive considering who you're dating."

That bursts my bliss bubble. "Hey, I take offense to that."

"He's lovely to you. That's what matters."

"My gentle giant," I sigh.

"Uh-huh, sure. Back to the no trespassing cactus," she prods.

A laugh escapes me as I study the goofy picture. "What about it?"

"Is there a reason you're making such a statement? Should I be concerned about safety in Knox Creek?"

"No, I think it's a joke."

She pauses. "You think?"

"I didn't buy it."

Her head shakes. "Who did?"

"I'm not sure. It just showed up one day."

"And you didn't think to question who put it there?"

"Not really. It's cute and adds charm. Besides, the message is punny."

"That's one way of looking at it."

My narrowed stare turns to her. "How do you see it?"

"This"—she gestures to the rug—"is the work of a certain neighbor turned boyfriend marking his territory."

"Really?"

Harper gives me a slow once-over. "We better get you to the doctor sooner rather than later. Ridge is going to man-handle your entire landscape once he gets a whiff of your blooming garden."

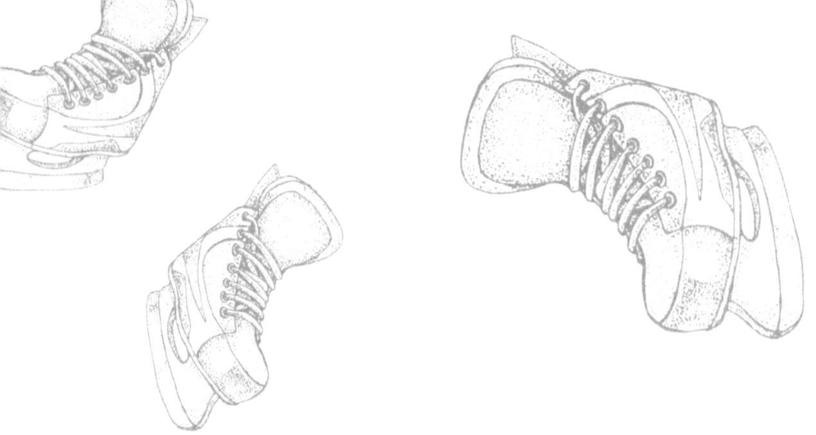

CHAPTER EIGHTEEN

Ridge

GRIND INTO THE SOFTNESS BENEATH ME. PRESSURE builds as the promise of relief nears. Just as I'm cresting the peak, something strange prods at the blurred edges of my brain. That nudge bleeds to awareness and I groan into the pillow.

My blissed-out state fizzles, taking pleasure along with it. I roll flat onto my back while simultaneously stretching. Several joints creak and pop in the process. Then it's silent.

The remnants of the dream taunt me. A hollow pang replaces the warmth that consumed me moments ago. My arm flops into the empty space beside me, confirming Callie isn't in my bed. The sheets are cold and untouched rather than tangled between a shapely pair of legs. I long for the day when she'll be cuddled against me every night.

Rather than dwell on wishful thinking, I grab my phone and unlock the screen to open our thread.

Me: good morning, sweetness

Callie: Hey, boyfriend. Right on

> time. You're more reliable than
> an alarm clock.

> Me: damn straight

> Callie: Your texts are the best
> way to start my day. I always
> wake up with a smile on my
> face. Thanks for that, along
> with everything else.

> Me: no need to thank me. it's
> an honor I take very seriously

> Me: how'd you sleep?

> Callie: Very soundly thanks to
> my new favorite nightgown.

> Callie: *image attached*

The phone slips from my grip and smacks me in the fore-head. I barely register the sting as I straighten to get a better look at the picture. It's her under the covers, with just the hint of my jersey visible. I bite my knuckles to muffle a grunt, as if I'll disrupt the scene. The rush of heat in my blood demands that I palm my cock through my boxers. A rough squeeze makes me dizzy, and I need more.

I stare at the photo Callie sent. My arousal stirs from slumber and I'm instantly hard again. Not that I'm surprised. There's an unfulfilled hunger gnashing inside of me whenever this woman is involved. It's been less than ten hours since I kissed her goodnight and held her in my arms where she be-longs but it feels like a week of tortured separation has passed.

After stacking the pillows, I prop myself into relaxed a position. My cock strains for attention within the confines of my shorts. I tug down the elastic waistband to free myself, and then fist the solid length. A hint of vanilla teases my nostrils as I begin a lazy pace. Another groan escapes me, but this one is heavy with promise of release.

Callie: Are you still there? Did you fall back asleep?

Me: nah, but I'm still in bed

Callie: What are you doing?

Me: just staring at you in my jersey

Me: might make it my wallpaper

Callie: LOL You really like seeing me in something of yours, huh?

Me: that visual speaks to my primal urges

Me: like I've gone feral and lost common decency

Me: I wanna dress you in my shit so other men don't get any ideas

Callie: Oh, that reminds me. Did you buy the cactus mat for my porch?

Me: sure did

Callie: Is that a message to keep other guys away from me?

Me: would it bother you if it was?

Callie: Not at all. You're the only man for me.

Me: telling me that is only gonna make my possessive streak worse

Callie: Is that a promise?

I choke on several expletives. If only this woman knew the force she wields over me. Protective instincts combine with burning lust. It's beyond my control. She'd be scandalized to witness me jerking off. I slowly pump my shaft while thinking about her lying next to me. My jersey protects her modesty, but it's too easy to imagine her naked underneath the mesh fabric. The fantasy is quick to take shape like every other morning. Callie's hand soon replaces mine, the grip delicate yet firm and confident. My eyes slide shut as the visual takes over.

Me: fuck, sweetness. what're you doing to me?

Callie: The same thing that you're doing to me. Can I see your tattoo again?

As if I would deny her. I pause my absent stroking to oblige. A pic of the healing ink appears in our chat. The design is simple, but the statement is bold.

Callie: Thanks for that. It's beautiful. I still can't believe you put my name on your body. Permanently. You can't just wash it off. Or maybe it's temporary. I didn't consider that before. It would make more sense if you were just testing out the design. Maybe to gauge my reaction. But by now, you're definitely aware how I feel about it.

Me: you're too cute, sweetness. it's very permanent. just like you are in my life

Callie: Wow. I'm a bit speechless, which doesn't happen often while we text.

Me: your approval is all I need

Callie: Well, you obviously have that. The fact that you... branded yourself for me is very... stimulating. Is this similar to how you feel about me wearing your jersey?

Me: yes. I'm extremely stimulated right now

Callie: Oh, my. This is beginning to remind me of a dream. Do you remember yours?

Me: only the ones that matter

Callie: What are those usually about?

Me: you

Callie: Me?

Me: it's always you, sweetness. I'm ruled by thoughts of you. awake or not

On cue, my dick twitches in my grip. She could tell me to come, and I'd climax without hesitation. The temptation to request her permission fondles me until I'm compelled to beg. But her reply distracts me.

Callie: You think of me that often?

Me: it borders on obsession

Me: I'm desperate to give you whatever your heart desires. whether that's kindness or protection or passion

Callie: Passion?

Me: that's the best part imo

Me: you're already my passion. it's only fair that I return the favor

Callie: This is definitely beginning to sound like a dream I just had.

Me: tell me about it

Callie: I'm not sure that I can.

Me: haven't we been over this? you can tell me anything

Callie: But this is difficult for me to talk about.

A shudder ripples through me as the possibilities assault my dirty mind. The screen goes fuzzy while I try to regain composure. It's a struggle, especially when my hips thrust into my fist.

Callie: Did you get up?

Me: probably not in the way you mean

Callie: How else do you interpret getting up other than out of bed?

Me: very easily when you're involved

Callie: I'm not sure I understand. Can you clarify?

Me: I'd rather show you. once you're ready

Callie: Funny you should mention that, boyfriend. It's actually what I wanted to discuss with you...

Me: now you need to offer more clarity

Callie: I'm ready for more... than kisses.

My focus is locked on her response. There's static where my normal functioning is meant to be. I'm too absorbed in trying to form a proper response. That's the only excuse for why I flinch when Callie's gorgeous face appears on the screen. The only improvement to this sight will be once I update my background. I swipe to answer and put the call on speaker.

"Sweetness?"

"Hello, Ridge." Her tone is a soft caress against my hard flesh.

I shiver despite the heat rushing through me. "This is a pleasant surprise."

She hums. "I figured it was my turn to call you."

"You'll never hear me complain about listening to your voice," I murmur.

"Okay, good." Callie's exhale is a loud puff. "What I have to say doesn't belong in our text thread. Then I won't have to type the words. I probably wouldn't send it."

"You think I'd use it against you?" I chuckle at what can only be a joke.

She laughs like I intended. "Nothing like that. But I might be humiliated reading it back to myself. It would be better not to have written proof. For my sake. Once I blurt it out, I don't have to reflect on the evidence of my impulsiveness."

My languid strokes pause from the concern in her explanation. "The suspense you're building is very intriguing. You have my full attention."

Callie blows out another heavy breath. "I've been having these… urges."

I squeeze my cock to the point of pain. That twinge tethers me to reality. Otherwise, I could be convinced I fell back into a fantasy.

"Urges?" I eventually croak.

"Uh-huh," she murmurs. "Whenever I think about you, there's this… longing. It's like an ache in my lower belly. Does that make sense? Harper—"

"Let's not discuss her right now," I rush to say.

"Oh… um, all right. Well, anyway, I was having a conversation about this yesterday. I've determined that yearning, down below, is desire for you."

Desperation distorts my vision and I falter. "Do you feel it now?"

"Yes," she answers immediately.

"Have you tried to ease the ache?"

Callie's inhale hitches. "No."

"Would you like to?"

She's quiet for several seconds. "Yes."

"That's good, sweetness. We're making progress. Have you ever touched yourself?"

There's another breathy pause. "What do you mean?"

I resume fucking my fist as if she can see me. "When you feel these urges, do you ever touch yourself where the throb is?"

She gasps. "No."

"What if we did it together? Right now," I add.

"Isn't that meant to be… private?"

"I'd much rather masturbate with you. Mutually." A tug party with Callie is the invite I've been waiting for.

"Mutual masturbation," she muses.

"Sounds fun, right?"

"But I wouldn't know where to start." The fact she's even willing to entertain the idea is a major win.

I don't bother masking my groan. "Are you blushing?"

"Yes, but that's nothing new. It's bound to happen when we're discussing such a delicate subject."

Heat rushes under my skin. "Are you warm in other areas?"

"I'm hot all over. It's never been this intense. Maybe I have a fever."

"That's just your body responding to the situation. It's totally normal. There's nothing to worry about," I promise.

"Why is there such a strong insistence? This hollowness demands to be filled." The slight whine in her voice could send me over the edge.

"That's what happens when you're ready."

"Like you've been hinting at for weeks?" Her huff is pure frustration.

"Yes, sweetness. You've reached a point where you want to explore these urges."

"But I don't know what I'm doing," she whimpers.

"You'll figure it out. Trust me. Should we play a bit and see what you like?"

"Only if you take charge."

"Gladly," I grunt and increase my pace.

The power she just handed over is a stronger adrenaline rush than being on the ice. Her request is like giving me free access to control every element. She might as well be beside me, studying my powerful strokes, with the amount of testosterone flowing through my veins.

I blindly grab for the lotion on my nightstand and squirt

a blob into my palm. The lubricant heightens the sensation. My grip turns slick, mirroring the slippery warmth of her pussy as I slide deep. Friction pushes and pulls while she clenches around me. The visual is so vivid, wrenching a curse from my parted lips.

"Ridge?"

"Mhmmm?" I don't trust myself to speak more than that.

"Are you okay? It sounds like you're panting."

"What if I told you that I'm already touching myself?"

She sucks in a sharp breath. "You are?"

"Abso-fucking-lutely," I groan. "I don't fight my urges when it comes to you, sweetness. Instead, I satisfy them. Often."

"There's much to learn," Callie mewls.

Those little noises are raw lust that I feed on. "I've got you. Want me to set the scene for us to do this together?"

CHAPTER NINETEEN

Callie

M Y THOUGHTS SPIN IN A RECKLESS LOOP AS I contemplate Ridge's offer. "Yes?"

His chuckle is rich and thick. "We'll go slow. Just relax for me. Imagine I'm kissing you."

My mouth tingles while I adjust against the mattress, sinking into the softness like when his lips are pressed to mine. "That's simple. It's practically all I think about."

He laughs again. "You're a natural, love."

"Only with you directing me."

Ridge clucks his tongue. "Nah, it's just us. Spontaneous bliss."

My memory is jogged. "Is that what happens after the unexpected part?"

"Yeah, sweetness. This comes easily for us now."

"Our connection is special," I agree.

"Even if it felt like a shock at first."

"I can't believe how comfortable I am with you. Right from the start." Which I'm further reminded of in my current position.

"We're about to explore new territory again, huh?"

"Yes." My quick response reflects eagerness.

"Are you ready?" There's rustling down the line. It's safe to assume he's preparing himself for whatever happens next.

"Please don't make me wait any longer," I beg.

"Fuuuuuck," he groans. "I can hear the desperation in your voice. You're such a good girl for asking nicely."

The praise sends a zing along my spine. Heat engulfs me, hotter than before. "I'm burning up."

"Are you still under a blanket?"

"No, I kicked off the covers."

Ridge expels a satisfied noise as if I've pleased him again. Or maybe he's visualizing me trying to cool off. "Are you wearing anything other than my jersey?"

"Just underwear."

"Is your phone on speaker?"

"Yes."

"That's perfect. Set it on the pillow next to your head. Think of me next to you. Can you do that?"

I slide my eyes shut from his command. My mind conjures an image of him stretched out beside me. His tall height matches the entire length of my bed. His spicy pine scent seems to waft in the empty space. I inhale a greedy breath as if I can actually smell him. The tie to his scent strengthens my imagination.

"Okay, I can see you." I shiver when he groans.

"You're doing such a good job for me. I want you to bend your knees toward the ceiling. Put your soles flat on the sheet."

"Ohhh," I breathe while getting situated in his directed pose.

"Are you comfortable?"

"Very." The chill settling over me is a welcome relief while I wait for further instructions. I can't help but notice that the ache has spread.

"Did the hem bunch around your hips?"

I don't need to glance down to confirm his prediction. "Uh-huh."

"You're on better display for me like this. I can't wait until I'm actually in the room, watching you splay your legs wide."

My bottom lip is trapped between my teeth to stifle a whimper. "I'm sure you will soon."

"Damn, sweetness. You're pure temptation. I'm stroking my cock while thinking about you in nothing but panties and my jersey."

Meanwhile, I choke on his vulgar statement. My mind instantly recalls the hard bulge that presses into me while we kiss. "That's very… explicit."

"Too much?"

The throb between my thighs suggests not. "No, I think… uh, I liked it."

"I can get really dirty for you, sweetness." Ridge's heavy breathing pairs with mine. "Do you want to hear more?"

"Yes. Please," I tack on as a wheeze.

A rumble applauds my efforts. "I bet you won't need much to get off."

"You mean have an orgasm?"

"Yeah, love. You're gonna come, which will trigger my release."

The pressure of performing halts my subtle movements. "I'm not sure I can do that to myself."

"You can. Trust me." His confidence sounds like a challenge. One that I hope is successful. "Rest a hand on your inner thigh. Imagine that's me touching you. Close your eyes if that helps."

"Okay," I exhale.

"Caress yourself there for a moment. Back and forth. Gentle motions. Get accustomed to the sensation. When you're ready, slowly slip your palm under your shirt. I want you to lift the fabric up your torso." Ridge's steady voice is at odds with the erratic gait of my heartbeat.

I follow his narration until my fingers are traveling along my bare stomach. Goosebumps rise on my skin while I tease myself. The delicate action is nice, but I want more.

"Now what?" My question is a breathy request.

"I've been kissing you, but my lips begin to drift downward. You tilt your neck to give me better access when my mouth travels there. My tongue leaves a wet trail, similar to the slick arousal in your pussy."

A strangled gasp rips from me. "My... pussy?"

The noise he makes is carnal, a physical declaration to note his approval. "We'll get to your needy sex soon. First, I want to play with your breasts. Are your nipples pebbled into stiff peaks? I bet they ache. Why don't you pet them a bit? Brush your nails against those hard points. You'll give yourself pleasure, sweetness."

Both of my hands wander as if compelled. When I reach my chest, a low moan tumbles from me. A shocking thrill sweeps across my awareness until I'm consumed. This part of my body is mostly ignored. Had I known the softest touch could deliver such ecstasy, I'd probably be rubbing myself constantly.

Tingles erupt in my lower belly and I jolt. The unfamiliar zap is strange. I pause my motions, which puts an end to the pooling warmth. Regret crashes down on me.

"Something is happening," I complain.

"Does it hurt?" Alarm clangs from his gritty timbre.

"Just the opposite. But it scared me," I whisper.

"Should we stop?"

"No," I blurt. "I want to satisfy the urge. It's almost relentless now. Tell me what to do, boyfriend."

Ridge grunts. "Fuck, my dick is so hard for you. I'm

thrusting into my fist, but it's not enough. Tweak your nipples for me. Imagine my teeth clamping onto your sensitive flesh."

I'm quick to comply. The cool air breezes along my flesh, but I imagine that sensation is from his mouth. My fingers pinch at the pointy tips. I cry out from the resulting sting.

"This is…" My comment fizzles with uncertainty.

"An awakening. You're learning what your body wants."

Shame threatens to steal my delight, but I allow Ridge's reassurance to wash over me. There's nothing wrong about doing this. Making myself feel good isn't bad.

On cue, another zing lashes at me. A whimper spills from my lips. I flex my muscles to alleviate the throb, but it only intensifies.

"You're almost there," Ridge rasps. "I can hear the demand for your climax to strike. Should we visit your clit?"

I shudder from the possibility. "Uh-huh."

"My eager girl. Gonna make me come being so responsive. We better hurry." The urgency in his tone spikes my pulse. "I want to soothe your ache. Should we touch your pussy?"

"Yes."

"Put a hand flat over where your panties are between your legs. Rock against the pressure. Set a pace and keep going."

Heat slaps my cheeks upon realizing that the cotton is damp. "I'm very wet down there."

Several expletives come from him. "Yeah? Tell me how wet you are."

Fire scorches my face, but I'm too far gone. "My underwear is soaked through."

Ridge expels a pained groan. "Take them off."

I don't question him. Not with the sizzling delight soaring to new heights. My thumbs struggle to tug down the elastic in my frenzied condition. The material stretches and tears in the process. I barely notice before discarding the ruined heap onto the floor. A tremble racks my limbs as the most intimate piece of me is fully exposed.

"Okay," I murmur while resuming my previous position. "I'm ready to finish."

"Your enthusiasm is very sexy."

"I'm a very motivated woman," I tease.

He laughs without restraint. "Have I inspired you?"

My thoughts wander to the hockey game and what I imagined Ridge doing to me on the ice. The vivid visual returns with graphic clarity. I moan openly.

"It's only you in my fantasies," I admit.

"Damn," Ridge croaks.

"Are you okay?"

"Couldn't be better." But he doesn't say more.

"Sure about that?"

"I was just lost in you, like usual."

My restless motions stop. "What do you mean? I'm right here."

"Yes, exactly. You're in this moment with me. That's what I needed to hear without realizing it. Now we gotta find out what works for you."

"I'm listening," I coax.

"Already such a dirty girl. Slide your fingers along your slit. Just touch and discover and decide what feels the best for you. There's some trial and error, but endless pleasure will follow."

"You're so much more experienced, Ridge." Not that I truly care. I'd never dare to wander into these depths alone.

"Only because I've been preparing for you." His tone is a gentle rasp as if a feather brushes on my naked skin. "Everything I've learned is meant to satisfy you. It's led us to this point. Feel how slick you are?"

I can hear it too. The sound is almost embarrassing. But I'm quickly absorbed in completing this task. My exploration bumps against an area that shoots a powerful surge through me.

"Holy shit," I spew.

"Found your clit?" His chuckle tappers off into a grunt. "Such a quick study. You'll want to focus on that spot."

"Yes, yes, yes…" The word babbles from me on repeat.

"Is your core clenching against nothing? You're empty and yearning to be filled."

"I need more," I whine.

"Move your fingers faster. Circle that precise spot until you fall apart."

A tight spring begins to uncoil inside of me. "I'm not sure how to handle this."

"Just keep going. Are you close?"

"I must be. Oh, gosh." My toes curl from the lusty onslaught. "I never knew anything like this existed."

It doesn't take much after that, just like he guessed earlier. I sweep across that swollen bundle while my muscles begin to seize. Tingles rise and begin to spread from where I'm swiping. My hips buck on their own, seeming to chase the sensation. Spots dance in my vision and a sudden rush hits me. I let go, leaping into the unknown.

"Oh, oh, oh," I chant.

"That's it, love. Right there."

But Ridge's voice is drowned out by the simultaneous waves crashing over me. The reward unleashes a warm flow into a continuous loop. My mouth drops with a soundless wail as my back arches. I'm a twitching mass as bliss floods into my veins. A floating sensation overtakes me. My free hand smacks against the blanket, gripping tight to root me in place. It's a very real possibility that I'll fly away and never return. Minutes seem to pass while I slowly regain composure.

Our labored exhales fill the lull that I'm certain is called the afterglow. I'm definitely feeling light and sparkly. A giggle escapes me at the connection.

His choppy breath resembles laughter. "Not a bad way to start the day, huh?"

More giddy laughter bubbles from me. "Did you…?"

"Mhmm," he sighs. "Might've blacked out for a moment."

I smile. "Likewise."

"Made quite a mess."

My fingers rub together to discover we share that as well. "Thanks for taking charge and handling my needs."

Ridge scoffs. "There you go again, giving me too much credit."

"As if I could ever give you enough." The list of favors he grants me grows by the hour.

"Trust me, sweetness. You call and I'll come running. The pleasure is all mine to give."

"Ours," I correct. "It was a mutual effort."

"In that case," Ridge drawls. "You can score on me whenever the mood strikes, sweetness."

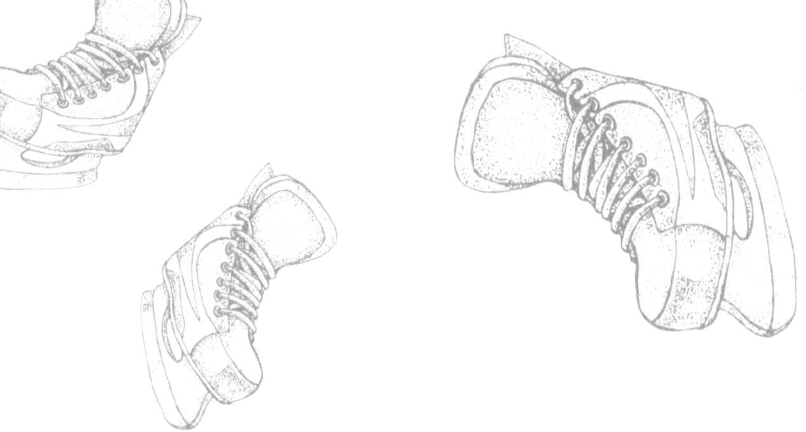

CHAPTER TWENTY

Ridge

I smirk at the suggestive texts while waiting for her response. We've gotten progressively more explicit over these past few weeks. It shouldn't be long until we have a playdate in the flesh rather than through a speaker. That's precisely why I ordered Callie a new gift for the impending occasion.

Those thoughts fade when the three bouncy dots don't appear. I frown at our thread and my unanswered messages. Silence mocks me while my screen remains the same.

But she's never complained about my dirty texts. Quite the opposite. Callie usually types something adorable that pumps my cock to bursting levels.

Her lack of response sets off warning bells. I shift my truck into park, and get out to confront this strange situation. The bell jingles as I step inside Pampered Pooch. My stride falters at the scene in front of me. That delay in processing lasts less than two seconds. Even so, I can't believe what I'm seeing.

First and most importantly, Callie is behind the counter crying. She's visibly afraid, practically trembling in fear. Her watery gaze lands on me and her frozen stance thaws slightly. That evident relief expands my chest.

That's right, love. Reinforcements have arrived.

What I notice next is more of an afterthought, but clearly the source of her upset. A man stands with his back toward me while he continues blabbering. The harsh tone spewing from him doesn't belong anywhere near Callie's ears. Then he makes the mistake of pointing a stubby finger in her face.

My protective instincts roar to the surface, ready to maim and defend against the threat. I stalk forward to place myself between him and Callie. The customer's rant cuts off at my interruption. His eyes bulge in recognition. He gulps audibly and stumbles backward.

"Done bitching and moaning so soon?" My muscles bunch and flex, itching for a fight.

The dude is still dumbfounded. His gaze tracks over my height like I'm a giant. Might as well be considering how puny he is.

"Not so tough now, huh? Found yourself an adequate opponent. C'mon, let me hear what you've got to say." I lean in and cup my ear.

He lifts a trembling palm as if that will stave off my attack. "I've got no beef with you, Crusher."

"No? That's interesting," I seethe. "The way I see it is that you've just given me a reason to kick your ass."

His knees look ready to buckle. "What? Why?"

"Give my girl trouble and you've just created a war with me." My even voice is a deception.

Meanwhile, his face shakes and cracks into broken shards. "Your girl?"

"Damn fucking straight. That's my future wife you're disrespecting."

Callie gasps, which is the first peep she's made since I entered. The asshole appears to be equally as shocked by my claim. His complexion turns ashen while he blanches.

"Shit," he mutters. His palm lifts higher to act as a shield. "I had no idea, man."

"Her connection to me shouldn't matter."

"But—"

Thunder booms across my expression and cuts him off. The urge to throttle him is a rabid beast inside of me. "Does verbally attacking an innocent woman make you feel bigger? Is your dick that tiny?"

He sputters. "My dog got hurt under her care—or lack thereof."

I don't spare the hound loyally sitting at his heels a glance. "That gives you the excuse to make her cry? Nah, wrong answer."

If possible, his eyes get bigger. "I was filing a formal complaint. It's not my fault she's sensitive."

Menace echoes off the floor when I shift to crowd his space. "Are you trying to make me mad?"

"Aren't you already?"

My chuckle is devoid of emotion, taunting him. "The fact you're still standing in one piece answers that stupid question."

His pinched lips remind me of a puckered butthole,

which almost earns him a genuine laugh. "What about Daisy Mae? Her ear is bleeding."

"Don't be a shit human. You signed a waiver. There are policies in place for this exact reason. Take your mutt to the vet like a proper owner."

He straightens as if regaining his backbone. "She's a purebred."

"That's what you got from what I said?" I growl under my breath. "If you've got a problem, take it up with me. Next time you wanna snivel and whine, let me know. I'll introduce you to my fists. Unless you'd prefer a proper greeting now."

He winces as I crack my knuckles. "That won't be necessary."

"You sure? It's been too long since I've knocked someone's teeth out. A broken nose is a decent alternative. Might fix the smug slope you use to look down at everyone else. There's something satisfying about that crunch of bone."

"Now you're just trying to intimidate me."

I wag a scolding finger at him. "We both know I don't have to try. But I suggest you get the fuck out before we test that theory."

"Messaged received. Let's just forget this happened."

"As if that's possible." My glare becomes lethal as he retreats toward the door. "Aren't you forgetting something?"

The dumbass glances around, searching for who's hidden behind me. "No?"

I sidestep to get my point across. "Apologize to the lady. Make her believe it. Otherwise, I'll be forced to have you beg for her forgiveness."

His posture deflates in surrender. He has the courtesy to look Callie in the eye. "I'm sorry, okay? My temper got the best of me. It wasn't my intention to make you cry. Daisy Mae got injured, but accidents happen. I shouldn't have blamed you. Please accept my apology."

My scoff reveals how I feel about his flimsy attempt, but it's not my decision. I glance over my shoulder. The sight of her tear-stained face reignites my rage to a chaotic boil. A deep breath is my attempt to calm the storm. Vanilla fills my lungs and gives me pause. Her scent provides comfort, as well as an important reminder. This is about her. If she gives me free rein, I'll gladly punch her assailant in the throat.

"Do you think that was sincere, sweetness?"

Her glassy stare doesn't move from mine. She blinks, but doesn't react otherwise. It's obvious she's uncomfortable voicing her opinion until the customer is removed from the situation.

"I hope you've learned a valuable lesson. If not, we'll be chatting again soon. You're free to leave."

He pauses before crossing the threshold. "No hard feelings, Crusher?"

"That's entirely up to you." I shoo him away like the exterminated pest he is.

Once the scum skitters off to a dark corner where he belongs, I turn to Callie and nearly double over from the pain lingering on her features. The tremble in her bottom lip is a knife to my gut and awakens the demand for retaliation. But he's already gone. More than that, she deserves my full attention.

In a swift maneuver, I hop over the counter and pull her flush against me. "I've got you, love."

Callie collapses into my embrace with a sob. "He was very mean."

My palm traces the length of her spine. "Should I beat him bloody?"

Her fingers curl into the front of my shirt. "No, don't leave me."

"Never." Which reminds me. "Why were you alone? Where's Stacey?"

"She went home early. The only pups left are overnight stays. That man picked up his dog early."

Anger burns and threatens to rise, but the fuse is smothered from her warmth against me. "He won't bother you again. I'll make sure of it."

Callie sniffles while peeking up at me. "I feel silly for being this upset."

"Don't even." I cradle her cheek in my hand. "If anyone is ridiculous in this scenario, it's that's douche canoe with an ego problem."

"I suppose," she huffs. "Thanks for coming to my rescue."

The arm I have around her waist tightens instinctively. "I'll always come for you, sweetness. I just wish I had sooner." My nose presses into her hair for a fresh hit of vanilla. "And you don't need to thank me. Defending you is part of my duty as your… boyfriend."

"If the roles are ever reversed, you can rely on me to save you."

My forehead touches hers and our gazes lock. "I look forward to it."

The cogs in her brain might as well be visible as she mulls something over. "Why did you call me your future wife?"

"That's how I refer to you in my mind. Might as well make it public knowledge." I rest her palm flat over the purposeful brand on my chest. "You're permanent to me."

"Maybe I should get a tattoo," she breathes.

My thumb absently rubs along the scar on her forearm. "Of what?"

"As if you have to ask." The blue in her unwavering gaze heats to smoldering levels.

I melt into her faster than liquid lust. Our mouths glide together in a practiced motion. The last drops of aggression evaporate as she opens for me. Chemistry sizzles from the slippery friction of our tongues. That crackle strokes my flesh and I groan against her lips.

An urgency seems to consume us. Callie rises onto the balls of her feet to get closer. The palm I had at the dip in her back lowers. She arches into me when I grip her ass. A feverish rush floods downward through my veins and sends me reeling. The mewls spilling from Callie confirm she's just as eager.

She bumps her hips into mine and nudges my dick in the process. There's no mistaking my arousal that's excited to greet her. Rather than shy away, she rubs herself against me. I'm shot with a feral dose of pleasure. The layers of clothes between us become insignificant.

Static streaks over me as if her skin is touching mine. My cock twitches and I thrust to alleviate the throb. She must sense the shift in my mood, whimpering for more. I swallow her pleasure while feeding her my own. We get swept away in each other for several blissful moments.

Claws clicking on tiled floor interrupt our fiery passion. Callie is the one to pull away and I muffle a protest. Her giggle might as well be foreplay for how hard the sound gets me. But we're practically on display for Main Street. It's probably in our best interest to move this make out session to a more discreet location.

Before doing so, I cast my gaze to the dog circling Callie's legs. "Who's this?"

"The doodle puppy I told you about." She scoops him into her arms, immediately nuzzling into his fur. "Meet Walter."

"He's… cute." In a cockblocking sort of way.

"And the fluffiest puffball. You're irresistible, aren't you?" Her laughter rises several octaves when the pooch begins licking her face. "He's very friendly."

"I can see that." The mutt pins me with a smug look that I can easily decipher. *Lucky little shit.* I find a good spot to scratch behind his ear to form a truce.

"We're practically inseparable during my shifts." As if she has to tell me. Their bond is evident.

Which prods at my curiosity. "Why haven't you claimed him as yours yet? Isn't he up for grabs?"

"It's a bit more complicated than that. Mostly because the owner hadn't committed to putting him up for adoption."

I quirk a brow. "Past tense?"

Callie bobs her head. "She just confirmed this morning that Walter can't move into her new apartment."

"Does that mean you're allowed to take him tonight?"

She narrows her eyes at me. "I don't see why not. You're being extremely encouraging."

"Why wouldn't I be? He makes you happy. That's my main priority. Let's bring him home. We can stop for supplies along the way."

Amusement twinkles in her eyes. "To your place or mine?"

"Both. Ours," I amend.

"Ours?"

I tip her chin up for a kiss. "Haven't you realized by now that what's mine is yours?"

"Maybe I need a reminder," she exhales against my mouth.

And I give her one. Gladly. Callie sags forward to accept my affection. Walter is trapped between us, but he doesn't seem to mind fitting into the equation. The three of us are already an inseparable unit.

As if listening to my thoughts, Callie notices our position and smiles. "I think he approves."

"Our meet cute is better than I expected."

Her brow furrows. "Oh?"

"Couldn't have been better." I ruffle the curls on Walter's head. "This smooth transition avoids the trouble I was facing of getting him out of here without you realizing he's gone."

"Why would you do that?"

"How else would I put him in a box on your doorstep to find?"

"You wouldn't." But her laughter is knowing.

My shoulder lifts in a half shrug. "I'd been planning on it ever since you mentioned him."

Callie blinks as unshed tears collect in her eyes. "What did I do to deserve you?"

"I could ask you the same. But if you want my honest answer." My lips brush her forehead. "You chose the path that led you straight to where I've been waiting for you."

Her sigh is dreamy and content. "This occasion calls for so many pictures. You've turned my evening right side up."

"The direction it always should be."

She points to the ceiling for emphasis. "What else are you planning, boyfriend?"

My smirk is stamped into her temple. "If I told you, I'd have to keep you forever."

"How convenient," Callie murmurs. "I'm not planning on going anywhere."

CHAPTER TWENTY-ONE

Callie

Me: Hey, boyfriend. Did you make it to your side of the yard okay?

Ridge: have I told you how much I fuckin love it when you check on me

Me: It's part of my duty as your girlfriend, right? Oh! That reminds me. I've never been to your half of the duplex. You always come to my place. What are you hiding over there? Should I be concerned LOL

Ridge: I've got nothing to hide from you

Ridge: you're always welcome but there's not much to see

Ridge: it serves a purpose. more of a house than a home

Me: I suppose that makes

sense. That solves the suspicion. You've just made me very curious.

Ridge: the gym is probably the only redeeming quality

Me: You have a gym in your house?

Ridge: fuck yeah. how else would I stay in shape to protect you?

Me: By going to an actual gym. Isn't that what most people do? LOL

Ridge: we've established I don't like most people and those dumps are crowded af

Me: I wouldn't know...

Ridge: never been to a gym, sweetness?

Me: Nope. Can't say that I have. I don't have a clue what type of... equipment you use. My exercise routine consists of walking.

Ridge: I have a solid cardio suggestion

Me: Oh, yeah? I'm not much of a runner.

Ridge: you don't have to be on your feet for this

Ridge: unless you prefer that position

Ridge: looking forward to trying them all and seeing what you like best

Ridge: we can start slow. build up your stamina

Ridge: I'll do most of the work. you can just spread out and enjoy yourself

Warmth stings my cheeks as his messages flood in. The tingling in my lower belly reveals where this topic has strayed. I'm no longer naïve in regard to his innuendos. Our conversations often trail in this direction, especially lately. That doesn't mean I'm going to make it easy for him.

Me: This all happens in your gym? Wow. I'm impressed. Do you allow other guests inside?

Ridge: just you

Me: Really? I assume Garrett and Drake would take advantage of your top-notch facility and personal training

Ridge: not funny

Ridge: it's bad enough when they drag me to their sorry excuse for a gym

Me: LOL

Ridge: only you get this deal, sweetness

Me: It's definitely something to consider. I should probably

> be more physically active.
> Health and wellness is
> important.

Ridge: just let me know when you're ready to start

> Me: I'll check my schedule, boyfriend.

I giggle to myself, which draws the attention of the pup dozing in my lap. He nuzzles into my arm and whines. His interaction is the ideal transition.

> Me: You just left, but I think Walter misses you.

Ridge: just Walter?

> Me: You already know I do.

Ridge: doesn't hurt to hear it

> Me: I miss you so very much!

Ridge: I miss you always

> Me: Maybe there's a way to fix that.

Ridge: what're you suggesting?

I gnaw on my lip while courage tries to evade me. My fingers hover over the necessary letters to type the message. Nerves tumble across the width of my stomach to distract me.

This is a major leap. It would be considered scandalous where I was raised. Probably worse. But the past doesn't matter. That was the old me, and I've evolved.

In just a few short months, my confidence has grown faster than weeds after a downpour. It's thanks to this man. There's an easy way to show him how far I've come. My progress is his to claim.

> Me: Would you like to have a slumber party?

My thumb presses send before regret can steal my guts. I squeal and force my gaze to the ceiling. Anticipation tickles me. This is going to shift our relationship into the fast lane.

But seconds tick by without the telltale chime of his response. My eyes lower to the screen to see nothing has changed in our thread. The beats that follow feel dipped in molasses. Still nothing. A sinking sensation weighs down my stomach.

I was too forward. He doesn't want me to initiate. This was a terrible idea. But those ugly thoughts don't match our dynamic.

The abrupt bang on my front door is a strike of thunder that rocks the entire foundation. A yelp rips from me and I whirl to face the disruption. Walter doesn't hesitate to run straight for the action. His paws slide on the wood while he prepares to greet whoever waits on the other side. My stride is far more cautious. I creep forward on shaking legs. The phone in my grip complains with a creak.

Sweat slicks my palm when I grip the knob. That gives me pause before I pry the door open a sliver. Ridge is visible through that narrow gap. Relief instantly floods me, and I straighten to grant him entry. But he doesn't move. Instead, he remains locked in position with his arms braced on the frame.

I take a moment to assess his disheveled appearance. Paired

with his silence and unannounced arrival, this behavior is slightly concerning. "Hey, you. Is everything… okay?"

The green in his eyes swirls with an emotion I'm too inexperienced to name. When he takes me in, standing on the opposite side of the threshold, I feel that fiery stare lick along my bare legs. He clenches his jaw, but doesn't respond otherwise.

My fingers fiddle with the frayed cuff of my jersey. "Did I do something—?"

"You look so fucking sexy," he groans.

"Really?" Surprise rings in my voice.

As if he didn't just see me twenty minutes ago. The only thing I did was change my clothes. I peek at my outfit that's practically standard issue at this point.

"And then you text me that dangling fruit. Fuck," he grunts. "I just need a second to collect myself before I maul you."

Which is evident by his state of distress. His chest is heaving. It appears like he can't catch his breath. My attention is riveted to the rapid rise and fall of his bare skin that's on display. The tattoo on his left pec becomes a focal point. I'm falling into a trance from the rhythmic motion and slump into the wall.

Walter chooses that instant to race circles around Ridge's ankles. Zoomies strike at all hours of the day, especially when a preferred person returns. The hyper pup yips in glee before dashing back into the house. I barely blink during that entire sequence.

Ridge adjusts his stance, which draws my gaze downward. The gray sweatpants he's wearing leave little to the imagination. His penis is stiff, and the outline is visible through the fabric. I lick my lips while contemplating the odds that he's naked underneath. A guttural sound cuts off those dirty musings, but my concentration lingers on that sizeable bulge.

"Sweetness," Ridge rasps. "It's rude to stare unless you're gonna make good on that shameless gawking."

"How might I do that?" My voice is pitched in uncertainty.

"Fuuuuuck." He rakes a hand through his hair while treating my angled pose to a slow once-over. Another animalistic growl rips from him and he bites at his knuckle. "Wanna let me in?"

My belly dips and swoops. I step aside to let him pass. Rather than brush by casually, Ridge prowls forward to cage me against the open door. Shock freezes me between the solid surface at my back and the insistent throb of his desire. Instinct arches me into him. A blaze instantly rushes under my skin, and I gasp.

Ridge takes advantage. His head dips until our mouths slam together. One of his arms lowers to loop around my waist, dragging me tighter against him. I lift both of mine to wrap around his neck. We're aligned in body and pleasure.

My tongue tastes his while his palm kneads my butt. The thick material of my jersey limits the sensation, but the tease sparks a desperation inside of me. This isn't nearly enough. An urge to lift my leg around him twitches through my muscles. Even that minimal shift draws awareness to the dampness between my thighs. I want him to touch me everywhere.

Heat blooms and spreads until I'm sweltering. Ridge holds me closer, as if feeding off my warmth. Flames spark hotter whenever we move. The friction builds into an inferno I can't ignore. I squirm against this relentless lust that demands to be satisfied.

This madness isn't mine alone. Ridge is feverish, a clammy urgency clinging to his exposed flesh despite the cool evening air. His pelvis grinds against mine. That's when I realize how aroused he is. The large bulge I admired earlier feels even bigger while pressed into me. I want more. Badly. My hips take control and begin rolling along his steely length. His fingers fist the fabric at my thigh, using that grip to drag us closer.

Dizziness swarms me when he inhales my next breath. Our tongues slide together in an erotic temptation. Passion explodes outward from our sealed lips. I want to be bold and grip him in my hand. The same nerves from earlier keep my wrists crossed against his nape.

As if possessing a direct line to my inner desire, Ridge severs the kiss. "Can I take you to bed?"

"Please," I beg.

His smirk is wolfish as he scoops me off my feet. I squeal and kick while he adjusts his grasp on me. Once I'm cradled in the balance of his bulk, he slams the door with his elbow. He rushes across the room toward the stairs but pauses before the climb. I follow his gaze to see what's distracted him.

"Were you crafting?" His squint is narrowed on the pile of supplies cluttering my coffee table.

"I started on Walter's introduction page. It has a welcome home theme," I explain.

"You never let me see your scrapbooks. I've been waiting for permission to admire your talents." Ridge creeps in that direction before catching himself.

I chew on my inner cheek. "We can go through that one if you want."

He seems to struggle with a decision. His first look at my beloved hobby is tough to beat. But we were in the middle of something else.

His hurried pace resumes on our original path. "Nah, you can show me in the morning."

The flutters bouncing in my stomach have little to do with him taking three steps at a time. I nuzzle against his chest while soaking in the confirmation that he intends to spend the night. As if his presence didn't provide enough proof. It's obvious to Walter who doesn't bother following us. That's probably for the best.

Ridge walks into my room like he owns the place, which I

suppose makes sense. We've never been in this space together, though. It's been off-limits like he wanted to respect my privacy and refuge. That phase has officially expired.

His gaze does a quick inventory of my meager belongings that I've been meaning to expand on. That task is much easier to complete now that I'm not required to pay rent. I roll my eyes up at my boyfriend, but he misses the sarcastic snark.

"So," he drawls. "This is where the magic happens."

I giggle and bobble in his hold, but he doesn't release me. "It's not much."

Ridge shrugs while edging closer to the mattress. "More furnishings than mine."

My nose wrinkles as I glare at the blank walls. "I find that hard to believe."

"You'll see when you dare to visit."

A huff lifts the hair off my cheeks. "I hadn't been invited until tonight."

"You're always welcome at my house," he reminds.

"That's very neighborly of you, boyfriend."

"I could say the same to you about hosting our long over-due slumber party."

"Long overdue? Is that why you couldn't get over here fast enough?" Which explains his lack of response.

"Mhmm," he says and presses a kiss to my forehead. "You call and I come running."

"Literally," I laugh.

"Should we find out what other liberties you'll grant me this evening?" Ridge sets me in the middle of the bed.

I turn to my side and watch as he gets himself situated beside me. "Do you want to get under the covers?"

"Not yet." He pauses, allowing his gaze to travel over my relaxed pose. "Damn, love. My fantasies didn't do you justice."

My throat goes dry while I admire him stretched out next to me. "You look right at home."

His smile mirrors my statement. "I might never leave."

"Okay, but you packed pretty light." I pretend to search for his overnight bag.

"All I need is you." Ridge catches my eye roll this time and chuckles. "What more could I need?"

"The essentials," I chide. "Like a toothbrush and clean underwear."

"I'm comfortable going without." He juts his hips.

That purposeful movement calls attention to the rigid column barely concealed by the gray sweats. The shape of him is fascinating. His girth resembles a thick and venomous snake. One I've only heard about in stories. It jingles an internal alarm.

I find myself wondering how we'll fit together. "You're… above average, right?"

A flash of a dimple tries to soothe me. "How kind of you to notice, sweetness. Top of the scale in every measurement that counts."

"That doesn't surprise me." But awe still tints my tone. "The evidence is a tad… startling."

"This isn't all me." He slides a hand into his pocket, which is on the other side and contradicts his claim. "There's something extra in here for you."

I wait for him to expand on that vague hint, but he doesn't. "Are you gonna whip it out or what?"

Ridge chokes and begins coughing until his eyes water. "Damn, love. Slow down. We gotta ease into this."

My inexperience is exposed, and I fumble into a backpedal. "Should I get my scrapbook?"

"Later," he breathes against my lips.

I float in his chaste kiss for a moment. "What happens now?"

His chuckle loosens the unease prodding at me. "Now that I'm in your bed, what're you planning on doing to me?"

"Um…" I stall on my innocence. My mind sputters along unknown avenues of how to please him. "Are you hungry?"

"What're you serving?" His bent knuckle circles my cheek.

I imagine my blush can be seen from the stars. "There's plenty of tater tot hotdish left from dinner."

Ridge rubs his stomach. "Nah, I'm still stuffed. Don't tell my mother, but I prefer your version."

"Really?"

"One of the best things I've put in my mouth." His eyes twinkle in the dim lighting. "I'm curious about what you'll offer me for dessert."

"Do you want cherry cobbler? I found a recipe."

He lifts his brows. "Is that so?"

"It takes an hour to bake. That doesn't include prep. Maybe there's a faster option," I mumble.

"Don't stress about time. We'll take as long as you need. I'm a patient man, remember?"

I frown. "You're going to make it with me?"

"When we've reached that point," he rasps. "I have to make sure you're ready for me."

That concept has returned to haunt me, but I appreciate the context clue. "You're talking about sex."

Ridge groans, dragging his bottom lip between his teeth. "Fuck, I'm going to worship every inch of you."

I squirm at the desire in his voice. "Please."

His palm rests on my waist. "What're you asking for?"

Warmth seeps into me. "I'm not sure, but the ache is there."

"Do you want to touch yourself?"

My hand instinctively trails down between my legs, but the jersey blocks me. "Will you help?"

He tugs on the hem, collecting the mesh material in his fist, but pauses at the middle of my thigh. "Tell me what to do. You're in control."

I gulp at the nerves threatening to suffocate me. "Just like when we're on the phone."

"Be specific," he urges.

"Kiss me."

Ridge's mouth is on mine in the next rapid beat of my heart. The fact he didn't hesitate to obey my command is an electric thrill. A tremble moves through me like a surge of power. He's giving me permission to use him for my pleasure. I have the authority to rule his motions. But only if I dare.

I tilt my face, sending his lips to my jaw. He smiles into my skin. That sign of encouragement from him is another boost to my confidence, giving me a push to explore uncharted territory.

"Cup my breast," I wheeze.

Again, there's no delay in his response. His hand roams upward along the slope of my waist to reach my chest. Ridge caresses me, circling the mound, before cradling the weight in his palm. A groan spills from him into the crook of my neck.

"No bra?"

"It's a nuisance."

He drags his nose along my throat. "Couldn't agree more. I love having unrestricted access."

Which he's provided me with as well. The reminder prompts me to rest my fingers on his abdomen. His muscles flex beneath my timid contact. He's warm and inviting. I begin tracing the definition sculpted there. If I didn't know better, I'd think he's chiseled from stone.

Ridge continues playing with me in return. I arch into him when he brushes over my nipple. The friction is more of a tease through the fabric.

My inhale tappers into a whimper. "Go under."

He immediately pulls at my jersey, dragging the mesh fabric up my torso. That slow graze against my skin is a stimulating tickle. I shiver as a chill offers a momentary reprieve from the heat. My nipples pebble and he tweaks one between his bent knuckles. The sting sends a zap straight to my core.

"Oh!" I cry.

His eyes study my expression. "Good?"

"Yes."

He repeats the process, clamping on and off to heighten the sensation. Tingles spread through my lower belly. I'm slick and needy, but too shy to announce it. My blunt nails curl into him. There's no excess to grasp. As if once again listening to my private thoughts, his head suddenly dips.

I grab his hair when he latches onto my breast. His lips pull at my nipple, sucking me deep. A squeal falls from my slack mouth. I bend to push more of myself into him. Ridge grumbles against my flesh, telling me just how much he enjoys this.

The throb in my center is an insistent demand. My thighs clench, but that does little to ease the yearning. He must notice my struggles and increases the pace. His tongue swivels and lashes my breast before he blows against the damp peak. That blast of cold sizzles through me.

I picture him lavishing my clit with the same attentions. Once that thought takes shape, I wonder if it's just a hopeless fantasy. Or would he willingly do that to me. Desire multiplies into a starving hole that needs to be filled.

"More," I plead.

Ridge pauses. "Where?"

The words stick together into a jumbled mass. Rather than spit it out, I lower my hand to where the ache blooms. My panties are soaked where I press down against the twinge. That only feeds the bottomless pit my lust has become. I punctuate my meaning with a roll of my hips.

He stares at my movements but doesn't take the hint. "Tell me, sweetness."

Frustration battles against the nerves holding me hostage.

Just before I beg him to take the reins, a guide materializes from the depths of my ambitious research. The idea forms and grows until I can clutch on. Inspiration blends with my imagination to create a scene fit for us.

"It was suggested that I read romance novels to gain knowledge. I've devoured several already."

Ridge blinks slowly. "Okay…?"

"The content is very… erotic."

Awareness gleams in his gaze. "Oh, I see where you're going with this. What did you learn?"

"We could… pleasure each other. At the same time."

"You wanna touch me?" He nods to the tented material camped in his lap.

"Yes, very badly." I giggle at the double entendre.

"The desire is very mutual, love." Ridge hooks his thumbs into the waistband of his sweats. "I'll show you mine if you show me yours."

I mirror his action. "Let's do it."

My underwear is halfway down my legs when he strips to reveal himself. Coherent functioning flees the scene. The sight in front of me defies logic.

"Holy shit," I sputter. "You're huge. Like way above average."

"Speaking from experience?" His nostrils flare.

"No," I rush to say. "But there's no way your penis is a normal size."

Ridge chuckles. "Are you impressed?"

"And stunned. Your penis is the size of… a footlong sandwich with extra meat."

His laughter booms, shaking the entire bed. "Close, but not quite."

My eyes are dry from lack of blinking, but I can't look away for a second. "I won't be able to wrap my fingers around you. Are you supposed to fit inside of me? That's meant to happen eventually, right? But I don't see how that's possible.

You'll rip me in half. I've heard it hurts, but this will cause permanent damage. Severe pain—"

"Hey," he murmurs to cut off my rambling. "That's a worry for a different day. I promise to prepare your body until I'm sure you're ready. You'll take all of me eventually. We'll work you up to it."

"I trust you." Even if my vagina doesn't.

"That's real good to hear, sweetness." Ridge kisses me. "I'll always take care of you."

My forehead nudges his when I nod. "You're my dream come true."

"It's the same for me. I can't believe luck blessed me with you." He splays my hand flat over the tattoo on his left pec.

I admire the design, like many times before. It's simple yet extraordinary. Those four words—Property of Calliope Rose—inked into his flesh is a sight to cherish. "We're stuck in this together. Permanently."

He grunts. "That makes it sound like a last resort."

"As if," I scoff. "You're my first choice. The only one I'll ever choose."

"That's better." He presses his lips to mine again.

My fingers wander to his shoulder, finding a line of raised flesh there. "Is this—?"

"The pain from the past," he murmurs.

"We match." I rotate my wrist until the burn mark is exposed.

Ridge rubs along my scar with his thumb. "If that's the way you want to look at it, I won't argue."

"What we've overcome makes us stronger. Together." I lean into him, which connects our hips. My gasp spills into his mouth. "You're very hard."

He groans against my lips. "That's what you do to me, even talking about tough shit."

"Really?" My wide gaze lowers. "Are you going to come

on me? Some is already leaking out. Does semen shoot out from your tip? That happens in the books. Can I watch? Is that a strange request? I'm just really fascinated by you—or is that strange?"

He coughs, but the sound is strangled. "Good Lord, woman. Warn me before you talk to my cock like that."

Fire ignites in my cheeks. "Too weird, huh?"

"No, not at all. But I'm about to blow my load and you haven't even touched me."

Realization dawns and I grin. "If it makes you feel better, I'll probably get off super fast too. I'm very… excited."

"Look at you, unleashing the sexy vixen," he croons. "I knew you had a dirty side."

"Not until I met you," I giggle. "This… sexual awakening is your doing."

"Should we find out what else I can do to you?"

"Yes," I breathe. "And teach me how to pleasure you in return."

"You don't need lessons for that." He shushes me when I start to interrupt. "Just spread out beside me. You're an irresistible temptation."

I pout. "But I want to make you come."

"And you will. Our goals are aligned, as always." Ridge's palm drifts along my thigh. "Get your fingers wet. Use your arousal as lube for me."

My hand is moving before he finishes speaking. I moan as tingles rapidly flare outward to bathe me in a familiar warmth. The slippery consistency greets me, allowing me to complete the task Ridge assigned. A jolt shocks me when I tap on my clit. Another passionate whimper hitches from me. His grip tightens on my hip as I drench myself for him.

I lift my arm to display the evidence practically dripping off my nails. "Is this enough?"

"Fucking exquisite," he rasps.

Ridge encircles my wrist and gently steers me toward his eager shaft. I stare shamelessly while coating his length in my essence. A glossy smear follows the snaking path of a vein. I trace that ropey line with my thumb, spreading the lubricant in the process.

The combination of our arousal satisfies a primal itch I didn't realize needed to be scratched. It's lewd but I'm mesmerized. This is allure wrapped in conquered inhibitions. I want to be worthy of his worship. Motivation infuses my motions as I begin stroking him. Much like my earlier prediction, I can't touch my fingers together while gripping him. But my grasp is slick, easily earning me a groan.

"Damn, sweetness. You're a natural," he praises. "Just like that."

Ridge brings his fingers to my center. His touch is sure and precise. He's quick to focus on my clit, swiping back and forth in rapid flicks. I tremble from the onslaught. It's too much but not enough. The nonsensical mewls babbling from me are meant to explain that.

"Does my girl need relief?" He taps at my sensitive bundle of nerves.

I jerk in his hold. "Yes. Please, please."

It's only then I notice that my arm isn't pumping him. The motions had been keeping a steady tempo but stalled somehow. That concern melts away as he increases his pace. Static crackles in my veins, and I release a soundless cry. My hips buck when he dips a thick digit inside of me.

"So responsive." Ridge smirks as if proud.

"You're really good at this," I wheeze.

He plunges deeper into my core. "My experience is meant for you. How does it feel?"

A spasm clenches my inner muscles. "Better than ever."

"That's right, sweetness. Your pussy is purring for me. I want to hear you fall apart."

My vision goes hazy as he starts fingering me. The speed matches his rotations on my clit. It's a combination that ratchets my bliss to the precipice. Pressure builds and expands until I'm certain I'll burst.

"Oh, oh, oh," I chant.

Ridge thrusts into my fisted grip. "Almost there?"

"Uh-huh," I mumble. "So close."

"Let go for me," he commands.

I'm compelled to listen. The rhythm he sets lulls me into feverish relaxation. Heat prickles my skin while he plays my clit like a finely tuned instrument. Meanwhile, I fumble my grasp on him.

Ridge doesn't complain. Determination wafts off him. His dedication to the task is admirable. My hips snap forward, colliding with his dick. We grind together in a mindless heap, chasing the promise of a simultaneous climax.

Tingles spread until I'm consumed. My breathing becomes labored as if I'm racing to a destination. Release is within reach. I surrender to the sensations, my body bowing in gratitude. Just a bit more…

When he slams his finger into me, I fly over the edge into oblivion. My pulse thunders in my ears. The ache blooms into a rush of pleasure. I'm barely aware of Ridge's string of foul curses seconds before a gush splats my stomach.

My muscles seize and lock. I thrash against the invisible bonds of euphoria. The content buzz finds me next. Ridge's woodsy spiced aroma fills my nostrils as I coast.

He sweeps through my center with leisurely strokes as I regain clarity. There's a quivering spasm from below that twitches the rest of me. Spots dance in my eyes and I try to focus. His sated smirk matches the calm radiating from me.

I shift, which reminds me of the puddle on my belly. "You totally came on me."

Ridge's eyes heat. "Does that bother you?"

My fingers swirl through his release. "No, it's kind of…
exciting. I imagine you couldn't hold back for another moment
and erupted."

"That's exactly what happened." His hand roams from
between my thighs to where I'm playing with the sticky substance. He rubs his cum into my skin like lotion. "Now you're
wearing more of me. Drenched in my love. No other guy will
dare to get close."

I giggle. "You're very protective."

"Are you just noticing?"

"Umm, no." More laughter bursts from me. I pause for
a moment to collect myself. "That's a thrill for me too. In a
different way. Nobody has defended me like you do. It makes
me feel special."

Ridge tilts my chin until our lips brush. "You're everything
to me. I'll do whatever it takes for you to believe that."

My flush resembles a fanned fire. "I already do."

"Doesn't mean I'll quit trying," he murmurs into another
kiss. Like this man even has to lift a pinky to please me.

Doubts creep in about my ability to return. "Was I okay?
At… uh, touching you. Did I make you feel good?"

He loops an arm around my shoulders and tugs until I'm
draped over him. "Do I need to come on you again?"

I snuggle into his solid warmth. "If you insist."

"Don't tempt me," he rumbles against my temple.

My fingers skip along his as a thought occurs to me. "Can
I ask you a question?"

Ridge chuckles, jostling our position. "My curious girl.
I'll answer whatever your heart desires."

I peek up at him, basking in the happiness shining from
his expression. "What did you bring in your pocket?"

CHAPTER TWENTY-TWO

Ridge: my new favorite thing is waking up beside you

Ridge: and falling asleep with you in my arms

Ridge: and hearing you whisper my name in your dreams

Ridge: Garrett and Drake are harassing me about grinning like a fool

Ridge: will you defend my honor?

Callie: Hey, boyfriend! My favorite thing, other than all those you already listed, is finding numerous texts from you. It tells me you're always thinking about me. Not that I ever doubt you do. Work has been busy, but you're always on my mind. I was in the outdoor run with the pups. The service is spotty at best out there. I'm back inside now. Tell Drake and Garrett they'll have to deal with me if they don't leave you alone. Not sure how I'll deliver their punishment, but that's only a problem if their behavior continues. Let's hope they leave you alone.

Ridge: knew I could count on you, sweetness

Callie: That seems only fair since you do so much for me. My knees are still weak from that last orgasm you gave me. Of all the objects I would've guessed to be hidden in your pocket, a vibrator wouldn't make the list. The books I'm reading didn't prepare me for that. I'm also a bit surprised you'd allow something else to give me pleasure, Mr. Territorial.

Ridge: a sex toy isn't my competition

Ridge: I'm more than willing to be a team player when it comes to getting you off

Ridge: but I'll be the only cock involved

Ridge: think of the bullet as an extension of me

Ridge: and another new nickname?

Ridge: you're stroking my ego really hard

Ridge: speaking of hard, my dick misses you. it makes walking difficult

Ridge: I'm gonna catch so much shit if the guys notice my third leg that won't go down

Callie: My goodness! You're very chatty, which you seem to reserve for me. I'm the only one who gets this talkative version of you. That means a lot. It's comforting to know that you're just as attached as me. My belly swoops are very active right now. I love how you get me going with a few simple words. My blush is probably going to concern Stacey soon. Maybe she'll let me take my break early.

Ridge: what're you gonna do on your break

Callie: Think of you. Obviously. That's all I do these days. I'm not complaining. You keep my brain occupied. It helps my shifts go faster. Soon enough we'll be together again. Gosh, I sound obsessed. Maybe I am. If you're not careful, I'll get addicted to you. But let's be honest. I am already.

Ridge: don't threaten me with a good time

Callie: Well, it's a done deal. You've already intoxicated me. I'll never get you out of my system. Does that make me sound deranged? If it does, I'll handle the consequences. We're stuck with each other, right?

Ridge: better be

Callie: I certainly plan to keep you around. You're the only one who makes my... kitty purr. Along with everything else. Not sure what I'd do without you at this point.

Ridge: lol you'll never have to find out

Ridge: can't type pussy?

Callie: No way! Especially not at work. It feels wrong. I'm sweating just thinking about talking like that. Stacey is really going to think I have a fever at this rate.

Ridge: why? pussy is another name for cat

Callie: Oh, please. That's not the definition you're using and we both know it.

Ridge: it turns me on when you're sassy

Callie: You're going to get me in trouble, boyfriend. I almost bumped into the wall.

Ridge: smh watch the corners

Callie: Those sharp edges are dangerous. Pretty sure one just tried to leap out at me.

Ridge: no more sexting you for, sweetness. I'll change the subject

Callie: TYSM. My concentration would appreciate it.

Ridge: how's Walter?

Callie: He's got a case of the zoomies, like always. Glitzy is here to play. They get along well. Sydney is very happy we have a dog. We made plans to take the pups on a walk later. I couldn't say no if I tried. Her enthusiasm is infectious.

Ridge: glad to hear it. still okay taking him to the park tomorrow?

Callie: Absolutely. I'm looking forward to getting to know your friends better too.

Ridge: don't get too excited or I'll be jealous and uninvite them

Callie: I wouldn't dream of it, Mr. Territorial.

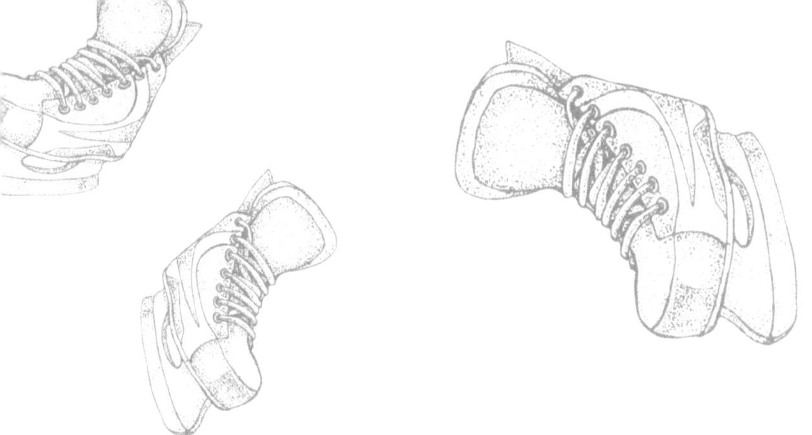

CHAPTER TWENTY-THREE

Ridge

THE WOOD BENCH CREAKS BENEATH MY WEIGHT while I wait for Garrett and Drake to pass another round of judgment. Somehow, I got stuck in the middle. Our seating arrangement is most definitely on purpose. These two instigators tag-team me at every opportunity. A family-friendly picnic in the park isn't safe from their heckling.

"Not sure what's got your thong in a twist, Crusher. This is tradition." Garrett's fresh attempt to get a rise out of me falls flat.

"Yeah, quit your bitching," Drake adds.

As if I've stooped to their level and given them a crumb to feast on. Instead, the goading rolls off my hunched form. I've been ignoring their presence for the better half of an hour. That hasn't stopped them from swarming like blood-thirsty insects since we arrived.

But it's nothing I can't easily swat away. Especially when Callie is within sight. She sits on a blanket beside Grace, Harper, and Sydney. Her smile brightens the sunny afternoon while she listens to whatever nonsense is being served from the peanut gallery. Glitzy and Walter race circles around the group to provide a secondary distraction.

My focus remains straight ahead while the cluckers flanking me decide what shit to spew next.

Drake does the honors. "When's the wedding, man?"

Garrett's scrutiny burns into the other side of my face. "Are you about to smile?"

"Told you," Drake hoots. "Smitten kitten in our midst. He's lost control of his facial muscles."

"Damn. Never thought I'd see the day." Garrett whistles like a plane is about to crash.

The urge to punch them shoots a tremble through my arms, but I don't break position. My bent elbows stay locked onto my knees.

Meanwhile, Drake chuckles at our buddy's sound effects. "You've become a helluva grill master, Foster. Did we pack wieners to roast?"

"Ridge has a kielbasa we can rake over the coals. Or he used to. Rumor has it, he's no longer in charge of his own meat. Better check in Callie's purse."

Drake nudges me after that eloquent comment from Garrett. "Get it? You're pussy whipped."

"Yup," I grunt.

"At least you can admit it," Garrett laughs.

"I've always wondered how it feels," Drake muses. "Wanna weigh in on this topic, Evans? You've got experience."

Jake flips him off from across our makeshift circle. The grumpy asshole makes me look like a fluffy unicorn in comparison.

Drake shrugs and chooses the lesser of two evils to annoy. "Do you surrender your balls completely or does Callie just fondle them whenever the mood strikes?"

My temper bubbles to the surface. "Yank that toothpick

you consider a dick from your ass and maybe you'll find out."

Drake claps after finally managing to provoke me. Such a pathetic victory to celebrate. "I bet getting head on the regular is worth it. Does she spit or—?"

I whack him in the chest with a clenched fist. "Better shut up or you'll make me mad."

He doubles over while hacking up a lung. "Shit, Crusher. I'm just fucking with you."

"Same," I return.

"Doesn't feel like it." He rubs his sternum.

"Find someone who cares." I blindly wave toward a crowd gathered under the nearby pavilion. "Maybe there's a single mom who will tend to your wounds."

After that, the dumbass duo decide to shift gears onto greener pastures. Garrett blows his fiancée a kiss. Feminine laughter snags Drake's desperation for companionship. Jake's attention hasn't strayed from where Harper and Sydney are sliding beads onto string to make bracelets. The fuck-off vibes he's exuding are potent enough to protect the entire park. That gives me the freedom to stare at Callie until my gaze is likely to burn a hole in her dress. She doesn't feel the heat of my unwavering interest as she joins in the crafting.

After Drake finishes perusing the options far out of his league, he realizes a comfortable silence has fallen over us. "How did I become the odd fuck out?"

"The fact that you even have to ask, dumbass," Garrett retorts.

Grace whirls to confront the crude interruption. "There are kids nearby."

His eyes bulge at her scold. "Did I say fuck? I meant duck."

"Always fucking with a perfectly good saying," I mutter.

"Not you too." The reprimand is aimed at me.

I hold up a palm. "The children are preoccupied. Except this pair."

"Oh, we're entertained."

"Me too," Sydney chirps. "But you both gotta put a dollar in the curse jar."

Grace and Harper pin us to our bench with a mutual glare. I tug my hat down to shield myself from their scathing ire. Drake smirks, far too pleased with himself.

Garrett scoffs. "Don't loop me in with these two, soulmate. I'm innocent."

His fiancée snorts. "You're many things, bartender. Innocent isn't one of them."

He scratches at his jaw, not bothering to hide a growing smile. "Got me there."

Callie squeals, which morphs into an untamed giggle. My concentration is redirected where it belongs to find Walter showering her with sloppy kisses. Lucky mutt. As if listening, the dog doubles his efforts to make me jealous.

Garrett cocks his head at the commotion. "Let me get this straight. Someone just gave a golden doodle away?"

"Apparently," I drawl.

"Aren't they a designer breed?"

I shrug. "Depends who you ask."

"How convenient for your wallet that this one happened to be free," Drake chimes in.

"I'd buy her a dozen puppies." The happiness shining on my girl's face is worth a fortune. A sideways glance from left to right suggests I'm not the only one to notice.

"She's poking out of her shell, huh?"

I jab Garrett's arm. "Don't refer to her as a turtle."

"Could be a snail," he grumbles.

"He's right," Drake agrees. "Callie is different lately. It's in a good way, don't get me wrong. Like she's more carefree or some cathartic shit."

"An oppressed seed that needed to be nurtured and watered by a particular hose to bloom into a flower."

I startle at the sudden appearance of Joy. "The fuck you come from?"

"Main Street." She points at the road as if I haven't lived in Knox Creek for years. "Cole and Belle are bonding over ice cream. I needed to stretch my legs."

Garrett studies his sister. "Are you a poet and I didn't know it?"

She wrinkles her nose as unshed tears collect in her eyes. "That little sonnet just sprang through the dirt to be heard. The hormones have me all up in my feels."

"Ah, thanks for the warning." Drake scoots to the edge of the bench.

"Don't be a dick," she blubbers.

He blanches. "What? How? I was just—"

"Being an insensitive prick," she snaps.

"Sorry," Drake mumbles.

"How's my nephew cooking in there?" Garrett pokes at Joy's small baby bump.

"Just fine, weirdo." Her hand smacks his away.

"Jeez." He shakes off the sting. "Do you need a snack? Maybe a punching bag?"

She straightens and blows out a slow exhale. "Apologies for the snark. It's something I'm working on."

"I can see that." Her brother adjusts on his seat as if seconds away from fleeing.

A beaming grin replaces the scowl on Joy's face. "Love is grand. Good for you, Crusher."

I bob my head in gratitude while trying to traverse the emotional whiplash. That leads me straight to Callie. Her head is tipped skyward, allowing the sun to bathe her silhouette. A gentle breeze billows the flowing fabric at her waist, a fantasy taking shape underneath. My mind is quick to wander along a path to where she's pregnant. Her stomach is swollen where our child grows and thrives. I stretch my fingers as if I can reach out to feel the life we're building. The vision is vivid, blurring the line between fact and fiction.

Motion in front of me steals the picturesque view. "What's got you grinning like you won the Stanley Cup?"

I scowl at Drake's waving arm. "Nothing."

"Isn't it obvious? He's tapping that hot ass over there." Joy lewdly thrusts her hips, but immediately pauses to fan herself. "Damn, I'm getting myself hot and bothered."

"She's a total banger." Grace sidles up beside Garrett to join our sidebar.

Garrett's mouth pops open. "Like you would bang her?"

I thump the back of his head. "Quit admiring my future wife."

"Can you blame us?" Joy blinks innocently.

"Solid choice. I'd put a ring on that." Grace flashes the diamond on her finger for emphasis.

I turn my gaze to the source of my obsessions. Callie is on her feet taking pictures. She spins and aims the camera at me. Before I can blink, the film is spit out from the top of the Instax.

The sneaky photographer winks at me. "I caught you looking."

My smirk is entirely for her benefit. "I'm looking at you."

"Luckily I'm behind the lens, huh?"

"C'mere, sweetness." I crook my finger.

Callie's hips sway to an exaggerated degree. I'm instantly hypnotized by the effortless flow of her stride. A slight curl quirks her lips as she approaches. It reveals this sultry strut isn't an accident.

Her sandal bumps my boot. "Hey, boyfriend."

Lust stabs me in the gut. "Missed you."

"I was right over there."

"Distance doesn't matter. Need a seat?" I pat my thigh.

A blush colors her cheeks but she inches forward to comply. I pull Callie onto my lap and tuck her flush against me. Vanilla swirls in the air to provide me with an instant sense of peace. In the next moment, my face is buried in the dip of her shoulder for another hit. But it's not enough. My hat gets flipped backward to grant me unrestricted access. Then I'm diving in for more.

A shudder rolls through my body. Callie gasps as if she can feel the desire swirling off me. The park fades into a colorful blob. Idle chatter goes mute. Nobody else exists but us.

"Um, wow. You're very… affectionate. Didn't know you had it in you, boss." Harper must've abandoned her spot on the blanket as well.

I couldn't care less about who's witnessing my unconditional attachment to this woman. Callie isn't as immune and squirms in my hold. The extra attention probably makes her uncomfortable. I slouch onto the bench and tip my legs upward. The change in position rests her head on my chest. Her face is aimed at the clouds, away from prying eyes.

"Just ignore them," I whisper in her ear.

Her exhale is choppy. "You're a cozy chair."

"Best seat in the house."

"Welp, that's our cue." Harper signals to Jake and Sydney. "We gotta get home and do the dishes."

The little girl pouts. "But I don't wanna clean."

"You actually have a playdate with Polly. Daddy and Mommy will handle the dishes while you're gone."

"Really?" Excitement raises Sydney's tone several octaves.

"Yep, we'll get them taken care of. Doing the dishes is very important." Harper puckers her lips at Jake.

The little girl spins on her heel to address us like an adoring audience. "Mommy and Daddy do the dishes a lot. Like all the time. Especially after I go to bed. Not sure why there are still plates and cups by the sink when I wake up in the morning."

Joy snickers. "They take their time on certain platters. Those big ones are tricky. You have to scrub really hard to get them clean."

"Daddy does best on those tough-to-reach stains. Really gets after it." Harper wiggles her brows.

"Dirtier the better," Jake says.

"Adults are weird," Syd grumbles.

"Yeah, kid." Drake appears perplexed while trying to follow their exchange. "But only certain ones."

Harper ignores him, turning her attention to Callie and me. "Have you started on any small plates? Maybe just spoons? Forks are fun. Especially in the afternoon."

"Pairs well with a nap," Jake offers.

Her eyes sparkle. "Oooooh, yes. Lay them all out on the counter. A nice kitchen is essential."

"You have to watch how hard you bang the pots together or you'll be eating for two." Joy pats her belly.

"Food for thought." Harper taps her temple. "Toodles."

But it's never that simple to part ways. Our group disperses in an extension pack of Minnesota goodbyes. The crude humor mixed in makes the long-winded farewells somewhat tolerable. Drake is last to amble off, leaving me on the bench with Callie.

"Why do they care so much about dishes? I'm confused." A furrow creases her forehead.

"They're talking about sex," I rasp.

"Oh! How sneaky."

"Very."

Her eyes trail after our friends as if she wants to chastise them. Before she can make good on that plan, a different idea seems to distract her. "Should we... um, do the dishes?"

"Not yet, sweetness." I chuckle and skim my fingers along her sides. "But we can definitely do a pre-rinse and soak cycle."

CHAPTER TWENTY-FOUR

Callie

PAUSE JUST OUTSIDE THE ENTRANCE. AN INVISIBLE BAND cinches around my ribs, making it difficult to take a decent breath. Familiar nerves join forces with doubt. The latter is what plagues me.

This is a bold move. Probably too fast and forward, considering the panic ready to send me skittering back home. But I'm supposed to be brave. Take chances. Discover the unknown. Become the best version of myself. That's the entire point.

Music thumps from inside as I gather my scattered courage. It's just like every other time I've stopped by. But the encouragement is a farce. I rub my clammy palms along the silky fabric hugging my curves. A downward glance confirms I'm still securely fastened in this impulsive purchase. All that's left to do is… leap.

I bounce on the balls of my feet in preparation. Fellow pedestrians send me curious looks, which does little for my confidence. Their interest is warranted. I'm loitering on the curb while giving myself a pep talk. That's my final cue.

Unfiltered noise greets me when I yank open the door.

Too many voices compete against the country song currently playing. I blink at the busy scene. How silly of me to assume a Wednesday evening would be less popular at the infamous cock den. Before regret can sink its claws into my guts, a shrill call freezes me on the spot.

The loud wolf whistle rips across the room. An abrupt quiet descends on the throng as all eyes shift to Harper. When people realize she's staring at me, they're quick to follow her lead. The urge to duck and cover trembles my knees. Instead, I square my shoulders and creep forward into the crowded space.

My heart races faster with each step I take. The attention I'm receiving is impossible to miss. Gazes skim over my face to concentrate on my chest. I focus on Harper, ignoring those hovering in my peripheral. A direct path to the rail forms as people move aside. The impulse to curl into myself clenches my muscles but I won't surrender. I'm not weak.

There's a riot in my flexed stomach as I approach the bar. Every stool is occupied. An awkward pause rattles me as I decide where to stand. I scoot into the gap between two seats and wave at my friend.

"Holy shit, babes." Harper's mouth hangs wide open. "You actually went through with it."

I fidget with the hem that ends at mid-thigh. "Did you doubt me?"

"Nope, I'm damn proud." Her smile couldn't get wider if she tried.

"Um, yeah. Thanks for the warm welcome. Everyone is staring." Including the men next to me.

"Can you blame them? Your tits are—"

"Fuckable," the guy on my right cuts in.

Harper lifts her brows. "You're not wrong, but I'd watch what you say to her."

His perusal roams over me at a lewd pace that makes my skin crawl. "And why's that?"

Her lips flatten into a firm line. "You don't need a reason, Roy. Get your butt off her seat."

He guffaws. "We reserving spots now?"

"For her? Bet your ass. This is Ridge's future wife."

My belly swoops and flutters at the title. This isn't the first time I've heard the claim. I certainly hope it's not the last.

Roy shifts to fully face me. His eyes widen. "Oh, damn. Are you the one Lonny yelled at? He almost pissed himself just recalling how Crusher almost beat him to a pulp at Pampered Pooch."

Another burst of pride shines from the sassy bartender. "Yep, that's her. The one and only."

"Well, shit. If you'll excuse me, I'll be on my way." The man snags his beer from the counter and ambles off into the swarm.

"There you go." Harper points to the available spot.

"That wasn't necessary." But I slide onto the leather cushion.

"If I didn't boot his ass, Ridge would."

"More than likely," I laugh.

"Zero hesitation. Guaranteed," she corrects. "Especially with you looking like a juicy snack dangling over dozens of salivating savages."

I follow her stare to my plunging neckline. Harper is responsible for this racy idea. Her role as instigator comes naturally, and I was happy to comply. Which reminds me…

"Not sure if you'll have time to play, but I brought Uno." I set the cards on the wood surface.

"Huh?"

"You told me to bring a game."

"That"—she points at the deck—"isn't what I meant."

I frown. "You don't like Uno?"

A gleam flashes across her gaze. "I do, but I'm gonna like seeing Ridge lose his shit even more."

"Why would he do that?"

"Let's find out." Her attention slides to a point over my head. "Someone's ears were burning."

I feel him before I see him. His warmth against my back is a comfort I'll gladly sink into. A tattooed arm slides around my waist and yanks. I recline backward against a muscular chest that moonlights as my pillow.

"Hey, sweetness." Ridge's warm breath coasts along my neck to awaken a shiver.

I sag into his capable grip, allowing him to support my weight. "Hi, boyfriend."

His coarse stubble rasps along my throat when he nuzzles into me. "You good?"

"She couldn't be better. I was about to make her a Slippery Dickery. Unless you wanna have at it, boss." Harper holds up a cocktail shaker.

"Nah, I'm good on this side."

"Where you can play guard dog," she quips.

On cue, tension radiates from him while he scans our surrounding area. I rest my palm on his and thread our fingers together. A calm quickly loosens the rigidity in his stance.

I swivel sideways on the stool, tipping my chin upward in a silent request for a kiss. Ridge dips to accept my invitation. Our mouths meet for a brief but electric moment. A sizzle sparks in my veins when his tongue sneaks out to lick my lower lip before he straightens. His relaxed grin mirrors mine, but then he glances down at my outfit. I teeter in limbo for his judgment.

"You look"—his throat works audibly—"incredible."

"Thanks, boyfriend."

He scrubs over his mouth. "Gonna get me arrested."

My ears must be deceiving me. "What was that?"

"These jokers won't be able to resist. Too damn tempting."

"She sure is." The comment comes from the man beside me.

"Must be fucking joking," Ridge snarls. The softness in his expression morphs into steel edges sharp enough to maim as he glares at the guy. "Care to repeat that?"

"Nope, just shooting the shit with my buddies." He turns away.

My boyfriend throws invisible daggers at the customer's back. I sit still while waiting for him to forgive the minor interruption. Meanwhile, the person sitting on my left must smell the anger wafting from him. He voluntarily vacates his seat before becoming the next target. Ridge claims the stool, seeming far too pleased with his ability to chase people away without a word.

"Where were we?" He lifts our connected hands to pepper kisses along my knuckles.

A sigh breezes from my parted lips. His eyes are pools of liquid fire as he shamelessly admires me. I might melt from his smolder. My dopey grin suggests as much.

"Good grief, Callie is sexy." Harper reappears from serving others in her section. She fans herself, looking positively giddy while assessing her boss's response. "Is it hot in here? Must be the fumes rising from her cherry cobbler."

I scowl at what I've recently discovered is a code for my virginity. "Very funny."

"You won't be laughing when he's gobbling it." She mimics the act of eating.

"Harper," I hiss.

"Don't pretend your cooter cake isn't eager for him to have a taste."

"You're incorrigible." I duck my head to hide the flames blazing across my cheeks.

"I'd suggest you knock it off unless you want to lose your job." Ridge's authoritative reprimand demands obedience.

It also gains the attention of the guy sitting beside him. "Hey, Crusher. This is unexpected." He leans over to glance at me. "Got yourself a yummy treat, huh?"

Ridge has the front of the guy's shirt in a fisted grip before the man has finished speaking. "Care to rephrase that?"

He flounders in the presence of such animosity. "Uhhh…"

Ridge's jaw ticks. "Is this a prank? Is every dude in my bar that desperate to send me to jail?"

"Nah, Crusher. We're solid. I was just… making polite conversation. Didn't mean any harm." There's a plea in his statement.

"Doesn't matter. Leave her out of it."

"Absolutely. I'll mind my business."

"That's what I thought." He tightens his hold for several seconds before releasing the latest victim to his wrath.

"This is even better than I thought!" Bliss drips from Harper's tone.

"It's not nice to take enjoyment from another's torment," I scold.

"Oh, puh-lease. Ridge is a big boy. If he can dish out the roast, he better be prepared to have a serving. Besides, I didn't encourage anything other than flaunting your newfound confidence. You're radiant, babes. Comfortable in your beautiful skin. Own that shit."

"She's right. Sorry, sweetness." Ridge rips off his hat, dragging a hand through his hair. "I'm a tad disturbed from these assholes objectifying you."

Harper snorts. "A tad?"

"What do you expect? They're acting like they haven't seen a woman before." He adjusts our position so my legs are framed with his. "I'm crazy about you, love. Clearly. My emotions can run aggressive and get the best of me."

Warmth bathes my entire face but I don't hide from him. "I think you're doing just fine."

His thumb traces the flush staining my cheek. "My reaction probably isn't attractive. Definitely not rational."

On the contrary, and the tingles spreading through my lower belly confirm as much. But I can't admit that in such a public space. "You're defending my honor."

Ridge smirks. "That's giving me far too much credit for acting unhinged and possessive."

"I don't see it that way. You haven't shamed me or made me feel bad for wearing a dress that's revealing."

"It's your choice. I'll never take that away from you. But these fuckers"—he blindly swats at the crowd—"can kick rocks."

"Always protecting me, right?"

"And I don't plan to fail." Which has him boldly pointing at a man sitting across from us. "Are you attached to your eyes?"

The guy nods but doesn't dare to speak.

"Then I'd recommend you take them off my future wife or I'll remove them from their sockets for you."

The man immediately averts his gaze like a chastised kid.

"Blatant pricks," Ridge grumbles.

I squirm in my seat, slightly ashamed to be turned on in this situation. "Maybe I should go."

He tightens his hold on me. "You're right where you're meant to be, sweetness."

"Not sure your customers would agree."

"They'll get over it." In the next instant, his thunderous expression strikes a guy sitting several spots down the rail. "Need an actual excuse to drool like a teething infant ogling a tit? How does my fist breaking your jaw sound?"

The man dashes out of sight before I can blink. Ridge is practically vibrating in place, scanning the room for anyone ballsy enough to test his nonexistent patience. One peeks over in our direction and an animalistic growl rips from my boyfriend. It seems the last straw has just been tossed down.

"Oh, shit." Harper whips a white towel in the air while backing away. "Crusher is about to unleash the beast."

As if scripted, Ridge leaps off his stool. The abrupt motion sends the seat crashing to the floor. But that doesn't properly announce his upset.

"Everyone get the fuck out of my bar!" His bellow is loud enough to tremble the walls. "Roosters is closed."

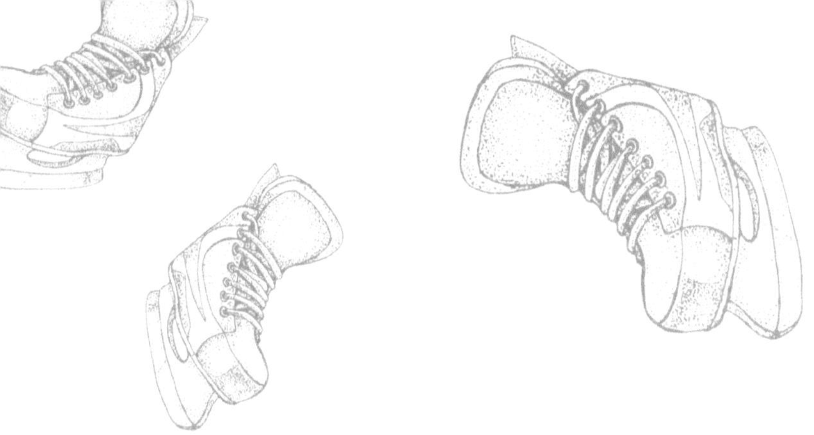

CHAPTER TWENTY-FIVE

Ridge

THE PLACE IS EMPTY IN LESS THAN SIX MINUTES. I counted the seconds while herding disgruntled customers to the exit. Receiving a free drink ticket on the way out diluted their intoxicated attitudes. Garrett and Drake will regret leaving me in charge for the night. But that's trouble for another day.

"Bold move, boss." Harper backs toward the door. "I'm impressed."

"You're not my intended audience."

The meddlesome bartender peeks around me. "She's sitting pretty. Ready and waiting for whatever you have planned."

"That's not for you to worry about. Get gone and drive safe." I usher her outside and lock the deadbolt before she can consider a response.

Harper was the final pain in my ass to vacate the premises. Now it's just me and Callie. If only it could always be this way. A guy can dream.

After shutting off the lights, I take a breath to calm the frenzy my brain has scrambled into. I turn around slowly. Only the soft glow from behind the liquor display illuminates the space. It's more than enough to define Callie's flawless beauty. But I'd be able to identify her in the pitch dark.

She's perched on her stool like the prim and proper queen she is. Her tits are nearly spilling out of that fucking dress. The sight is an erotic fantasy on steroids.

It's a shame so many others got to witness the view. The reminder threatens to rekindle my frustration, but she couldn't care less about them. Callie showed up tonight to see me. She won't even speak to them, reserving her words for my ears. I'm the only man she deems worthy to worship her.

"Looks like you've got me all to yourself, love."

"Just the way I like it," she murmurs.

"Should've said so sooner. It was my pleasure to kick those fools to the curb."

"That was rather entertaining." Callie tilts her head, admiring me from across the room. "How long are we staying here?"

My eyes narrow playfully. "Got somewhere else to be?"

She giggles. "Not really, but Walter is home alone."

"Well," I drawl and begin striding forward. "That's entirely up to you."

"How so?"

"You hold the power. Indefinitely, sweetness."

"In that case…" Her sentence trails off when she begins rummaging in her purse. "Can I snap a picture of you?"

I freeze. "Now?"

"Mhmm," she breathes. "You look… intense."

"And you like that?"

"Very much so."

My chest expands and I spread my arms wide. "Then take your best shot."

She whips out the vintage Polaroid as if this is a memory to cherish. The thought almost drops me to my knees. But I'm not close enough yet.

Lust pumps into my veins as I stalk toward her. I don't

want to scare her, but my need for this woman is slightly terrifying. Although she never cowers from my obsessive version of devotion.

To prove my point, Callie takes the opportunity to capture an image of me in this state. Her fingers pluck the film free and she fans herself with it. She smiles when I rumble my approval, as if we're equal parts infatuated.

I arrive in front of her and immediately kneel at her feet. My mouth goes dry while I inhale her addictive elixir of vanilla and sexual ambitions. Her legs are the finest silk beneath my palms. I roam along the smooth expanse until she noticeably clenches.

"What're you doing down there, boyfriend?"

Rather than answer, I chew on anticipation and delayed gratification. "You chose this dress for yourself, but did you think it would drive me to the brink of insanity?"

Callie bites her bottom lip. "Do you like it?"

"Fuck," I chuckle. "That's an offensive understatement. I contemplated burning the bar to the ground to get rid of the distractions. My attention is solely meant for you."

Her gaze heats. "I'm all yours."

"Did I mention you look edible?" I rest on my heels to appreciate the full scope.

"You said incredible."

"That too. But now I'm going to feast on you. Consider it my way of apologizing for acting like a brute."

Her faithful blush makes an appearance. "It doesn't bother me. Does that make me just as… naughty?"

"Fuck yeah," I groan. "You wanna be my bad girl?"

"Uh-huh."

"You shouldn't admit that to me."

Callie wiggles on the stool. "Why not?"

"It'll make me even more irrational." Not to mention hard, but this isn't about me.

"Give me your worst, boyfriend."

"Seductress," I rasp while shuffling forward on my knees. My hat gets flipped backward in the process. "Remember you asked for it."

I bunch the bottom half of her dress around her hips. She shivers as I expose her modesty but doesn't protest. Not yet, at least. My thumbs hook underneath her panties. I remove the barrier in a practiced motion, and pocket the lace like the trophy it is.

"Lean back, sweetness. Brace yourself on the edge of the rail. Get comfortable."

She gets situated as requested, angling herself into an optimal position. "There."

"Perfect." I hook her legs over my arms.

"Can people see?" Her focus is pinned on the front windows that offer us an unobstructed view of Main Street.

"Nah, it's tinted. I'd never put you on display for others."

Callie stares at me hovering just above her splayed core. "This is very... intimate."

"Which is why I've saved this act strictly for you. My future wife."

Confusion pinches her expression. "You've never done this before?"

"Nope. It felt too personal in the past. Whatever happened before you is a muted blur that lacked substance in every shape and form. I never had the desire for more, until the day I saw you." I press a gentle kiss to her inner thigh. "You'll be the only woman I eat from."

She trembles in my grip. "Oh, my."

"Just relax for me," I exhale across her sensitive flesh. The glistening sheen reveals she's turned on. Salvia pools on my tongue, desperate for a taste. "Maybe find something sturdy to hold."

That's the final warning I provide before burying my face

in her essence. The tangy punch of her arousal consumes my senses. I'm instantly drunk, my thoughts spinning on how to drench myself in her. My shoulders stoop to spread her wider and grant me unrestricted access.

After flattening my tongue, I swipe through her center from ass to clit. The latter is where I land and home in on. That bump of nerves is my Everest. I'll conquer the climb and challenge her to another. My lips seal around the designated target, sucking deep.

"Holy shit," Callie wheezes.

She arches against the onslaught. Her palms fumble to get a grip on me, quickly swatting my hat to the ground. Then she grabs fistfuls of my hair and uses that hold as an anchor.

I rumble around a mouthful of her. Tart honey slicks my lips like a healing balm I didn't know I needed. My suction increases while simultaneously flicking her clit. She bucks into me, spewing praises that are mostly unintelligible.

Control is a slippery slope and I'm sliding down. Callie seems to be fighting a similar battle. Her hips rock at a feverish pace, urging me faster. I drape her right leg over the neighboring seat, using the shift in position to bring my hand into the mix.

Her pussy accepts two fingers easily. I add a third, which is a tight squeeze. True to my word, I've been preparing her for my cock. She'll be ready to take me soon.

"Oh, oh, oh," she chants.

Her inner muscles become a clamp and I'm sure she's close. Before I let her tip over the edge, I pull my mouth away. I slow the motions of my fingers to pump into her at a lazy pace. Without breaking stride, I stand and use my unoccupied hand to reach for the condiment dispenser on the counter.

"What're you doing?" Her glazed stare searches mine.

I grab what I'm searching for, hiding the item in my hand. "A little something extra."

"For what?

"Dessert." I hover my mouth over hers.

Before I can return to my spot on the floor, she presses her lips to mine. The move is unexpected and provocative. Satisfaction strokes me, but this is her exploration. I remain still while she tastes herself on me. A soft mewl spills free. Her tongue sneaks out for more and I'm quick to deepen the kiss. She opens for me, eager to match my enthusiasm. Her complex flavor blends with our mutual desire.

Callie pulls away, licking at the gloss that remains. "I was curious."

Carnal fuckery grips me in an unrelenting fist. "What do you think?"

She rolls her lips between her teeth, mulling over the answer. "Not bad. A bit odd. I'm not sure how to define it."

"Indescribable," I say. "A unique blend that can't be replicated."

And I'm about to add another element.

My knees meet the concrete while I change tactics. I drag the fruit by its stem through her slickness. My fingers pinch the sticky orb before sinking into her. The combination dips an inch into her pussy. I swirl and rotate for good measure. A slow pull removes my saturated treat for consumption.

A garbled noise spews from Callie. "Did you just—?"

"Make my own version of cherry cobbler? Abso-fucking-lutely."

I pop the much-improved fruit into my mouth. The sugary syrup intensifies her rich taste into an irresistible cocktail. My eyes roll back and I groan. I'll never get enough.

Callie's jaw is hanging slack as she watches me swallow the ingenious creation. She doesn't get the opportunity to reply before I'm tonguing her clit again. Her squeal reaches for the rafters. My fingers glide into her pussy while I send her toward relief.

Heady lust crashes over me as her climax peaks. I'd follow her over the edge if it wouldn't leave me in a messy situation.

A spasm twitches her limbs and she cries out. That's my cue to double my efforts. After a final swipe, her release floods down my throat. I can't seem to gulp fast enough. My girl is a squirter, quenching my thirst from this point forward.

A startled squeak escapes her as if she can feel how much is flowing free. When my mouth isn't full, I'll explain what just happened. She thrashes against my hold while I guide her through euphoria. I drink every drop until she's wrung dry.

Callie slumps against the bar. A daze blankets her features into a thoroughly pleasured expression. There's a dreamy droop halfway covering her eyes that almost has me diving straight in for seconds. Her labored breaths crack into the post-coital bliss.

"Um… that was definitely something extra," she croaks.

"Yeah, love. I got you to squirt for me."

Her lashes flutter, but she doesn't avert her gaze. "Is that what the… gush was?"

"Best thing I've put in my mouth. Fucking exquisite." I lick my fingers clean.

"Wow." A flush stains her skin while she regains composure. "A cherry, huh?"

I smack my lips. "Almost an adequate substitute. Might sate me until I get the real deal."

The momentary lapse clears and she perks up. "When will that be?"

An idea springs to my cloudy mind. "Do you have plans this weekend?"

"Only if you're making some for us."

"I was thinking we could get out of town for a while."

"For a date?"

My shrug is feigned nonchalance. "Or two. Probably three. We'll make it an extended stay somewhere… romantic."

Callie gasps. "Like a vacation?"

"Yeah, sweetness. I'm gonna whisk you away."

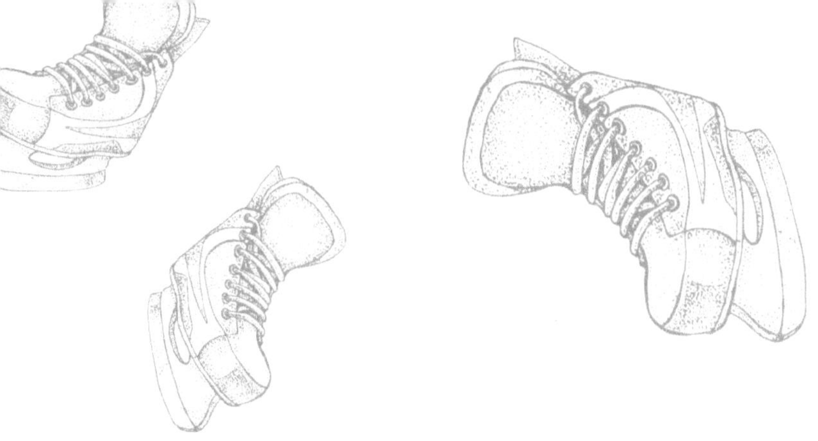

CHAPTER TWENTY-SIX

Ridge

CALLIE GAWKS AT OUR HOME FOR THE NEXT THREE days and two nights. "You rented a… mansion for us?"

I shift the truck into park and cut the engine. "Not quite. My buddy owns this place. He's on the road and offered to let us stay for the weekend."

Her lips replicate a tiny circle. "That's very nice of him."

"He owed me one."

"Well, I'll happily help you reap the reward. What're we waiting for?" She gathers the pile of pictures taken along the trip and tucks them in her purse. The camera remains clutched in her grasp, ready to capture more memories.

"Before we go inside"—I pop the latch on the center console and snag the three envelopes stashed there—"choose one."

Callie studies the fanned-out formation I'm holding for her picking. "What are these?"

"A selection process. We'll do them all but you decide the order." I shake the options.

"Ooooh, I like this game." She plucks the middle choice from my grip and rips open the tab. "Dinner and a massage."

"Solid start, sweetness. The fridge is stocked with your favorites. I'll be the chef."

She falters. "You're going to prepare dinner?"

"Don't look so shocked. It won't be the first time," I chuckle. "But don't give me too much credit either. The prep is mostly done."

"Does that still count as cooking?"

"You tell me."

"I think you're getting off easy," she giggles.

"That remains to be seen."

Her eyes narrow. "Are you talking about sex?"

My dick jerks on command. "When it involves you? Always."

"Allow me to repeat myself," she whispers. "What're we waiting for?"

"Trust me, it's in the best interest of both of us." I lean over to give her a kiss. "Get your sexy ass in there while I grab the bags."

Her happiness grins against my lips. "Yes, boyfriend."

But Callie hasn't made it beyond the foyer when I arrive with our stuff. Her wide stare swings in every direction. I stand beside her to appraise the interior that's more than likely professionally decorated.

To our left is a sitting area that has more couches than a hotel lobby. The paintings are probably originals to further boast about Luke's wealth. On the right, there's a long hallway that leads who knows where. A grand staircase promises more riches to behold on the second level. The vaulted ceilings trail to the polished floor. Straight ahead is an entire wall made of glass, providing a panoramic view of the rural property.

It's too damn fancy for my style, which is why I barely notice the features. My gaze rarely strays from Calliope Rose.

She spins in a slow circle while admiring the crystal chandelier. "I can't believe someone lives here."

"Do you want a house like this?"

Her gaze meets mine. "No, it's too… much. I'd get lost every day."

My arm cinches around her waist, pulling until we're locked in a hug. "Don't worry, sweetness. I'll always find you."

She sighs into my embrace. "This is really nice."

"It's my goal to please you," I murmur into her hair.

Callie draws in a deep breath, which I imagine fills her lungs with my scent. "You've gone above and beyond."

My laughter jostles her head on my chest. "I've barely begun. Can I feed you?"

She peers up at me from under hooded eyelids. There's a rosy blush staining her cheeks, leading me to believe she's in the mood for something other than food. "Yes."

I link her fingers with mine, steering us toward the kitchen. The open concept demands recognition and has more square footage than my entire first floor. Luke is probably overcompensating for what he lacks in other departments. "Showy bastard. He's gonna catch a bunch of shit for this."

Callie giggles. "It's extremely elegant."

"Sure," I grunt.

"Walter would've worn himself out sliding on these tiles." She taps the nearest white slab with her toe. "I wonder if he feels abandoned."

I scoff. "He's in very excellent care."

"Sydney was honored when we asked her to watch him."

My head bobs. "She takes puppy sitting very seriously."

Callie suddenly gasps, peeking through a set of French doors. A huge arrangement of chrysanthemums sits in the center of a massive dining table. "Oh, my! Those are stunning."

"Glad they arrived on time," I note absently.

Her focus swings back to me. "You ordered them?"

I nod again. "There should be more in our room."

Unshed tears glisten in her stare. "You went through a lot of trouble for me."

I cage her chin between my thumb and forefinger, tilting until her lips are upturned for me to kiss. "There's never trouble when you're involved."

"Tell that to your customers," she teases against my mouth.

"That's their own damn fault." But I can't be too pissed considering where that night led. And once my mind wanders between her legs, it's impossible to stop.

I've feasted on her at every available opportunity since that evening. The memory of Callie's taste on my tongue from breakfast in bed this morning is still fresh, but hours on the road have passed since then. Something gleams from beside me to snatch my attention. I smirk at what's waiting for recognition.

The granite island is large enough to serve as a buffet. My mind travels to a more explicit meal. Callie splayed out, wriggling in rapture. I'd lick any excess that dribbles onto the smooth surface. Arousal pulses from behind my zipper, making the denim stretch tight.

I widen my stance while glancing behind me. "What're the chances we can find cherries in there?"

Warmth melts the blue in her eyes into a lustful shade. "You're bad."

My smirk is dipped in filthy intentions. "You love it."

"I do."

"Only one way to find out." I back to the fridge, refusing to let Callie leave my sight.

She follows my lead until we're perusing the contents in the fridge. "Is that tater tot hotdish?"

I remove the covered casserole dish. "My mother's recipe."

"How?"

The container thumps on the counter. "I didn't ask questions."

"Sounds like magic."

"Or good fortune." I motion to our surroundings. "My buddy asked for a list of stuff to order. This was at the top."

"I can't wait to try it." Suggestion leaks from Callie's reply.

My dick throbs in response while I preheat the oven. "Want a salad on the side?"

"Are you going to toss it yourself?"

I choke on my own spit. "Good Lord, woman. Do you know what you're asking for?"

She blinks, the picture of innocence. "A tossed salad?"

The possibility—slight as it might be—of me getting in her ass is enough to blow my load. I blindly reach for the nearest stationary object, gripping the edge until my knuckles bleed white. It takes several moments to talk myself off the ledge. "Coming right up, sweetness."

She doesn't react to my uneven tone. "Can you check if there's ranch? Extra creamy is best."

I clench my eyes shut, begging for a reprieve. My feet stumble forward to do her bidding. "Take a seat. I'll get this whipped up for us."

"Can I help?" Her temptation is right behind me, far too close to remain unaffected.

"Nah, I got this. Relax for a bit."

The scrape of a chair announces Callie doing as requested. "If you insist."

It doesn't take long to gather supplies. All the fixings we could ever want are available, including her desired dressing.

My motions are a blur as I dump the pre-packaged ingredients into a bowl. It's about muscle memory at this point.

"Are you okay, boyfriend?"

I can feel her interest scalding my back. "Couldn't be better."

But that's a lie, and she must hear it. "Are you sure? Your movements are very… stiff."

I hang my head, allowing a tortured groan to spill free. "Just hungry."

"Want me to put in the hotdish?" Callie is already off her chair, sliding on bulky mitts. "How long should I set the timer for?"

My mind whirls in a useless cycle when she bends to set the pan on the rack. "Um…"

"Twenty minutes is usually sufficient for reheating."

"Perfect," I breathe.

She glances over in my direction. Her eyes widen at whatever state she finds me in. "You're really… excited."

I don't need to look down at the evidence bulging in my jeans. "Occupational hazard."

"From tossing salad?"

Another punch of lust jabs me in the gut and I almost fold in half. "Just from being around you."

She begins reaching for me. "Do you want me to—?"

My arm straightens outward to halt her advance. "We should eat first."

"What if I'm not hungry?" Callie twirls a lock of her dark hair, a sneaky glint entering her gaze.

"You said I could feed you." My voice cracks in a plea for willpower.

Her focus slips downward. "Mhmm."

"Sweetness," I rasp.

"Yes, boyfriend?"

"Be careful what you wish for," I recite the phrase like the warning it is.

She licks her bottom lip. "I prefer throwing caution to the wind. Let's do it. Together."

"You're testing my restraint, love."

Callie steps up to me, gripping the front of my shirt in her fist. "How do I make it break?"

"Fuuuuuck," I exhale across her forehead. It appears my earlier aspirations might come to fruition after all. My palms roam to her ass and I press into her. Hard against soft. She gasps at my rigid need. I begin lifting her to the ledge of the island. The height will put her pussy directly in my face once I'm seated.

But then she struggles against my intentions. "No, not here."

"Do you have something against this pristine eating surface?"

"I'm ready to have sex," Callie blurts. "In a bed, if that's… agreeable."

CHAPTER TWENTY-SEVEN

Callie

MY REQUEST CAUSES A CHAIN REACTION. RIDGE KEEPS me lofted in his grip and turns to exit the kitchen with purpose. His lips carve a sizzling path along my throat as he navigates our course. Through the desire he's stoking, common sense filters in.

"Wait! The oven." Won't make that mistake again.

He's quick to comply, retracing our steps before resuming his progress to wherever we're going. As it turns out, the guest bedroom where we're assigned to sleep is at the end of a very long hallway. In the minutes it takes to get there, nervous anticipation has tangled into a knot that consumes my stomach.

I cling tighter to him as we approach our destination. My inner muscles clench, empty and demanding to be filled. The stimulation ripples through me and I have to stifle a moan. I wonder if Ridge can feel the tremble in my legs.

The door opens with a creak. That ominous sound echoes the unknown about to come. His stride is steady while he carries me toward the mattress that monopolizes the space. The size is even bigger than the California King he recently purchased for me. Although he's been staying over every night, which makes the purchase mutually beneficial.

My butt sinks into the memory foam when Ridge sets me down. He's quick to step back, as if needing a brief pause before proceeding. I take the opportunity to stretch my courage.

There's a visible quake in my hands as I grasp the hem of my dress. The cotton whispers against my skin. Cool air prickles the fever scalding my flesh with every curve I expose. Once the material is pulled over my head, I'm bathed in goosebumps. Only my bra and panties conceal me.

Ridge's gulp is audible. It draws my focus to the tension cutting into his expression. He flexes his fingers, clutching nothing but invisible desires. The swell in his pants tents the material outward. It reminds me where that girthy shaft is expected to go.

I want this. Badly. But there's a decent dose of concern injected into me along with the lust. He's a very large man.

"I won't hurt you." His low timbre is soothing.

My exhale sputters in return. "I know."

"You look worried."

I smooth my features. "Just general curiosity about how you're going to fit."

"We'll go slow."

My head jerks in false bravado. "I'm ready."

Ridge reaches over his shoulder to grip the collar of his shirt. A single tug reveals his upper half to my hungry stare. The sight of my name inked on him puts me at ease. We belong together. This will work, along with everything else.

The clink of his belt knocks me from those assurances. His zipper lowers next, offering a peek at his boxers. The green fabric strains over his erection. My mouth goes dry and I instinctively scoot backward. An undeniable warmth is summoned to my lower belly. I squirm at the slick sensation that soon follows. Ridge smirks, undoubtedly guessing where my mind has traveled.

With a downward shove, the denim pools at his ankles and he stalks forward. "Make yourself comfortable, sweetness. Just like at home."

"Is this the massage portion of the date?"

His mouth pulls up on one side. "Only if you're referring to me rubbing you on the inside."

There's no arguing with that. I get situated in the middle. My upright position is supported by a stack of pillows. The silk comforter beneath me is like a cozy embrace. "This bed is luxurious."

"Only the best for you."

"Did you plan this part too?" My palms rub along the softness surrounding me.

"Only in my depraved imagination. One thing remains constant." He climbs onto the end of the bed, crawling to where my legs are parted in invitation for him. "I'm always on my knees for you, love."

"The view is steamy."

"Couldn't agree more. You're so fucking wet for me." He brushes across the damp lace that betrays my arousal.

I try to squeeze my thighs together, but he's blocking my attempt. "Mhmm."

"We should ditch these, yeah?" Ridge doesn't wait for permission to peel off my underwear.

Not that I expect him to. I've already waved the green flag.

Before adding the crumpled bundle to the discard pile, he shoves the soaked section against his nose. His inhale is savage, like a hunter catching the scent of what he's about to chase. The act is crude and obscene and an extreme turn-on. My hips shift in urgency, the insistent ache becoming more demanding.

He lowers to the gap between my splayed limbs, his broad

shoulders spreading me wider. His tongue traces the outer edge of my center. Close, but more of a tease. I buck upward and he chuckles.

"Impatient?"

"Yes," I admit.

That's all I have to say. His lips seal around my clit with purpose. The suction is forceful, as if he's trying to slurp through a straw. It's strong enough to curl my toes.

Tingles erupt and I arch against the friction. He swipes that sensitive spot at a pace meant to send me over the edge. I squeal as pleasure immediately spreads outward. The pressure builds, growing in magnitude until I can't contain it a moment longer.

"Oh, yes. There! I'm gonna—" My sentence cuts off on a wail as I climax.

A spasm rocks my core, searing through my veins like electric shocks. Those zaps heighten the bliss already crashing over me. When the static rush subsides, an quiet buzz sweeps in.

"Fucking exquisite." He licks me from his lips.

"Gosh," I wheeze. "You're really good at that."

"It comes easy when I'm passionate about the end result."

"One of these days, you'll let me return the favor."

"We'll see."

I huff. "That's just a polite no."

"Do you want to have sex?" He points from his penis to my vagina.

The gesture is a tad mesmerizing. "Uh-huh."

"Then let's focus on that." Ridge shifts to hover over me, keeping his weight balanced on a bent elbow. His eyes search mine. "You sure about this?"

"Positive." To prove my point, I wiggle and rotate sideways to remove my bra.

His gaze lowers to my breasts. His swallow is thick. "We can wait."

"Nope, I'm ready. Please."

"No need to beg, sweetness. Although I do love when you ask nicely." His grin would incinerate my panties if they weren't already stripped from me.

Ridge kicks off his boxers and then we're naked. Together. I inhale sharply when his arousal comes in contact with mine. A gentle rock from his pelvis has him gliding along my slick center.

"Do you want to be on top?"

"Absolutely not," I blurt. The thought is too intimidating, especially my first time.

"I've got you, love. Let me grab a condom."

"Why?"

His lips quirk into a wolfish grin. "For protection."

"Oh, we're already protected. I'm on the pill."

Ridge goes still. "Did you do that for me?"

"I didn't want anything between us," I murmur. "Even a thin layer of latex."

"Fuuuuuck, sweetness. Not sure what I did to deserve you." He's made a similar comment before.

The significance pulses through my bloodstream while I cradle his cheek. "You heard me when nobody else would listen."

"I was just waiting for you to speak the words that are mine," he breathes. It seems like he's about to join us as one but pauses. "Are you worried about STDs?"

"Should I be?" The doctor mentioned something about those at my appointment.

"Nah, my dick is practically a monk. Definitely cleaner than my mind."

"Me too. Obviously. Other than a variation in anatomy." I laugh to myself, which nudges him against me.

His eyes slide shut for a moment. "Not gonna last long. I've never gone without."

"Another first?"

"Saved for you."

I'm nodding too fast, trying to stave off the threat of tears. "Ready when you are, boyfriend."

His forehead lowers to mine. "Don't be scared."

"I'm not. This is natural. My body will stretch for you." Even if that's to my maximum limits.

"We've prepared for this. Just relax. I'll only feed you a few inches at first." Ridge shifts until I can feel him aligned at the most intimate part of me.

"Is it going to hurt?" Pain already leeches from my voice.

"Not if I do it right, which is why I'm not gonna pop your cherry quite yet. This is just an introduction for much more to come. We'll get loosened up first." He could be talking in a foreign language and I'd be less confused.

But that's mostly due to the chaotic mush that is my brain right now.

I circle one arm around his middle, gripping on for a sense of stability. My other palm rests on his shoulder. In return, Ridge cups my jaw. I tilt into the caress and he smiles down at me. His thumb smooths along the heat flaring in my cheek. The touch is tender and reverent, as if I'm precious. This man makes me feel that way in this moment and every other we've spent together.

Our eyes remain fastened as he enters me. Just his tip slips in at first. There's pressure, but it's like when he fingers me or uses a vibrating toy. His pace is careful and patient. When he sinks a bit deeper, that thick presence doubles. I part my mouth on a silent gasp. My core clenches, struggling to accept him.

"Relax for me, sweetness."

I nod while blowing out a long breath. The strain in my

middle decreases to accommodate him. Between that and my arousal, he's able to slide in a little more. The familiar sensations become a dull sting when his girth forces me to stretch wider. I don't move, not wanting to interfere. His wild gaze searches mine. Whatever he sees halts his forward motion. The pause allows me to adjust. After several beats, the slight discomfort fades.

"There we go," he rasps.

His solid force retreats but immediately glides in again. From there, a shallow in and out starts. He doesn't go beyond his previous stopping point. The push and pull is rhythmic, lulling me into false complacency. Waves of pleasure roll through me, but it's too soon to be content.

The arm holding Ridge's weight off me trembles. That guides my concentration to the rigid flex throughout his entire form. He's restraining himself. There's so much more he wants from this.

"Give me all of you," I whisper against his lips.

He shakes his head. "Tell me to come."

"You can just do that? On command?"

"If you demand it. Besides, I'm wound tighter than tape on a hockey stick."

I analyze the comparison, but my attention strays when he gives another pump. "Come for me." A term of endearment appears in my mind and I add, "My future husband."

That's the trigger he needed. He shudders, a groan spilling from his lips. The tension seems to escape him as well. There's a noticeable increase in wetness where we're joined.

We rest at that breaking point for a minute. His labored breaths paint my mouth in pleasure. I sip at the passion he releases, eager for more.

Ridge pulls out and sits back on his heels, focused on what I can only assume is a mess between my thighs. "Fuck, sweetness. Look at you drenched in me."

I squirm under his intimate scrutiny. "Why did you leave me? Don't stop."

"Let me play for a second. I don't want you to lose any." His fingers are there, gently probing.

A whine escapes my parched throat when I feel him slide inside of me. I realize he's pushing his semen back into me. It's totally on-brand for him. My face heats at the realization that I love his obsessive side. More than I should admit.

Ridge slathers the combination of our essence on his length, which is still very erect. If I hadn't witnessed the evidence of his climax, I'd be likely to believe he hadn't finished. Those thoughts flee as he reclaims his previous position over me.

His dick nudges my opening. "This might hurt, but just try to relax. Let me take care of you. I'll make sure this is good for you once the worst is done."

My eyes widen. "What're you gonna do to me?"

"Make you mine."

Before I can fully process the words, Ridge drives himself into me. Pain pinches from where he breaks through my virginity. The burn blazes and spreads, but I ignore the sharp twinge. That was the final barrier between us.

He slams forward until his shaft is buried inside of me. There's nowhere left to go. The thick length breeches depths that were previously untried. I'm full of him. Stretched and claimed and no longer innocent. I love the upgrade.

His breathing is harsh as he dips to press our foreheads together. "Are you okay?"

I nod. "This is already more special than I expected. Better in every conceivable sense."

"How do you feel?"

"Complete," I sigh.

A rumble rolls through him. "Yeah, sweetness. You took a broken man and made him whole."

Emotion blurs my vision. I crane my neck until our lips connect. His tongue swipes out to meet mine. We get lost in the exchange as our bodies join in the most natural sense.

My tears drip onto his skin, bringing us impossibly closer. "I didn't feel like I belonged or had a home until you."

"This is us, love." He kisses the next droplet that escapes. "And see? We fit."

I wince when he rocks slightly. But that painful jab evaporates almost immediately. Pride bursts from my chest. I've taken every inch of him. My inner muscles squeeze in victory.

Ridge groans. "Damn, you're with me in this madness."

"Wouldn't be anywhere else," I confirm.

After that, he begins to move. He resumes his motions from earlier. Except now, his strokes are longer and more powerful. Ridge seats himself deep within me on every fluent entry.

"You're tight and wet for me," he praises.

"Uh-huh." It's undeniable. I'm slick to the point it's excessive.

"Gonna make me come again. Sooner than I planned." He chuckles as if that idea is amusing.

The sound of our shared arousal is obscene. Every steady slap from our bodies merging is a countdown to climax. Each beat fills me with more of him until I can no longer identify us as individuals.

The ache fades, replaced by a muted throb. That pulse matches the excitement thundering in my chest. Pressure and comfort battle for recognition. The mixture heightens my need. I can't fathom losing this connection. Or how I survived so long without him.

Ridge's movements are fluid and steady. I slant my hips to greet his timed thrusts. A muffled curse rips from his clenched jaw. My grin reveals the satisfaction thrumming through me.

His face dips into the curve of my neck. He nibbles on

the sensitive flesh there until traveling lower. When he latches onto my nipple, I bend to his will. He smiles against my breast while suckling me.

Tingles soon emerge from my lower belly. The telltale cue has me grinding against him, chasing the relief. His hand snakes down between us. My eyes flutter when he thumbs my clit. An onslaught of stimulation crashes over me.

"Please," I whimper.

"Such a good girl. Do you wanna come?"

"Yes, yes, yes."

A flick from his thumb shoots me to the stars. At the last moment, I lift my legs and lock my ankles against his butt. I want to cage him in me. Deep and hard and permanent. The shift in angle shoves him straight down to the hilt.

Ridge bellows his release. I tip over the peak beside him. Pleasure floods my veins and I'm thrashing against the force. His motions become disjointed and jerky as he erupts. My thighs spread to allow him to give me more. Every ounce belongs to me.

Our erratic frenzy calms as we float in orgasmic bliss. Ridge lowers himself to rest on me. His burly weight is still mostly balanced to the side, otherwise I'd be crushed to dust.

We remain like that while lounging in the afterglow. There's no rush to move or separate. My fingers rake through his damp hair while he draws patterns into my skin.

"I love you, sweetness."

My heart soars, swatting through the fog. "Really?"

"Thought it was obvious," he laughs.

"Doesn't hurt to hear it, boyfriend." I kiss the tip of his nose. "I love you too."

"You better."

It's my turn to giggle. "Or what?"

"I'd be forced to take more romantic measures."

Flutters erupt in a flurry. "I'm not sure I could handle that."

"We'll see," he teases.

"But I love you already." The complaint is weaker than tissue paper.

"How much?"

"To infinity," I announce.

"And beyond?" Amusement sparkles in his eyes.

I shrug. "One of the only movies I was allowed to watch as a kid."

He nuzzles into me. "My deprived sweetness."

"Not anymore, thanks to you."

"Are you sore?" He works his hips along mine.

An unmistakable stab slices through my core. "Maybe a little."

"How does a bath sound?" Ridge slowly removes himself from me.

I flinch at the loss, but my vagina is grateful. "Will you join me?"

He rises onto a crooked elbow. "Whatever you want."

"You're in the mood to spoil me?"

"Always. I'll wash your hair and pamper your properly." He dips down for a kiss.

"In that case, a soak would be lovely."

"Consider it done, love."

I find myself contemplating a frequent curiosity. "How did I manage to capture your devotion?"

"Took control of your destiny." He makes it sound so simple.

"That hardly answers my question. You could have anyone."

"Only want you, love." Ridge's nose drifts along the slope of my jaw. "Have I thanked you lately?"

My brain sputters. "For what?"

"Everything."

"That's not very specific," I quip.

"No? It encompasses my debt to you."

Laughter bursts from me in a hysterical stream. "Don't be ridiculous. You definitely don't owe me. Not a single thing."

"That's where you're wrong. I was hollow without you, existing without purpose. That day I first saw you changed my entire outlook. I suddenly had a vision for a future worth living. You've taught me how to dream bigger. Strive for better. Trust openly. Honor always. Love unconditionally. Put someone's needs above my own. I'm this man you believe can have anyone, but I'd be nothing without you. Isn't that the value of everything?"

"Oh," I breathe.

Ridge chuckles. "There we go, sweetness. Bathe in my gratitude while I prepare your bubbles. That'll get me one step closer to evening the score."

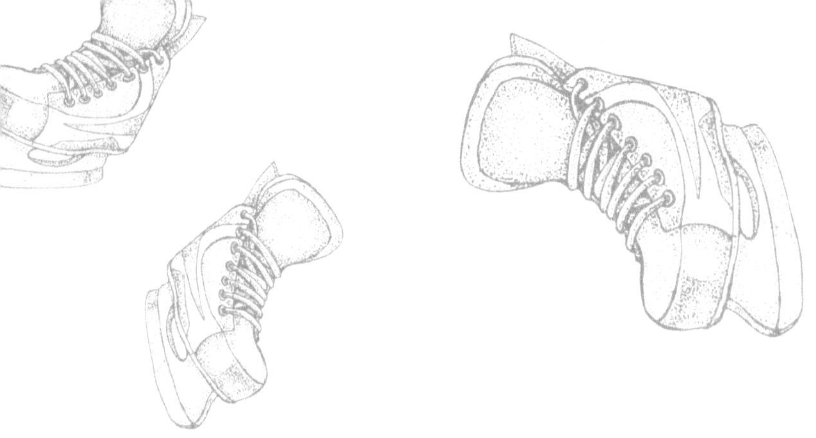

CHAPTER TWENTY-EIGHT

Ridge

THE WARMTH TUCKED TIGHT AGAINST MY FRONT shifts in a suggestive manner to rouse me from a peaceful slumber. My morning wood twitches on impact. Callie moans, pressing her ass into me even harder. Our cuddles are the best part of waking up.

"Fuck, sweetness." My palm curls around her hip, roaming to splay flat over her stomach. I use that hold to lock us together. "Still dreaming?"

She hums, but doesn't answer otherwise.

"Is my cock in your pussy? Am I thrusting balls deep? I bet you're wet for me."

"Such a romantic," Callie mumbles.

I grind forward, her crack cradling my dick. "You love me."

She squirms back into my advance. "I do."

"This jersey is a cockblock." I pluck at the thick fabric concealing my easy access.

"Since when?" Her eyes remain shut, but she smiles into the pillow. "It's more of an aphrodisiac."

"Only if I can strip you of it." I drift my hand downward to slip under the hem and cup her bare center.

Callie hisses. "My vagina hurts."

"Say less, love." My touch returns to above her waist. "We'll do a low-strain activity today."

She peels one eyelid open when I hover the envelope within reach. Excitement brightens her features as she flings into an upright position. "Our next date. What could it be?"

"Only one way to find out." I pass it over, allowing her to do the honors.

Her nail breaks the seal and she whips out the paper. "Visit Beaver Rush."

I chuckle. "Excellent choice."

"As if there's another option. Is this an actual place or just code for you having breakfast in bed?" She points between her legs.

"My naughty girl catches on quick, but we'll give your pussy the rest she deserves." I stretch beside her, several joints popping in the process. "Beaver Rush is a park just down the road. It's somewhat of a hidden treasure, like the G-spot. Only those willing to work for it will get to enjoy the benefits."

Callie giggles. "You have a special way with words."

"It's part of my appeal." I wink. "Get dressed and we'll go."

She rolls off the mattresses like a limber gymnast. "Yes, sir."

A rumble rises from my chest. "Or maybe we should stay here."

"Nope, too late." Her sexy ass sways toward the bathroom.

The shower turns on a moment later, which has me bolting into action. I knock on the closed door with my knuckle. "Need a hand?"

"I think I can manage," she calls over the noise.

"Then how about a penis?"

"In my mouth?"

I glance down. My cock is practically begging for the

opportunity, tenting my boxers to campsite proportions. "It's impossible to deny you."

"Then don't."

"Only if you let me eat you in return. Sixty-nine?"

The knob turns and her flushed face appears through a small crack. Steam billows behind her. "My lady bits are on a hiatus."

"Raincheck?"

Her gaze rakes over my mostly naked form, landing on my insistent dick. She licks her lips. "Absolutely."

I step back from temptation before lust replaces logic. "If you start moaning my name, I can't be held responsible for what happens next."

"Is that a promise?"

My thumb gets clamped between my teeth to stave off a growl. "Dirty girl. Clean yourself up and we'll be on our way."

She winks before disappearing from sight. I throw on clothes and force myself out of the bedroom. If I get a look at her dripping wet, all bets are off. Those thoughts cloud my mind as I aimlessly wander around the house. Instinct leads me to the kitchen where I pack a cooler. Soon enough, footsteps come from down the hallway.

"Ready," Callie announces.

My focus feasts on her as she approaches. A flowy dress tries to hide her figure, but I can easily map every curve. I blindly grab for the keys on the counter and meet her in the foyer. "Stunning as always, sweetness."

She tilts her chin in invitation. "Thanks, boyfriend."

I give her the kiss she seeks. "Love you."

Her sigh puffs against my lips. "I love you more."

A disgruntled scoff rips from me. "Don't start with that. It's not a competition, at least not one you can win."

She pouts while snagging her purse and camera from the hutch. "But you owe me."

"Which is why I love you the most." I escort her outside, pausing while the automatic lock engages.

"I see what you did there," she scolds half-heartedly.

"To be fair, I warned you."

Callie's laughter floats to the cloudless sky. Sunlight dances across her upturned features and I almost trip over my own feet. This woman has no clue how much power she wields over me.

With a palm notched at the base of her spine, I guide her to the truck. She snuggles against me along the way. I gobble the affection as usual, planting several kisses on her forehead. Once she's situated and buckled, I round the hood and get settled behind the wheel. Her hand is clasped protectively in mine as I turn onto the street.

"This is a scenic route," she notes while admiring the lush landscape.

My attention veers between her and the nonexistent traffic. "Have you ever thought about learning to drive?"

She peeks over at me. "It holds appeal, but you're a wonderful chauffeur."

"I don't mind taking you wherever you need to go."

"Precisely," she chirps. "I've become somewhat of a passenger princess."

"The offer stands if you ever want a private lesson," I hint.

"Can I sit on your lap? You can work the pedals while I steer." She leans across the console as if she's about to hop over.

The tires squeal when I swerve into the opposite lane before getting back on track. "Keep it together, woman. We don't wanna crash."

"Just testing your restraint."

"I think we've determined it's nonexistent whenever you're involved."

She squeezes my fingers that are linked with hers. "Your reaction time is stellar too."

"Which includes a safe arrival." I pull into the empty lot. "That was quick."

"Which is favorable in this situation." Not sure how much longer I could tolerate her intoxicating scent without unzipping my fly.

Callie waits patiently for me to open her door. A dreamy smile quirks her lips as she allows me to help her down from the cab. I remember to grab the snacks at the last second, and then we're wandering along the gravel path.

The unmistakable sound of rushing water increases our pace. A break in the trees widens into a grassy expanse. At the edge is a rocky cliff that drops off into the water far below. Across the river is another bluff. That's where the waterfall cascades down in an endless stream.

"Wow." Callie's breathless response is aimed straight ahead.

"Do you approve?"

She nods while shuffling forward. "You pick the best locations."

My focus follows hers. I've stood in this very spot on several occasions. It's served as an escape more than anything.

Experiencing the natural wonder through her perspective is striking. There are suddenly new sights to see. Purpose and meaning lingers on every surface. Fuck, I'm getting sentimental about Beaver Rush of all places.

"What do you think?" I bring us to a stop where the vantage point delivers from every angle.

"Remember our first kiss?"

"How could I forget?"

She spreads her arms out, letting the wind swirl around her. I move behind her to mirror the pose. Our fingers skim and connect.

"That's how this is. We're free to fly and soar and reach new heights," she says.

I recall her using a similar line on the darkened porch all those nights ago. "Can I copy your answer?"

She giggles. "Yours was way better."

"Nah, you've proven to conquer any challenge. Me included."

Her eyes find mine. "As if you made it hard for me."

"No?" I bump my cock into her ass.

"Other than your happy penis."

I snort. "Happy penis?"

"That sounds like happiness," she laughs.

The words repeat in my head. "Very fitting."

"We do fit together quite snugly." She rubs along my length with precision.

"Sweetness," I rumble against the blush heating her cheek.

"Oh, right. Ummm… the view is beautiful. There's something calming about rushing water. I'm very relaxed." Callie inhales slowly, allowing her eyes to flutter closed.

"Can we take a picture?"

Her startled gaze meets mine. "You're asking me?"

"Just seems like a moment worth capturing." Along with all the others.

She bends to retrieve the Instax. "Where should we pose?"

I turn until the waterfall is crashing behind us. "This is what Beaver Rush is known for."

"Perfect." Callie tucks herself tight against me and lifts the camera.

My chin rests on her shoulder while I stare at the lens. I see her peeking at me from the corner of her eye. She returns her focus ahead to snap the shot. At the last second, I dip to press a kiss to her cheek.

"Gah," she complains as the film spits out. "Thought I had you."

"Can't make it too easy for you."

"One of these days, boyfriend." She wags her finger at me.

"I let you get that one of me in Roosters. Coming for you," I remind.

A sigh slips from her. "As I recall, I was coming for you that night."

"That's my dirty girl. Should we sit?" I lower to the ground and part my legs.

She doesn't hesitate to collapse in the spot I created for her. I support my weight on one arm, circling the other around her. She accepts the offer to recline against me. We're quiet for a moment, but I can hear her curiosity burning.

After another minute, her gaze seeks mine again. "What're you thinking about?"

I reach for her left hand, lifting until her ring finger brushes my mouth. "Can't wait to marry you."

"Me?" Her pitch reaches the tallest branches above our heads.

"Do you see another love of my life nearby?"

She elbows me, but there's no punch behind it. "That's just very… shocking."

"And tattooing your name on my chest isn't?"

"Well…"

"How about calling you my future wife?"

"Yes?"

I chuckle at her apparent confusion. "Didn't you refer to me as your future husband last night?"

Callie doesn't bother denying what we both heard loud and clear. "I'm worried something will go wrong. This seems too perfect."

"That sort of thinking will lead to unnecessary doubt."

Her lips squish into a pucker meant to tease. "Maybe."

My hold on her tightens. "Fate is on our side. There are no guarantees. We take what we're given and be thankful. I'll never take the gift of you for granted."

Moisture gathers in her eyes. "Gosh, is this a fairytale?"

I press my forehead to hers. "One of those spicy books you're reading is probably more accurate."

"Sexy romance," she muses. "They end in happily ever after too."

"The brooding hero can't believe his luck when the gorgeous virgin deems him worthy of vigorously claiming her before they stroll off into the sunset. Couldn't write our story better myself."

Her thighs visibly clench, followed by a loud grumble from her stomach. She covers the noise with a palm. "Yikes. Way to spoil the mood."

"I need to feed you."

She scoots backward until her ass once again cradles my cock. "What's on the menu?"

My fingers clench on her hip. "Naughty girl. Real food."

She hums. "Worth a shot."

"I'll let you have your way with me soon enough."

"But in the meantime?" Suggestion trickles from her tone.

"Just let me hold you close."

Callie smiles, snuggling into my embrace. "Only if you promise to never let go."

"That's a deal I'll never refuse, love."

CHAPTER TWENTY-NINE

Callie

WOBBLE AGAIN, NEARLY FALLING ON MY BUTT. THE ache from my last tumble still hurts. "This is hard."

"That's what she said," Ridge jokes.

My shoulders lift in a shrug, which sets me off balance and I slip. "I did say that."

He's at my side instantly to offer assistance. "Damn, you're too cute. Sexy as fuck in skates too."

"Um, thanks?" I pinwheel while attempting to gain any sense of traction. "A baby deer is more graceful."

And that makes one of us.

Ridge's movements are effortless. He might as well be a shark slicing across water. Other than the fact we're on ice and it's freezing. The comparison stands.

I don't, nearly capsizing for the fourteenth time in the same amount of minutes. "Does beginner's luck not exist in this sport?"

"Use the toe pick."

"You don't need one," I mumble.

"Sweetness," he chuckles. "Hockey blades don't have a

pick. I got you figure skates because they're easier to learn in. More stability."

I huff. "Tell that to my sore bottom."

Ridge cuts across the glassy space separating us, braking to a halt so fast that ice shavings fly in every direction. "Need me to rub it for you?"

My brain sputters while trying to process his smooth moves. "You're really hot."

"Do my skills impress you?" He glides backward without concern.

Warmth gathers and spreads from my lower belly. "Mhmm."

"Want me to take you for another spin?" He slides to a stop in front of me and holds out his hands.

The offer is tempting, and would make this process much easier. It would also contradict my earlier desire for independence. I stubbornly told him I wanted to try on my own. What a foolish decision.

"How did I get myself into this situation?" But the question is strictly rhetorical.

The final envelope contained a vague statement about playing hockey. For a gullible moment, I thought we were going to watch another game. As it turns out, we're providing entertainment for ourselves. Mostly Ridge. Unless this is meant to be a comedic performance. At least no one else is in attendance since this is a private arena his friend owns.

Ridge's frown is a punch to the stomach. "You're not having fun?"

My lack of talent manages to propel me straight into his arms. "I love you."

"Love you, and your knack for deflections." He supports my clumsy efforts without fail. "Are you about done?"

"How about an intermission? I recall something about hot chocolate."

A twinkle gleams from the green in his eyes. He digs in his pocket and whips out a puck. "How about a quick game first?"

I rock my hips into his. "And here I thought you were excited to see me."

His scowl scolds my attempt at humor. "You'll get frostbite on your ass if you're not careful."

"How—?"

"I'll start by stripping you from this sorry excuse for pants." Ridge pinches at the flimsy material of my leggings.

"You told me to be comfortable."

"Might as well go naked for all the padding these offer. No wonder you're sore."

"Sorry I didn't dress properly for an occasion I've never attended before." Sarcasm is becoming second nature for me.

"You can make it up to me later… if you win," he adds ominously.

Intrigue narrows my eyes. "Tell me more."

Ridge reaches over the boards and grabs a hockey stick. "This is for you."

I wrap my fingers around the proffered end that has a taped section. I clutch it awkwardly, testing the weight as I try to swing it back and forth. It's heavier than I predicted and barely moves. "Where's yours?"

"I don't need one."

We're in motion before I can question him. It requires zero labor for him to pull me across the rink. He puts me no more than three feet from a net and drops the puck in front of my stick. I'm trying to solve this riddle as he backs himself into the goalie position.

Ridge squats. "Take your best shot, sweetness."

My laughter echoes off the rafters. Even at this

distance, my chances aren't awesome. "You think I'll be able to score on you?"

"Won't know until you try."

"What happens if I get a goal?"

"You can have whatever you want." A smolder ignites in his gaze.

I'm certain mine reflects a similar heat. "Anything?"

He nods. "Pick your prize."

Determination digs my toe pick into the ice. I try to aim, but I doubt it will make a difference. My motions lack finesse and speed. Despite the odds, the puck glides straight into the net. The only sound is my heartbeat drumming to the tune of disbelief.

"Not fair. You didn't block it!" I finally sputter.

Ridge's smirk is holding secrets. "I wanted you to win."

"And why is that?"

"Oh, I have a hunch what you choose will benefit both of us." His stare hasn't left me. "What'll it be?"

"You," I say.

He points to himself. "Me?"

"I want you," I clarify.

"You already have me. Completely. Forever."

"Not completely."

He chuckles. "I beg to differ."

Warmth blazes in my cheeks regardless of the chill in here. "You haven't let me…"

Ridge lowers his gaze to where mine has settled. "What's that, sweetness?"

"Um, I want to…" Nerves muffle my request.

"Say it," he urges.

"Put your penis in my mouth," I blurt.

He rolls his lips between his teeth, most likely trying not to laugh. "You wanna suck my cock?"

I nod as my face flames. "Uh-huh."

Ridge slides forward. "Give me a blowjob?"

"Yes," I breathe.

In a fluid maneuver, he scoops me off my skates and rushes to an opening in the boards. "Want a private tour of the locker room? It's not much, but the floor is padded."

"How can I resist an offer like that?" I don't, obviously.

He slams through a door and puts me down. I've barely regained my equilibrium when he lowers to undo my laces. Relief sighs from me once I'm freed from the torture devices. Ridge shoots me a grin before removing his own. While he does that, I take a moment to examine where we are.

The space is what I expect. Two walls have storage stalls. A bench occupies another. Rows of hooks are drilled above, available to hang whatever equipment players strip off. The final side is occupied by a large shower. A sterile scent hangs heavy in the air.

I turn in a slow circle. "Smells... clean."

Ridge snorts. "Luke is very particular when it comes to this facility."

"And he won't mind that we're about to..." I still can't get the words out.

His mouth slants into a wolfish smile. "Defile each other?"

"This isn't about me." I gesture to a certain part of my anatomy.

"We'll see." He unfastens his jeans, dropping the denim to mid-thigh.

My eyes widen at his erection that's practically waving for attention. "No boxers?"

"Nah, I chose to be optimistic." His bare butt meets the wood bench with a slap.

"That's going to leave a mark," I giggle.

"The imprint of my ass will give this place character." He twirls a thick roll of tape around his finger.

"Where did that come from?"

"My dirty mind." An efficient yank loosens a long strip from the spool. "I might be out of the game, but I'll never forget how to wrap like a pro."

"Wound tighter than tape on a hockey stick," I recall.

His wink caresses my arousal until I'm squirming. "The same applies in this instance. It's gonna come in handy."

I watch his precise movements. "What're you doing?"

"Restraining myself." The creation in his palms is beginning to resemble a pair of cuffs with a long strand attaching them.

My mouth drops. "Why?"

"I want you to feel safe. Secure and in control," he adds.

Confusion pinches my expression. "You've given me those luxuries from the start."

"Extra precaution. Just humor me."

I swallow any additional rebukes. Ridge slips the connected binds on his wrists. While reclining against the wall, he stretches overhead to loop the makeshift rope onto a hook. His biceps replicate the appearance of chiseled boulders in this suspended pose. A slight tug from him tests the effectiveness.

My brow quirks. I'm not delusional enough to assume this contraption can actually contain him. His strength could easily snap the middle. It's the implied significance behind the gesture that counts.

Satisfaction is a sharp jerk of his head. "All right, sweetness. Have your way with me."

"Uh, okay." I scoot forward to accept my prize. Uncertainty hitches my approach and I stumble while kneeling in the gap between his legs.

His smile is reassuring. "Any touch you give will blow me away. You can't go wrong."

"Doubt it." I gulp at the saliva pooling in my mouth.

The size of him from this angle is intimidating. "Think of my cock as a huge piece of hard candy. Kiss, lick, suck… maybe a few strokes from your fist."

My fingers flex and I curl them around his base. "I can do that."

"There we go," he groans. "Do whatever you want to me. It won't take much. The memory of you tightly laced in skates really does it for me. Don't even get me started on how you gripped that stick."

"Got it." I rise slightly to hover my mouth over the crown of his penis. My eyes find his from under hooded lids. "Just relax for me, boyfriend."

His hands clench against the pliable shackles. "Damn, you're a natural."

A lollipop enters my thoughts and I swirl my tongue around his tip. There's a salty flavor that greets me. It's not unpleasant, which is a welcome surprise. I'm encouraged to seal my lips at the bottom of the flared top and add suction. Ridge jolts, shoving more of himself into my experimental descent.

"Shit, sorry." His retreat is a smooth glide that removes him almost entirely.

Rather than provide a verbal response, I repeat the motion of pushing him deep. His groan is a boost to my confidence. I try to take more of him, but his tip bumps the back of my throat. It's not even half of his generous size.

"Look at you," Ridge rasps. "Trying to devour me whole on your first try."

There's a tease in his tone. A challenge too. One I can aim to please after I've gained experience. My jaw is already complaining from the strain.

Before withdrawing, it seems wise to cover my teeth. His sigh might as well be a thumbs-up. I hollow my cheeks, sucking him deep again. He curses and a tremor racks his limbs.

"Shit, that's good." The vibration from his praise rumbles into me.

Slickness gathers between my thighs, but I ignore my needs. This is about getting him off. The reminder of my desired outcome emboldens me to increase my pace. Hesitancy fades and my rhythm becomes more fluid. Ridge jolts again. The bench squeaks beneath him. His reactions are a sure sign I'm doing something right.

"Not gonna last," he murmurs absently.

I smile around his girth on my next downward glide. His chuckle is pure satisfaction. In reply, my tongue flattens against the protruding vein that snakes along the underside of his manhood. Saliva acts as a natural lubricant. My grip is slippery as I roll my wrist to stroke him. The combination of my hand and mouth seems to really excite him.

A tremble rocks through him as he adjusts on the seat. I pump him faster, the slick friction fueling my goal. More expletives spill from his aroused state. He's fighting with himself not to move.

"Fuuuuuuck, I'm gonna come."

I moan my approval, almost missing the clank of metal knocking into a solid surface. My gaze wanders to where the hook dangles from a scrap of broken drywall. Ridge grunts while breaking the cuffs in two. He lunges for me, and I'm suddenly detached from his shaft. Before I can protest, Ridge is rearranging our position.

He sprawls flat on the floor while guiding me to straddle his lap. My vision blurs and I belatedly realize he set me on him backward. The switch puts my face in direct proximity to his penis, which serves the original purpose. It doesn't explain why he encouraged the shift.

That is until he rips the fabric directly over my sex. The seam of my leggings doesn't stand a chance. My panties suffer a similar fate. Cool air kisses my slick arousal as the shredded material gapes wide open.

Ridge groans. "Need your pussy in my mouth."

I'm not about to argue, especially when his exhale spears into me. He grips my hips seconds before his tongue begins lashing my clit. Heat immediately floods me, spreading out in a fiery wave. My body sags forward and I grasp onto his length like an anchor. Through the lust stealing my focus, I manage to get my lips around his flared tip.

We operate in this tandem formation to strive for release. Ridge isn't taking it easy on me. His lips latch onto my sensitive bud and the pressure is exquisite torture. I double my speed, bobbing while sucking him as hard as possible. It's almost like a competition. One I'm certain not to win.

On cue, tingles build in my lower belly. I mewl around his length. The intensity forces me to pause my attempts to win this round. To be fair, it's mostly his fault.

The blame flings from focus as my orgasm strikes in the next second. I shatter with a muffled cry, my mouth still stuffed full. Relief explodes like a balm to cool the feverish rush. Ridge hums, the vibrations sending me to new heights. Quakes ripple through me while I ride the peak.

When the quivers fade and I regain functional mobility, I resume my methods to deliver him pleasure. My hand strokes his lower half while I suckle his tip. Ridge thrusts softly against my onslaught. His face is still buried in my core, but that doesn't stop him from urging me on.

I swirl my tongue rapidly, which earns me a fresh round of garbled compliments. There's a noticeable pulse in his penis. It appears as if his balls are shrinking. Maybe these are signs he's close.

Ridge's palms drift across my lower back in a tender caress. "Gonna swallow?"

My throat works on reflex and I nod. That must be the answer he was waiting for. Seconds later he erupts in my mouth. A salty burst announces his release has arrived. I quickly gulp in order to catch it all. The taste is a tad bitter, but not bad. My tongue takes several laps along his tip before I finish the job.

I straighten from his lap while dabbing at my lips. There's a definite swell lingering there, evidence of my labors. The harsh breathing behind me reveals my boyfriend has exerted himself as well. In a graceless dismount, I collapse in a heap beside him.

Ridge is staring at the ceiling. There's a dazed gleam in his eye. I'm sure my gaze is twinkling with stars and hearts. The blissful calm settling over me suggests as much.

After several minutes of floating in mutual relaxation, I decide to creep on the silence. "Was my blowjob okay?"

Ridge blinks, a bit of the haze clearing. "Might not recover."

My pulse skips to a happy beat. "I did well?"

He makes a gruff sound. "You literally blew my mind. I'm... speechless."

A giggle peals from me. "Another victory, and so soon."

"Fuck, sweetness." Ridge scrubs over his face. "If that's your choice of a reward, I'll gladly lose. Score on me whenever you want a rematch."

"But you flipped the scene on me," I chide.

"Are you complaining about me cashing in that raincheck?"

I shake my head. "Your friend might. His wall is busted."

"He'll get over it. Me on the other hand?" He touches my cheek with a bent knuckle. "I'm altered to the very foundation of my existence."

"Uh-oh, that sounds serious."

"It sure is." He sneaks an arm under my shoulders and tugs until I'm acting as his personal blanket. "Good thing you're already stuck with me."

"Permanently?"

A rumbles rises off his chest. "And then some."

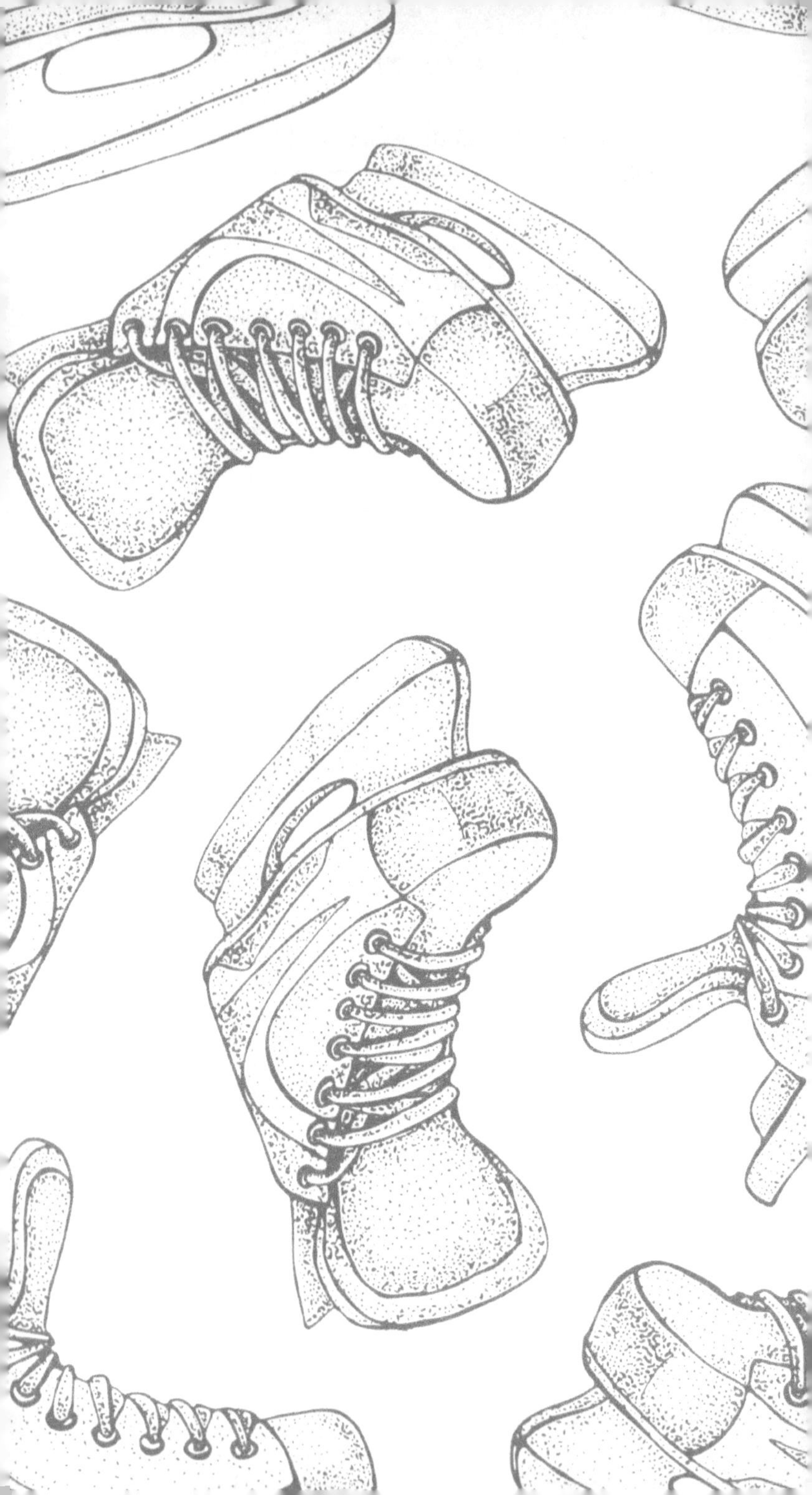

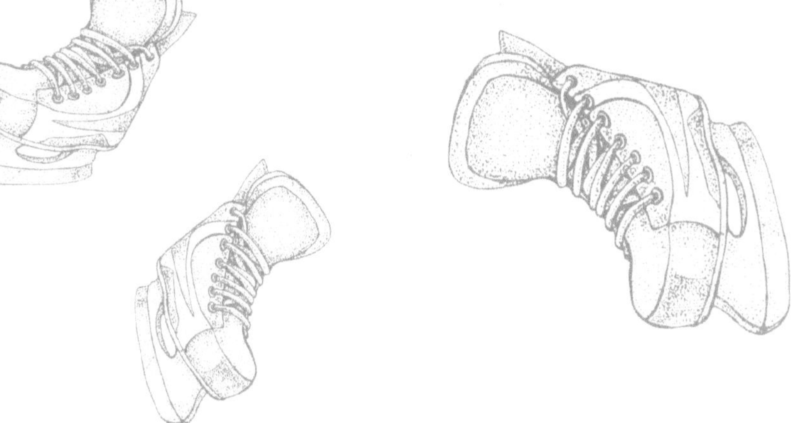

CHAPTER THIRTY

Ridge

"Did you miss us?" Callie coos at the pup wiggling on her lap. "We missed you every single second."

I grunt. "Don't lie to the guy. You were preoccupied for most of the weekend. If not, I didn't do it right."

She shivers and sends me a sly glance. "You did me right, boyfriend."

My chest expands while I idle at a stoplight. "That's what I thought."

"But our good boy needs reassurance that we still love him." Her voice returns to the pitch reserved for babies. "We'll never leave you for too long. No, we won't. And when we take another vacation, maybe you can come with. If not, Sydney will gladly watch you. She did such a great job. Didn't she?"

Walter yips and bathes her face in sloppy kisses. The spoiled dog looks extremely confident in his pampered state. I'm certain he's aware that we're his forever home. Especially since rules are already bending in his favor. He usually isn't allowed in the front seat while I'm driving, but the distance from Jake's garage to our house is just a short ride. Nothing too eventful happens on this stretch.

"Stop!" Callie's screech is paired with her palm slapping against the passenger window.

I almost swerve into oncoming traffic. "The fuck?"

"Pull over. Right now. Hurry. Please." Her punctuated statements are as close to a demand as she's ever given.

I'm quick to follow orders, finding an empty spot along the curb. Walter detects the change in mood, leaping into the backseat without a command. Callie is out of the truck the second I'm parked.

My rushed stride quickly eats the lead she gained on me while chasing… a person? Confusion muddles my thoughts until Callie touches a lady's shoulder. The stranger whirls, fright trembling her already shaken form. Recognition sparks in her troubled expression and she visibly relaxes.

"Mother," Callie exhales.

A broken sob rips from the older woman when she realizes her daughter is there. Her bottom lip trembles, drawing my focus to a bloodied split in the middle. There are faded bruises on her cheek as well. Those are the only wounds I can see. The haunted look in her eyes is most likely from injuries that go far beneath the surface.

Callie's mother collapses forward into her daughter's open arms. They embrace as shared relief and sorrow shudder between them. The contact is obviously long overdue.

"How is this possible?" Callie's voice cracks over the disbelief.

Her mom doesn't answer. She quietly basks in the comfort her daughter's hug provides.

Callie rubs a palm down her back. "You're here. That's all that matters."

And that's an undeniable truth. It's obvious this woman is seeking refuge. I'm not a gambler, but I'd bet my fortune she wasn't granted permission to leave the compound. Against the odds, she managed to escape. Much like her daughter.

Emotion quakes through their bond as they sway together.

Callie's eyes squeeze shut, spilling tears down her face too. The sight physically pains me but I remain on the sidelines.

I'm not alone in my place on the outside looking in. What's meant to be a private moment is becoming a public display.

A crowd is gathering to witness their reunion. Rumors will soon follow. I highly doubt either will be comfortable with that.

"Sweetness, we should get her away from prying eyes." I motion to the busy street and nosy pedestrians.

Her watery gaze finds mine as she straightens. "Yes, good idea. Come on, Mama."

But her mother is stumbling backward, away from me. Her fretful motions and unblinking stare reflect years of torment I wouldn't wish on many. Only the ones responsible for creating this fear deserve such punishment.

I hold out my palms in an attempt to appear harmless. The horrors she's been dealt probably make my efforts futile. To prove that assumption, she shrinks into herself as if wishing to be invisible.

Callie is there, crouching to console her. "Mother, be calm. Ridge is safe. I promise."

The assurance from her child, most likely the only soul she trusts, slices through the terror. The older woman rises to her defeated height and nods. She allows Callie to guide her to my truck where they climb into the backseat.

I paste on a signature scowl to alert the onlookers to fuck off. Most scatter like the pests they are. That doesn't stop several others from whispering as they flee.

"Fucking vultures," I spit.

My boots smash into the concrete as I stalk to the driver's side and get behind the wheel. A glance in the rearview mirror reveals Callie clutching tight to her mother. Walter has his head on the older woman's lap, providing his own form of moral support. The battered survivor is still crying, but she's trying to muffle the upset. More than likely for my benefit. It serves to remind me of the insecurities Callie still drags around like a shackle she can't escape.

"Mother," Callie whispers. "What happened?"

Strained silence is the only response. I catch her mother's gaze for less than a blink before hers lowers to the floor. It's an ingrained response, one I'm familiar with. Callie relied on the same avoidance to protect herself.

Not long ago, my love was stuck in this petrified state. Similar defense mechanisms echo from her mother's mannerisms. It's no surprise she passed the knowledge to her daughter. But damn, Callie has shed many of those traits. She's flourished in the months we've been dating. I can't even picture how oppressed she was after first fleeing Billmoore.

The leather creaks under my unforgiving grip as I pull onto the road. If only a certain man's neck was the victim of my chokehold. He'll get what's coming for him. Either from my hand or a punishing force greater than me.

Callie brushes over the discolored skin on her mother's face. "Did Father do this?"

Her nod is subtle, but might as well be a scream.

Fury burns in my veins, and I barely manage to swallow a furious shout. "Fuck."

The older woman flinches, which stabs guilt directly into my gut.

"I'm sorry," I rasp. "Forgive me. I didn't mean to scare you."

She appears stricken by my apology.

Callie laughs, but the tune lacks her usual humor. "See, Mama. Ridge is a good man. We'll take you to our home. You can live with us."

"What's your name?" My question is aimed at Callie's mother, regardless if she's the one to respond.

"Althea," my brave girl replies. "She'll let you call her Thea once she trusts you."

"And that's a goal I'll strive for," I openly admit. "You'll be safe with us, Althea. We're family."

Fresh tears pool in her eyes and she exhales what I imagine is years of repressed panic.

That's a start I can appreciate. Eventually, her mother will deem me as a reliable source she can lean on. Then she'll accept my presence without terror blanching her expression. Until then, I need to respect the healing process.

The truck rolls to a stop after I pull into Callie's half of the driveway. I shut off the ignition and step out, opening the rear door for them. Althea skitters past me in a frightened blur. Callie's exit is far more composed.

Confidence exudes from her movements while she purposefully presses into me. Her soft grin is a luxury I bask in, which immediately snuffs the anger roiling through my veins. Those lips demand to be kissed and I eagerly bend to do just that.

"I'll be next door." My head tilts in the direction of the house I haven't slept in for weeks.

It hurts to separate myself from her, even for a single night, but this isn't about me. They need time alone. I'm more than capable of providing that at the very least.

Callie holds my stare for several moments as if there's something she's holding in. After another brief pause, she must decide it's better left unsaid. "I'll text you once I get her settled."

"Take your time, love." I plant a peck on her forehead.

Callie snuggles against my chest. Her inhale is long and deep, as if she's taking a piece with her. "Thank you, future husband. For everything."

CHAPTER THIRTY-ONE

Callie

WATCH AS MY MOTHER REACHES FOR HER MUG ON THE table. Her movements are still skittish after three hours in my home. She was never this scared when we lived together before. A year and a half has passed since we've seen each other. This jumpy version is a shadow of her former self. It's almost as if she expects someone to appear from thin air and crash down on us from the ceiling.

Steam rises from the tea I steeped for her, but the soothing blend has done little to ease her nerves. The spoon rattles against the rim when she takes a small drink. There's a persistent tremble in her hands that won't cease. It's concerning, much like this stressed silence between us. I wait with bated breath for her to speak.

Mother clears her throat, refusing to meet my imploring gaze. "I'm grateful you found me, but you're not safe if I stay here."

The implication behind her warning is evident. "Did you tell him where I went?"

Her eyes leap to mine for a brief moment. "Of course not."

"Then how will he find us?"

"He's dangerous," she says in response.

I shiver from the ice in her tone. "Ridge won't let anyone hurt us."

Mother hums to a disbelieving tune. "He's very… tall."

"My gentle giant," I muse.

"How did you meet him?"

"Through a mutual friend." Not that my boyfriend would willingly claim the bubbly blonde as such.

Mother takes another sip of her tea. "Harper?"

I smile at her impressive memory. "Yes. She's been vital to my… revival."

"Is that what we're calling this?" She motions to the luxury furnishings Ridge included in the rental.

My attention drifts to the fireplace. Framed photos from the past months sit on the mantel. "It feels that way. Like I've been given the gift of a second chance. You're on the road to recovery too."

Mother winces. "That makes me sound like a victim."

"You are, Mama. Were," I amend. "But control is yours now. You can choose how to move forward."

"I'm not sure I can believe that. Not yet at least."

"Give it time. You've just arrived."

She allows a lull to enter our conversation as her attention wanders. "You called him your future husband."

Heat stings my face. "I didn't mean for you to hear that."

Mother raises her brows. "It shames you?"

"Not at all. It's more of a… joke between us." Except that explanation turns my stomach. I let my heart speak for me. "He's become my favorite person. We're very attached to each other."

"You love him?" She signals to the wall our houses share.

My gaze follows her motion, as if I can see him on the other side. "I love Ridge very much."

Approval twitches her lips. "It's the same for him."

Flutters erupt in my belly like this is new information. "How do you know?"

"He wears his devotion for you like a badge of honor."

"You think so?"

She nods. "It's a relief to see you're doing well. I've been extremely concerned without a way of contacting you."

The ominous edge in her statement prickles my skin. "What happened after I left?"

A faraway look enters her eyes, as if she's in a different house entirely. "Your father has a mistress."

I balk at her abrupt reveal. Although, on second thought, it's not surprising. Affairs are quite common in that narrow-minded society. Many men in Billmoore believe it's suitable to have multiple wives.

"Once you left, our marriage changed. Your father stopped speaking to me. The blame for your… betrayal was placed on my shoulders. That was expected, as we discussed before you fled. But I wasn't prepared for his anger. He began treating me like a servant. If I dared to mention the shift in his behavior, I'd be punished. How foolish of me to assume he'd forgive my deception. Most recently, he threatened to replace me. I would have preferred that option." She gingerly touches her bruised cheek. "Even though he has someone new, he wouldn't release me. I don't believe he'll ever let me go."

A bitter taste fills my mouth. Father could be cruel, but he always had a sense of justice. It seems my absence stole his humanity.

"He's a monster," I murmur.

Mother agrees with a dip of her chin. "I'm worried he'll find me."

I place my palm over hers, offering a reassuring squeeze. "Ridge will protect us."

A loud bang on the door startles both of us. Walter wakes from his snooze at my feet and rushes to greet the visitor. His happy bark pairs with the scratching on the wood to announce his impatience.

As usual, I'm more leery as I turn to the entryway. My brow furrows, wondering why Ridge would bother to knock. Then it occurs to me that he's probably being respectful of my mother's privacy. He's considerate like that.

I go to let him in, only to immediately regret that decision. My feet are quick to backpedal away from the threat. Walter whimpers and slinks off to find shelter from the approaching danger. Lucky pup. I wish I could do the same.

Instead, I'm forced to confront my past. "Father."

The man who took the liberty of ruining my youth darkens the stoop. "Calliope." His upper lip curls in a sneer as he enters without permission. "I've come for my wife."

My mother gasps from where she remains seated on the couch. Father's glare narrows in on her before I can blink. I sidestep to block his view of her.

"She's staying here." I hate the tremble in my voice.

Thunder booms in his expression. "Get out of my way, child."

"No," I blurt.

My father goes still. "What did you say?"

"I said no," I repeat. "Mother left for a reason. She wants a new life, one that doesn't include you."

"You dare speak to me this way?"

The urge to cower knocks my knees together. There's a painful knot forming in my stomach that makes it difficult to breathe. But then a voice whispers to remind me that I'm not this tortured girl anymore. He can't intimidate me unless I allow it. I'm in control.

My posture straightens from under his mean intentions and bully mentality. "You're not welcome in my home. Please leave."

"How bold you've become while living in sin." His chuckle

is cruel, a wicked sound meant to deliver fear. "Where's your *boyfriend* to defend these actions? He left you alone."

For a split second, I fear my father did something to Ridge. Then I remember who my boyfriend is and what he's capable of.

Father takes my silence as surrender. "I can't believe you'd expose your mother to such depravity. Shame on you, Calliope."

"Shame on me? You're the shameful one. Look what you did to her." I boldly point at the marks on Mother's skin.

"You've forgotten your place since leaving the compound, daughter. Allow me to remind you." Father raises his arm as if to backhand me.

"I fucking dare you." The voice is more menacing than my father's could ever be.

But such contempt hasn't sounded like a morally gray knight storming the castle to save the day. Until now.

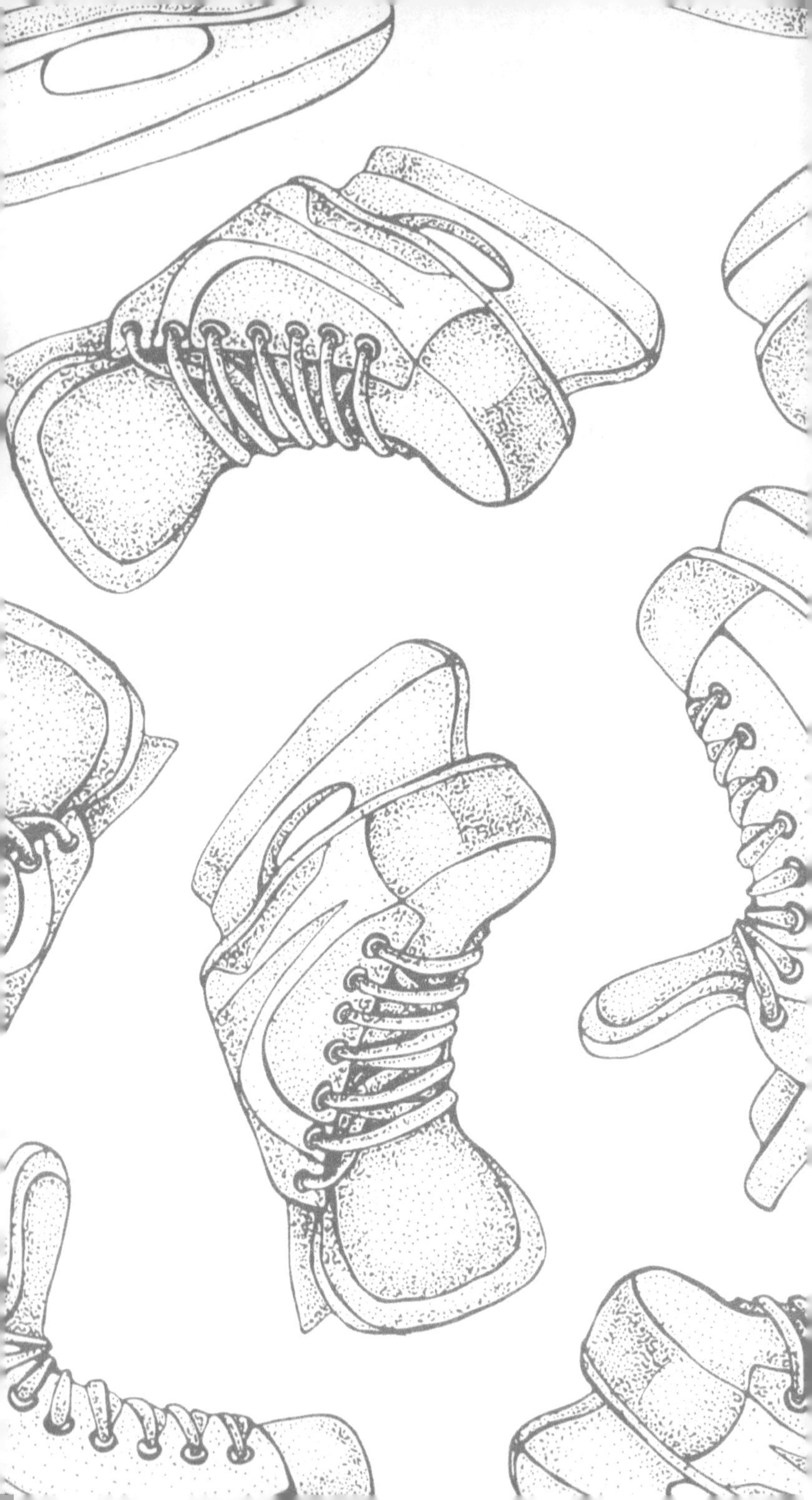

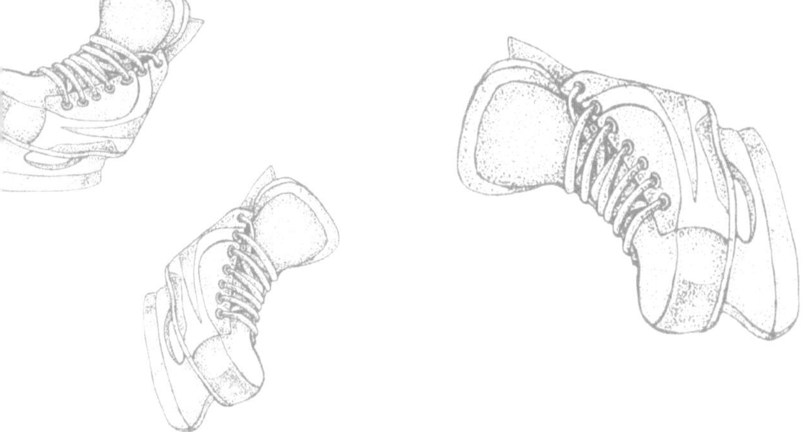

CHAPTER THIRTY-TWO

Ridge

THE SCENE I STEP INTO FREEZES MY BLOOD. CALLIE'S father is seconds away from slapping her across the face. Had I arrived a moment later, she'd be battered and bruised.

It's a damn good thing I followed the gut instinct that urged me to check in over here. Something didn't feel quite right. Now I know it's this piece of shit stinking up the place.

The man whirls to face me after my blatant interruption. "Well, look who decided to join us. You must be the boyfriend."

"Damn straight, and that makes me your worst nightmare. I'd suggest you get the fuck out before I break your ability to do so."

"Is that a threat?"

"Depends on your response," I drawl.

He widens his stance, as if that will make him appear like an adequate opponent. It's pathetic.

"This is a family matter. It doesn't involve you." He has the courage to point at me.

I almost laugh in his face. "Nah, you're the intruder in

this situation. That woman you're disrespecting is my whole world. I'll be damned if I'm gonna stand back while you try to make her feel less than. That goes for her mama too. The way I see it, you owe them both an apology."

The ass blubbers soundlessly like a fish out of water. "I'll never apologize for fulfilling my duty as the head of our household. Over my dead body," he adds.

"That can certainly be arranged."

His face takes on a reddish hue as he snorts like a bull. "Are you even listening to me?"

"No."

"Those two"—he blindly points at the women who have the displeasure of witnessing his rant—"need to be taught a lesson."

I go still when that venom spews from him. The suggestion strikes a match and hovers the flame over my short fuse. Consider me triggered.

A memory assaults me, and it's not even mine. The scar on Callie's arm might as well be seared into my own flesh. That burn mark spreads into a lethal blaze fueled by countless injustices from this waste of oxygen. Revenge is the only extinguisher.

My hands clench into weapons that won't quit until he's properly dealt with. I glance at Callie taking a stand against her tormentor. She returns my stare and must see the desire for vengeance overtaking me. Her head shakes, just slightly. That refusal diffuses the bomb set to detonate. He's still her father. I probably shouldn't kill him.

My exhale releases the fire in my veins. "For their sake, I'm gonna pretend you didn't suggest that."

His eyes bulge to cartoon proportions. "You're defending their behavior?"

"Bet your sorry ass. Not only that, I encourage them to

be independent. They have my full support to chase their wildest dreams."

His molars audibly grind. "I didn't come here for jokes."

"Could've fooled me," I grunt.

Especially when he talks about his wife and daughter like they're disobedient dogs. If anyone has earned a one-way ticket behind the barn, it's this ugly fucker I'm forced to stare at. I'd be doing us all a favor by putting him down.

He swats at my most recent retort. "Just release my wife and we'll be on our way."

"Haven't we already been over this? That's not gonna happen unless she willingly goes with you."

His glare swivels in her direction. "She belongs to me."

"Like a piece of property?" I thump his forehead to regain his attention. Maybe knock some sense into him too. "You're a real sack of shit. Who gave you this power over her? Did she volunteer?"

He hesitates after my corrective action but makes no move to reciprocate. "That's the structure Billmoore thrives on. My wife will be prosecuted for the harm she caused."

"The harm she caused," I echo. The impulse to smack him again heats my palm. "What crimes did she commit?"

He blinks, scrounging for an answer that doesn't exist. His corrupt rules hold no value. "She stepped out of line."

"Didn't take you for a hypocrite."

His temper flexes and strains against whatever is holding him back. "I've about had it with your insults."

My chuckle is a taunt. "Now we're getting somewhere. Why don't you tell me about your off-season hunting practices? Or maybe you'd prefer to share the details of your gambling circuit? Both are illegal, and that's by government law. Not some fictional justice scheme you've cooked up."

He visibly pales. "How do you know about that?"

"I paid a visit to your backwoods community. It didn't take much to get the dirt I went for."

"Are you trying to blackmail me? That's extortion."

"It's hilarious that you're trying to use legitimate legal jargon when it suits you."

His throat bobs with a thick gulp. "We don't need to get the authorities involved. Just give me my wife—"

"The answer is still no," I interrupt.

He sputters. "I drive all this way to fetch her—"

"Gonna stop you there," I cut in again.

Before I continue, Callie appears at my side. She squares off against her dad. "How did you know where to find her?"

"I don't have to answer to you, Calliope."

"Guess again," I growl.

He looks positively perturbed by my frequent redirection. "I suppose it won't hurt to reveal my ingenious methods."

"The fucking ego on this guy," I mutter. "Your dick must be the size of a Tic Tac. No wonder your wife left you."

His mouth pinches into a pucker that would be very popular in prison. "As I was saying, I took precautions after Calliope left. I figured her mother might get the same idea, but I made sure she couldn't get far. Stupid woman is dumb enough to believe that gaudy bauble on her wrist is an actual token of my affection."

An uncharted level of disgust twists Callie's features. "You're tracking her?"

"Have been for over a year now." The schmuck has the audacity to appear proud.

A shrill noise cuts across the room seconds before Althea chucks the bracelet onto the floor. She stomps on the fake jewelry as if crushing his balls beneath her heel. Satisfaction raises her chin to a haughty tilt when the task is complete.

I nod in approval. "Couldn't have said it better myself. Who else feels vindicated?"

Callie's father trembles with barely contained fury. "I can't believe you're allowing them to act like this."

"In case you missed my statement earlier, they're free to do whatever the fuck they want. You and I aren't the same." It's an offensive slur to my moral code that he assumes otherwise. "Which leads to you taking the hint and showing yourself out. Or I can go with you. We can put an end to this dispute once and for all."

"I'm not going anywhere without my wife," he repeats.

My head tilts as a thought occurs to me. "Was there a wedding?"

His expression is dumbfounded. "Huh?"

"Did you exchange vows? Sign a marriage certificate? Make it legitimate?"

"That's not how—"

"Then she's not your anything, except maybe by common law. But I doubt you believe in that either."

"I've had enough," he barks. "Come, Althea. We're going home."

"She already said no. Is that word foreign to you? Does she need to repeat herself?"

Althea is trembling like a leaf but she meets his glare. "No."

"You don't have a choice." He launches himself at her, but I have his shirt in my grip before he moves an inch.

I stride toward the door with him in tow. "Excuse me, ladies. It's time for me to take out the trash."

He's fussing and kicking like an insolent toddler the entire trek to the driveway. "You can't do this."

I shove him off me. "It was very unfortunate meeting you. Let's never do it again."

His beady gaze narrows. "As if I plan to make this a habit."

"Glad we have an understanding. Not sure where you

parked, but I suggest you run for it before I beat you to it." I make a shooing motion to scurry him along.

"This isn't the last you'll hear from me. I'll be back with reinforcements."

"Like a party? Fucking awesome. I love big groups of people. While you're doing that, I'll compile a list of the laws you're breaking. In addition to the two I already mentioned, this is private property and you're trespassing. The cops are good friends of mine, which makes them your enemy."

"All I hear are more empty threats," he snarls.

Clearly, nobody ever taught him not to poke the bear. I stroll at a leisurely pace to where he's loitering in the street. "This can go two ways, old man. I can kick your ass before letting you leave town, or you can get the fuck out on your own with some of your dignity still intact. Either way, if I ever see your face again, you'll regret it."

"Fucking prick," he sneers.

"That's not very nice. I was trying to be considerate by giving you a choice, not that you deserve it. Now I'll just do what I want." I pretend to lunge at him. It's more posturing than anything.

The fake intimidation tactic does the trick. He tucks tail and dashes into the dark, which fills me with more joy than I thought he was capable of providing.

I wave at his retreating form. "Tootle-fucking-oo."

Vanilla carries on the breeze like a reward for my valiant efforts. That welcome scent has me retracing my steps until I'm hovering over the threshold. I grip onto the doorframe, stopping myself from imposing. These two have tolerated more than their fair share of masculine energy for one evening.

Before I can take my leave, Callie rushes forward and climbs me like a tree. Her legs cinch my middle while she peppers my face with kisses. "Thank you, thank you, thank you."

Althea is more demure in her appreciation. Her smile is

small, but present. A sure sign she's going to be okay. That alone is worth the senseless sniveling I just endured.

I band an arm under Callie's ass to brace her weight against me. "No gratitude necessary. It's an honor to protect you, sweetness."

She huffs. "Um, you're our hero. The dragon is slayed."

"Didn't we decide this isn't a fairytale?"

"It feels pretty dreamy," she breathes.

"Mhmm." My agreement is pressed against her lips. "I should go."

Callie arches away to study my expression. "Why?"

"I'm sure you want to decompress after… that." My free hand points to where her dad was last seen.

She shakes her head. "Don't leave. What if he isn't really gone?"

He'll meet my fist, but I don't reveal that. "Would it make you feel better if I camp in the yard?"

"No, stay in here." She rocks her hips into my lower abdomen as if that will persuade me.

If I'm being honest, temptation clouds my judgment. But I refuse to overstep. "Your mom would probably be more comfortable if I left."

"Let's ask her." Callie releases her hold on me, sliding down my front before pivoting to face her mother.

"Althea has been through enough," I rumble.

The older woman straightens in her spot on the couch. "Call me Thea, and please, take a seat."

CHAPTER THIRTY-THREE

Callie: Hey, boyfriend. Just thinking of you, like always. Missing you too. How's the couch?

Ridge: lonely af

Callie: Thanks for staying over. We really appreciate it. Do you want me to send Walter down there to cuddle with you?

Ridge: we both know he's not gonna leave your side

Callie: Who said he was coming to visit you by himself? I want to join the cuddle session.

Ridge: nah, keep your mom company. she needs you

Callie: I'm not too sure about that. She's snoozing soundly. Like actually snoring. It's adorable. You gave her peace of mind.

Ridge: least I could do

Callie: Such a humble gentleman. You went above and beyond like usual. It's okay for you to admit that you're the best. I won't tell anyone.

Ridge: I'm only the best for you

Ridge: also me and gentleman

don't belong in the same sentence

Callie: I disagree. But you did go a bit feral on my father. It was very… attractive. Is that weird to admit? Obviously by now, you know I find every side of you extremely sexy. The growly protective mode version fits in the top five.

Ridge: what's number one

Callie: You're not supposed to ask about favorites. That's not fair to the others. They're all you, though. Maybe it's fine in this case. It is, right? I'm talking to you while typing like you're going to answer. It's been a long day. Wow, I'm on a tangent. Okay, I had to choose in this moment, it would be when you're extra romantic.

Ridge: I'll keep that in mind, sweetness

Ridge: and I didn't mean to make that so hard for you

Callie: No? I'm pretty sure you love getting hard for me. LOL

Ridge: damn. there's my dirty girl

Callie: So… should I come cuddle?

Ridge: if you come down here, we won't be cuddling

Callie: I like where this is going.

Ridge: sweetness...

Callie: Yes, boyfriend?

Ridge: don't tempt me. I'm trying to be decent

Callie: We already determined you're the best, especially when it comes to me. A quick hump and pump session won't sully your reputation.

Ridge: until your mother wakes up and finds me in a compromising position lol

Callie: She's out cold. Besides, Mama approves. That moment when she told you to call her Thea? Too precious. You've earned her trust.

Ridge: I'd like to keep it that way

Callie: Fine. How about we discuss our next trip?

Ridge: my girl is a traveler

Callie: I'm definitely ready to explore more places. Expand my horizons. There's a certain location I'm curious about. Maybe you can take me there.

Ridge: what's it called

Callie: Pound Town. Does that tickle your fancy?

Ridge: lol I can't even with you

Callie: You love me.

Ridge: with every molecule of my being

Callie: There you go again, being such a romantic. And my personal savior. How am I expected to resist? Allow me to thank you properly.

Ridge: you already did

Callie: Not with my vagina. Unless you'd prefer my mouth.

Ridge: good lord, woman. keep it in your pants

Callie: I'd prefer to get in yours.

Ridge: damn, I've created a sex fiend

Callie: Are you complaining?

Ridge: absolutely not

Callie: Alright, I'll cool it for now. I'd really like to find a way to repay you for everything you've done for my mother and me, though. Maybe you'll actually let me pay rent for a change.

Ridge: nope just let me love you

Callie: That comes easily.

Ridge: sounds like you

Callie: Now who's being dirty?

Ridge: you've created a sex fiend too

Callie: And yet, we're not sleeping together.

Ridge: just temporarily. maybe you should move in with me.

Ridge: your mother can have this half

Callie: Are you being serious?

Ridge: there's nothing to joke about

Callie: You'd do that for her?

Ridge: for us. we're in this together

Callie: Swoon alert. The belly swoops are in full swing. Does this mean I'll finally get to see the inside of your house?

Ridge: not sure why you haven't snuck over there already

Callie: I was waiting for a formal invitation.

Ridge: sweetness smh

Ridge: there's nothing formal about me

Callie: I beg to differ. You're very dashing and charming when you want to be. How else did you captivate such a shy damsel without even trying?

Ridge: fine. this is me asking if you'd like a private tour of your new home

Callie: I'd love that. Does tomorrow work for you?

Ridge: my schedule is wide open

Callie: Mine is too. How convenient.

Ridge: almost like we included an additional day in our vacation to recuperate

Callie: That was smart thinking.

Ridge: I'm more than a bartending jock with an obsessive streak for a certain sexy brunette

Callie: Oh, yes. Your list of strengths is longer than your

penis, and that's really saying something. Most impressive is that you're mine.

Ridge: definitely my most redeeming quality

Callie: Too modest. Love you, boyfriend.

Ridge: love you, sweetness. dream of me

Callie: Always! xoxo

CHAPTER THIRTY-FOUR

Callie

RHYTHMIC BREATHING SENDS ME TO THE BASEMENT to expand my search. I descend the steps leading to the lowest level that Ridge converted into a personal gym. He wasn't exaggerating about the quality of his facility. The space is impressive, even to someone with zero experience with fitness centers.

I yawn and scrub at my face, trying to ditch the sluggish lag from a deep sleep. That drowsy haze makes this downward trek feel endless. Walter didn't bother following me at such an early hour. Can't say I blame him.

After entirely too many stairs, my bare feet slap against the mats when I reach the bottom. What I find inside the mirrored space boosts my energy faster than a bucket of coffee.

Ridge is sprawled on a bench and lifting what looks to be an enormous amount of weight. He's shirtless, which is always a tasty sight. Chiseled muscles flex and release for my viewing pleasure. Too bad I don't have my camera.

That disappointment fades as I notice what he has on. A pair of familiar gray sweatpants cover his bottom half. My mouth waters at the sight. It seems this man is on the break-fast menu. Yummy.

On Ridge's next rep, he spots me lingering in the corner. A grin instantly cracks through the stony concentration. "Good morning, sweetness."

I wiggle my fingers at him while approaching in a lazy stride. "Hi, you. Why didn't my roommate boyfriend wake me?"

His lips lift at the term. "My plan was to slip back between the sheets before my roommate girlfriend noticed."

"As if I wouldn't feel your absence," I admit freely.

"You're just as attached to me, hmm? It was tough leaving your warmth, but there's a restless energy inside of me that demanded an outlet. I didn't want to take all that out on you."

A hot flush spreads through me. "I wouldn't have minded."

Rather than take the bait, he drops the heavy barbell on the rack with a soft *clink*. It's only then that I process he was still holding the weight. Such strength is unfathomable to me.

Ridge sits upright and grabs a towel from the seat. "Love living with you."

"We already were," I chide.

"Not officially."

I cup his scruffy cheek. "Thanks again for letting my mother move in over there."

She's adjusting faster than I predicted. It's only been a week, but her progress is encouraging. Her support system is top-notch, of course. Harper took it upon herself to introduce my mom to several local ladies, and she's made fast friends with them. They've been very accepting and welcoming.

As if listening to my inner musings, Ridge hums his approval. "Thea is right where she's meant to be. The house would've just sat empty otherwise."

"Oh?"

"Now that I have you in my bed, I want you there forever." He nuzzles into my touch.

A thought occurs to me. "Why do you sleep in the smaller room? The master is much bigger."

Ridge bites his bottom lip, dragging the flesh through his teeth. "The one we're in now shares a wall with yours on the other side. I liked the idea of being as close to you as possible when we weren't together."

My knees wobble under the intensity of his devotion. "That's very…"

His mouth quirks at my delayed pause. "Romantic?"

I nod and rest my palm over his tattoo. "My favorite."

"Now you're here to stay, and we can relocate to the suite fit for a queen."

"Am I still dreaming?" My breathy voice is fit for a fantasy.

"If you are, so am I." His gaze grows hotter the longer he stares at me in my makeshift nightgown.

"I'm a bit dizzy. Maybe I should sit down." I take the liberty of straddling his lap. My fingers clasp onto his shoulders for support.

Ridge's hands automatically roam the expanse of my bared thighs, sneaking under the hem of the jersey I'm wearing. "Have you eaten?"

"No, and I'm famished." A clench in my lower belly confirms as much.

"What should I feed you?"

"Protein," I blurt.

His hips roll, which grinds my core against him. The sweats do little to hide his arousal. "Would you like a sausage in your bun?"

I'm nodding too fast, focused on the hunger gnawing at me. "Yes, please."

"Fuck, you ask so nicely." His touch wanders higher and abruptly stops. "No panties?"

"I was optimistic."

"That's my girl," he croons against my upturned jaw. "I like your style."

A downward tug frees his penis from the loose confines of his pants. My slick center glides along his length, drenching him in me. I shiver while warmth quickly spreads through my veins. Ridge groans in return, as if he's succumbing to a similar heat. My scalp prickles where perspiration gathers and I'm suddenly burning.

"Too hot," I complain.

He strips the jersey from me in a fluid motion. "Better?"

Cool air bathes my fevered skin and I sag into the relief. "Much."

"Where were we?" His fingers dig into my waist as he slides me back and forth. "Soak me, sweetness."

I'm turned on to the point of almost dripping.

On the next forward motion, his tip bumps my opening. We expel a mutual groan. My grip on his shoulders tightens as I lift slightly. Ridge's eyes widen on mine. "Gonna ride me?"

My head jerks in the affirmative. "Straight to Pound Town."

He chuckles, which jostles our position. That jolty movement nudges him into me. The humor evaporates from his expression, replaced by a blissful smile. My mouth curves to match his while the desire to be filled becomes a need.

I stretch around him, accepting his wide girth into the most intimate depths of me. There's an abundance of arousal to ease his entry. My gaze locks on his as more wetness builds. The resistance loosens with every inch he gains.

We sigh in unison once I'm fully seated on him. We start at a cautious pace while we get accustomed to this flipped dynamic. Before this, I'd been too unsure to go on top. The onslaught of pleasure has me questioning why I waited so long.

I shift my hold to the bench rack for leverage, rising and

falling at a steady pace. My pebbled nipples rasp against his chest. That friction sparks into flames that are ready to set me ablaze. An urgency pushes me to increase my tempo until our hips smack together with each rushed contact.

A purposeful tilt of my pelvis sends him impossibly deeper. Ridge's hands travel to my butt, cradling the soft curves before squeezing. The combination of tender and rough pairs with his hardness driving into my pliable warmth.

Through the clouds of lust, I notice Ridge's attention is fixed on a spot over my shoulder. It's only then I remember we're on display at every angle. The mirror straight ahead provides a direct view of him looking back at me. He returns the awe in my expression, a smirk waiting on his lips. I keep my gaze forward, which allows me to witness what's happening from behind.

His fingers lewdly part my bottom cheeks, exposing where we're joined. He uses that grip on me to slow our frenzied pace. "Look how we fit."

I moan at the visual of our bodies becoming one. A spasm ripples through me, clenching my inner muscles. Ridge falters at the pressure.

"Fuck," he grunts.

That response encourages me to repeat the clamping action. "I love how you feel inside of me."

It's obscene how such a thick shaft slides easily inside of me. His manhood glistens from how stimulating I find the improbability to be. Our difference in size should be a challenge, but it only brings us closer. That point is punctuated into fact as I watch him fill me to the brim again.

I can't remove my eyes from the erotic performance we're putting on. Every movement is caught in explicit definition. Even my puckered hole is visible, and I absently wonder if he could ever fit there. But that's a curiosity for another day. Right now, we're chasing our pleasure to new heights.

Our reflection urges me on. I watch while Ridge fights for restraint. Climax hovers within reach. Our tempo works faster to deliver us to the peak. That push and pull flows directly to the demand gaining momentum.

I get swept away in our passion, unsure where he ends and I begin. Tingles collect strength and propel outward. Surrender is mine to give and I fling myself over the edge.

A soundless scream parts my lips. Ridge's shout could punch a hole in the roof. Trembles vibrate through me and ripple into him. We latch onto each other as the flood washes over us. The calm that follows sends me floating down until the room stops spinning.

Our sticky foreheads meet to keep us upright as we catch our breath. My grin kisses his. Ridge loops his arms around me as we bask in our simultaneous orgasms.

I slump against his chest in a useless heap. "That was… satisfying. Better than eggs and bacon."

His laughter fluffs my hair. "Still hungry?"

My stomach chooses that moment to growl. "I could be convinced to have seconds."

Ridge stands, managing to keep us connected. "Let's see what I can do to you in the kitchen."

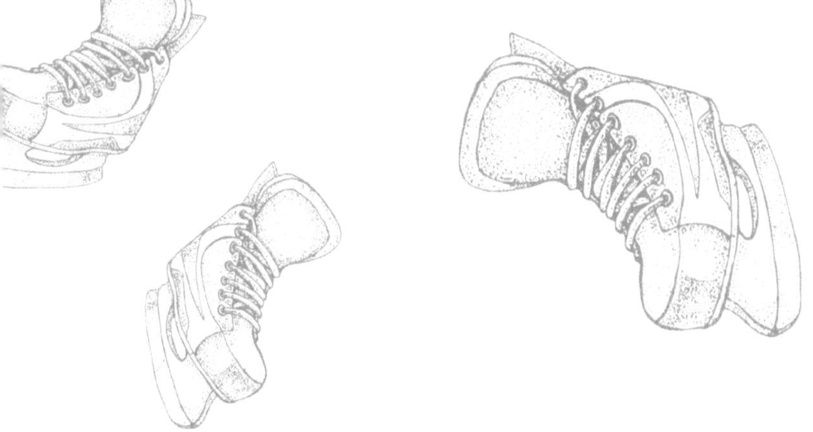

CHAPTER THIRTY-FIVE

Ridge

CALLIE GLANCES OVER AT HER PURSE AGAIN. THAT'S the fifth time in three minutes. I quit polishing the glass in my hand to give her my full attention. She doesn't notice, too preoccupied with her bag on the neighboring stool.

"You look suspicious," I tell her.

"Me?" Callie points at herself.

"Do you see anyone else capable of captivating me on a constant basis?"

She doesn't bother checking our surroundings. Roosters closed half an hour ago. The room emptied of the last stragglers not too long after. Her ass wiggles on the seat, as if she can't sit still.

I toss the towel over my shoulder and prop an elbow on the bar, putting us inches apart. "What's up, sweetness?"

"I have something to show you." The statement rushes out of her in a whoosh.

"Are you hoarding cherry cobbler?"

"As if I could get away with that. You gobble every bite the moment it's out of the oven."

"But you're hiding something. Should I be concerned?" A tightness spears into me.

Callie giggles, which eases my mind. Her hand dives into the depths of her purse, pulling out a hardcover journal. There's a tremble in her fingers as she passes it to me across the counter. "Here."

I study the nondescript cover that reveals nothing of the contents. The bulging size is slightly suspect. "What's this?"

She shoots me a flat stare. "It's not going to bite you."

"Can't be too sure," I mumble.

"You've only been asking for a peek at what I'm crafting since we started dating."

That's the incentive I need. I flip open the cover and a title page greets me. In a neat script that I could never replicate, Callie wrote our names. It's the doodled hearts that really do it for me, though. Talk about a throwback I didn't realize I needed.

A creak from her stool announces that she's leaning forward. "This is our journey so far from my perspective. Obviously. It's separated into two sections. The beginning is more of a diary. Just a few random occasions when our paths happened to cross. Most of them were at Roosters, which is why I thought it was fitting to let you read them here. Not that you knew I existed back then."

My eyes lift to hers. "I always knew you existed."

"Okay, fine. Before we ever talked," she corrects.

"That's better." I wink at her and flip to the next page.

"This is after I saw you for the first time." Her smile reflects the fond memory.

"Let's see if I made a good impression."

My gaze drops to feast on her jotted thoughts from February of last year. The date is significant to me, but not for a reason she would recognize.

Hey, stranger.

I'm not sure what else to call you. Diary is too common. Not that stranger gives you a real identity. It feels a bit odd writing to myself. This way I'm picturing you as a new friend. I don't have very many of those, but that's not the point.

Something unexpected happened today. I was walking through town on Main Street, like I've done many times in the past two months since arriving in Knox Creek. But there was this sudden urge to stop on the sidewalk. I can't really explain it other than I felt compelled to pause. That led to me looking around, and I saw a bar across the road.

Roosters is the name. I'll never forget the pull to go inside. That was odd too. Why would I be drawn to a bar? I've never been anywhere close to one. But a gut instinct should be followed.

Once I got close enough, I saw him. He's so... handsome. A stranger, like you. Maybe I should be writing this to him. As if I'd ever dare to let him read my inner thoughts. That's almost as crazy as me approaching the bar to begin with.

I'm ashamed to admit that I watched him. I think he might work there, but I'm not sure. Minutes flew by as I stood there in the winter cold. The icy chill didn't bother me. It could've started snowing and I wouldn't have noticed. My feet wouldn't budge from the spot.

If only I had the courage to go inside. There's a flutter in my belly that feels like a swooping sensation. I wonder if that's another sign from this man. It doesn't seem possible considering where I came from.

I ran from Billmoore to escape men, but I think he's different. No. Scratch that. I know he's different, especially when compared to the monster who raised me. I find myself *wanting to meet this stranger. Maybe even talk to him. But that's never going to happen. I can't even walk into a bar. Forget talking to a man, even if he could be special to me.*

I rest my hand flat on the window. A foggy imprint appears, as if I'll leave a lasting mark on the glass. That's all I'll ever be. A bland outline that's mostly invisible. Too afraid to be noticed. Unless I make the choice to change.

Until then.

xx

Callie

My breath falters as I reread the passage. It's as if my eyes are deceiving me. The words remain the same, though.

I flip through the rest, just at a quick glance until we're home where I can truly appreciate the magnitude. She's recorded every interaction we've shared. Heat blurs my vision and I blink against the sting.

"Sweetness," I croak. A rare emotion clogs my throat. "This is… the most thoughtful gift I've ever received."

And I'm not even talking about the journal.

Callie's eyes widen in alarm. "You don't get to keep it yet. I mean, it's not done."

I chuckle and rub at my wet lashes. "Well, damn. There goes my smile."

She swoops in for a kiss. "Don't pout. There's more to come for us, right? I was planning on keeping track of our entire first year as a couple."

Which gives me an idea for her next entry. I vault over the bar and land by her side. "Come with me, love."

Callie startles from my abrupt movement, but accepts my proffered hand. "Where are we going?"

The explanation is waiting outside where I turn her toward the front window. I press her palm to the glass before placing mine on top. "Do you know what else happened on February 23rd last year?"

A furrow dents her brow as she glances up at me. "I'm not great at guessing games. Can you give me a hint?"

"I saw you," I breathe.

She whirls around until our gazes clash. "What?"

"I was bartending and something told me to look up. My focus went directly to the window. You were there with your hand on the glass. Could've sworn you were staring into my soul."

A lone tear tracks down her cheek. "How is that possible?"

I slide my palm along hers, joining our fingers with a gentle squeeze. "Just one more reason twenty-three is my favorite number."

She nods. "It's lucky for us."

"Unexpected bliss," I exhale.

Callie grins. "And spontaneous."

That's my cue. My heart is thumping loud enough to be heard over incoming traffic. She tracks my smooth descent as I bend down on one knee. Thanks to the late hour, nobody is awake to spoil our private moment.

Callie blinks when I remain on the ground. "What're you doing?"

I pull the velvet box from my pocket and open the lid. The musgravite solitaire sparkles under the street lamp. "Making you my wife. Well, fiancée first. But that's only if you agree."

More tears collect in her eyes as she stares at the grayish-green gemstone. Her awe alone covers the hefty price I paid. "You're proposing?"

"Trying to," I tease.

She tucks her wobbly lips between her teeth. "Is this really happening?"

"I got permission from your mom." Thea couldn't approve

fast enough, practically shoving me out the door to get the job done.

Callie's brows fling to the overhang. "You did?"

"I sure as shit wasn't going to ask your dad."

She laughs, but it's a choked sound. "Good call, boyfriend."

I cluck my tongue. "Let's see about a permanent upgrade, hmm? I've been picturing you as my wife since… well, February 23rd of last year. It's no secret I'm obsessed and clingy and slightly unhinged. But I'll love you until my last breath. Will you marry me, Calliope Rose?"

Her head is bobbing to the rapid beat of my pulse. "Yes. Yes, yes, yes!"

I slide the platinum band over the knuckle on her left ring finger. My lips peck just above where the rock sits to seal the deal. "Fuck, that's a beautiful sight."

She twists her wrist until the lone jewel twinkles. "Was it expensive? I hope you didn't spend too much."

It's endearing as fuck that she thinks I'm referring to the stone. "It's unique like us, and that's what matters. Love you so much, fiancée."

"I love you." Callie collapses into my waiting arms, smashing her mouth to mine. "Thanks for seeing me when no one else did."

My grin curls against hers. "Thanks for showing me where to look."

She inhales long and slow. "It's the least I could do to score on you."

"Ready for a rematch?"

"With you at my side?" Callie molds herself to me. The musgravite solitaire gleams when she tries to wiggle impossibly closer. "I'm ready for everything, future husband."

EPILOGUE

Callie

W ALTER YANKS ON HIS LEASH, ALMOST DISLOCATING my shoulder in the process. "Jeez, someone is excited to get home."

Ridge chuckles while steadying me with an arm around my waist. "I'm convinced that dog never gets tired."

"He'll calm down eventually, once the puppy phase passes."

His gaze slides down to where our golden doodle is spinning in aimless circles. "If you say so."

I free the rowdy rascal and he clears the three porch stairs in one leap. We follow at a normal pace. A sting lashes up my arm when I reach for the banister. I wince and tuck the sensitive area against my side.

Ridge immediately hovers over me. "You okay?"

"Just itches." And burns like fire ants attacked my flesh. I don't dare reveal that last bit to him. If I did, this would be my first and only tattoo.

His mouths stoops into a frown. "It gets worse before it gets better. I'll apply more gel once we get inside."

My eyes drift to his shoulder, but the fresh ink is covered by his shirt. "You're not bothered in the slightest."

"I'm a pro."

"Really?" My eyes widen to mimic saucers. "That doesn't fit your vibe."

"Sarcasm is very sexy coming from you." The growl in his tone curls my toes.

I don't bother hiding a squirm. "Keep it up and you'll see plenty more come from me."

"Does sex fiend want to play?"

"Always," I return while swaying into him.

"That's real good to hear, sweetness. I'm already up for you," he rasps and presses the hard evidence into my hip. "Better get your ass in the house or we'll give the neighbors a show."

I trot forward, nowhere near bold enough to put our private intimacy on display for others to witness. Not that I believe Ridge would actually allow that to happen.

The door swings open before Ridge can grab the knob. Three very large men fill our entryway. I yelp and jump into motion, ready to flee without hesitation.

My fiancé doesn't share that flight plan. His presence turns darker than a midnight storm as he stares down these intruders. I'm not ashamed to admit that I duck behind him. One strange man is cause for concern. Three smashes the panic button on repeat.

I grab onto Ridge's shirt and yank. It's not a shock when he doesn't budge. My hold tightens for a second attempt but I'll rip the fabric before I get him to move. He's like a grizzly bear ready to dismember the wolves dumb enough to trespass into his den.

"What. The. Fuck?" He spits the punctuated expletive through clenched teeth.

Meanwhile, I'm tugging on his arm. "You're super strong

and everything but I don't love these odds. Let's go. They can have the cherry cobbler in the fridge."

"Don't antagonize them," I whimper. "Your ability to inflict damage is above average, but these odds aren't in your favor. Think about our future children."

Which is especially crucial considering our fur baby is two seconds away from meeting his doom. Walter's preservation tactics are another problem entirely. He paws at them, whimpering for their affection as if they're old friends. His plan is to beg for mercy. Maybe he's got the right idea.

"There's cherry cobbler in the fridge. I just baked it this morning. Give them the whole pan," I suggest.

"They don't get shit," Ridge snarls.

"It's not worth fighting over," I plead.

"I'd like to see them try." Ridge straightens to towering proportions. His presence appears to double in size and intimidation to confront the intruders.

"Let's check on my mom. She might be in danger." I pair the last ditch effort with a futile pull on his arm.

"These dipshits aren't much, but their loyalty is solid. They'd never hurt family."

I pause my evasive measures. "You know these guys?"

"Unfortunately," he grunts. "Meet my brothers."

My exhale becomes sputtered relief as the danger evaporates. Courage dares me to glance around the shield of my fiancé's broad frame. The imposing trio doesn't look too bothered by Ridge's frosty and lackluster introduction. One of them is even smiling, like his brother's abrasive attitude is hilarious.

Once my pulse returns to a semi-normal rate and logic scolds me, I notice the resemblance. My gaze sweeps over their similar traits before skittering away. They return my curiosity, but their attention is more bold and direct. That focus is a bright beam putting me on the spot.

My cheeks heat while I seek shelter behind Ridge. Acting naturally around men is still a challenge. The freedom to speak casually with them evades me as well. I manage to collect a few words and aim them at the only guy I trust.

"Do they have names?"

Ridge reaches an arm back to embrace me. His steady heartbeat calms mine, always offering support. "Bryson on the left is the oldest. Hudson is stuck in the middle. Literally. And the baby on the right is Soren."

The youngest brother is still wearing a grin. He wags his eyebrows and steps forward with a palm outstretched in my general direction. "It's a pleasure to meet you, Callie."

Ridge intercepts the gesture, swatting his hand away. "Don't touch her."

"Just being friendly." Soren winks at me.

A menacing noise thrashes from the wall of muscle in front on me. "That's the problem."

"Damn, you've always been possessive with your stuff but I've never seen that translate to a woman." He whistles as if a bomb is dropping and the other two nod in agreement.

"Callie is everything to me." Ridge's explanation pins their interest on me again.

"You were supposed to warn me if they were going to visit," I remind him in a rushed whisper.

This isn't the first impression I'd choose to make. It will certainly leave a lasting mark in the shape of my embarrassment.

He glances at me from over his shoulder. Any traces of frustration are smoothed from his expression. "Trust me, sweetness. I would've told you if I'd known."

"This wasn't planned?" My voice is a squeak.

"Nope." Irritation clouds his features when he scowls at the trio again. "These assholes took the liberty of letting themselves in, which means I need to change the lockbox code. Why don't you tell me what the fuck you're doing at our house."

"Just wanted to congratulate you on the engagement," Hudson drawls.

"Is your phone broken?"

His lips twitch in what I recognize to be amusement. "Would you answer if I called?"

Ridge's shrug is noncommittal. "Maybe."

"Liar," is rumbled from Bryson.

"Haven't seen you since Christmas and I'm already sick of your shit."

"Likewise, kid." The nickname almost makes me laugh.

My fiancé doesn't approve. "Move your asses."

Ridge shoves through their barricade as if they're nothing more than a mirage. His brothers are wise enough to split apart, clearing a path for us into our own home. I dip my chin and allow him to steer me toward the kitchen. Footsteps follow, but my mind is traveling elsewhere.

My face burns as I recall what he did to me on the counter this morning. There were more cherries than my cobbler recipe needed. Ridge gladly gobbled the excess while feasting on me. A distinct whoosh comes from the rear porch entrance to knock me from those memories.

"Finally," Harper huffs. She slides the glass door behind her and rushes toward us. "How long is a tattoo session? Did you have to wait for Ridge to get his done? You've been gone for hours."

I ignore her remark about the appointment to redefine our scars. "Where did you come from?"

"Outside." She points over her shoulder as if I didn't just watch her step inside.

My gaze wanders to our other three unexpected guests. "But why are you here?"

"Oh!" She laughs, but it's strained. "Don't be upset, okay?"

My pulse quickens while Ridge turns to stone beside me. "What did you do?"

Harper fidgets before gripping onto the handle. "Um… well, maybe it's better if I show you."

I creep forward until the backyard is in view. My eyes bulge at the unpredictable sight.

Tables and chairs are arranged in a socially receptive formation. Bright pink decorations fight against the natural scenery. Clumps of balloons sway in the breeze as if greeting us. Upon closer inspection, a few appear to have a phallic shape. My blush reignites until I'm sure the clouds can tag me as scandalized.

Our friends are spread across the grass in clumps of two or three. My visual sweep pauses on Drake and a woman I don't recognize. They seem to be caught in a heated moment, which encourages my focus to move along. Under the shade of our large oak tree sits my mother and an older couple. An undeniable longing pushes me to move in that direction.

"Surprise!" A loud bellow erupts from right behind me.

My soul vacates my body for a second as I jolt. Ridge looks ready to punch his youngest brother. I grab his clenched hand, prying his fingers open to weave through mine.

Soren's announcement has the desired effect on everyone else. They turn in a unified pivot to where we're standing on the deck. Applause and cheers boom from our suddenly captivated audience. Harper is bouncing on her toes, clearly pleased with the end result.

My friend hops next to me and gives my shoulder a gentle nudge. "Go on. Enjoy your engagement party."

"Our what?" The slice of Ridge's tone could sever the head from a statue.

She rolls her eyes. "Oh, hush. It's just a small gathering. The invite list almost got away from me. I had to remind myself that you two aren't fans of crowds. Jake was convinced this would backfire. It totally makes me want to throw him a huge extravaganza."

"Ridiculous," Ridge mutters.

"That's exactly what Jerky Jake said. Twinning," she chirps.

"It's not so bad." I bump Ridge with my hip.

The thunder fades from his expression when he smirks down at me. "Are you happy?"

A giddy tingle spreads through me. "I think your parents are over there talking to my mother."

His gaze doesn't shift from mine to confirm my suspicion. "They wouldn't miss the occasion."

"It's very special," I breathe.

"Hold off on the compliments until you get a load of Abbie's swag." Harper rolls her lips between her teeth.

I catch sight of Grace's friend straight ahead. She's pointing to a stack of metal tins that are neatly organized on a table. Garrett is visibly laughing at the colorful contents that he's holding in his hand. After a shrug, he dumps several pieces in his mouth.

Grace shakes her head, trying and failing to hide a smile. She motions to the little girl standing with her daddy near the fence. Sydney appears preoccupied, but my curiosity is piqued.

Ridge remains glued to my side as I approach them. Once again, shock widens my eyes as I discover what they're arguing about. My earlier concern about the balloons was warranted.

"Hi!" Abbie doesn't hesitate to hug me, but makes no attempt to touch Ridge. "Congratulations. I'm responsible for providing the risqué items."

Grace snorts and points at what appears to be candy. "That's one way of describing these."

"Every party needs a theme. I took the honor of deciding this one." Abbie taps a label while pride stretches her grin. "Same pecker forever. It fits with the cock den."

Ridge nods. "I don't see a problem."

"They're not bad." Garrett shakes the box that's filled with tiny dicks. "Wanna try? They're sugarcoated for your pleasure."

Ridge shoves his lofted arm away. "I'll pass."

"Your loss." He pops more onto his outstretched tongue.

Grace inspects a blue piece. "Aren't these reserved for bachelorette shenanigans? Like after dark when it's only adults."

Abbie cackles. "This is tame compared what I have planned for you. Just wait and see, bride-to-be."

"We can't bring you anywhere," Grace mutters.

Before she can defend herself, an excited squeal cuts into our social circle. "Is that candy?"

Abbie falters at the appearance of Sydney. The little girl has her sights very much set on the inappropriate treat. My face goes up in flames and I'm not even in the hot seat.

"Oh, sh—crap. Yep. But it's not very good." Garrett rushes to swallow his recent mouthful.

Sydney frowns. "I wanna taste it."

"Sorry," he mutters to Harper in advance.

My friend arrives on the scene, bending in half to catch her breath. "You're too fast, superstar."

But her daughter isn't listening. She's poking at the rainbow selection. "Is this sperm? You shouldn't eat that."

Harper chokes on her laughter. "This should be entertaining."

Abbie glances from the blonde to Sydney. "Why not?"

"You'll get pregnant," the little girl states loud and clear.

Abbie glares at the candy as if it's suddenly toxic. "Who told you that?"

"Payton and Gage. Their mama swallowed lotsa sperm. That's how she got two babies in her belly at the same time."

I clap a palm over my lips to disguise the amusement. The others aren't as discreet. Humor glistens from Harper's gaze, just waiting for us to crack. Soon our group falls victim to a fit of giggles. Sydney is beaming like a shining star in the center.

Ridge rubs over his forehead as if he can erase the last five minutes from memory. "And on that note, let's go see our folks."

They rise from their seats as we approach. My mother smiles, her chin tilted in newfound confidence. She's found the best version of herself and it shows. Ridge's mom and dad look gleeful as well. Their matching grins capture a sense of familiarity. I blindly grab for my camera, but belatedly remember it's in the house.

"I'll get it for you in a moment," Ridge says. His awareness of me never rests.

"Love you, future husband." I rise onto my toes and kiss his scruffy jaw.

He stoops to grant me better access. "And I love my future wife."

The collective sigh from our parents brings my attention forward. I instinctively seek comfort in my mother's embrace first. She's quick to open her arms for a hug. We exchange a soft squeeze before separating.

"Hello, Thea." If I'm not mistaken, Ridge bows slightly to acknowledge her.

She titters like a flustered beehive. "Oh, you. That's a tad overboard, hmm?"

"Never," he assures. His palm settles on the small of my back, guiding me flush against him. "Sweetness, these are my parents. Fern and Forrest, this is my Calliope Rose."

His mom is already crying, letting the tears fall freely. "It's wonderful to finally see you in person, Callie. Ridge talks about you nonstop whenever we call. I managed to convince him to send me a picture. One glimpse and I knew you belonged together."

Warmth spreads through my chest. "Really?"

"Absolutely, dear. It feels like we're already family."

Forrest hums his approval. His eyes crinkle in the corners as he smiles. Kindness reflects from his expression, filling me with a sense of belonging. It's easy to see where Ridge gets it.

Gratitude slams into me and I blurt, "Can we hug?"

They don't give me a second to doubt the request. Together, the four of us merge in a silent exchange of understanding. Fern reaches for my mother, bringing her into the fold. We remain in the huddle for several moments, but the bond we formed is permanent.

My bottom lip trembles as emotion tries to conquer my composure. "Thank you for raising Ridge to become such a good man."

"Don't give us too much credit," Forrest replies. "It's you who captured his heart and gave him the other half of his soul."

Fern gazes at her husband with unfiltered adoration. "Isn't it something?"

He mirrors her devotion. "Rather indescribable."

Ridge presses a kiss to my temple. "Spontaneous and unexpected."

I snuggle against him. "That sounds like our happily ever after to me."

That's the end… mostly. Are you curious about the tattoos mentioned in the epilogue? Well, I have that scene as well as two others from Callie and Ridge for you here!

And read on for glimpses at more Knox Creek romances…

Curious about Garrett and Grace? Their friends to lovers, opposites attract romance is called *Yours to Catch*. Here's a sample for you from Garrett's point of view.

I smile at the approaching trio, but a lone figure snatches my focus before they reach me. The woman is instantly recognizable. She drove me to distraction last month, which led to Harper transforming Roosters into a dance club for an entire night. It's been impossible to forget her hypnotic allure. That trance once again renders me useless.

Harper is talking to her, but I only hear the erratic thrash of my desire. The bombshell that's wrecking my composure is breathtaking in a plain t-shirt and jeans. No frills or fuss, which suits my style just fine.

Her shapely figure commands my full concentration. As if tethered, I'm incapable of looking away. She's lush curves and endless pleasure wrapped in one fuckable package. My mouth goes dry as I treat myself to a languid perusal of those supple lines that connect to create an irresistible form. Somewhere in the recesses of my lust-addled brain, I realize that it's not polite to ogle her this way.

My creeper status warns me to retreat when Sydney joins their conversation. A slow blink does little to alleviate the pressure in my groin. In a weak attempt to sever this daze—and regain control from my cock—I forcefully avert my gaze off her tits. The button on her purse strap halts my decent intentions. I cough to free myself from the stupor.

"Holy shit," I blurt. "You're my other half."

Harper squeaks in outrage and claps her palms over Syd's ears. Then she pins me with a glare. "Can you watch your language?"

The pinch in my features is meant to be apologetic. But in reality, I'm too transfixed by the raven-haired beauty to notice much else. "We're meant to be."

She raises her hands to strike my wayward nonsense. "I just want a cocktail."

"Hold the tail?" I wag my brows to regain the trustworthy charm that never steers me wrong. "We can save that for later. For now, we need to celebrate. Your number is the same as mine. Fifty-three."

Her gaze narrows on the button I have proudly displayed on my shirt. Then she glances at the identical pin attached to her purse strap. "I forgot about that."

"It's tradition," I hoot and spread my arms wide. "The anticipation of meeting your match keeps you searching the crowd."

My exaggerated reaction makes this casual game sound like the stars aligned to bring us together. Maybe there's a bit of destiny involved. Not that I believe in fate. In reality, every attendee is given a button at the entrance with the incentive of a prize. The festival ritual is forgotten more often than not. I'd been guilty of doing just that until this chick returned to my sights.

"That's quite a romantic sentiment." She gives me another once-over. "Front and center, huh?"

"Didn't want the one meant for me to miss it." I tap the number pinned smack dab in the middle of my chest. Then I tack on a smirk to showcase my dimples. These weapons of destruction have an undefeated record against panties. The protective layer melts off before the ladies know what hit them.

This girl is my latest target and appears caught under the influence. After staring openly for several seconds, she rips her gaze off me. "And now that you've found her?"

"Pretty sure you found me, soulmate."

Did you notice that mention in the epilogue about Payton and Gage? They're the kiddos in my double single parent romance called Mine for Yours. Take a peek at this snippet from Rylee's point of view!

Rhodes mirrors my gesture. "Damn, Firefly. Your circumstances might be more brutal than mine."

I release a sigh steeped in drama best left unsaid. That's not a competition I want to win, but he's probably right. "Maybe we'll gather the nerve to exchange our horror stories someday."

Before he can reply, conspiring whispers of the non-contempt variety swarm us. Gage and Payton are gathered in a conspicuous huddle right in front of us. How they got this close without me noticing further proves the previous topic should be avoided. Permanently.

Giggles erupt from their collaboration. My gaze narrows into a squint. It's obvious these two are up to something. Payton nods and breaks apart from the suspicious formation. I brace myself as she steps toward me, clearly elected to take the lead in whatever this is.

"You're Gage's mom, right?" Her question is a lyrical chirp, rhetorical as it might be.

I peek over at my son, who's taken a sudden interest in tying his shoes. "Yep, that's me. You can call me Ms. Creed or Rylee… or Gage's mom. I'll answer to any of those. Is your name Payton?"

"It is!" She beams, showing off her gap-toothed grin. The Tooth Fairy has been busy with this one.

"Such a lovely name for a young lady. It's very nice to meet you." I glance at Rhodes, who's stifling a laugh with his fist.

"You're pretty. Like really pretty." She blinks at me with pure innocence before turning those doe eyes to her father. "Isn't Rylee super pretty, Daddy?"

Now it's my turn to muffle an obnoxious cackle. With my lips sealed tight, I realize just how wrong my earlier attempt had been. Amusing, yes. But definitely a mistake.

A delayed concern overshadows my humor. The term could be tainted for him. I'm almost afraid to look, preferring to remain blissfully ignorant. But the guy looks cool and calm, with no signs of distress or cracking up. He must recover faster than me.

Gage and Payton share a quizzical shrug. I shake off the inside joke before they can ask. That flub isn't worth dissecting while more important matters are being discussed. I bat my lashes at Rhodes, waiting for his verdict.

His chocolate stare locks on mine. "She's stunning."

My breath catches. It shouldn't be a shock that he's set on knocking me sideways. I'm jostled from the misplaced romantic bubble by Payton's giggles. She's returned to the huddle stance with Gage. The whispers and flailing continue soon after.

"We're in trouble now," he whispers from the corner of his mouth.

I cross my ankles and recline against the hard seat. "Let them have fun."

"Famous last words," he mumbles.

Gage straightens, scrawny shoulders rolled back. "Payton is my girlfriend."

Rhodes' eyes bulge. "What?"

Payton's smile could replace the sun. "Gage wants to be my boyfriend."

Her dad struggles to form a response, jaw hanging slack. He's not so cool and calm anymore.

I let my own giggle roam free. "Oh, yeah. We're in so much trouble."

Rhodes looks to me for advice, or a way to defuse this premature dating situation. Something seems to occur to him, the wheels spinning wildly behind his gaze. He pins Payton with a protective father mean mug that could make me quake in my boots. "Henry is already your boyfriend."

She flips her hair. "I can have two."

That barely registers. I'm too busy studying Gage. "Yeah, let's talk about this. Don't you already have a girlfriend?"

"I have six girlfriends." Pride sings from his voice.

I gape at him. "Excuse me?"

He proceeds to prattle off their names, ending with a pleased grin. "But I want to marry Payton the most."

Rhodes chokes on nothing but shock. "Marry?"

I make a slicing motion to Gage. "We've talked about this."

My son's focus slides to the bristling body beside me. "Uh-oh. Are you gonna get me with a shotgun?"

"The fu—fudge?" Rhodes is glaring at me.

I hang my head with a groan. "It's just something I told him once when he was caught flirting. The dad wasn't impressed that his little girl was blowing kisses and looking lovesick. I was kidding. Obviously."

"That was funny," Gage laughs from his belly.

"Okay, whatever." Rhodes slashes the air. "You aren't getting married."

Payton stomps her foot. "Are too. We're in love."

"You're really not," he retorts.

She rolls her eyes. "But that's no fair. You're gonna marry Rylee."

"Oh, no. We aren't getting married," I insist.

Gage squishes his lips into a pout. "But you're holding hands."

I lower my gaze to confirm that we are, in fact, still holding hands. Rhodes drops me like a hot potato. The kids double over in a fit of laughter. Apparently, our spoof is more believable than I thought. Especially to a pair of second graders.

Rhodes grips the back of his neck. "We were, uh, practicing."

Payton wrinkles her nose. "For what?"

His expression blanches in a panic I feel deep in my gut. It seems my partner in crime isn't too stellar on the fly. He has to go and prove me wrong, of course. "Our staff meeting on Friday."

Want to read more? Check out *Mine for Yours* here!

ABOUT THE AUTHOR

Harloe Rae is a *USA Today* & Amazon Top 5 best-selling author. Her passion for writing and reading has taken on a whole new meaning. Each day is an unforgettable adventure.

She's a Minnesota gal with a serious addiction to romance. There's nothing quite like an epic happily ever after. When she's not buried in the writing cave, Harloe can be found hanging with her hubby and kiddos. If the weather permits, she loves being lakeside or out in the country with her horses.

Broody heroes are Harloe's favorite to write. Her romances are swoony and emotional with plenty of heat. All of her books are available on Amazon and Kindle Unlimited.

Stay in the know by subscribing to her newsletter at;
bit.ly/HarloesList

Join her reader group, Harloe's Hotties, at
www.facebook.com/groups/harloehotties

Check out her site at www.harloerae.com

www.ingramcontent.com/pod-product-compliance
Lightning Source LLC
Chambersburg PA
CBHW061108310726
48974CB00002B/447